CRITICS ~~...~~ LEIGH ~~GREENWOOD'S~~
THE COWBOYS!

CHET

"*Chet* has it all! Romance and rustlers, gunfighters and greed . . . romance doesn't get any better than this!"
—*The Literary Times*

"CHET's plot moves with the speed of stampeding cattle. Supporting characters spring to life and swing into action. Tension is as sensitive as a hair trigger. Leigh Greenwood tops my list of favorite romance writers."
—*Rendezvous*

BUCK

"*Buck* is a wonderful American Romance! Leigh Greenwood remains one of the forces to be reckoned with in the Americana romance sub-genre."
—*Affaire de Coeur*

"A rip-roaring good time. Leigh Greenwood pens the finest stories in romance fiction."
—*The Literary Times*

"If anyone can write a perfect historical romance, it has to be Leigh Greenwood!"
—*Bell, Book & Candle*

MORE PRAISE FOR
THE COWBOYS

WARD

"Few authors write with the fervor of Leigh Greenwood. Once again [Greenwood] has created a tale well worth opening again and again!"

—Heartland Critiques

"Leigh Greenwood captivates readers time and time again! If you enjoyed the *Seven Brides,* you will fall in love with *The Cowboys*!"

—The Literary Times

"Leigh Greenwood is synonymous with the best in Americana romance."

—Romantic Times

JAKE

"Reminiscent of an old John Wayne/Maureen O'Hara movie, *Jake* kicks off what is sure to be another popular series from Leigh Greenwood."

—Robin Lee Hatcher

"*Jake* is an exciting, fast-paced Reconstruction Era romance . . . . Readers will definitely want more from this great writer and will want it soon. Leigh Greenwood has another winning series in the works."

—Affaire de Coeur

"Only a master craftsman can create so many strong characters and keep them completely individualized. Greenwood's books are bound to become classics."

—Rendezvous

SWEET MELODY

"I like you," Melody managed to say. This time her voice sounded fuzzy and weak. "I've so much reason to be grateful that it would be—"

"I don't give a damn if you're grateful or not," Chet barked, his voice so sharp she jumped. "Do you like me, or is it my guns?"

"I hate your guns," she snapped, not sounding the least bit faint now. "I can't imagine why I should like a gunfighter as much as I like you, but I can't help myself. It has nothing to do with drawing fast or chasing cows about in the middle of the night or burning haystacks or—"

He'd crossed the room in a few swift strides. Before she could ask what he meant to do, he'd swept her into his arms and was kissing her so fiercely she wondered if she'd survive. His arms wrapped around her, gripping her in an unbreakable embrace. Only she didn't want to break it. After the initial shock, she felt wonderful, exhilarated.

The Cowboys

CHET

LEIGH GREENWOOD

LEISURE BOOKS   NEW YORK CITY

*To my agent, Natasha, and her sidekick, Oriana.
I couldn't get along withou you.*

A LEISURE BOOK®

Published by

Dorchester Publishing Co., Inc.
276 Fifth Avenue
New York, NY 10001

Cover Art by John Ennis

ISBN 0-8439-4594-X

The name "Leisure Books" and the stylized "L" with design are trademarks of Dorchester Publishing Co., Inc.

Printed in the United States of America.

The Cowboys

CHET

Chapter One

Central Texas, 1880

Melody Jordan paused on her way from the corral to the ranch house. Someone was riding up. Another one of those rough, unkempt cowboys from the looks of him, probably looking for a place to lie up for a few days, or weeks. They always said they wanted work, but they never stayed. Sooner or later they saddled up and rode off into that limitless horizon.

Melody glanced up at the metallic-blue sky. She loved the feeling of openness and freedom this country gave her as much as she loved the violent shifts in weather. But she still got nervous whenever she had to ride out of sight of the ranch house. After growing up in Richmond, Virginia, with its well ordered streets, she didn't understand how anyone could find their way across this limitless expanse of flat, featureless prairie.

The rider dismounted just short of the ranch yard and started to walk the rest of the way. That made her pause. She hadn't figured out very much about Texas in the three months she'd been here, but she did know a cowboy would almost rather go hatless than walk. Melody peered at him, her hand shading her eyes from the glare of the sun. His horse walked slowly behind the cowboy, as though each step was an effort. Melody found it surprising that a Texan would walk just because his horse was tired. She wouldn't go inside yet. She wanted to know more about this man.

Catching sight of his weapons—a rifle and a gun—she felt a chill. She had lived through the destruction of Richmond, the aftermath of the Civil War. She had seen at first hand what guns could do to people's lives. She hated guns and couldn't understand why every man in Texas felt naked without one. Despite his concern for his horse, apparently this man was no different.

The merciless sun beat down on her bare head, and she retreated to the porch. That was something else she couldn't accustom herself to. It got hot in Virginia, but there were huge trees and thick grape arbors for shade. For the more adventurous, there was swimming in the James River.

There were no arbors here, few trees—the only ones she'd seen were gnarled pines, stunted and misshaped by the wind—and barely enough water to quench the thirst of the thousands of cattle that wandered the inhospitable land. Melody couldn't imagine how they found enough food to stay alive, much less grow fat.

She didn't understand Texas at all, but she had

to learn quickly. She had to choose a husband, and the only candidates were her foreman and the owner of the neighboring ranch.

Chet Attmore felt no embarrassment over leading his exhausted mount. At twenty-nine he was too old to suffer from the vanities that afflicted young cowboys. He was what he was, a gunfighter, a label that would haunt him for the rest of his life.

He liked what he saw. Wood frame ranch house, bunkhouse, and barn. The lumber had been brought in, maybe from as far away as Fort Worth. He was used to sod houses, brush corrals, and rickety sheds. The corral here was constructed of barbed wire and cedar posts. The owner of the Spring Water Ranch was more progressive than his neighbors. The horses in the corral looked strong and well fed, like the cattle he had seen riding in. There must be ample water somewhere, maybe in the spring the ranch was named for.

Chet had already noticed the woman. At first he'd made himself look elsewhere. Looking at what he couldn't have was an irritation he didn't need. Now he was so close, it would be rude not to look at her.

That wasn't a hardship. He could tell at a glance that she was young and fresh from the East. She was still pretty; her skin looked soft and creamy instead of burned to the color of new leather, and she still shaded her eyes rather than peered from between eyelids that formed bare slits. She wore shoes rather than boots. Despite the effects of the wind, he could tell she had taken time to fix her hair. Her dress was made out of a soft, flowered material which the never-ending wind whipped around her body. If she hadn't been wearing some sort of stiff petticoat, he would have had a disturbingly graphic outline of her lower body.

She looked achingly soft, pretty and feminine.

Chet felt his body begin to swell. He cursed. He had no business reacting to her this way, but he couldn't help it. He was in the prime of his life. She looked to be in the prime of hers. The trouble was, their primes were separated by too many men faced over the barrel of a gun. He had come to buy a horse. He would leave as soon as he got one.

He didn't really have to leave to keep from seeing her. She'd run inside and send her father or the foreman out to see him. He'd buy his horse, then be asked to stay for dinner. She would help her mother serve the meal, then disappear again. She and her mother would eat after the men. During the rest of the evening he would hardly see or have a chance to speak to her. It was just as well. What could they have to say to each other?

They might invite him to spend the night in the bunkhouse and eat breakfast with the hands next morning. After that he'd pay for his horse, mount up, and ride out toward Pecos country. He'd rather be going in the opposite direction, to the Broken Circle, Jake and Isabelle Maxwell's ranch. It seemed like years since he'd seen them. It seemed like a lifetime since he'd lived there, one of their many adopted sons.

The memory of those days had followed him all through his time as a hired gunman—when he was exhausted from the chase, when he faced a man anxious to kill him, when he questioned why he lived his life as he did. Yet now that he'd given up hiring out his gun, he couldn't go back to the only place he'd ever felt at peace. He was forced to head in the opposite direction. All he wanted from this girl was a horse to help him on his way.

She didn't go inside as he expected. She stood at the bottom of the steps, waiting. She was even younger and prettier than he had thought. Her hair was a rich brown. Cut short, it clustered about her face in a profusion of curls kept in constant motion by the wind. That would soon change. She'd let it grow long, gather it in a bun, and tuck it under a bonnet. He was glad he wouldn't be here to see that. She was utterly charming in her refusal to yield to the harshness of the land.

She watched him with huge, brown, doe-like eyes. Most likely she thought he was just another wandering cowhand. She'd probably seen more than enough of them already. The Spring Water was one of the most prosperous ranches in the area. Every freeloader within a thousand miles probably drifted this way sooner or later.

It annoyed him that she'd think he was a cowboy living off the hospitality of the country, but there was no point in getting upset about something he couldn't change. People were always getting the wrong idea about him. Most of the time that suited him just fine. He didn't know why it should start to bother him now.

"Howdy," Chet said.

"Good morning," she replied. "What can I do for you?"

Virginia. He couldn't miss that accent, its soft vowels and slurred consonants. Probably from some old family with roots going back before the Revolution. She probably grew up in one of those

13

old brick mansions his father used to tell him about. If so, what on earth was she doing in Texas?

"I'd like to talk to your father, miss. Or the foreman if he's around."

"My father's dead, and the foreman's not here. Maybe I can help you."

Virginia manners, too. Calm, self-assured, with a trace of condescension she probably wasn't aware of. People in Virginia just naturally thought they were better than anybody else. He wondered how many generals and signers of the Declaration of Independence she was related to. He was related to one.

"I need a fresh horse, miss. Mine's worn out." They both stared at the sorrel gelding. His coat wasn't dull, he didn't look too thin, but he stood with hanging head, his legs slightly spread.

"How can you tell?" she asked.

Clearly she hadn't been out here long. She was probably used to seeing Thoroughbreds, Morgans or some other fancy breed, kept in a stall at night and growing fat on a diet of grain.

"He had a little trouble outrunning some Indians a while back. The first time, he outran them with no trouble."

"You were twice attacked by Indians?"

"Not attacked, precisely. I don't make a practice of getting that close. They saw me passing through and decided to hurry me along."

"They aren't supposed to be here."

"They were here first. They still don't understand why they have to leave." Being from the East, she probably thought all Indians were dead or chased somewhere on the other side of the Pecos.

14

"The buffalo's gone," she said. "If they don't settle on reservations, they'll starve."

She understood a lot more than many Texans, but he wasn't here to discuss the Indian problem. He wanted a horse. "How about that horse?"

She eyed him more closely now. He could bluff his way through a high-stakes poker game. He wouldn't hesitate to chase bandits or rustlers beyond the Rio Grande or across the Mexican border, but this woman made him nervous. His years as a hired gunman had brought him into contact with many women, but none like this one.

He ought to be thinking about a horse. Instead he was thinking about her soft, rounded chin. It had a tiny crease down the middle, just enough to keep it from being perfectly rounded. And that hair! It was alive. Colored with all the richness of dark chocolate, it moved about her face in a kaleidoscope of shapes, framing her face in never-ending variety. She was any woman, and all women at once.

"I can't afford to trade a good horse for one you say is worn down," she said. "Why don't you stay and work for us for a couple of months? If you do a good job, I'll see you get a good horse."

He could pay for a horse, but he would prefer a trade. He'd need his gold where he was going.

"I had a mind to move on," he said. He didn't want her to think he was going to stay long. If they needed permanent hands, her foreman ought to get the word out in Fort Worth or Abilene. No point in depending on whoever happened by. "I want to be as far as Santa Fe before the first snow is on the mountains."

"You can earn enough money to pay for your

15

horse and still make it to Santa Fe before winter," she said.

Why was she so anxious to have him take a job on her crew? She didn't look like the kind to hire just anybody who passed by. Besides, he didn't know if she had the authority to hire him. He didn't know a single foreman who would take kindly to having a female move in on his job. But then, maybe she hadn't been out here long enough to know that. She certainly didn't know enough to dress appropriately.

"You don't have to decide right away," she said. "Turn your horse into the corral. You can put your things in the bunkhouse. We have dinner at six. Of course you'll eat with us."

Southern hospitality. You had to feed anybody who stepped on your place and look like you were happy about it, even if you hated their guts. He saw no sense in that. Eating with people he didn't like gave him indigestion.

"There's no need, miss. I can eat with the crew."

"Guests always eat with us." She paused as though considering something. "Why do you keep calling me miss? I'm old enough to have been married years ago."

He didn't know. He guessed he'd just looked at her and decided no married woman would look this young and fresh. The energy of life still flowed strong in her. She didn't look discouraged or weighed down by defeat. She hadn't given up believing in and hoping for the fulfillment of her dreams.

"I didn't mean to hurt your feelings. You just look so young, I figured you had to be an unmarried girl."

She smiled. "Unmarried, yes, but hardly a girl. Surely I don't look that young."

"When you get to be my age, anybody under twenty looks like a babe."

"But you can't be more than twenty-five," she said.

"Twenty-nine."

She cut a spurt of laughter off in the middle. "Then you'd better unsaddle that horse and shuffle on over to the bunkhouse while you still have the strength."

She was laughing at him. He heard it in her voice, saw the amusement in her eyes.

"Things haven't gotten that bad yet, but I confess my bones do ache worse than they used to."

"If you've been running from Indians, you're lucky you have no more serious complaints than aching bones. Now you'd better tell me your name. I can't tell my foreman I've hired a man without at least knowing his name."

But she had. And that was something else he couldn't explain. People from Virginia usually wanted a four-generation pedigree before they'd let you in the door.

"My name's Chet Attmore, and I only agreed to think about it," he reminded her.

"My name's Melody Jordan. Our foreman is Tom Neland. I'll send him out to talk to you as soon as he gets back."

"No need to bother," Chet said. "I can see him at dinner."

"Suit yourself," Melody said. She turned and mounted the steps, but turned back before she reached the door. "Do consider the job," she said. "We've been short-handed since my father died,

17

and we're having a little trouble. We could use a good man."

"How do you know I'm a good man?" Chet asked.

She smiled at him, a truly friendly, welcoming smile with all the feminine warmth he'd missed for so long. "A woman can always tell that kind of thing." She turned and entered the house.

Not the kind of women Chet knew. Most of them were as ready as any man to pick your bones. The rest of them could be trusted to gravitate to any drunk, liar, or thief with a ready tongue. Chet figured it didn't say much for him that they were the only kind of women he knew.

As he led his horse over to the corral, Chet wondered if this might not be just the place he needed for the next few weeks. He hadn't made up his mind exactly where he intended to go or what he intended to do. His reputation as a gunfighter complicated every decision he made. Maybe this would be a good place to lay up for a while and see if his past came looking for him. If not, he could start looking for some out-of-the-way place to settle. If it did, well, he'd face that bridge when he got to it.

He admitted to himself that Melody Jordan had something to do with his decision. Though he'd steered clear of entanglements with respectable women, he couldn't see a woman in trouble and not want to help her. He didn't know anything about Melody's problems, but if they were as bad as she was pretty, then she was in a heap of trouble. Past experience told him it would be easier to walk away before he became involved.

Past experience also told him he wouldn't.

*   *   *

"Who is that man?" Belle Jordan asked as Melody straightened the pillows behind her stepmother's back. "He's not one of the crew."

"His name is Chet Attmore. He rode in asking about a horse. His is played out."

There was something about that she didn't understand. The animal was obviously of much better quality than a man of his appearance could afford. It was possible he had stolen it, but somehow she was certain he hadn't.

"I hope you didn't give him one."

"No, I offered him a job so he could earn the money to pay for it."

"But you know nothing about him," her stepmother protested. "He could be one of the rustlers."

"That's true," Melody admitted, "but I'm sure he's not."

"How can you tell? Did you ask him?" Her stepmother leaned forward. She could see the ranch buildings from her window. She watched as Chet walked his horse to the corral and let down the bars. "He's certainly making himself at home."

"I invited him to supper. He hasn't made up his mind about the job."

"I wish you hadn't hired him. That's Tom's job," Belle said.

"I couldn't risk his leaving before Tom got back. Lantz Royal's bullying has driven off three hands since Pa died."

"I still wish you hadn't. Women don't know anything about hiring hands."

"Tom can't tell any more by looking at a man than I can."

"We still shouldn't interfere."

19

"Tom works for us, Belle. If you or I want to hire a hand, we can."

"I wouldn't think of doing such a thing," her stepmother declared, her eyes still on Chet as he unsaddled his horse. "I wouldn't know how."

"I didn't think I did either," Melody confessed, "but it was easy."

"What's Tom going to think when he comes back and finds a strange man in his bunkhouse?"

"He'll think we have a new hand."

Melody had never been able to get her stepmother to understand that now that her husband, Melody's father, was dead, they were the bosses of Spring Water Ranch. Robert Jordan's will left half his ranch to Melody and half to his widow and two sons. Since the boys were both under age, Melody and Belle Jordan had equal votes in all decisions.

But decision making was beyond Belle's ability. The habit of depending on men to make all decisions was so deeply ingrained, she had instinctively turned to her foreman when her husband died. She had been shocked when Melody arrived from Richmond and immediately tried to discuss the future of the ranch. Months later, Belle still felt the same way.

"He looks rather old for a cowhand," Belle remarked as Chet replaced the bars in the corral and headed toward the bunkhouse. "He can't have much ambition."

"He's only twenty-nine," Melody said.

"You know his age?" Belle asked, shocked.

Melody felt herself grow warm. "He said to a man of his age I looked like a mere child. I said he couldn't be more than twenty-five. That's when he told me he was twenty-nine."

"You shouldn't discuss your age with a stranger."

"I didn't. We were discussing his."

"It's all the same," Belle said airily. "I wish you'd given him that horse. I'm not sure I feel comfortable about him."

"You have nothing to worry about. He seems a quiet, dependable man. If there are any problems, we can fire him as quickly as I hired him. Now lie back and take your nap. I'll wake you when dinner's ready."

Belle Jordan obediently leaned back against the mound of pillows and closed her eyes. Melody pulled the curtains against the light.

"Have you thought any more about who you're going to marry?" Belle asked.

Melody felt something inside her clench. She had been in Texas less than three months, yet she was expected to marry Tom Neland or Lantz Royal before the summer was out.

If she weren't in Texas, where there was a desperate shortage of respectable women, Melody would have to consider herself practically on the shelf. Here she was in the fortunate position of being able to choose between two good men. Belle didn't understand why Melody didn't jump at the chance to marry one of them at the earliest possible moment.

Melody didn't know how to tell her stepmother that she had remained unmarried because she had never found a man who could touch her heart. All she'd ever wanted was to be loved. Now she felt as if she had been set down in front of two cages and told to choose which one she wanted to be locked in for the rest of her life.

"I haven't made up my mind yet."

Melody left quickly, before Belle could begin her lecture on the folly of waiting too long and running the risk that one or both suitors might get away.

"Is Mrs. Jordan sleeping again?" Bernice asked when Melody entered the kitchen.

"I hope so," Melody said. "I closed the curtains. Now if the boys will just stay outside."

"Why would they want to be inside?" Bernice asked.

"To cause trouble," Melody replied without hesitation. "I think they lie awake at night thinking up things to do the next day."

"They're boys," Bernice said. "What do you expect them to do?"

"Have a little consideration for their mother."

Bernice snorted. "Boys that age are too full of devilment and sass to understand sickness, or care much if they did. They'll bust if they're not going all the time."

Bernice turned back to her stove. She cooked for everybody on the ranch. She thought nothing of preparing meals for as many as twenty men at a time. Melody helped whenever she could, but she suspected Bernice could have done just as well alone.

Bernice claimed to be half Indian and half Irish. Melody figured that when Bernice began to take form in her mother's womb, the Indian had fought the Irish and won hands down. Except for having one blue eye and one brown, Bernice looked completely Indian, and she reveled in it. She threatened to scalp the boys at least once a day. They threatened to tie her to a stake and do much worse.

Melody wondered where they learned half of

what they knew. She'd had suitors in Richmond with less knowledge of the world. She was certain none of them knew half what Chet Attmore probably knew.

Melody imagined he was familiar with just about every trick the world could throw at him. He seemed quiet and unassuming, but she hadn't missed his air of confidence. He could afford to keep a low profile because he knew he could handle anything that might come his way. He just had that look that said he didn't have anything to prove.

He was tall and lean, tough and brown. She wouldn't be able to tell much about his hair until he took off his hat, but he had thick blond lashes and eyes as blue as sapphires. He didn't talk much, didn't seem to be in a hurry. Melody hadn't expected that. Everybody here seemed to be in a lather to get things done. In a minute was never soon enough.

It was nothing like Virginia. Life there seemed to have stopped since the war.

Everyone out here had expected her to adjust practically overnight. More than that, they expected her to marry and be content. She couldn't be content, not as long as she felt like a stranger in a foreign land still struggling to learn the language. She certainly couldn't choose a husband until she could understand Texas men.

"Who was that man that rode up?" Bernice asked.

"He said his name was Chet Attmore," Melody replied.

"What'd he want?" Bernice asked as she pulled three cake pans out of the cabinet and began to grease them with lard.

"He wanted a horse. His is worn down. I offered to let him work to pay for one."

"What did he say?"

"He's thinking about it."

Bernice poured thick, golden batter into each pan. She was almost as famous for her cakes as she was for her donuts.

"You see he stays."

"Why?" Melody told herself to stop standing around. She opened a drawer, took out an apron, and tied it around her waist.

"Strange things have been going on since your pa died," Bernice said as she started putting the cake pans into the oven. "You can use a man like that."

"How do you know what kind of man he is?" Melody asked. She turned to Bernice, forgetting she had work to do.

"You can tell just by looking," Bernice said. "Don't take no words."

Melody had felt the same way the minute she'd set eyes on him. That was why she had offered him a job. She'd never done such a thing before. She must have wanted him to stay. But why?

Melody could see him walking into the yard just as clearly as if it were happening all over again. She remembered he looked big. Strong. The holstered gun at his waist still disturbed her. She hadn't yet learned to accept a gun as part of a man's everyday dress. From the ease with which he wore it, the look of the well-worn leather, it was obvious he had.

He hadn't shaved in several days. His beard was heavy, but it was too blond to hide his face. It wasn't your typically handsome face. At first glance, one might be inclined to dismiss it. His face wasn't smooth and rosy-cheeked. Nor was it chiseled and aristocratic. Nevertheless, his face intrigued her. She wasn't certain what it was. She thought it had an element of heavy sensuality— something she found disturbing—but she couldn't be sure. It was rugged and rough, but through the lazy ease, the dust and fatigue, she saw a very handsome man, one who seemed aware of how she was looking at him, even what she was thinking.

There was strength in his face, a kind of strength that had nothing to do with money or bloodlines or anything else external. He had the charm of a Southern man, an easygoing manner, a gentle way with his horse, even a respectful attitude toward her. Melody had first seen these qualities in some of the men who'd survived the war. Here she saw it in a man who'd just reached his full maturity, and it drew her like a magnet.

"No, I don't guess it does take words," Melody said. The sound of gunshots caused her to start. She looked up at Bernice.

"Sydney practicing to be a gunfighter," she said. "According to Neill, he means to take care of all our troubles by himself in a month or two."

"I wish his mother would talk to him."

"What for? She can't stop him doing anything. Never even tries as far as I can tell."

"She ought to be concerned for his safety, as well as about the crazy ideas he's getting into his head."

"Don't make a bit of difference. Some people have no backbone. She's one. Depended on your daddy to tell her when to breathe. It's a good thing you're different."

"Not much. I can't make up my mind what to do about marrying Lantz or Tom."

"That's because you don't know this place yet. Once you do, you'll make up your mind fast enough."

"You make me sound hard and bossy."

"No, just tough and sensible." Bernice closed her oven door and fanned herself. "Maybe you can talk that drifter into finding out who's at the bottom of all this trouble."

Before Melody could answer, the back door burst opened and her younger brother, Neill, burst into the kitchen. "Did you know we had a new cowhand?" he asked, breathless with excitement.

Melody nodded.

"Well, Sydney just shot him."

Chapter Two

"Merciful heavens!" Bernice exclaimed. "If I told his mother once, I told her a dozen times—"

Melody didn't wait to hear what Bernice had told Belle. She followed Neill as he ran from the house toward the bunkhouse. Visions flashed through her mind of Chet dead with blood streaming from a hole in his chest, Chet dead with blood all over his face, Chet dead with . . . She stopped herself. Neill had said Sydney shot him. He hadn't said a word about killing.

She followed Neill around the corner of the bunkhouse only to be brought to an abrupt stop. Chet was very much alive, though blood covered the side of his neck. That didn't seem to concern him so much as what he was saying to a very startled-looking Sydney Jordan.

"Only a fool shoots a gun near ranch buildings," Chet was saying.

"I didn't mean to—"

"Good thing you hit me instead of one of your horses," Chet said. "Nobody will miss a drifter, but a good horse can mean the difference between living and dying."

"How was I to know you would be walking around that corner?" Sydney said, angry and embarrassed. "All the hands are out."

"Somebody's always around a ranch," Chet said. "Suppose it had been your mother?"

"She'd never come out here," Sydney said. "She's scared of horses. Now give me back my gun."

Startled, Melody shifted her gaze to the gun in Chet's hand. It was Sydney's. What was Chet doing with it? Sydney never let anyone touch it.

"Does your mother know you have a gun?"

"Of course. I'm not a baby. I'm fourteen."

"Where I come from, fourteen is considered too young to be wearing a gun."

"Where do you come from, some place like Austin?"

"I've been there, but I don't call it home."

"This is the Texas plains," Sydney said. "If you don't wear a gun out here, you're either a woman or a coward."

"Or a kid."

"I'm no kid!" Sydney shouted. "Now give me back my gun."

"I'll make a deal with you. You promise not to shoot it around the ranch buildings, and you can have it back."

"I don't have to make deals with saddle tramps," Sydney said. "This is my ranch, and that's my gun."

"Give it to me," Melody said, walking up to

Chet, her hand outstretched. "I'll keep it until he develops some manners. Sydney, you know that's no way to talk to a stranger. I've told you a hundred—"

"You're not my mother!" Sydney shouted. "And I'm not one of your fine Virginia gentlemen. If one of them was to come to Texas, he wouldn't last a week."

"Pa lasted a lot longer than that," Melody said. "Now I think you owe this gentleman an apology. Not even Texans make a practice of shooting strangers in the face."

"I didn't mean to shoot you," Sydney said, "but I'm not sorry. You had no right to take my gun."

"My usual reaction when someone shoots at me is to shoot back," Chet said. "Would you rather I had done that?"

Melody felt a shiver. That possibility hadn't occurred to her. Despite his easygoing style, this man looked like the kind to shoot first and sort out the situation later. Sydney could so easily have been lying there dead.

"Sydney might not be sure, but I'm very grateful you didn't shoot back," Melody said.

"He probably couldn't hit anything," Sydney muttered, his expression sullen.

The words had hardly left his mouth when a pistol shot shattered what was left of Melody's nerves. A small shriek escaped from behind the hand that had flown to her mouth. Sydney looked startled at the speed with which Chet had drawn and fired.

"If you'll check that tin can you were shooting at, you'll find a hole in the middle of the peach on the label."

Quick as a flash, Neill ran to where the can had

landed. He picked it up, and his eyes grew wide.

"Wow!" he exclaimed, looking from the can to Sydney. "Right through the middle. You coulda killed Sydney deader than a skinned steer," he said, turning to Chet.

Melody swallowed.

"Who the hell *are* you?" Sydney demanded. The angry red in his cheeks had changed to a dull pallor.

"Are you a gunslinger?" Neill asked.

"Neill Jordan!" Melody said, recovering her voice. "Apologize to Mr. Attmore right now."

"I'm sorry," Neill said. "I just wanted to know. I never saw anybody who could shoot like that."

"I used to be foreman of a large ranch," Chet explained. "I found it very helpful to be able to shoot better than the outlaws who tried to steal our cows. But I guess you could call me a gunfighter. A lot of people do."

"Wow!" Neill exclaimed, his eyes getting big. "A real gunslinger! Wait till I tell Mama."

"Maybe you'd better tell Bernice," Melody said. "I don't think your mama would appreciate it the way you do."

Neill ran off, taking the prized can with him.

Her remark might have sounded offhand, but Melody felt anything but casual about what had just happened. The thing she disliked most about Texans was their firm belief that guns and violence were the answer to every problem. Now she'd invited a man to work for her who admitted being a gunslinger. If that peach can was any indication, he had probably killed a lot of people.

She couldn't have a gunslinger working for her. She had enough trouble with Tom wanting to arm the men in response to Lantz's bullying, especially since the rustlers had shot Speers. Then there was Sydney. He was angry at Chet for showing him up and taking his gun, but he longed to become a gunman. He'd forget his anger if Chet offered to teach him how to shoot. No, Chet had to go.

But she wanted him to stay. She couldn't offer any reasonable explanation for it, but she'd been strongly attracted to him from the very first. Why else would she have offered a job to a complete stranger? She'd thought this man was different. Even Bernice agreed he was someone special. It hurt to find she'd been mistaken.

"I guess you could have killed me," Sydney said.

"I wouldn't have," Chet said. "My adopted father always said I had to see what I was shooting at before I pulled the trigger. The one time I didn't, he nearbout knocked my head off my shoulders."

"Nobody'd knock me in the head," Sydney said, bristling.

"Better to get a lump on your skull than shoot the wrong person and have to live with it for the rest of your life," Chet said.

Chet held out the gun to Sydney. The boy practically snatched it from Chet's hand. Melody opened her mouth to reprimand him, then closed it again. If Sydney was going to listen to anybody, it would be this gunman. He had nothing but scorn for her and her Virginia manners.

"If you'd like me to help—"

"I don't need any help from you," Sydney said.

Melody hoped Sydney's continued rudeness stemmed from embarrassment at having been caught in the wrong, but she didn't count on it. He was determined to prove his manhood. She

31

was the only one who made any attempt to convince him he was going about it in the wrong way.

"I wasn't aiming for the can when I shot you," Sydney said. "I was angry because I'd missed it."

"Never shoot in anger. If you do, it'll kill you one day."

"Nobody's going to kill me," Sydney said. "I'm going to be the best shot in Texas."

"If you stay alive long enough."

But Sydney had turned and marched off toward the house. Chet turned to Melody.

"I've tried, but I can't do anything with him," she said before he spoke. "I told you we were having some trouble. Well, Sydney thinks being able to shoot fast is the only solution. I've tried to tell him there are lots of other choices, but I haven't met a single man since I came to Texas who can see anything but fighting and guns. Sorry," she said, when she realized he probably thought her remarks referred to him as well. "I'm not used to this, and I don't understand it. Let me see about your wound."

"It's nothing. Barely a scratch."

"Even scratches can become infected. Let me look at it."

She could tell he didn't want to, but he was too polite to refuse her offer of help. Or maybe he just thought it was easier that way.

She hadn't realized just how tall or how big he was until she reached up to touch his neck. She was of medium height for a woman, but he must have been at least a foot taller. He seemed much bigger now that she was close to him—his arms, his chest, even his neck, all thick and broad and well-muscled.

32

"It seems to have done little more than take the skin off," she said.

"I told you it was nothing."

"I'll have to clean it."

Melody found it hard to concentrate on his wound. An aura of sensuality seemed to surround him, to envelope her as she stood next to him. When he looked down at her with those incredibly blue eyes, she felt herself sinking in a pool of mesmerizing warmth. It seemed to draw her in, to promise something unique. It was so strong that, despite her dislike of guns, it made her regret he couldn't stay.

Melody had had her share of admirers. In a Richmond devastated by the Civil War, the daughter of a well-to-do Texas rancher was energetically pursued. She had made her debut at sixteen, had been a veteran of the courting ritual by seventeen, almost an old maid by the time she was eighteen and her aunt's death caused her to move to Texas. But not once during those years had any man so powerfully affected her.

Yet Chet wasn't doing anything. He simply was.

She didn't know how long she might have remained standing there, virtually immobilized, if Tom Neland hadn't ridden in.

"What's going on?" Tom asked as he dismounted.

"This man stopped by to ask about buying a horse," Melody said as she fought free of the lethargy that gripped her. "Before he'd had time to drop his bedroll in the bunkhouse, Sydney shot him."

"It's just a scratch," Chet said.

"What were you doing to make Sydney take a shot at you?" Tom asked, his suspicions aroused.

"I came around the corner of the bunkhouse just as Sydney was taking a shot in frustration," Chet explained.

"Chet took his gun away," Melody said. "When he got it back, he went inside in a huff."

"I should think he would," Tom said. "Nobody takes another man's gun away."

"A fourteen-year-old boy who fires random shots in a fit of temper in the vicinity of ranch buildings is still a child and should be treated like one," Chet said.

"I'd like to see you try," Tom snapped.

"He's not my responsibility."

It wasn't hard to see that the two men weren't going to be friends. Only Tom showed overt signs of dislike, but it was clear Chet wasn't impressed with the Spring Water foreman. That shouldn't have come as a surprise. Melody had been in continual disagreement with Tom Neland from the moment she'd arrived.

"He's not my responsibility, either," Tom Neland said.

"Miss Jordan just said you were her foreman," Chet said.

"What of it?"

"It could have been one of your men coming around that corner."

"What goes on around here is none of your business."

"That's where you're wrong," Melody said. "I just hired him."

What was wrong with her? She'd just decided he had to leave and here she was telling Tom she'd hired him.

"Hiring's my job," Tom said.

"You weren't here."

"How do we know he can do the work?" Tom asked, glaring at Chet. "Just because he looks like a grub line rider doesn't mean he's any good with cattle."

"He used to be a foreman on a cattle ranch," Melody said.

Melody could see Tom bristle immediately. "That doesn't mean anything," he said. "If he were any good, he wouldn't be at loose ends now."

"Have you ever heard of the Randolph family's Circle Seven Ranch or Jake Maxwell of the Broken Circle?" Chet asked.

"Sure. Everybody's heard of them, especially the Randolphs."

"I worked three drives to Abilene with Monty and Hen Randolph. Jake Maxwell is my father. I was his foreman until I was twenty-two."

Melody was careful not to smile at Tom's look of chagrin. From being a nameless, drifting gunslinger, Chet Attmore had turned out to be a cowman with better credentials than Tom. Maybe he wasn't a gunslinger after all. Maybe her instincts had been right.

"Then what the hell are you doing here?" Tom asked, his mood not improved by being proved wrong.

"I told you, he needs a horse," Melody said. "I talked him into working to pay for it."

"If he really is Jake Maxwell's son, he can buy a whole herd of horses," Tom said. "That man owns a half dozen valleys in the Hill Country."

"Jake owns two," Chet said. "Various members of the family own the others. And yes, I can buy a horse. But I only wanted to trade until my horse has time to recover."

Melody stared at Chet. That accounted for the

quality of his horse. It didn't account for his down-at-the-heels appearance.

"Then I can't see why you'd want to hang around here," Tom said. "We're not nearly as grand as you're used to."

"I'm only an adopted son," Chet said. "Jake doesn't owe me a dime."

He said it dispassionately, as if it didn't bother him one way or the other. Melody felt a bond of sympathy. She wasn't an orphan, but she'd lost her mother at birth. Aunt Emmaline had done the best she could, but no one could take the place of a girl's own mother. And though her father had sent money regularly, she'd always felt that if he really loved her, he'd have wanted her with him in Texas.

"I still don't think you'd be happy here," Tom said.

"In that case it's a good thing I'm not planning to stay," Chet said.

"I thought Melody said—"

"She offered me the job. I agreed to think about it. It's clear you don't like me. I'd be a fool to stay under those conditions."

He certainly didn't mince words, Melody thought. "But you will stay for dinner," she said. "After being shot, that's the least we can do." She regretted he was leaving, but it was probably better this way. She already had two men to deal with she couldn't understand. She didn't need a third.

"You could trade me a horse," Chet said, a faint smile on his lips.

"You can have any horse you want," Melody said, "on condition you stay until tomorrow morning and let me take care of your wound."

Chet looked at Tom.

"Of course you'll stay the night," Tom said. "There's plenty of room in the bunkhouse. Bernice feeds the hands in the kitchen at five o'clock."

"He'll eat with the family," Melody said.

"A place in the kitchen is all I'm used to," Chet said. "I'm not dressed for anything else."

Melody had every intention of arguing with him, but she was distracted by the sound of a rider approaching. She looked up to see the very impressive figure of Lantz Royal.

Lantz was thirty-eight, big, handsome, and the richest cattleman in the area. He was used to getting everything he wanted. When people called him greedy, he laughed and said he didn't want much, just all the land that bordered his. Her father had stood up to him, but Royal had run most of the ranchers out of the area. Now that Bob Jordan was dead, Royal had made it plain he meant to have the Spring Water.

He wanted Melody as well. She sometimes got the feeling that if she didn't agree to marry him, he'd take the ranch and leave her and her brothers nothing. So far, he'd been patient, willing to get what he wanted by guile rather than force, but she didn't know how long that would last.

Not long if he was as impatient as his son. Blade Royal was wild and willful, and fancied himself a gun hand. He was not above doing something rash or downright foolish, but Lantz was always around to see that Blade didn't have to suffer the consequences of the trouble he stirred up.

Blade had wanted to marry Melody, too. She didn't know which man would be more dangerous if they ever squared off against each other.

She did know that at eighteen, Blade Royal was too young to be thinking of becoming anybody's husband.

Chet was irritated with himself for bandying words with Melody's foreman. He had been toying with the idea of staying at the Spring Water for a short time, but Tom Neland obviously didn't like him and didn't want him there.

It was just as well. He'd been thinking too much about Melody, and that wouldn't do anybody any good. A woman like her would see him as a curiosity at best, at worst somebody to avoid at all costs. He'd seen the way she reacted when he admitted to being a gunslinger. After all these years, he still couldn't get used to it. He kept making the mistake of thinking he was as good as anybody else.

Men like him had a place, and it wasn't anywhere near women like her. He might as well get her out of his mind right now. She was just another good-looking woman. He'd forgotten at least a dozen. He'd forget her, too.

Yet he had been thinking about changing his plans because of her. That was a dangerous sign. A smart man wouldn't have needed Tom's dislike to know it was best to leave. Chet had lived through too much danger to start making foolish decisions now.

The arrival of the arrogant newcomer wouldn't normally have concerned Chet. He had started to turn away until he noticed Melody's reaction. Her body seemed to stiffen; the expression on her face become set. But it was the glance she threw in Chet's direction that caused him to pause, the fear at the back of her eyes that caused him to take a closer look at this man.

Chet had seen his type before—big, handsome, strong, rich—a man who seemed to think success gave him the right to do anything he wanted. His overbearing attitude, even the way he sat forward in the saddle, told Chet he was probably worse than most.

It bothered him that Tom Neland reacted in much the same way as Melody. If her foreman was uneasy around this man, how could he be depended upon to stand up to him? Chet decided to stay right where he was for a few more minutes.

"Good afternoon, Miss Jordan," the man said. "You're looking as beautiful as ever."

Chet disliked him at once. It wasn't that Melody wasn't beautiful or that she didn't deserve the compliment, but coming from this man's lips it sounded like a slur.

"I'm feeling hot and dusty," Melody said. "You're going to have to excuse me. I've got to see to Chet's wound."

"Has another one of your hands been hurt?"

He showed no concern. In fact, Chet thought he looked pleased.

"It's just a scratch," Chet said, facing the man who was rude enough to have remained in the saddle.

The visitor ignored Chet. "I don't recognize him," he said to Melody. "He's not one of your hands. What's he doing here?"

Chet knew it was foolish to rile this man, but he wouldn't be dismissed by anybody's oversized ego. "I don't recognize you either," he said.

"You're certainly not a hand. What are *you* doing here?"

"My name's Lantz Royal." The man's angry irritation communicated itself to his mount, making the animal restless. "I'm Miss Jordan's neighbor. I've come to make sure she's doing all right."

"My name's Chet Attmore. I'm just passing through. I'm sure Miss Jordan would welcome any gentleman concerned about her."

"I—" Melody began.

"But you are not a gentleman."

Royal reached for his gun. He stopped, his hand in the process of closing around the handle. Chet's gun was pointed directly at his heart.

"I was about to say no gentleman would stay in the saddle while talking to a lady." Chet intentionally spoke in a soft, unhurried voice. "Nor would he attempt to shoot down a man he didn't know in front of her."

"You insulted me," Royal said, his color high.

"I just wanted to say you weren't treating Miss Jordan with the respect she deserves," Chet said. "I'm sure it was an oversight. You were so anxious to know she was okay, you forgot all about your manners."

Chet eased his gun back into its holster, but he didn't take his eyes off Royal. Nor had he made any attempt to keep a slight sneer from his voice.

"I wasn't going to kill you," Royal snapped. "I was just going to teach you a lesson."

"How? By giving me a *scratch* on the other cheek?"

Royal muttered something under his breath and turned to Melody. "I'm sure you know I meant no disrespect," he said as he swung out of the saddle. "I'd never be rude to the woman I hope to make my bride."

Chet hoped his face didn't show the shock he felt. He hoped she hadn't given any serious consideration to this proposal. He couldn't read her thoughts, but he did know she wasn't comfortable around Lantz Royal.

"I'm perfectly fine," Melody said to Royal in a flat, controlled voice. "It was kind but unnecessary for you to check on me three days in a row."

"I had to come," Royal said. "I heard another one of your hands had been attacked. What happened?"

"We don't know," Tom Neland said. "They shot from ambush. Speers's partner was more interested in seeing he got help than in going after the coyote who tried to drygulch him."

"I've been telling you this country is too dangerous for an unmarried woman," Royal said to Melody. "If you would just agree to marry me, I'd have my men all over those hills. Wouldn't a rustler dare come within a hundred miles of the place."

"What makes you think it was rustlers?" Chet asked. "I haven't heard of any around here."

"They just started within the last year," Tom said. "I won't know until roundup, but I think we've lost cattle."

"Me, too," Royal said.

Chet turned back to Royal, careful to keep his expression neutral. "If your men can't protect your own herds, how're they going to protect Miss Jordan's?"

Royal flinched, as if he'd started to draw his gun and thought better of it. Chet decided no one had tweaked Royal's nose in so long, he thought he could do or say just about anything he pleased. It was about time somebody told him otherwise.

"I would hire a dozen extra men if necessary," Royal said, making a visible attempt to rein in his temper.

"You'll be pleased to know you needn't go to so much expense," Chet said. "Miss Royal has just offered me a job. Seeing as how I'm right handy with a gun, she won't be needing your dozen extra men."

Hell, why had he gone and said that? He had already made up his mind to ride out the minute he could get his leg across a fresh horse. He'd let a pair of brown eyes and a fearful glance egg him into throwing down a challenge to this loud-mouth. Now he couldn't leave until he was sure Royal wouldn't take his anger out on Melody or her crew.

"We don't want your kind in Concho County," Royal said. "You drifted in. You can drift right out again."

Chet had had trouble with his temper all his life. The one thing that made him madder than anything else was some big rancher thinking his money and the number of men he had working for him entitled him to push other people around. It just naturally overpowered his good sense.

"I couldn't go, not after Miss Jordan has prac-tically begged me to take her job." He smiled in-wardly at the look she darted in his direction. He bet Melody Jordan had never begged anybody to do anything in her life.

"*I* didn't beg you," Tom Neland said, "and I don't want you here."

"It's a shame what you want doesn't count much," Chet said, again speaking softly.

"I'm foreman around here."

"Which means you take your orders from Miss Jordan."

"I . . . Miss Jordan leaves the running of the ranch to me."

Just as he'd thought. Tom Neland didn't want anybody telling him what to do, especially a woman. Chet suspected they'd already had a few run-ins on that score.

"Are you trying to run me off before she can look at my wound?" Chet asked Tom.

"Nobody's trying to run you off," Melody said. "And I did offer you a job, so it's yours if you still want it. Now if you'll excuse me, Lantz, I need to tend to Mr. Attmore's neck. Thanks for coming by. Good day."

"Melody, there's no need for you to take care of every tramp who wanders onto your place," Royal said. "Let Bernice see to him. I wanted to talk to you about—"

"Did you hear Miss Jordan?" Chet asked.

"Huh?" Royal stared at Chet as though he'd forgotten he was there.

"She told you good day. That means you're to leave."

"Now look here—"

"Forget your manners again? You'd better buy yourself a book. That way you can brush up on them before you come over here again."

"Come on," Melody said to Chet. "I want to get something on that wound before it becomes infected."

"Who the hell is that man?" Chet heard Royal ask Tom.

"I don't know," Tom replied. "Seems he stopped

here wanting to swap for a run-down horse."

"Well, get rid of him. I don't want to see him when I come back. If I do, I'm not going to be responsible for what I do."

Chapter Three

"Are you trying to get yourself killed?" Melody asked as they walked toward the house.

Chet was feeling annoyed with himself now that his temper had begun to cool. Once again he'd let anger force him into something he'd already decided not to do. But he'd learned long ago that he couldn't do much except ride it out and patch things up when it was over. He'd inherited his temper from his mother. He couldn't remember her when she wasn't screaming at someone. His father was just the opposite; he never seemed to care about anything.

"Why would you think that?" Chet asked.

"You deliberately tried to provoke Lantz Royal."

"He made me angry."

"Do you always provoke people who make you angry?"

"Usually."

"I thought you said you had been a foreman. How did you get your men to work together?"

"It caused some problems."

"I expect it did."

"None I couldn't handle."

"Other people may have stayed out of your way, but Lantz won't. He's the most important rancher in this area."

"He certainly thinks so."

Melody looked askance. "He has more cows, more land, and more cowhands than anybody else."

"And more arrogance and more certainty that he ought to have anything he wants. You meaning to let him have you?"

She turned on him. "That's none of your business."

"I didn't say it was." She started toward the house. "You going to answer my question?"

She stopped and turned again, irritation showing in the set of her mouth. "If you know as much about manners as you pretend, you know it's rude to ask such a question."

"My manners don't count. His do if you plan to marry him. I was just trying to shape him up a little for you."

"You were not. You were trying to provoke him. Why?"

"I don't like men who go for a gun for no reason."

"In Virginia, telling a man he's no gentleman is one of the surest ways to start a fight."

"I guess that makes him more of a gentleman than I thought."

"You're just playing with me," she said, irritably, "like you did with Lantz."

"I don't like Lantz."

She stopped abruptly and directed a questioning look at him. "And you like me?"

"Sure."

"Why? You know nothing about me."

"You're prettier. Besides, you offered me a bed and a bandage."

She studied him for a moment. "I don't understand you. You dress like a drifter, yet you're connected to two of the biggest ranchers in Texas. You seem to know how to act like a gentleman, yet you admit to being a gunslick."

Chet laughed. "I bet you didn't learn that word in Virginia."

"Don't try to sidetrack me. I thought you were going to go, but you tell Lantz you've hired on. You act like nothing in the world matters to you, yet you defended my honor like an old-fashioned cavalier."

"You can blame that on my adopted mother. She brought Savannah etiquette to Texas, whether we wanted it or not."

"I doubt she taught you to insult rich and powerful men with no regard for the consequences. I'm trying very hard to convince myself you're not crazy."

"If you're not going to look at my neck, I think I'll wash it in the trough."

"And poison the horses!"

Chet grinned. "I bet you created a stir in Richmond society." He felt a momentary qualm when he noticed a slight tinge of color in her cheeks.

"I speak my mind, if that's what you mean. As you no doubt know, men aren't very fond of that."

"Especially those with limited minds."

She smiled in spite of herself. "Especially those. Now let's go inside before Lantz and Tom come to see what we're talking about."

"We could tell them you're trying to decide if I've been out in the sun too long."

"I expect they've already reached that conclusion themselves."

Neill came tumbling out of the house just as they reached the kitchen.

"Wait until Tom sees this!" he said, holding the tin can with the peach wrapper aloft.

"I'd rather you didn't show that to him," Chet said.

"It's too late now," Melody said when Neill didn't slow down. "If you're determined to show off, people are going to talk about it."

"That's what Isabelle said."

"Who's Isabelle?"

"My adopted mother."

"The one from Savannah?"

"Yes."

"But she married a Texan."

"Isabelle has wonderful manners, but underneath she's just as ruthless as Jake. She'd make mincemeat of Lantz Royal."

"I'd like to meet her," Melody said as she opened the kitchen door and stepped inside.

Those innocent words spiraled into a chain of thoughts Chet wouldn't allow his mind to follow.

"You'd like her, but she's a bit bossy, just like you're going to be once you get a handle on this place," he said as he started to follow her through the doorway.

Melody slammed the door in his face. He grinned. The lady had a temper. He pushed the door open and peeped in to see if she was going to throw something when he entered.

"I am not bossy," she said when their gazes met. "And what makes you think I have any desire to get a handle on this place? I might decide to sell my half of the ranch and go back to Richmond."

He came in and closed the door behind him.

"It won't sell so good with the doors off the hinges," remarked a woman up to her elbows in flour. "You the fella Sydney shot?" she asked Chet.

"Yes, ma'am."

Her hands stilled in the dough as she looked him up and down. "Maybe we'd better send him out hunting more often. He never brought down anything half as good-looking as you."

"Bernice, how can you say such a thing?" Melody exclaimed.

"Because I've got eyes in my head," Bernice said. "And if you don't think he's better looking than anybody you've clapped eyes on—here or in your precious Richmond—then I say you're telling a lie. Look at him, honey. There's a smoldering look in those eyes that could light a fire in the dark and musty corners of any woman's heart."

"That's not the point," Melody said, the color rising in her cheeks again.

"Then what is?"

"This blood on my neck," Chet pointed out, winking at Bernice.

"Do clean him up," Bernice said. "I hate to see such a pretty man all bloody."

Melody pulled out a chair and motioned Chet to sit down. With something short of the best will in the world, she filled a bowl with water and prepared to wash his neck.

"You don't like it when people tell me I'm nice looking?" He didn't flinch when she touched the wound.

"I imagine you've been told that far too often."

"Have you been told too often that you're beautiful?"

Bernice burst out laughing. "He's got you there."

"I don't believe in pandering to a person's vanity," Melody said.

"I like being pandered to," Chet said. "It helps make up for the times people decide they'd rather point a gun at me."

"That was your decision."

"That's why I decided to hang up my gun. Sadly, I'm still long on guns and short on compliments."

This man was full of surprises. If she interpreted him correctly, he'd given up gunfighting. Or at least he was thinking about it.

"Don't look to me to even the score," Melody said.

"Me neither," Bernice said with a chuckle. "You bat those eyes at me, and my poor old heart would give right out."

"Bernice, I never thought I'd hear you talk like this."

"I'm old, child, but I've got a good memory. I'm not blind either. Now you stop worrying about me and get him cleaned up so he can make himself presentable for dinner. Belle will have a fit if he comes to the table looking like he's been dragged across the corral first."

"I thought you said I was beautiful," Chet said.

"I did, boy. Beautiful, but dusty."

It had been a long time since anyone had called

Chet a boy. He wondered if Bernice's eyesight was as good as she thought.

"When I think of how easily this wound could have been fatal," Melody said, "I feel weak in the knees."

"Don't worry. A gypsy in Mexico said many bullets would be fired at me, but I would die in my bed."

"You can die in your bed from a bullet wound," Melody pointed out.

"I asked her about that, but she said her crystal ball had gone cloudy all of a sudden."

Melody stepped back so she could look at him. "Are you ever serious about anything?"

"Most people like me this way. They say I'm usually too serious."

"I expect you do it to keep people at a distance. You needn't bother since you're leaving."

Chet had never met a woman who could cut through his defenses quite so quickly. "You might not like me serious."

"As I said, you're leaving. It won't matter what you're like."

"Melody doesn't believe in sugarcoating things," Bernice said.

"So I see. You don't have to put a bandage on my neck. It'll make it hard to swallow."

"It's still bleeding."

"It'll soon crust over."

She chose a clean pad and poured whiskey into it. "This is going to sting."

"You mean it's going to feel like the Devil's got his claws in his neck," Bernice said.

"I don't suppose it'll hurt worse than the bullet," Chet said.

"Okay, I won't give you any sympathy."

He hadn't meant it that way, but he had obviously riled her. It did sting, but he'd experienced much worse over the last seven years.

Besides, he was distracted by the smell of gardenias. The smell had danced around the edge of his consciousness ever since he entered the house. When Melody leaned over him the first time, he'd identified the fragrance. When she leaned over him a second time, he was certain it came from her. It was a sweet smell, strong but not cloying. He liked it. He thought it suited her.

"You don't have to be so stoic," she said.

"What do you want me to do, yell and scream?"

"No, but a wince would let me know there's somebody inside that shell, that you can feel things."

He grimaced. "There. Are you satisfied?"

Her expression said she wasn't. She handed him a clean pad. "Hold this to your neck until it stops weeping. After that you can get rid of some of that dust Bernice mentioned. We sit down to dinner at six o'clock."

"I don't want to eat with the family."

"It would be bad manners to refuse. And you know what happens to men who behave badly toward a lady."

She left the kitchen without giving him a chance to respond.

"No point in arguing with her," Bernice said. "Once she makes up her mind, she don't change it."

"She and Royal ought to make a great pair."

"Don't wish that on her," Bernice said.

"Why? The man's rich and wants to marry her."

"There's a curse on that house," Bernice said.

"What are you talking about?" He'd been joking

about the Mexican gypsy. He didn't believe in signs and portents or witchcraft.

"His son's dead set on marrying her, too. If she goes to that house as a bride, at least one of them will be dead inside a week."

The sooner he got out of here, the better, Chet thought to himself as he walked back to the bunkhouse. He felt as if he'd stepped into the middle of a bad play where all the protagonists ended up dead by the final curtain.

He noticed his saddle and bedroll weren't outside the bunkhouse where he'd dropped them. He looked around but didn't see them anywhere. He stepped inside the bunkhouse. It took a moment for his eyes to adjust to the dim interior.

"You the fella Sydney shot?"

The voice came from the gloom of one of the bunks.

"Yes," Chet said, turning to the sound, struggling to make out the shape of the young man lying in the bed.

"Tom put your gear on the bunk over there." He offered his hand in a friendly greeting. "I'm Tim Speers. Tom said you'd probably come looking for it."

"I'll need it to ride out of here tomorrow."

"Tom said Miss Jordan had offered you a job. I sure wish you'd take it."

"Why? You don't know whether I can tell one end of a cow from the other."

"I wouldn't care if you couldn't tell a heifer from a steer. I saw the way you stood up to Lantz Royal. That's all I need to know."

Chet pulled up a chair and straddled it, his arms resting on the back. "Why is that so important? You've got a foreman."

53

"Tom will face Royal, but he can't stand up to him. There's a difference."

"You mean Tom has courage, but Royal doesn't think him dangerous enough to worry about."

"Something like that."

"Why would I be any different?"

"He already knows you can draw like lightning and ain't afraid to do it."

"It seems to me this whole question rests in Miss Jordan's hands. She can send him away or not as she wants."

"Between Lantz Royal's boys shooting at us to scare Miss Jordan into marrying him and rustlers shooting at us for real, a cowhand's life ain't worth much around here. I'm thinking about asking for my time as soon as I get well enough to travel."

"I'm not hunting a shooting job," Chet said.

"Neill said you drilled a peach can."

Chet felt like kicking himself for doing something so stupid. "I guess old habits die hard."

But that wasn't the way he usually behaved. He didn't insult powerful ranchers, either. Anyone who knew him knew he drew his gun only as a last resort. He never went around shooting at targets to show off his marksmanship. Yet he'd done all those things in the space of half an hour. What had gotten into him?

Melody Jordan, that's what. Something had happened to him the moment he set eyes on her. He didn't know whether it was lust or fascination, but he did know that even thinking there might be a possibility of something developing between them was crazy.

Even if he was fool enough to consider getting married, she was wrong for him. She was old Virginia society. He was an ex-gunfighter who couldn't do anything but punch cows.

He stood up. "I guess I'd better get out of here before I do anything else stupid."

"How do you figure that?"

"I got Miss Jordan thinking I can handle her job, you thinking I can handle Royal, and Neill thinking I can handle a gunslinger. It'd take a very tough man to measure up to all that."

"Something tells me you could do it."

"As I see it, Melody holds all the cards. She only has to play them and the game will be over."

Chet was uneasy about joining the family for dinner. He never liked meeting strangers. They always expected him to be something he wasn't. The women took one look at him and decided it was open season. The men preferred someone willing to talk too loud, drink too much whiskey, tell too many tall tales. He was quiet, a loner, a disappointment to all. He'd tried to get Bernice to let him eat in the bunkhouse with the wounded cowhand. Much to his surprise, Speers was summoned to the table as well. He wasn't happy about it either.

"I never ate at the house," Speers said when Chet helped him through the door.

"Don't worry about it," Chet said. "They're doing this to punish me and Tom."

"Why?"

"Because I'm not doing what they want me to do."

"Tom doesn't want you to stay."

"Tom didn't invite me to dinner, either."

"I see what you mean."

The ranch house didn't have the same comfortable, lived-in feeling Isabelle's had. Everything about it made Chet feel out of place. It was larger than he had ever seen in this part of Texas. Expensive-looking rugs made him afraid to step on the floor. The walls were covered with fancy paper decorated with French ladies and gentlemen in elaborate clothes. Mirrors in ornate gold frames and pictures in heavy, dark frames covered much of the walls. Beneath these someone had placed several fragile tables, all of them loaded with vases of colored glass or painted with pastoral scenes. The parlor was filled with furniture that looked as uncomfortable as it was fashionable. Victorian. Chet didn't like that style one bit. Too fussy.

"Makes you afraid to breathe deep," Speers said.

On the opposite side of the hall a pocket door slid open. Melody stood just inside.

"I think you men will be more comfortable in Pa's study," she said, standing back to let them enter.

Chet could see Speers visibly relax, whether at the sight of a room full of sturdy, leather-covered chairs with rag rugs and a stone hearth or of Tom Neland relaxing in a deep chair, he couldn't tell. Tom didn't look pleased to see Chet. Nor did he offer to give Chet a hand getting Speers settled into a chair. His sour expression indicated that his mind was taken up with things that displeased him even more.

"You sure you don't need a doctor to look at that leg, Speers?" Melody asked.

"There's no doctor between here and town," Tom said.

"I can look at it," Chet offered.

"What can you do?"

"I know a little bit about gunshot wounds."

All three people looked at him expectantly.

"I've had a few," Chet said.

An expensively dressed woman floated into the silence that followed.

"I thought I'd find you in here," she said, her East Texas drawl mixed with an accent Chet didn't recognize. "Why is it men never like to sit in the parlor?"

"Rooms like that make men nervous," Melody said. "They remind them too much of the baths their mamas used to make them take before company came."

"It doesn't stop the boys," the woman said, turning to Chet as he finished helping settle Speers. "They'd flop down on anything if I let them. . . ." Her voice trailed off as her gaze fixed itself on Chet. Her eyes narrowed, then grew wider. Her entire physical posture changed from fairly brisk to positively languid. A hand automatically smoothed a ruffle at her breast that wasn't out of place.

"Who are you?" she asked in a voice that was at once husky and excited.

"I already told you," Melody said. "He walked in earlier wanting to trade his horse."

Chet figured a wash and dress clothes made him look so different, she didn't recognize him.

"You're welcome to any horse we have," the woman said.

"This is my stepmother, Belle Jordan," Melody said. "Please ignore her offer. She knows nothing about horses or the ranch."

"I do know it's impolite to refuse a man in

need," Belle said. "Especially such a handsome one."

Chet noticed Melody roll her eyes heavenward. "His looks don't make any difference."

Chet couldn't resist nettling Melody. Acting as he thought one of her Virginia beaux would, he bent over Belle's hand and brushed it with his lips. "You don't have to worry I'll beggar the ranch, ma'am. I only want to borrow one for a while."

"Melody, I don't see why he shouldn't have any horse he wants if he means to return it."

"What if he doesn't mean it?" Tom muttered.

"I'm certain he does. A dishonest man couldn't look this handsome. But why don't you stay here while your horse rests up? You could . . . merciful heavens! Have you been shot?"

"By Sydney," Melody informed her stepmother. "I told you about that, too."

"I know, dear, but I didn't know you meant him."

Melody rolled her eyes once more. "Speers is more seriously wounded."

"But he's one of ours. This man is a guest."

"I doubt Speers hurts any less for not being a guest."

Belle ignored her stepdaughter. "You really must stay until you've had a chance to recover."

"It's his horse that's tired, Belle, not him."

"If his horse is worn out, you can be sure he is, too."

Fortunately, since Melody's high color indicated that she had reached the end of her patience, Neill stuck his head into the room. "Bernice said dinner's on the table. Sydney is already eating."

The head disappeared. Chet assumed Neill had gone to make sure Sydney didn't get too much of a head start.

"I have tried to teach those boys some manners," Belle said to Chet, "but I might as well be talking to the wind."

"It would help if you gave them some consequences and meant it," Melody said.

"Darling, you know Sydney is too strong-minded for me. I expect Neill will start running over me soon, too."

"He is already," Melody said as she swept past them.

"I sorely miss my husband," Belle said to Chet as she took his arm and followed her stepdaughter. "He was such a strong man. I'm afraid I depended on him for everything."

Chet had seen her type before. She wasn't really a bad woman, probably even quite a nice one. She simply didn't have any backbone, or preferred not to use it if she had. She thought a man, especially a handsome man, was the answer to everything.

He knew most men preferred such a woman, and he could certainly see why. She'd never disagree with him. She'd keep herself pretty and soft, be ready for him whenever he wanted her. She'd make certain everything in the household was ordered to please him. She'd flatter his vanity and mean every word of it. Yes, he could see how a man could grow mighty attached to a woman like Belle Jordan.

Melody wasn't a bit like her stepmother. She had more energy than a yearling colt, limited patience, a tongue with two sharp edges, and a stubborn streak he bet ran from the nape of her neck to her tailbone. The man who married her was in for a thorny marriage. She'd be yapping at his heels from dawn to dusk, keeping his toes to the mark, his shoulder in the harness.

But . . .

Isabelle was a dynamo, and his sister Drew kept the entire clan hopping to her tune. Not that he would want to be married to Drew. As much as he loved her, she'd drive him around the bend inside a month. If Drew loved you, she was all over you.

Still . . .

If he'd been able to consider marriage, he'd prefer a wife strong enough to take over if something happened to him. With his reputation with a gun—not to mention his brother Luke's—something probably would. It was just as well he wasn't planning to get married. He wouldn't want to make the woman he loved a widow.

They arrived at the dining room to see the end of a confrontation. Melody had apparently taken Sydney's plate from him. He was intent on getting it back.

"Give it back, or I'll punch you."

"You will wait to eat until your mother is seated," Melody said, her voice rigidly controlled. "And if you ever again serve yourself before a guest even enters the dining room, you'll eat in the kitchen."

Sydney drew his fist back.

"I'd think very hard before I did that," Chet said.

Sydney looked around, angry at the interference. "What business is it of yours?"

"Probably none. But if you hit your sister, I'll have to break your arm."

Chapter Four

Melody hadn't heard Chet and her stepmother enter the dining room. She looked up, embarrassed to have him witness still another example of her family's faults. She certainly hadn't expected him to come to her rescue in such dramatic fashion. If anyone supported her, she would have expected it to be Tom. He'd been trying to convince her that he'd make her a good husband, that he could be the male authority figure Sydney and Neill needed so badly.

Sydney's body jerked. He turned toward Chet, his eyes filled with anger. "You wouldn't."

"There's one way to find out," Chet said.

The coldness of his voice chilled Melody right through. She didn't understand how he could be teasing one minute and deadly serious the next. The change was too fast, too confusing for her.

"What are you doing here?" Sydney demanded.

"Cowhands are supposed to eat in the kitchen."

"I invited him to eat with us," Melody said. The diversion gave her the opportunity to hand Sydney's plate to Bernice, who set it on the sideboard.

"He's a guest," Belle said as Chet held her chair for her. "Guests always eat in the dining room." Tom held Melody's chair.

"He's a cowhand," Sydney insisted.

"That's what you'll be when you grow up," Melody said.

Now that the ladies were seated, the men sat down.

Sydney flushed. "I'm already grown up, and I'm not a cowhand. I'm the owner."

"Your mother and Melody own the ranch," Tom said, shaking the folds out of his napkin and putting it in his lap. "You won't come into your share until you're twenty-one."

"I don't see why," Sydney said. "Blade Royal is only eighteen, and he runs his ranch."

"Blade only does what his father lets him do," Tom said.

"That's more than I get to do," Sydney said with ill grace.

Bernice set Sydney's plate before him and he began eating immediately. He didn't normally behave this badly. Melody suspected he was only doing it because he knew he was in the wrong over shooting Chet. Sydney was having a difficult time entering his teens. He was old enough to think he ought to take over his father's position at the ranch but too young to do it. He resented Melody's attempts to restrain him and to teach him how to behave. As far as he was concerned, the mark of manhood was ability with a gun. He practiced constantly. If he'd had any natural aptitude, Melody doubted they would have been able to restrain him this long.

"I'm sure Tom would be happy to take you out with him," Belle said. "It can't be very dangerous. All he does is ride around and look at things."

Melody turned to Tom, but he only shrugged. He'd heard his work belittled so often, he was getting used to it. She glanced at Chet but could tell nothing from his expression. She imagined he would have nothing but scorn for any woman who understood so little of what it took to manage a ranch. Melody didn't know much yet herself, but she knew it involved more than just *riding around.*

"I don't think he ought to ride with Tom while things are so unsettled," Melody said.

"He's practically a man," his mother said. "He ought to be learning how to manage his inheritance."

"It'll be safer when we don't have Royal's men shooting to scare off our cowhands and rustlers shooting to kill," Tom said.

"I insist that you stop making such accusations against Mr. Royal," Belle said. "He wouldn't do anything like that."

"His cowhands are doing it," Tom said. "There's no question about that."

"Then I'm sure he knows nothing about it," Belle insisted. "It's absurd to think he would be shooting at us when he wants to marry Melody."

"He's doing it because I haven't agreed to marry him," Melody said. "He's trying to prove to me that I can't survive without his protection."

"He's right," Belle said. "Every woman needs a man."

"Possibly," Melody said, not willing to embark

on an old argument in front of Chet, "but I don't need Lantz Royal."

"Then marry his son," Belle said. "He's crazy about you, too."

"He's a few months younger than I am," Melody said. "It would almost be like marrying Sydney."

"Well, you've got to marry somebody," Belle said. "There aren't any better candidates around."

"I'm here," Tom said. "I'm not as rich as Lantz, but I'm older than Blade."

"You're a hired hand, Tom. Melody can't marry you."

Melody wondered how a woman ordinarily so sensitive could be so cruel on occasion. She supposed that came from considering Tom in the class of servants who weren't allowed to have feelings. Lantz and his son, on the other hand, were on Belle's social level, so she endowed them with all the qualities she attributed to herself.

"I am not going to marry anyone," Melody stated. "I've told you before, I want to go back to Virginia."

"Please!" Belle said, holding her hand up to halt any more words. "Don't tell me you won't consider a marriage to Lantz or his son. I don't think I can stand it."

"Very well, I won't tell you," Melody said. "But—"

"I don't know what's to become of us, Mr. Attmore," Belle said, turning to Chet, who'd sat like a stone statue through this whole monumentally embarrassing discussion. "I've tried to be a mother to her. I understand that she might feel uncomfortable in Texas. Our ways are strange to her. But I can't understand her threatening to go back to Virginia when the whole state is in ruins."

"Only part of it."

"You told me the Union army burned Richmond."

"They did."

"Then what they didn't burn doesn't matter."

Melody had given up trying to explain the war or its aftermath to her stepmother.

"Mr. Attmore, you talk to her," Belle asked. "I can't, and I promise you I've tried."

"I've never set foot outside of Texas, ma'am, unless it was to go into Mexico or the New Mexico Territory. I couldn't very well advise Melody either way."

Why was it the sound of his voice was like velvet against her skin? It ought to be rough and raspy from all the years he'd spent in the heat and the dust. But it was just as sultry as a summer afternoon with the breeze wafting up from the James River, bearing the smell of fresh water and the deep forests on the south side of the river.

"You could at least appeal to her on behalf of— what's your name?" Belle said, turning to Speers.

"Tim Speers, ma'am."

"Mr. Speers," she said, forgetting him immediately. "I'm sure he doesn't want to get shot again. Lantz's cowhands would stop this irresponsible shooting at people if they had a good woman to tell them how to behave."

"I was shot by a rustler, ma'am," Speers said.

"It's all the same," Belle said. "Rustlers wouldn't dare attack a ranch with a lady in residence."

"They attacked our ranch," Melody pointed out.

"I'm sure they didn't know we were here. You never ride out."

Melody gave up. When Belle wanted to prove a

point, she ignored reality as completely as she ignored other people's feelings.

"Much of Richmond has been rebuilt," Melody said, trying to give the conversation a new direction. She couldn't endure any more of Belle's embarrassing revelations. "Some of the neighborhoods are even nicer than they were before. It's an exciting time to be in Virginia. If I were to sell my half of the ranch, I'd have enough money to start my own business."

"Melody! How can you even think of doing anything like that?" Belle asked.

"I'll have to support myself."

"Your husband will do that."

"I will have to support myself until I find a man I wish to marry."

"I don't see why you don't wish to marry Lantz. He—"

"You won't be able to sell the ranch," Tom said.

Belle turned sharply to Tom. "What do you mean? I don't wish for Melody to sell her half of the ranch, but she can if she wants."

"Nobody's going to touch it as long as Royal has his eye on it." Tom seemed to be struggling to control both his anger and his frustration. "They know he'll run them off like he ran off everybody else in the county except your husband. He's always had his eye on this place, and he means to have it. If he can't get it by marrying Melody, he'll take it."

"Really, Tom, don't be absurd," Belle said. "Lantz shouldn't be shooting at the men—that's bad of him—but he's just trying to convince Melody to marry him. You can't blame him for that. As for taking our ranch, I'm sure he'd do no such thing."

"I'll go after him for you," Sydney said. "I'll kill him. Then you can do anything you want."

He'd been quiet so long, and Belle's conversation had been so embarrassing, that Melody had almost forgotten Sydney was at the table.

"I have no objection to your riding with Tom," Belle said, "but you're not to take a gun."

"Then there's no point in going," Sydney said, his enthusiasm turned to sulks.

"None of you seem to understand what I'm saying," Tom said. "Royal intends to have this ranch. He'd prefer to get it through marriage, but he'll take it any way he can." He turned to Melody. "Marry me and let me hold it for you. I'm not afraid to stand up to Royal."

Melody felt cornered. When she'd first arrived in Texas, she'd been confused, disoriented, shocked by the unexpected death of her father. Lantz's attention had been a comfort and a support. She hadn't felt so lost or so helpless when he was around. His proposal of marriage had been as flattering as it was unexpected. It had also seemed like an answer to all her problems.

Melody had come to Texas hoping for a new start, even a new kind of life. She had come to maturity at a time when the destruction caused by the war had given her aunt great freedom and responsibility. For years Melody had shared that freedom and responsibility. But as society recovered and men resumed their usual positions, she found herself being hedged in by social conventions she couldn't accept. She had looked toward the freedom of Texas.

Now she found herself in a place where men respected women even less, gave them even less freedom, and were quite ready to coerce her into marriage against her will. Worse still, they lived by a code of behavior based on guns and violence, a code she found reprehensible.

And now, if she wanted to return to Virginia, she couldn't. She couldn't return to Richmond without money. What little her aunt possessed had gone to her own children. Her half of the Spring Water Ranch comprised Melody's entire inheritance.

"I don't want anybody getting into a fight because of me," she told Tom. "I'd marry Lantz Royal if it would keep people from getting hurt."

"Thank goodness you're finally being sensible," Belle said.

"But it wouldn't," Melody added. "All anybody out here thinks of is guns and fighting and shooting people. Even Sydney wants to be a gunhand. And why not? Mr. Attmore does it for a living, and people look up to him. Lantz and his son bully people, and everybody looks up to them. Now we've got rustlers willing to shoot people so they can steal our cows. Why should I want to stay in a place like this?"

"Melody, you exaggerate. I'm sure Tom didn't mean—"

Melody threw down her napkin, pushed back her chair, and stood. "Excuse me."

She left the room as quickly as she could, before she burst into tears. She had suspected for some time that she was caught with no means of escape, but she'd kept telling herself she was mistaken, she'd find a way if she just kept looking. Tom's brutal statement of the truth had ripped that soothing hope to shreds.

She had to face marrying Royal or losing the only inheritance she and her brothers had.

She tried to tell herself that marrying Lantz wouldn't be so awful. He was a handsome man and had shown every desire to please her. Belle would have a chance to remarry—she was too young and beautiful to stay a widow long—and the boys would have an opportunity to discover there was something more in life than cows and guns.

There was only one good reason to hold out. She didn't love Lantz. No man had ever been able to touch her heart. But if she was going to remain loveless for the rest of her life, why not marry Royal and save herself and her family from ruin?

An image of Chet, even more stunningly blond and handsome in his dress suit, sprang into her mind. No. In reality, it had been there all the time. He was certainly the most attractive man she'd ever met, but she knew nothing about him.

Yet there was something about him that wouldn't let her ignore him. Maybe it was that he seemed to be so completely in control of his life. If he had demons, he'd come to terms with them. If he'd had unrealized ambitions, he'd decided he was better off without them. If doubt and indecision had tormented him, he'd arrived at a state of inner peace.

Or maybe he was so good-looking that she just thought he must have reached a state of near perfection.

No, he was a gunfighter. He depended on his ability to shoot people before they could shoot him.

Yet Melody was sure he was the strongest man she'd ever met. There was no posturing, no covering up for some lack. There simply wasn't any. That didn't seem right when she compared him to Royal. Royal had money, position, and power. This man had nothing. Yet the feeling persisted. She was drawn to Chet, yet was wary, trusting but not able to understand him.

Whatever the source of this feeling, it wouldn't matter after tomorrow. He'd be gone, and she'd be left by herself to decide what to do about Lantz and the ranch. Everybody's future depended on her answer. But the answer they wanted would bind her to a life that looked more and more like bondage to an insensitive bully. Could she agree to that, even to save her family?

"You can't pay any attention to half the stuff Mrs. Jordan says," Tom Neland said as he and Chet headed back toward the bunkhouse. "She doesn't understand about ranching."

"It doesn't matter what I think."

Chet matched his stride to Tom's. He'd seen some silly women before, but never one like Belle. She seemed to think any man would make a good husband as long as he was rich.

"She ought to get married again," Tom said. "Those boys need a father."

"Looks that way."

Chet didn't know about Neill, but it was clear Sydney was headed for trouble unless someone managed to turn him around soon. Not that being named Sydney wasn't a cross to bear in itself. Chet could recall more than one boy who'd had to fight his way through his formative years because of his name.

"I try my best with him, but it's not the same."

"It never is when you're the hired help."

Tom flinched. No man liked to be labeled as inferior. Chet knew that from experience, but

Tom was headed for bigger trouble. He didn't lack courage or determination, but he lacked what it took to successfully stand up against a man like Lantz Royal. Tom didn't have the commanding presence to make a troublemaker stop and think, the brains to out-think a man like Royal, or the brash courage to gamble everything on the chance of winning. He'd end up in a fight, and sooner or later somebody would kill him.

"I may be hired help," Tom said with a flash of temper, "but Belle depends on me for everything."

"Miss Jordan strikes me as a young woman who knows her own mind and likes to use it."

"Melody doesn't know anything about ranching either," Tom said. "Besides, she's too much a lady to want to be involved in the day-to-day running of a ranch."

Chet didn't pretend to know much about Miss Melody Jordan, but he was certain Tom Neland knew even less. How could a man think he was in love with a woman when he didn't have the slightest idea what she was like? And how could Melody consider marrying him when she must know he couldn't tell her thoughts from those of a longhorn cow?

Melody held the key to the whole puzzle of Spring Water Ranch, but Chet didn't know which way she would jump. If she did the most logical thing, she'd marry Royal. He seemed fond of her. He might even treat her right most of the time, especially if she knew how to handle him. And Melody struck him as a woman who could handle just about anybody once she set her mind to it.

"You got any preference in horses?" Tom asked.

"Not as long as they're strong and surefooted."

"Look them over and take your pick."

"No rush," Chet said. "We can do it in the morning."

It worried him that he wanted Melody to turn Royal and Tom down flat. It worried him even more that he kept playing with the idea of staying around to see how things turned out. It didn't add to his comfort to know he'd already been thinking of what he could do to turn Sydney's mind from guns. Then there was the advice he wanted to give Tom.

Nobody wanted him to stay. Belle Jordan thought he was a handsome cowhand, but Lantz's money was more important than Chet's looks. Tom Neland just flat wanted to get rid of him. After two run-ins, Sydney probably would prefer to shoot him. Neill, on the other hand, was certain he was a gunslinger.

Melody didn't like gunslingers.

Chet shouldn't be concerned about what she thought of him. He shouldn't be concerned about anything but getting a horse and going on his way. He could too easily become emotionally involved with this woman. That could only cause unhappiness for both of them.

"Then we'd better turn in," Tom said. "We get up early."

"And I have a long way to travel."

But he didn't have a destination.

Melody had told herself she wouldn't get up to see Chet off. He was just a cowboy who'd stopped over for the night. He'd gotten his horse. Now he'd pass out of her life just as suddenly as he'd entered it.

"I'm sorry to see that one go," Bernice said as she cleared away the breakfast table.

"He's such a nice-looking man," Belle said. "He must have come from a good family that has fallen on hard times."

"Maybe," Bernice said, "but some people are born to be gunslingers."

"Why do you say that?" Melody asked.

"It's just a feeling. He didn't say much and he didn't do much, but you knew he was around."

Melody had already figured that out for herself. She had lain awake for hours last night unable to forget that he slept just a short distance away in the bunkhouse. She tried for a long time to understand just why she couldn't ignore him.

There were his looks, of course, but it wasn't simply that he was attractive. When he looked at her, he made her feel attractive, desirable. He made her acutely aware of his physical presence, of her own body. He made her so sensitive that the movement of her clothes against her skin ignited a fire in her body. He was a whole different breed of man than what she was used to. He wasn't Virginia, though he had that smooth charm. He wasn't Texas, though he had the guns and something like metal under his easygoing style. Maybe it was heat. He was like a volcano, slumbering, warm, and inviting, but capable of . . .

But it was still more than that. There was something sensual about his look, about him. His eyes were never quite open. He didn't look quite directly at her, yet somehow he created a feeling of intimacy, of something secret and precious shared. His look almost seemed to reach out and touch her, caress her. It drew her in until she felt enmeshed in a web, drawn close to him whether

73

she wanted to be or not. It gave her chill bumps just to think about it.

Then there was his body. It was impossible to forget that. He wore ordinary clothes, worn and soiled from his journey, but on him they seemed just right. Yet when he changed for dinner, the dark coat, white shirt, and tie seemed just as much a part of him as tight brown pants and tan shirt. He seemed almost too relaxed, his weight resting more on one foot than the other. Self-assured. Reassuring. Inviting.

And those lips, which seemed made for kissing. And his arms—strong enough to still even the most vigorous female objection.

Melody jerked her thoughts back to the present. Thinking about that man could hypnotize even a strong-minded woman.

"I suppose it's best he's gone," Belle said. "Tom says he made Lantz very angry, and Sydney is still mad at him."

"Lantz is just mad because someone stood up to him," Melody said. "Tom is jealous because he knows Chet is more of a man than he'll ever be, and Sydney's angry because someone finally pulled him up short. It would have done them all good if he had stayed for a month."

"A man like Mr. Attmore isn't one to take orders," Bernice said.

But Spring Water Ranch desperately needed someone who could give the right kind of orders. Melody didn't know what kind that was, but she had reached the conclusion that Tom Neland didn't know either.

"We couldn't have him making Lantz angry," Belle said. "We don't want to discourage his coming over as often as he likes."

But Melody found herself even more dissatisfied with Lantz Royal than before, and the possibility of becoming his wife was more grim. Though she had nothing concrete to base it on, she couldn't get rid of the conviction that everything would have been quite different if Chet Attmore had agreed to stay.

Chet didn't like having to leave his horse. Until he could send someone back for it, his borrowed mount would be a continual reminder of the Spring Water Ranch. He wanted to put the last twenty-four hours completely out of his mind. He needed to forget they had ever happened, that there was such a place as the Spring Water Ranch . . . such a woman as Melody Jordan.

He let the buckskin walk at its own pace. It was a beautiful morning, but it would be hotter than a skillet by noon. Some people said central Texas had a beauty and grandeur all its own. To Chet, nothing could equal the Hill Country, the mountains, deep valleys, and rushing streams that made up the home he'd left behind, the home he could never return to.

He'd never had a real home as a child, just a series of cheap hotel rooms. His father had been an outcast from an old Southern family, his mother a barroom songstress. Their passion for each other had burned out almost as quickly as it had ignited. His father never said much after his mother ran off, just that she was a whore gone to a whore's reward. Back then, Chet hadn't known what that meant. Now he knew it meant someday she'd die from disease, starvation, or some man's anger.

His father had been a gunfighter with a penchant for high-stakes card games. When his enemies couldn't get him fair, they shot him in the back.

His parents had had nothing to leave their sons but their weaknesses. They'd gotten Luke first, turned him into a gunfighter like their father. Then they carried Chet down the same swift-running stream. That was all the more reason not to get married. No point in raising a third generation of gunfighters. There was only one end for such a man. Chet didn't want to think about what could happen to his daughters. A man taking up a gun was bad enough. But how could a man watch his daughter sell her body?

He didn't know about anybody else, but he couldn't. He'd kill half the population of Texas before he let that happen.

Chet muttered a string of curses. He didn't know why he'd let himself get started thinking along these lines. He'd decided years ago marriage wasn't for him. Now after just a few hours in Melody Jordan's company, he was trying to convince himself he'd made a mistake.

He knew Melody was the reason. He knew himself too well to be mistaken. Long, lonely nights around a campfire or in a hotel room had given him plenty of time to think, to get to know himself. His job had forced him to be brutally honest. There was no room for vanity. That could mean death.

No, he was trying to find a reason for continuing to think of Melody, maybe even to go back and accept her offer of work. But he wasn't a weak man. He could stick to his decisions even when he hated doing so. This was better for him. It was better for everyone else.

He turned his attention to the land around him. He'd been told most of it belonged to Lantz Royal. It seemed flat, arid, and colorless compared to Jake's ranch in the Hill Country. No eagles soared, no birds sang, and the cattle grazed the barren land in isolation.

The land seemed empty. That made it all the more unexpected when two men seemed to appear straight out of the ground in front of him.

Chapter Five

Chet knew immediately there would be trouble.

The riders looked tense, on the prod. There was no avoiding them. He wondered if they had followed him or lain in ambush. A man with a reputation with a gun was always a mark for anyone wishing to build his own reputation. A gunslinger was known by the number and caliber of the men he'd killed. It was a vicious circle. The harder you worked to stay alive, the more someone wanted to kill you. That was why he'd quit. Now he wondered if he'd left it too late.

He let his horse slow to a walk. He recognized one man. Billy Mason. He had a small reputation as a gunhand, more as a hired gun than a gunslick. He was also known to be a petty thief and cattle rustler.

He didn't recognize the other man. He knew he'd never faced anybody that young, but something about him looked familiar. Maybe he was somebody's younger brother.

They stopped about four yards apart.

"Howdy, Billy," Chet said. "I see you're out of jail."

"You didn't tell me you'd been locked up," the young man said to Billy.

"Yeah. I got mixed up with the wrong crowd and got blamed for what they did."

There'd been more than enough evidence to connect Billy to the rustlers, but Chet didn't bother to remind him. "You got a job around here?"

"Yeah. I'm working for the LR Ranch," Billy said.

"I'm not familiar with the ranches in these parts," Chet said.

"You must be familiar with one. You're riding a Spring Water horse."

"I borrowed him," Chet said. "Mine was worn down."

"Tom Neland doesn't lend his horses," the young man said. "I say you must be working for the Spring Water."

"I heard they was short of hands," Billy said. "A gunslick might be just what they was looking for."

The other man suddenly looked alert.

"I'm not working for anybody," Chet said. "But why should you care if I were?"

"We've been having trouble around here," the young man said. "Some from the Spring Water, some from rustlers. I figure if you're not one, you might be the other."

"Who's your friend?" Chet asked Billy.

"Blade Royal," Billy said. "His father owns the LR Ranch."

Chet relaxed slightly. So this was the young man who'd developed a crush on Melody only to find she was more likely to become his step-mother than his wife. He couldn't help feeling sorry for the boy. No matter how it worked out, it was bound to be hard on him.

"I met your father yesterday," Chet said.

"You the cowboy who drew on him?"

"He started to draw on me first."

"Is he that fast?" Blade asked Billy.

"Yeah."

"Can he hit what he aims at?"

"That, too."

"Then you ought to be working for us," Blade said. "We can pay you more than the Spring Water."

"I'm not working for the Spring Water," Chet said again. "I'm just traveling through."

"Where're you going?"

Chet was beginning to be irritated by this youngster. "Haven't made up my mind yet."

"Don't let us keep you," Billy said.

"You'll be on LR land for the next ten miles," Blade said. "Make sure you leave it as empty-handed as you came."

Chet felt the anger build inside him in a rapid crescendo. He tried to tell himself Blade was little more than a boy, that he was suffering from un-requited love and was probably already regretting his words. He reminded himself that Melody would probably be the kid's mother before Christmas. Anything Chet did would rebound on her because she'd given him the horse he now rode.

It didn't work. His temper got the upper hand.

"I'll make a trade with you," he said. "I won't

rustle your cows if your men stop harassing the Spring Water cowhands."

"Our men wouldn't bother with the Spring Water hands," Blade said.

Chet couldn't decide whether his contempt was for the smallness of Melody's ranch or the hands' ability with guns.

"Somebody shot the Speers boy," Chet said. "He said it was rustlers. You wouldn't be trying to steal a few cows on the side, would you? No, I guess not. Despite that gun you tote, you still look wet behind the ears."

Blade's eyes blazed with fury, and a little of Chet's anger ebbed. The young cockerel didn't like being treated with his own medicine. He apparently thought being his father's son gave him a right to do what he pleased. It was high time he learned different. "I'd better be on my way," Chet said as he touched his hat and started his horse forward. "Nice talking to you."

"Dammit!" Blade cursed as Chet rode past. "I'll show you I'm a man."

"Some other time," Chet said without turning around. "I've got a long way to go."

"Come back here!" Blade ordered.

Chet kept going, dipping down into the depression from which Billy and Blade had sprung so unexpectedly.

"Blade, let it ride," Billy said.

"The hell I will! Nobody's going to call me a child."

"You can't—Blade, don't!"

Chet would have sworn somebody hit him on the side of his head with a hammer, except it felt hotter than a branding iron. Only when he found himself falling out of the saddle did he realize he'd been shot. A futile curse rose to his lips as blackness closed around him.

He'd left it too late. A young fool had finally gotten himself a reputation.

Luke Attmore thrust his spurs into his mount's flanks, driving the horse into an easy gallop. That gunshot could mean nothing, but it could just as easily mean trouble. Billy and Blade were out together. Luke didn't need Lantz Royal to tell him that was a dangerous combination. If Lantz really wanted to protect his son, he'd fire Billy Mason instead of telling Luke to keep an eye on Blade.

Luke didn't usually babysit anybody. He was a professional gunman paid for his skill and his willingness to use it. He'd been hired to find rustlers. Lantz had added keeping an eye on Blade afterwards. When Luke threatened to quit, Lantz doubled his salary. Nevertheless, Luke was sick of Blade's company. The boy was spoiled and vicious. He was smaller and weaker than his father, and he pushed people just to prove himself. His self-image had suffered badly when Melody Jordan refused his offer of marriage, saying he was too young. The relationship between father and son had turned stormy when Blade discovered his father was courting Melody with every sign of success. Now they couldn't be in the same room without shouting at each other.

Luke topped a rise. The nearly flat piece of West Texas plain stretched out miles before him. Some distance off he saw two horsemen riding away. Billy and Blade. He recognized their horses. Maybe one of them had taken a shot at a pronghorn antelope, but Luke didn't see any game. He didn't see another rider, so they couldn't be chasing anyone.

Yet they were riding too fast. A horse wouldn't last long at that pace, and only a fool wore down his horse without a reason. Luke slowed his horse to a canter, a trot, and then a walk. Something had happened—he could feel it—but he didn't know what. He realized there was a dip in the ground ahead when the tips of a horse's ears appeared, followed by the head. Now he knew there was something wrong. The horse wore a saddle. Where was his rider?

Luke spurred his horse forward. Twenty yards later, the bottom of the dip opened before him and he saw the body of a man lying face down on the ground. Even at a distance, Luke could see the blood in his hair. He could also read the brand on the horse's flank. Hell, Blade had shot some poor Spring Water cowhand. Everybody knew Lantz was putting pressure on the Spring Water to force Melody Jordan to marry him, but up until now he had stayed within the law.

This killing could blow things wide open.

Luke rode forward. He wasn't about to help the sheriff do his job, but he couldn't leave a man to the coyotes. He'd tie the body to the horse and send it home. The Spring Water foreman could take it from there. There wouldn't be any way to tie the killing to Blade or the LR Ranch.

Uneasiness spread through Luke as he drew close to the body. Something about this man looked familiar. The blond hair, the tall body. He couldn't pin it down, but he was certain he'd seen this man before.

Luke dismounted, picked up the hat that had fallen several feet from the body, and caught up the horse's reins. He led the horse over to the body and untied the rope from the saddle. He knelt down and turned the body over.

Shock, cold and sickening, rolled around in his belly. He stared, unbelieving, at the still face. It was his brother.

Luke hadn't seen Chet in three years. Hard words has passed between them before they parted. Chet had insisted Luke quit hiring his gun to people outside the law. Luke had told Chet to mind his own business. When Chet said Luke was like their father, Luke had slugged him. It took half-a-dozen men to separate them.

Luke had not forgiven Chet. But now, looking down at his brother's inert form, he felt only tremendous guilt. Chet had given up his job as Jake's foreman to follow Luke, to keep an eye on him. That had always made Luke mad. He didn't need Chet's protection. He was faster than his brother.

But none of that mattered as he stared at Chet's body. A murderous rage toward Blade Royal filled his heart. The boy would die. Chet had been shot from behind.

Luke also felt a great sense of loneliness. He had no one else now. His father was dead. His mother had disappeared shortly after he was born. Luke had turned his back on Jake and his family when he hired his gun that first time. Only Chet had never given up on him, had begged him to give up a life that could have just one ending.

But Chet had been the one to die first.

For a moment Luke couldn't decide what to do. He couldn't bury him here, but where could he take him? Then he knew he had to take him home to Jake. They might be outcasts, but Jake's was the only real home he and Chet had ever had.

Luke knelt on the rocky ground. Sharp-edged stones cut into his knees as he slid his arms under Chet and tried to lift him. He didn't succeed. He'd never realized how hard it was to pick up two hundred pounds of dead weight from a kneeling position. He readjusted his hold and tried again.

The groan startled him. He hadn't been aware of making a sound. Then he realized he'd heard *two* groans. He quickly laid Chet down, unbuttoned his shirt, and slipped his hand inside. His brother was alive. Luke could feel his heart beating.

A feeling of relief came over him, one that was so strong, it robbed him of his strength. He had to drop back down, resting on his heels, until the weakness left him. As soon as he recovered, he checked the wound. The shot had grazed Chet's head, causing a lot of bleeding. It looked as if the bullet had traveled along the line of the skull and exited over the eye. It was a good thing Chet had such a hard head.

Chet opened his eyes. He looked confused at first. "Luke?"

He sounded relieved, as though he knew everything would be all right now that his brother was there. That made Luke feel more guilty than ever.

"What . . . are you . . . doing here?" Chet asked. He spoke haltingly, as though it took a tremendous effort to think of each word.

"Never mind that. Who shot you? Why?"

"Blade. Thought I was . . . working for Spring Water . . . riding . . . their horse."

"Don't try to talk. I've got to get you to a doctor."

"Melody."

"What?" Chet's voice was so weak, Luke couldn't understand what he'd said.

85

"Melody," Chet managed to say. "Take . . . me . . . to . . . Spring Water."

"Why should you want to—"

There was no use asking him. He'd passed out again. But why would he want Luke to take him to the Spring Water? He couldn't have been working for the Jordans. Chet had been Jake's foreman too long to work under Tom Neland or anybody else.

But how was he going to take care of his brother? It would be impossible to take him back to the LR Ranch. Blade would have to kill him to keep from being hanged himself. Wherever he took him, it had to be somewhere Blade wouldn't find him until Chet got well enough to defend himself. Luke couldn't leave him in a hotel room. Everybody in town would know most of the story within the hour. Besides, Luke wasn't a doctor. He didn't know anything about taking care of a wounded man.

Melody Jordan seemed to be his only choice. Chet seemed to want her. He'd send the horse back to the Spring Water. Maybe somebody there would come looking for him. If not, he'd take him there. If necessary, he'd pay them to take care of him. Luke looped the reins of Chet's horse over the saddle and slapped the horse on the flank to start him on his way. The horse set off at a brisk trot.

Luke knelt back down beside his brother. He'd build a fire and heat some water so he could clean the wound. Then he would wait.

Melody had felt moody and irritable all morning. She had argued with Tom over his intention to confront Lantz rather than bring in the sheriff, had a flaming row with Sydney, then walked out when Belle tried to defend her son's decision to keep practicing with his gun. Melody didn't understand why they couldn't see that their policy of confrontation would only cause more shooting. Not only were they a smaller ranch with fewer hands, but she'd heard Lantz had hired a gunfighter after the rustling started.

Melody had gone to the parlor with the intention of writing some overdue letters, but twenty minutes later she still sat with the blank paper before her. She couldn't decide whom to write. Or what to say. Things were really too unsettled to say anything except that she would be back in Richmond as soon as possible. But that was the one thing she wouldn't say. Without money she'd be a pensioner. Melody would stay in Texas for the rest of her life, herd those dreadful cows herself, before she'd accept charity. Besides, she couldn't leave her family. At least, not until things were settled.

Neill entered through the front door.

"Don't slam the door, and wipe your feet," she called out. It was a litany she repeated several times a day. It had made Sydney so angry that he now entered the house through the kitchen.

Neill stuck his head into the parlor. "That fella's horse came back."

"What fella's horse?" she asked, though she knew instantly whom he had to be talking about.

"That fella who left here this morning."

"I guess he didn't like our horse after all," Melody said, experiencing a spurt of anger at such rudeness. "He probably got another one at the LR."

"Tom said the saddle had blood on it." Neill

withdrew his head and started for the kitchen.

Melody was out of her chair, gripping Neill by the shoulders, before he'd gone five steps.

"What do you mean, there was blood on the saddle?"

"I don't know. Tom said it." Neill tried to wriggle away. He wasn't interested in anything except the morning snack Bernice always saved for him.

"Where's Tom?" Melody asked.

"At the corral, I guess."

Melody hurried out of the house. Why had Chet's horse come back? Why was there blood on the saddle? She could think of only one reason.

He'd been shot.

Tom was turning the buckskin out into the corral when she found him.

"Neill said Chet's horse came back with blood on the saddle."

"There's the horse, and here's the saddle," Tom said, pointing to the saddle resting on the corral rails. "See for yourself. There was blood on the horse's withers, too."

"What happened?" Melody asked. There were two spots and a smear on the saddle.

"Ran into some trouble, I guess."

"What kind of trouble? He was just riding through."

"I don't know. Maybe he ran afoul of some of Royal's hands. He had to ride through their range."

"You have to go find him. If he's hurt, somebody has to take care of him."

Tom looked at her as though she'd lost her mind. "I've got work to do. I can't be chasing after every cowboy who wanders onto this place. Hell, he could be so clumsy, he fell out of the saddle and hit his head."

"Then there'd be blood on a rock, not on the saddle."

"I don't know, and I don't care. I just came in because my horse went lame. I'm heading back out as soon as I saddle up."

"Then I'm going after him."

"You'll do no such thing. Decent women don't go gallivanting across the country by themselves."

"Decent women don't leave wounded men to die unattended," Melody retorted. She didn't know when Tom had gotten into the habit of telling women what they could and couldn't do, but he would soon learn he couldn't order her around.

"I doubt he's even hurt bad. The buckskin probably spooked at a snake or something and threw him. Chet will ask Royal for a horse or walk back here before nightfall."

"Hitch up the buggy. I'm going to find him."

"Melody, this man is none of your concern."

"I can't ignore anybody in trouble."

Tom's expression turned stubborn. "That's still no reason for you to get mixed up with him. I won't let you go after him."

"Won't let me!" Melody's voice carried a full load of indignation and not a little of the hauteur she'd inherited from a long line of Southern ancestors. "Let me remind you, Tom Neland, that you're my employee. You can't forbid me to do anything. If you try again, I'll fire you on the spot."

"You can't—"

"I can, and I will. If you don't hitch up that buggy right this minute, you'll find out just how quickly, too."

"Who'll run this place for you?"

"That won't be any of your concern."

"Belle won't let you."

"I own half this place. Sydney would vote with me. Give him a week, and he'd talk his mama into letting him take your place."

Apparently the reality of Tom's position began to sink in.

"I want to marry you, Melody, to take care of you and of this place."

"This has nothing to do with either of those things," Melody said, refusing to be sidetracked. "It has to do with extending Christian charity to a man who's been hurt."

"If he has been hurt, you'll need a buckboard, not a buggy."

"Okay."

"And I'm coming with you."

"Fine. I'll probably need your help. I'll get my medicine kit and be right back."

She also stripped the bunkhouse of its extra blankets and threw them into the back of the buckboard.

Tom had a great deal to say about a lot of things, and the long drive gave him plenty of opportunity to say them. Though Melody didn't answer, she did listen. It kept her from thinking about Chet and imagining all the terrible things that could have happened to him.

It also kept her from asking herself why she was so worried about this man. She checked on Speers regularly, but she didn't worry about him. She worried about the men when there was danger, but that didn't keep her from her regular duties. Chet had not only kept her from doing anything useful, he'd occupied her mind to such an extent that she wondered if she'd had any thoughts at all that didn't include him.

She told herself it was guilt over Sydney's shooting him, appreciation for his support at dinner. This was her way of paying him back.

She knew it wasn't the truth, but it kept her from having to consider some truly disturbing alternatives.

After what seemed like an endless ride, she spied a horse in the distance. It wasn't moving. A little later, she was able to make out two men on the ground.

"Someone seems to have found him," Tom said. "We didn't have to come, after all."

"He can't move him on a horse."

She was kneeling next to Chet before Tom could get out of the buckboard. Chet's head was covered in a bloody bandage. She looked up at the man who had found Chet, but the sun was behind him. She couldn't see his face.

"What happened?" she asked.

"He was shot in the head," the stranger said. "I think he'll be all right, but he'll need careful nursing."

"I'll see that he gets it. Help my foreman put him in the buckboard." Melody spread the blankets to minimize the jolting from the rough trail as much as possible. "Careful!" she scolded when Tom dropped one of Chet's legs while trying to lift him into the buckboard.

"I'm trying, but he's not a light man."

She positioned his face so it would be in the shade and laid him out as straight as she could, but that didn't satisfy her. "I'll ride in the back," she told Tom. "I want to hold his head."

"I don't see why."

"So his head won't bounce all the way back to the ranch." Once she settled herself on the blankets, Chet's head in her lap, she turned to the man who'd found Chet. The sun still came from behind. She wished he'd move so she could see his face.

"Thank you for taking care of him," she said.

"You know him?" The man's voice sounded strange, as though he was forcing it lower than usual.

"He stopped by our place yesterday to borrow a horse while his got over being used too hard. When it came back, I knew something was wrong."

"You should take him to town. He needs a doctor."

"The doctor will come to the ranch," Melody said.

"That'll cost money. If you need—"

"Thank you, but the expense is not a problem."

"If you're sure, I'll be on my way."

"Thank you, Mr. . . . I didn't catch your name."

"It's not important. Just take good care of him."

"You sound mighty interested in him," Tom said.

"I don't like to see a man left to die. He came to a while ago."

"Did he say who shot him?" Melody asked.

"No. He just asked me to take him to Melody."

"I'm Melody."

The man looked relieved. "One more thing. He said he was shot because he was riding one of your horses. Do you know why?"

"No."

He didn't look pleased with her answer, but he

mounted up. "Good day, ma'am," he said and started down the trail.

"What a strange man," Tom said.

"Get us home as quickly as you can," Melody said, the stranger forgotten. "Send Sydney for the doctor the moment we arrive."

Luke had no trouble finding Billy and Blade. They hadn't made any effort to hide their trail. Luke walked straight up to Blade and knocked him to the ground with a smashing punch to the jaw. Then he leaned over and jerked Blade's gun out of its holster.

"What the hell!" Billy exclaimed, reaching for his own gun. Luke moved quickly. He clipped Billy behind the ear with the butt of Blade's pistol. Billy dropped to the ground like a shot steer.

"What's the matter with you?" Blade asked as he wiped blood from his lips with the back of his hand. "Have you gone crazy?"

"When your daddy told me to look out for you," Luke said, his voice deliberate, his anger molten, "he didn't say you had a cowardly habit of shooting strangers in the back."

"Give me my gun and say that."

"What the hell did you think you were doing?"

"What do you care about it? He was just a Spring Water cowhand."

"No, he's not."

"Then why was he riding a Spring Water horse?"

"His was worn down. I imagine he told you that."

"Why should I believe him?"

"Why should you shoot him?"

"He said I was wet behind the ears."

93

"So you shot him in the back. I guess you're not only a kid, but a yellow-bellied coward as well."

Blade jumped to his feet. "I'll kill you for that."

"Come on," Luke said when Blade just glared at him. "Are you helpless without your gun, or are you afraid to face me alone? Maybe I ought to turn my back." He started to turn. "Will that buck up your courage?"

Blade came in cursing and swinging. He was no match for a man ten years older and several inches taller. The end was inevitable.

Blade lay on the ground, unable to get up again. "As soon as I tell Pa what you've done, you're a dead man," he managed to say between bruised and bloody lips.

"You won't tell your father anything about it. If you do, I'll inform the sheriff you shot that man in the back. Billy will back me up. If he doesn't, he'll hang with you."

He bent over and hauled Blade up by the front of his shirt. "If either you or Billy comes within a mile of that man before he gets well, I'll kill you. If he dies, I'll kill you anyway."

"What's he to you?" Blade asked, defiant to the end.

"Shooting a man in the back is trouble, and I don't like trouble. Besides, you just might decide to tell people I did it." A slight widening of the eyes told Luke that was exactly what Blade had intended to do. "I do a clean job. Nobody's going to push the work of a coward off on me. If that happened, people would start to think I was an easy mark. I'd have reputation-hunting fools following me."

He tightened his hold on Blade's shirt. Blade tried to break the grip, but Luke was too strong.

"Your father's a proud man. I'd hate to have to tell him what a cowardly worm he has for a son."

Luke pushed Blade away from him.

"Now you think up some real good tale to explain why your face looks like raw meat."

Luke turned and walked off. He didn't worry that Blade might try to shoot him in the back. He couldn't. His eyes were already swollen shut.

Chapter Six

"You can't bring him in here," Belle Jordan said.

Melody ignored her stepmother. "Be careful," she warned Tom and her brothers. "Don't drop him." Tom had Chet's shoulders; each boy had a leg.

"Where are you going to put him?" Belle asked. "We don't have any spare bedrooms."

"In my room," Melody said.

"You can't. Where will you sleep?"

"With Bernice. Watch the railing, Sydney! You're going to trip and fall."

There had been a spare bedroom on the main floor, but that had been turned into a sitting room for Belle. Now there were only four bedrooms in the house. Belle had one, Melody another; the boys shared one, and Bernice had the fourth.

"You shouldn't have brought him here," Belle said. "He belongs in the bunkhouse."

"He's got to be where I can watch him until he's better," Melody said. She held the door open for the men to carry Chet into her room, then ran to pull back the spread and the sheet.

"He'll ruin your bed," Belle said.

"I can wash the sheets," Melody said.

"I don't see why we have to be the ones to look after him."

"He got shot because he was riding one of our horses. That means our trouble got him hurt. We're responsible for him."

"I don't see how."

"Who shot him?" Sydney asked once they had Chet on the bed.

"I don't know," Melody told her brother. "The man didn't tell us. Tom, take off his boots."

"What man?" Sydney asked.

"The man who found him. I didn't ask his name."

"You'll have to undress him, too."

"I'm not his servant," Tom complained.

"Then I'll have to do it."

Tom gave in to the inevitable and began to remove Chet's clothes.

"Have the boys take everything downstairs," Melody said. "They'll have to be washed before he can wear them again."

"It's not proper for a single woman to take care of a single man," Belle said once they were outside in the hall.

"Do you want to do it?" Melody asked.

"No. I wouldn't have minded if he hadn't upset Lantz. I like him—how could I not like such a handsome man?—but Lantz will be upset if he finds him here again."

"Then he'll just have to be upset."

"There's no point in making him angry."

"Maybe there is. Maybe it's time he learns not everybody jumps when the great Lantz Royal snaps his fingers."

"That's no way to talk about a man who's asked you to marry him."

"Maybe it's the best way to tell a future husband you won't be bullied by him."

"Melody! A wife should never do that."

"You and I are very different, Belle. You like men to think for you, tell you what to do."

"But they're smarter than we are. They know best."

"I don't admit that any man's smarter than I am until he proves it. Even then, I wouldn't give up my right to have an opinion and have it listened to."

"You'll never catch a husband if you talk like that."

"I've already had three offers despite my talk."

"Accept one before they change their minds."

"No."

"Why not?"

"I don't love any one of them."

"It's a wife's duty to learn to love her husband."

"And if she can't?"

"Then she must endure."

"I could never do that. I've never had a real family. I've always been a guest in somebody else's home. I want to belong, to be loved. I will love my husband before I marry him, but he'll have to love me as well."

"You're asking for a great deal."

"I'd be offering a great deal. Myself. Did you love my father before you married him?"

"Of course I did. Your father was a wonderful man."

"That's exactly what I want, and I don't mean to settle for less."

"But Lantz loves you. He—"

"I'm not certain Lantz can love anybody but himself. Besides, I'm not sure I could be Blade's mother."

"He is a little wild, but he'll settle down."

"You can't know that. Now I've got to change Chet's bandage. I can't be sure that man cleaned his wound properly."

When they reentered the bedroom, Belle gave Chet a quick but careful inspection. "He'll probably heal anyway. He looks remarkably healthy."

Healthy didn't begin to describe Chet Attmore. Even unconscious, he set Melody on edge, body and mind. No man had ever affected her like this. When she first started discovering men, her friends related ecstatic experiences, times when they had trouble breathing, felt too weak to stand, unable to speak, think, or act. Nothing like that had ever happened to her, and she had finally put all of it down to wishful thinking.

Now she wasn't so sure.

Chet became aware of the incredible pain in his head before anything else. He felt as though someone had tried to split his skull with a dull ax. He didn't even try to open his eyes. He just lay there, perfectly still, hoping the pain would subside enough for him to think.

Try as he might, he couldn't remember what had happened to him. Images of his brother and two other men kept fading in and out. He must have been shot. He could tell he was in a bed, but where? He had been riding through open country far from any dwelling.

He opened his eyes. The stabbing pain was worse than he'd expected. He closed them for a few minutes more before opening them again. The pain had eased off enough so he could see, but he had no idea where he was. Even more confusing, he was in a woman's room.

His head was turned to one side. He lay still, looking at a window framed by what looked like blue silk and white lace. A velvet perfume box filled with cut glass and silver bottles, brushes, what looked like a lace handkerchief, and an oil lamp with an elaborate shade lay scattered about a dressing table next to the window. A large mirror with a gilt frame hung on the wall just above the table. The chair in front of the dressing table was an odd little thing with rolled arms and no back. A deep blue cloth decorated with large white flowers and a border of green vines entwined around golden trumpets and horns covered the table and hung to the floor.

Clearly not a man's room.

Then Chet became aware of the fragrance of gardenias. He couldn't tell if it came from the pillow beneath his head or whether it hung in the air of the room, but it was definitely there and it was definitely gardenias.

The only woman he'd ever known to smell of gardenias was Melody.

A rush of excitement sent the blood surging though his veins, making the pain in his head worse. He tried to will himself to be calm, to tell himself not to be foolish. Melody would have no way of knowing he'd been hurt. There must have been some other ranch close by. There must be another woman who smelled of gardenias.

He closed his eyes again. He was too old to be indulging in wishful thinking, too sensible to be thinking of Melody Jordan even if he did. Besides, he finally remembered what had happened. He'd been shot by either Lantz Royal's son or Billy Mason. His brother had found him.

Chet didn't know what Luke was doing in this part of Texas, but he was certain it had something to do with Lantz Royal. That shouldn't surprise him. Luke always hired out to the man who paid the most money. Luke had turned out just like their father.

Chet turned his head and an excruciating pain ricocheted inside his skull like buckshot in a barrel. He closed his eyes and tried to relax. He'd worry about Luke later.

Neill opened the door, tiptoed in, and set the lamp on the table. Melody followed with a basin and bandages, which she set on the table next to the bed. She looked down at her patient.

"He's not dead, is he?" Neill asked in a nervous whisper.

"Just sleeping. Go tell Bernice I'll want his dinner as soon as I change the bandages."

Chet looked very different from the man who'd ridden into the ranch just yesterday. Even as a stranger, there had been so much that was attractive about him—the sensual quality of his looks, his incredibly blue eyes, his smile, his easy, open manner, his quiet but respectful attitude toward her. Even though he preserved his privacy, he had never closed her out. His smile curved his lips, danced in his eyes, invited you to smile with him.

Yet all the while she sensed the inflexibility of his will, the steel of his courage. Everything about him said here was a man who was a rock, an anchor, a protector who would never fail.

But now he lay asleep in her bed, stripped of his armor, vulnerable, so very human. She wanted to reach out and draw him close, to keep him safe. She smiled at such a ridiculous notion. This man might be wounded, but he was far from helpless. He'd awakened while the doctor checked him. He had lost blood and the pain was so great that it exhausted his strength, but he had been awake and alert. Chet was just as casual about his wound as he was about everything else.

But in his sleep he looked vulnerable. The muscle in his jaw had relaxed. His entire expression had softened; his body had lost its tension; the watchfulness was gone. He looked very much like a man she would like to get to know. After all, she wasn't likely to meet anyone else this handsome for a long time. And if she had to marry Lantz . . .

Melody pushed all thought of Lantz aside. She would concentrate on Chet. Once he was well and on his way, she would decide what to do about Lantz and her family.

She had to change the bandage, and it was impossible to do so without waking him. The wound extended from front to back, and the bandages were wrapped around his head like a turban. She brought a chair and placed it next to the bed.

"Time to eat, I hope."

She jumped. He hadn't opened his eyes before he spoke. Now he did. It was hard to believe that their intense blueness could still startle her, but it did. His eyes seemed to glow.

"I didn't know you were awake," she said.

"I heard the door open. I recognized your tread."

That surprised and pleased her. It seemed so intimate.

"It could have been Belle or Bernice."

She thought she saw a hint of a smile. "Belle doesn't want me here. There's an irritated thump to her footsteps. Bernice is so small, she has to take half again as many steps as you."

Melody sat down next to the bed. "Do you analyze everything like this?" she asked.

"In my business, you have to know everything you can about your enemy, or you die."

She began to unpin the bandage. "But you said you weren't a gunslinger anymore."

"Old habits die hard."

"I'm afraid you're going to have to lift your head."

"It might be easier on both of us if I sit up."

"The doctor said—"

"If I did everything the doctors told me, I'd have been dead years ago. Just put these pillows behind me when I lean forward."

The covers fell back to reveal a broad, powerfully muscled chest. When he pulled himself up into a sitting position, the muscles in his biceps and shoulders tensed and bulged. Their size and movement mesmerized Melody. She decided she probably wasn't a very good nurse. Surely a proper nurse wouldn't let her concern for her patient's wound be overcome by a fascination with his body.

She'd never seen a man's chest. The mere sight was a far greater intimacy than she'd ever experienced with any man. The intimacy of their being alone, of his body exposed to her gaze, suddenly overwhelmed her. It nearly caused her to miss the onset of some strange feeling deep inside her, something that affected her very much like a fever. What else could have caused the sudden flush of heat in her face, the unaccountable trembling of her hands?

She didn't like this feeling of being out of control, of being at the mercy of something unknown. She averted her gaze, fighting the powerful urge to look at Chet once more, to reach out and touch him.

Merciful heavens! If Aunt Emmaline could know the thoughts passing through Melody's mind, she'd rise straight up out of her grave.

Marshaling all her willpower, Melody forced herself to concentrate on Chet's wound. She could tell it took great effort to endure the pain, but it showed only in the compression of his lips. Sympathy would be wasted on this man. She quickly unwound the bandage. The bullet had burrowed under the skin at the back side of his head, traveled around the curve of his skull, and exited at the front. She could only assume he had a skull of extraordinary thickness, for which she was grateful. It was impossible to imagine him dead. A passion for life burned fiercely in this man. He appeared to take everything so lightly, but he fought his pain and weakness with grim determination. Such unyielding resolve hid a great desire for something, only she didn't know what it was.

"How does it look?" he asked.

"Almost like you weren't hurt at all. Tomorrow I may leave the bandages off."

"Good. Then I can give you back your bedroom."

Her shock at the thought of his leaving surprised her. How could he have become so important to her so quickly?

"You probably have a concussion," she said, sounding breathless. "You must be careful for the next few days."

"I couldn't stay in bed if I were out on the trail."

"Then be thankful you're not. Now hold still while I try to get this pin in the bandage. I don't want to stick you. Or myself."

A knock sounded at the door.

"Come in," Melody called.

Neill entered, carrying a pitcher and a glass, followed by Bernice bearing a bowl. Neill set the pitcher and glass down on the dressing table.

The presence of others in the room did little to ease the tension in Melody's body.

"Can I see where you were shot?" Neill asked eagerly.

"I've already bandaged it up," Melody said, relieved to see her brother was completely unaware of her strained state.

"But I've never seen a real wound."

"If your sister will undo the bandage, it's all right with me," Chet said.

"This is ridiculous," Melody said.

"Come on, Mel," Neill pleaded. "I brought the milk and I didn't spill a drop."

"He was very careful on the stairs," Bernice said.

Chet looked up at Melody. "Let him see."

When he looked at her like that—with the smile transforming his face and laughter dancing in his eyes—she couldn't refuse him anything.

"Only if he promises to go away immediately."

"Sure," Neill said. He waited eagerly while Melody unwrapped the bandage. "Is that all?" he asked, visibly disappointed.

"Gunshot or rifle wounds are usually small and neat," Chet said. "If you want to see some real gore, shoot somebody with a shotgun."

"Is it really nasty?" Neill asked, excitement wreathing his face.

"I've seen strong men faint."

"Did you faint?"

"No."

"I wouldn't either."

"Then neither one of you has any sensibilities at all," Melody said.

"Men aren't supposed to," Neill said.

"Certainly not at eleven," Bernice added.

"Not ever, if some men I know are an example." Melody started to replace the bandage. "Now run along. Mr. Attmore has to eat his dinner."

"Come along," Bernice said. "You can bring his dessert later."

"Why?" Neill asked. "I've already seen the wound."

"Why do men always have to be bribed?" Melody asked when the door had closed behind them. "Why can't they do things out of the goodness of their hearts?"

"It's very hard for a man out here to be good as well as respected. Most of us settle for trying to stay alive."

"What do you mean by *out here?*"

"Back East you have the rules of society to protect you. You have laws and courts when they fail. Out here you often don't have anybody but yourself. You do what you have to, and you learn to live with it."

Melody had never heard it stated quite so straightforwardly before.

"I can see you want to argue with me," Chet said. "But I wish you'd wait until tomorrow. The delicious smell coming from that bowl Bernice brought has made me hungry. While I eat, you can tell me how you came to be living in Central Texas."

Melody was tempted to argue with him anyway, but a sudden smile disarmed her. "You sure you don't want me to feed you?"

"Quite sure."

She almost laughed. He acted as if the idea affronted him. She picked up the tray and placed it in his lap. "Milk will be better than coffee."

"I've never had milk."

"Never?"

"I don't remember it. Now talk. This soup smells too good to ignore."

So she talked. She told him her mother had died when she was three months old. Her father was fighting in Texas, so she had gone to live with her mother's sister in Richmond. After the war, her father stayed in Texas, started a ranch, remarried, and started raising a second family. She stayed in Richmond.

She told him how her aunt lived in a cabin while she worked to restore her land to production so her children would have an inheritance. She told him of the new house her aunt built on a ridge above the James River, of the fun her aunt had furnishing it, of her first party.

When her father and aunt died within a month of each other, the allowance her father had been sending stopped. Her cousins had invited her to live with them, but Melody had inherited half of the Spring Water Ranch, so she decided to come to Texas. It had shocked her to discover her step-mother had neither the knowledge nor the desire to run the ranch. She let her sons do as they wished and left all decisions to her foreman. She had encouraged Melody to do the same.

"She doesn't even know what we're having for dinner until we sit down to the table," Melody said. "I couldn't accept that."

"I don't imagine you could."

She looked to see if he was mocking her, but he kept his eyes lowered.

"I considered going back to Richmond, but I can't go back without any money. I refuse to be my cousins' pensioner."

"So you are caught here," he said, "unable to realize your assets."

"I suppose it looks that way now, but that's not what I thought at first. I was determined to learn to run the ranch, to help my stepmother raise my brothers to be effective managers of their inher-itance when they grew up. Then Lantz decided he wanted to marry me. When I didn't say yes right away, he had his men bully our cowhands in an effort to convince me I can't manage without him."

"Are you going to marry him?"

"He never gave me a chance to find out if I could love him. He assumed asking me was enough. Now that I know him better, I'm not sure I could ever love him. He only understands force."

"Marrying him would solve all your problems."

"Not all, but I'd rather not think about that now. It's your turn to tell me about yourself."

"There's nothing to tell."

"There must be something."

"Very little. My mother ran away before my brother could walk. My father dragged us around with him, leaving us in hotel rooms scared and hungry most of the time. He was a gambler and a gunfighter. He died the way all men of his stamp do, with a bullet in the back. My brother and I got thrown out of one orphanage after another. If Jake and Isabelle hadn't adopted us, we'd probably be dead by now. It'll probably happen anyway. My brother hires his gun to the highest bidder. One day he'll meet a man faster or luckier. I expect some day the brother, friend, or son of a man I've killed will succeed in getting even with me."

Melody didn't know what to say. The war had given her an understanding of violence and loss, but here she had strayed into a raw land where nearly all men considered gunplay an ordinary part of their lives.

"You're horrified," he said.

"Surprised," she said, trying to get her expression under control.

"No, you're horrified. You think we live like savages. We do, but my brother and I, and men like us, will make it possible for the men who come after us to live differently. Find yourself one of those. Not Lantz Royal. No matter how much he tries to disguise it, he's one of us."

Melody didn't know what to say. For a brief moment, the barriers had come down. His eyes warmed; his expression became intense. For a moment he wasn't so easygoing and uncaring. He seemed passionately concerned about what might happen to her. For a moment, she caught a glimpse of the fire that burned so brightly inside him.

Then he closed the shutters once more. But she

didn't feel so completely shut out this time. She now knew there were two sides to his relaxed manner. One was his enormous confidence in himself. The other was a shield to keep people from reaching the man inside.

"I'm not sure what I want to do," she said. "I want to escape this trouble, but I can't desert my stepmother and brothers. Belle knows even less than I do. She could lose everything, and my brothers would be penniless."

"Leave everything to Tom and go back to Richmond. You don't belong here."

Having Chet say it like that made it sound as though she was running away, as though she wasn't strong enough to survive.

"Why do you care what happens to me?" she asked.

The shutters closed with a bang. He didn't answer.

"Don't you think I'm clever enough, or strong enough?" she asked.

"I don't know you. I have no right to think anything about you," he replied.

But Melody couldn't accept that. She didn't know what he really thought, but she intended to find out.

Chet told himself that for a man who talked very little, he sure as hell could put his foot in his mouth in a hurry. Why did he think he had the right to tell Melody who she ought not to marry? Sticking his nose into something like that was a good way to get another bullet in the head.

That must be it. His head wasn't working right. All his common sense had leaked out through those two little holes or been knocked out by the concussion. Or maybe her sitting next to him as if it was the most natural thing in the world, talking to him as if they'd been friends forever, had caused it to wither and die. Maybe he liked the feeling so much, he wanted to feel she cared what happened to him.

Yes, he'd definitely lost any common sense he'd ever had. His sense of self-preservation must have taken a leave of absence as well. He was putting his head on the chopping block and just begging someone to lop it off. If he was going to be that stupid, he might as well have kept working until the day somebody shot him.

Now he was talking like an idiot. And all because of a woman. All he ever wanted out of life was exactly what Jake and Isabelle had. The irony was that holding on to family, giving up what he had to protect Luke, had cut him off from the very life he wanted. Doing the honorable thing had brought him into dishonor.

He knew all this, accepted it. Going over it again wasn't going to change anything. If he knew what was good for him, he'd pack his concussion into a tight bandage and hitch a ride on the first horse going east, west, north, or south. He'd traveled in worse condition and probably would again.

Chet eased down into the softness of the mattress. It was too late to leave today. Besides, Melody would make a terrible fuss.

Tomorrow would be soon enough.

Chapter Seven

"You had no right to put armed men at the water holes just because somebody put a little trash in them," Melody practically shouted at Tom Neland.

"It wasn't *a little trash*," Tom said. "It was dead coyotes. If we hadn't removed them right away, the water wouldn't have been usable for weeks. As it is—"

"And while the men are sitting around watching the water, rustlers could be driving our cattle from the range by the hundreds."

"Melody, dear, you've just come from a burned-up city," Belle said. "You can't possibly know as much about the ranch as Tom."

"Even in a *burned-up city*, men can't be in two places at once."

"I'm sure Tom has that all figured out. You ought to leave everything to him. It never does

112

any good when women interfere in men's work."

Melody was so angry, she didn't dare let herself speak for fear she'd say something unforgivable. Once more Tom had ignored her wishes—practically a direct order—and done what *he* thought should be done. And Belle was backing him up. Not because Belle had any ideas of her own on the subject. Belle never had any ideas. She left all the thinking to men. Any man.

That was what infuriated Melody the most. It wasn't in her makeup to defer to anyone just because he was a man.

She'd be the first to admit she hadn't known anything about ranching when she arrived in Texas, but she did have some firm principles, and the indiscriminate use of guns went squarely against them.

"Why can't they just check the water holes more frequently?"

"Lantz could ruin them."

"He wouldn't do that. He wants them to be his water holes. He's just trying to help me make up my mind to marry him."

"If you'd marry me—"

"Then you could have the men carry guns all the time and shoot at anything that moves. No, thank you."

"If you married Lantz, neither of you would have to worry about guns," Belle said. "The boys and I wouldn't have to worry about losing the roof over our heads."

"I mean to love the man I marry," Melody declared. "I don't love Tom or Lantz."

"But I love *you*," Tom said. "I have almost from the beginning."

"Yet you won't do what I ask."

113

"Lantz loves you," Belle said. "I bet he'd do anything you wanted."

"Lantz Royal has never tried to please anybody but himself in his entire life," Tom said. "If she wants a husband who'll give her the consideration she deserves, she'll marry me."

"Then pull the men off the water holes."

"You know I can't do that. I already explained—"

"So much for your consideration. I *order* you to pull the men off the water holes."

"You can't. You aren't the majority owner."

"Belle, back me up," Melody said.

"Darling, you know I leave everything to Tom."

"So he can do whatever he wants, and I can't do anything about it."

"If you'd marry Lantz, you wouldn't have to worry about any of this," Belle said.

"Then you'd advise me to leave everything up to him."

"Of course. Women should never interfere in men's business."

"Not even when they're wrong?"

"How are we to judge?"

"Because we're not stupid!" Melody said. She practically ran from the room. If she stayed one minute longer, she was surely going to hit somebody. She ran up the stairs and into her room before she remembered it was no longer unoccupied.

"You look upset," Chet said.

He had been lying down, but he sat up when she entered.

Melody should have left immediately, but she needed to talk to somebody before she started screaming. "I didn't mean to barge in, but I'm so angry I hardly know what I'm doing."

"I promise not to provoke you as long as you tell me what I'm not supposed to say."

She closed the door behind her and virtually threw herself into the vanity chair. "You're not to say a woman must yield to a man in everything, that a woman can never understand how to run a ranch as well as a man, or that a woman should never ask a man to explain himself."

"One of the cleverest outlaws I ever went up against was a woman. She got two bullets into me."

A spurt of laughter escaped, despite her mood. "I'm sure Belle and Tom would be glad to attribute my wayward disposition to a lawless streak."

"More likely they doubt anyone reared in tradition-bound Virginia could understand anything Texan."

"My father was able to learn enough to build this ranch and stand up to Lantz Royal's bullying. I'm his daughter. I can learn, too."

"I'm sure you can, but do you want to?"

She'd been letting her irritated gaze move randomly about the room. Now it focused on Chet. "What do you mean?"

"You said you wanted to sell your half of the ranch and go back to Richmond. Why waste your time learning how to manage a ranch you're going to leave the minute you can?"

"I had hoped . . . I'd thought . . . I don't know what I thought, but I'd never run away and leave my family. I was a guest in somebody's house for the first eighteen years of my life. Now that I have a home of my own, I don't mean to leave it." Even though it was raw, sometimes cruel, and seemingly full of guns, she was part of Texas.

"I thought I could learn to run this place on my own. My aunt always let me help her. She talked to me about what she was doing, even took my advice occasionally. I felt a part of everything she did. Here I feel like Tom and Lantz would like to lock me up inside a house and never let me out again."

"We don't have many good women in this part of Texas. We tend to want to protect them as much as possible."

"I don't mind being protected," Melody said. "In fact, I rather like it. But I don't like being suffocated."

"You don't like being told no."

"That, either," she admitted reluctantly. She'd bet he told people no all the time. It was probably his favorite word. He had that look. "But I can take it if I feel it's justified." He didn't look as if he believed her.

"Do you think Lantz Royal would let you run his ranch?"

"I'm not interested in running Lantz's ranch. If I married him, I probably wouldn't interfere except to stop him bullying people. I don't think that's fair."

"I'm sure his neighbors would agree with you."

She stiffened. "Now you're laughing at me."

"No, I'm serious. He doesn't have a good reputation."

Her ire evaporated. "That's what Tom said, but I thought he was just jealous."

"What else do you object to?"

"Guns. People here think they're the solution to everything. I hate them. I know too many women who lost husbands and sons in the war. I couldn't

116

stand it if my husband were killed. I'll forbid him to use guns."

"Then I suggest you head back to Richmond as soon as you can. You're not likely to find a husband to please you out here."

She didn't like that. He made it sound as if she was somehow defective, that she didn't measure up.

"I've already had three offers." She hadn't meant to say that. It sounded as if she was bragging, but this man irritated her. He said he wasn't making fun of her, but who could tell what he was thinking behind that inscrutable look?

"Weren't you just telling me that Lantz is still trying to bully you and Tom is still depending on guns?"

"Yes, but . . ." What could she say? Did she really believe either of them would give up using guns if she asked? "They would if they really loved me," she said. But she didn't sound convinced, not even to herself.

"I have a feeling not everybody sees love the way you do."

"What's wrong with my way?" He was beginning to make her angry. It was a shame he was so handsome that she couldn't stop thinking about him. He deserved to be ignored.

"I didn't say it was wrong. Just different."

"How?" It seemed he didn't want to answer. "You may as well explain. I don't intend to leave this room until you do."

The hint of a smile. Why was the blessed man so stingy? Didn't he know he had a smile that could bring a strong woman to her knees? Maybe he didn't want a woman like Melody, even on her knees? That thought sent a chill all the way through her.

"I don't have a wide experience of women. I couldn't say."

"You're not going to weasel out now. You've made a statement that implies I'm doing something wrong. You may think me hard-headed, but I do want to learn."

"All I meant to say is that you seem to interpret love as meaning one person will give up things he believes for the other. Another way to look at it is that you would have enough faith in the man you loved to believe he was making the right decision."

"Even about guns?"

"Yes."

"Why should I do that? I know what they can do."

"So do Texans. We depend on them for hunting, protection, even as a way of making a living. There isn't much formal law out here—none in some places. Men who have anything took it and fought to hold it against men equally determined to take it from them. That may not be a pretty picture, but it's the way things are."

"And you think they ought to stay that way?"

"No. Things will change, but that change will be slow in coming. Guns will be needed for a long time in some places."

"I don't understand you," she said. "You defend the use of guns, but you won't use yours anymore."

"I didn't say I wouldn't use it, only that I won't use it for money."

"I still don't understand you."

He did smile. It was like sunshine. "Don't

worry. I'll be leaving tomorrow. You won't have to worry about me again."

"You can't go. You're not well yet." He was always throwing her off stride. Now she had gone from being angry at him to being worried about his injury, about his leaving.

"I should have left today. If you hadn't made me so comfortable, I would have."

"Where are you going in such a hurry?"

"Nowhere."

"Is anybody waiting for you?"

"No."

"Then there's no reason to go."

"I can't continue to trespass on your hospitality."

"You don't know much about Virginians. You have to stay at least a month before even the most unsociable hostess begins to wonder when you'll leave."

"I do know Texans, and your brother, foreman, and stepmother all want to see the back of me."

"Not really. Belle is just worried about Lantz. Sydney is upset that you showed him up, and Tom is jealous of anybody taller than he is. He may start liking you just because you're even taller than Lantz."

"That's no reason to stay."

"And you call me stubborn. It's stupid to leave until you're well, especially when you have no place to go and you're perfectly welcome to stay here. Besides, I like talking to you. You're the only one who doesn't treat me like an idiot. Well, at least not like a complete idiot."

"I never meant to—"

"I know. I'm still irritated, but you've got to promise to stay."

"Why?"

"If you stay a few more days, you can ride your own horse." She didn't understand why he was so anxious to leave, but she could tell he was weakening. "Belle doesn't really want you to go. She hasn't had a new man to talk to in months. Neill wants you to stay. He's still showing that peach can around like he did it himself."

"I thought you didn't admire guns."

"I can admire a skill without admiring the use to which it is put."

"You're a complicated woman."

"Not really. Everybody is expecting you to eat dinner with us tonight."

"Everybody?"

"Yes. Bernice is preparing something special. She doesn't get the chance to cook for company often."

"You don't have to cook anything special for me."

"She's not. I've been teaching her to cook some of my favorite dishes. You can't imagine how much I long for something that isn't seasoned with a bushel of peppers or served with beans. You're going to get a traditional Virginia dinner, at least as traditional as we can get in Texas. Now I'll leave you to take your nap."

Melody decided she was a fickle woman. She had entered that room liking Chet. Ten minutes later she was thoroughly out of patience with him. Now she was begging him to stay. She was as bad as Belle. Considering some of the things she'd muttered under her breath about her stepmother, that was a terrible indictment.

She would have to figure out just what it was about this man that made it impossible to think of his leaving, of never seeing him again. It wasn't just his looks. She recognized and understood the tingles she felt when she watched him sleep, the strange feelings in her belly when she sat close to him, knowing he was virtually naked under those sheets.

But there was something else about him that caused her to beg him to stay, something that made her want to know he was near, that he would be in that room when she opened the door. It was a new feeling, something she didn't understand because it had never happened to her before.

That bothered her. She didn't like things she didn't understand. But she liked Chet, and she didn't understand him at all.

Chet had made a list of all the reasons why he shouldn't go down to dinner with the family, why he should have left the ranch the day before, why he should have moved to the bunkhouse if he had to stay, why he was crazy to walk into the midst of a group of people he knew didn't want him around.

There was only one reason to stay. Melody had asked him. It was just that simple. Stupid, but simple.

He scowled at himself in the mirror. He looked like a regular dude. Someone had ironed his shirt and pressed his black suit. He hadn't worn these clothes in years. Why had he now worn them twice in three days? Vanity and the inability to avoid making a fool out of himself. He wanted Melody to admire him. He knew she didn't think much of what he'd done with his life, so he was banking on his looks. He didn't understand the hold this woman had on him, but he'd been hooked hard and fast by a woman who disapproved of him.

He was nuts. Maybe he ought to go chase a few murderers and rustlers to get some sanity back in his life.

He opened the door and started down the hall. He didn't feel quite steady on his feet. The stairs were more of a problem, but he negotiated them alone. It would have humiliated him to ask for help.

Though Belle's house didn't look at all like Isabelle's, there was one similarity. The decorations were clearly feminine. It seemed all women wanted a fancily decorated nest, no matter how remote or inhospitable the country surrounding it. But this house lacked the dash of rough masculine strength that Jake and the boys had contributed. There was no boisterous seesaw battle between the masculine and the feminine. The feminine had won in a rout.

Chet shook his head. Maybe that bullet had done more damage than he thought. He'd never before muddled his head with thoughts like this.

"My, don't you look handsome," Belle Jordan trilled to Chet from the parlor, "not like you've been injured at all."

Chet directed his steps away from the office and toward a room filled with ornate Victorian furniture. Jake rarely denied Isabelle anything, but he'd put his foot down when she had wanted a roomful of similar furniture.

"Don't tell him that," Melody said, "or he'll be on a horse and out of here before nightfall."

"I'm not as steady as I look," Chet said, deciding

to stand rather than sit. "You've kept me in bed too long."

"You're trying to hurry things too much," Belle said, patting the sofa next to her. "Come sit down."

The dinner bell rang, sparing him. The office door opened, and Sydney and Neill came out, followed more slowly by Tom Neland. Chet looked at Melody in surprise.

"I won't let them sit in here," Belle explained. "They'd ruin the upholstery."

Isabelle expected Jake and the boys to wash and clean their boots. But once they entered the house, they were free to go anywhere they liked.

Not waiting for Melody and their mother to precede them, Neill and Sydney ran for the table and sat down. Chet held the chair for Melody, Tom for Belle.

"A gentleman waits until the ladies are seated to sit down," Chet said.

Neill bounced to his feet, a confused look on his face. Sydney remained seated, looking mulish.

"You can stand on your own or be lifted," Chet said to him.

He knew he was interfering too much, but this boy was being intentionally rude. Chet had spent most of his life without a home or a family that cared for him. This spoiled young man didn't appreciate what he had.

"You can't stand up without wobbling," Sydney said. "You couldn't lift a baby."

The boy's attitude was such an impudent challenge, Chet couldn't stop himself. He walked around the table, grasped Sydney by the collar, and lifted him straight out of the seat.

"Are you going to stand up, or do I drop you?"

Sydney stood and stared at Chet, his look mingling surprise and anger with the possible beginnings of respect.

Chet seated Melody, then sat down himself. He was greatly relieved to be off his feet. Lifting a 140-pound boy was no easy feat under the best of circumstances. A cruel pain throbbed in his head. *It's what you get for showing off.*

The meal got off to a hesitant start, but it wasn't long before conversation flowed easily. Chet mostly listened.

"If Melody would just marry Lantz, it would solve everything," Belle said.

"You've said that a dozen times," Melody said, her tone a little less than cordial. "It's not fair to keep putting the burden for solving the problems of this ranch on my shoulders."

"Well, you have to marry someone. It may as well be Lantz."

"I will not marry a bully," Melody said.

"He's not really trying to bully you," Belle said. "He's just trying to show you what could happen to a woman alone. He hasn't hurt anyone."

"Tell that to Speers."

"I don't like Lantz and won't defend him," Neland said, "but that was rustlers. They've been hitting everybody, including Lantz. He's furious, but they seem to know where everybody is all the time. If Speers hadn't gone off on his own, he wouldn't have been anywhere near them to get shot."

"If you'd let me ride with you, I'd stop those rustlers," Sydney said.

"You're not to go anywhere near any rustlers,"

Belle said. "I would lose my mind if you were shot."

Chet started to remind Belle that just two days earlier, she'd argued *for* letting Sydney ride with Tom but decided against it.

"I'd shoot them," Sydney said. "I'm getting better all the time."

"You're hardly more than a child," Belle declared. "You're to stay here where you're safe."

Sydney turned red. "Stop treating me like a baby. We need extra men in the saddle." He turned to Neland. "I'm old enough to ride with you, aren't I?"

"You are not," Belle said, her languid, helpless air vanished. "I'll fire any man who lets you ride with him."

"Only if I agree with you," Melody said. Her voice was quiet, a strong contrast with Belle's shrillness.

"What do you mean?" Belle demanded.

"You told me you could cancel any orders I gave Tom. Well, if that's the case, then I can cancel your orders as well."

Belle looked outraged. "I can't believe you would throw your own brother into the path of a bullet," she said, her eyes bright with anger. "I never believed you'd go that far to get controlling interest in the ranch."

"Sydney's share would go to Neill. I wouldn't get control unless both of the boys died. Even then, you would have control of their shares until your death."

Chet was surprised Melody could respond so calmly. He'd have been fighting mad if anybody had made such an accusation against him.

"I forgot," Belle said, suddenly transformed

into the wispy-voiced female Chet knew. "I can't think straight when I'm worried about one of the boys being hurt."

"Then you shouldn't have encouraged him to develop his gun skills."

"But he's a man. He has to be able to use a gun."

"Then you shouldn't be surprised he wants to prove he's better than anybody else. That's what men do."

"I wish your father were here," Belle complained. "He would know what to do."

"He'd let me ride with the men," Sydney said, still sullen.

"What do you think?" Melody said, turning to Chet.

"I think you ought to leave it up to Tom," Chet said, not wanting to get into the middle of this argument. "He's the one who'd be responsible for the boy."

"Nobody's responsible for me," Sydney said. "I own the ranch. Tom works for me. I'm *not* a boy."

"But you must have some experience of boys," Melody said to Chet. "You had a lot of brothers."

"And you were a foreman, too," Belle added.

Both women had ignored Sydney's outburst. Chet decided that was the crux of the problem. They ignored the boy when they shouldn't and came down heavy when they realized he was on the verge of growing into manhood. But women never wanted to let their children grow up and assume adult responsibilities. Even Isabelle had trouble with that, and there wasn't any female Chet admired more than his adoptive mother.

"You won't like what I think," Chet warned.

"Why not?" Melody asked.

Chet didn't want to make Melody angry with

him, but he'd been doing it ever since he arrived. There seemed little point in stopping now.

"I think he ought to be riding with Tom. I don't think it's sensible for a man to own a ranch or any other kind of business and not know how to run it. He'll be cheated and robbed if he's ignorant. He won't be respected by other men."

"But he's only fourteen," Belle objected.

"That's almost a man out here."

"See, I told you," Sydney said, flashing a smile of thanks at Chet.

"However," Chet added, "I'm disturbed by his carelessness with a gun. I wouldn't let him carry one for at least a year."

"What do you know about ranching?" Sydney demanded. "We got rustlers, we got—"

"He grew up on a ranch," Melody said. "He was foreman."

"Then you can tell us what to do to keep the ranch," Belle said.

Chapter Eight

If he had any sense at all, he'd excuse himself and disappear into his room. "I don't know anything about your situation. I couldn't give advice."

They weren't going to let him off that easy.

"Lantz Royal wants to marry me," Melody said. "I don't know which he wants more, me or the ranch, but he's made it plain he means to have both. He's putting pressure on me by hazing the men."

"Why does he want your ranch?"

"He wants to own everything within his reach."

"Then you have a choice—sell out, fight, or marry him." He couldn't imagine Melody married to Lantz without wanting to shoot the man.

"We can't sell because Lantz won't buy," Belle said.

"And no one else will offer because they're afraid of Lantz," Melody said.

"We can't fight him because he's got three times as many men," Tom added.

"And I refuse to marry him," Melody said. "I wouldn't even if he weren't a bully."

"Tom says if he pushes us off our grazing range, it'll leave us with nothing," Belle said.

"I expect your husband didn't own the land he grazed."

"Nobody does," Neland said. "We graze the land we can hold."

"Then you ought to buy the pieces that are essential, the land around springs, along streams, good grazing or hay meadows. If you owned those, there wouldn't be any point in anyone trying to run you off. You could also inform your local law officers of what's happening."

"That won't do any good. Lantz controls everybody."

"Then write the marshal's office. And document every incident with names of people who can vouch for you."

"They only help people with money."

"If you like, I'll write for you."

"Why should you do that?" Tom asked.

"Writing a letter isn't much."

"But it'll get you into trouble with Lantz Royal."

"That won't make any difference. I'll be gone in a few days anyway."

"We've been having some rustling, too," Melody said. "What would you do about that?"

"I'd have to know more about your operation here."

"Even general advice would be a help."

He found himself wanting to tell her to ask him to stay. He'd get rid of any rustler fool enough to set foot on her ranch.

"Organize night watches. It's harder to steal cows when people are around. Since the rustling at all the ranches started about the same time, it's probably being done by the same outfit. It's likely they're taking all the cattle to the same place. It ought to be easy to find out where. Once you do that, you have a chance of finding out who's doing the rustling."

"That doesn't sound very difficult," Melody said, looking toward Tom.

"I'm not finished yet," Chet said.

"What else?"

"When you find the rustlers, you've got to go after them. That'll mean using guns."

"But you said we ought to notify the law."

"If you wait for the law to do the work for you, you won't have any cows left. I told you before, people have to be their own law out here."

"Like Lantz?"

"I imagine he did a right good job before he got greedy."

"Pa faced him down," Sydney stated proudly. "He told him if he so much as touched a single Spring Water cow, he'd burn him out."

"How did your father die?" Chet asked.

"He and his horse fell into a ravine in a storm," Tom said.

"He had no business being out in that kind of weather," Belle said. "I begged him not to go."

"Why did he?" Chet asked.

"He wouldn't tell me," Belle said.

"He was certain we were losing cows," Tom said. "He thought the rustlers would raid during the storm and he could catch them."

That didn't make sense to Chet. No intelligent man went out alone in a storm. Besides, an experienced rancher knew the location of every ravine and canyon on his land. It wouldn't surprise him to learn there was something fishy about Bob Jordan's death. But Chet had no intention of voicing that thought. Putting it into this family's heads would just cause trouble and unhappiness. It was probably too late to find out what really happened anyway.

The door to the kitchen opened. One of the cowhands entered the dining room.

"We got hit by rustlers again," the man announced without waiting to be invited to speak. "They didn't get many steers, but they hit Toby."

"Is he dead?" Belle asked, her hand clutching her breast.

"It was just a graze, but they tried to kill him. The boys want to saddle up and go after them."

Tom crumpled up his napkin and pushed back his chair. "Saddle my horse. I'll be with you in a minute. I was afraid they weren't going to be satisfied with just a few yearlings," he said, turning to Melody. "They mean to keep it up until they've picked us clean."

"Chet just said—"

"This is no time for thinking and planning," Tom snapped. "It's time to *do* something. I'm going to hire a gunslick to take out these rustlers."

"No," Melody said. "You've got a crew. They can—"

"They're cowhands, Melody, not gunhands. You can't expect them to risk their lives unless they get gunhand wages. That's at least twenty dollars a month extra."

"I'm not hiring a gunman."

"Lantz Royal did the minute they touched his herd. They say he's lightning with a gun. Blond, like this fella here," he said pointing at Chet. "Name's Luke something."

So Luke was working for Lantz. Chet had feared as much. He tried to keep track of his brother, but Luke liked to keep his movements to himself.

"I'm not hiring a gunfighter," Melody said.

"But if Lantz did it—" Belle began.

"I don't care what Lantz did," Melody said, interrupting.

"Mama and I can vote you down," Sydney said. "We can cancel anything you say."

"We can talk about this later," Tom said. "Right now I've got to see if we can track those rustlers before they get too far away."

Chet hoped Luke had nothing to do with the rustling. Chet had always made sure he hired out to men he believed were trying to defend themselves, men who had right on their side. Luke hadn't always been as careful, but he'd never stepped over the line. Or not very far.

Chet hoped he was here purely to look for the rustlers. But that wasn't Luke's style. He wasn't much on riding through rough country, chasing down thieves and outlaws. He'd left that to Chet. So far that had kept them out of each other's way.

"I said, what do you think?" Belle was saying to Chet, a sharp edge to her voice. She didn't like knowing a man could be at the same table as she and not be aware of her presence.

"What do you want to know?" Chet asked.

"What do you think about hiring a gunfighter to go after these rustlers?"

"A lot of people do it."

"But would you do it?" Melody asked.

"No," Chet said, looking her full in the face. "I'd

go after them myself. And I wouldn't stop until I caught them. If I brought any back alive, they'd hang."

Melody blanched. "You don't seem to feel any mercy."

"Not for thieves," Chet said. "I work for what I have. I see no reason to let any man take it from me. Besides, a man who steals once will steal again."

"But he could change, decide to—"

"We're all what Nature made us, ma'am. Just like the leopard, we can't change our spots."

"Then you'll be a gunman for the rest of your life."

Chet couldn't see his own expression, but it apparently had been enough to make Melody regret her words.

"I didn't mean it like that."

"You're right," Chet said. "My father was a gunfighter. So is my brother. We are what we are, and we can't do anything about it."

"But you've left the profession."

"I don't want to kill anymore, but I'll pick up my guns again if I need to. I may not want to kill again, but I wouldn't hesitate to defend myself."

The look of horror on her face—maybe it was revulsion—told Chet he had put himself outside the limits of her understanding. He was someone she could never accept. Chet would rather have bitten his tongue than said what he had, but it was just as well. He'd known from the first that there could be nothing between him and Melody.

But he kept hoping something would occur to prove him wrong. It was better that he put an end to all possibility right now, before it became impossible to forget her.

"If you're always going to be a gunfighter, why don't you work for us?" Belle asked.

"Belle, you can't mean that," Melody said.

She said it as if she was talking about an infectious plague. She tried to eliminate the disgust from her voice, but he heard it.

"You already hired him once," Sydney said. "He can go after the rustlers with Tom."

"He'll get 'em," Neill said, "just like he got that peach can."

"I don't see why you're acting so shocked," Belle said to Melody. "We can't allow rustlers to keep stealing our cows. He said he'd shoot any rustlers he found stealing his cattle. Well, I don't see any reason why he can't shoot ours as well."

"Because I don't want a gunfighter around here. It'll just attract other gunfighters."

"I don't see why we have to be the only one without one," Belle said.

"I say we hire him," Sydney put in, his eyes shining with excitement. "Then he can get together with Lantz's gunfighter. I bet they'd wipe out those rustlers in short order."

"I'll do anything I can to protect you while I'm here," Chet said, "but I turned down Melody's job and I'm turning down any other offers. Leave the rustlers to Tom and Lantz," Chet told Melody. "These men are criminals, and they have to be treated that way."

"We have criminals in Virginia," Melody said, "but we don't ride after them with guns blazing, shoot them down, or hang them from the nearest tree." Her scorn for such actions was blistering. "They're brought to justice. A judge and jury decide their fate."

Chet was getting tired of being treated like

some kind of wild animal. He could admire spunk but not ignorance.

"Someday it'll be that way in Texas," he said, "but not for a few years yet. It'll be best if you go on back to Richmond and leave this ranch to Sydney and Neill. Maybe someday your daughter can come back without feeling that she's living among savages." Chet pushed back his chair and got slowly to his feet. "Now, if I'm to get well enough to give you back your bedroom, I'd better get some rest. The dinner was delicious."

He knew she wanted to think of some reason, to fabricate some excuse, why her remarks didn't include him, but he didn't wait long enough to give her the chance. He would have forgiven her. He could feel himself wanting to do it already. He had to get beyond temptation before it was too late.

Melody couldn't remember when she'd ever felt worse about sticking to her principles. She couldn't change her mind—she didn't intend to try—but the pervasive feeling of dissatisfaction wouldn't go away. She felt the way she did on those mornings when she woke up feeling out of sorts. Nothing felt good, even the things that were supposed to.

She didn't want to sit and talk with Belle and the boys. They wouldn't talk of anything except gunfighters. Sydney and Neill admired them. Belle saw them as the answer to at least part of their troubles. Melody saw them as the introduction of still more trouble.

She couldn't go to her room. Chet was there, and that would lead to an even more difficult conversation. He was the source of all her frustrations. She just couldn't make herself feel that Chet was a gunfighter. He'd told her he was. She'd seen him draw on Lantz without a moment's hesitation. She could even believe he would have used his gun, but she still couldn't believe he was a gunfighter.

Gunfighters were cruel, heartless men who didn't care who they killed as long as they got paid. They were nothing more than a lethal weapon pointed and fired on command.

She couldn't believe Chet was like that. She was beginning to accept that guns were a tool, possibly a necessary tool in Texas. She could also accept that she was wrong to assign them any kind of power, good or evil, and that they were only what a man made them. Maybe Chet could actually use his gun for good. She would have scoffed at such a notion a few days ago, but she hadn't met him then. She still hadn't known him very long, but you didn't always have to know a person for years before you could discern the quality of his character. Chet was honorable. She would wager her half of the ranch on that.

Her half of the ranch! There might not be any ranch to worry about if she didn't marry Lantz Royal. But the longer she waited, the more certain she became that she could never marry him. He hadn't seemed too bad at first, mostly willful and determined to have his way. She knew many men like that, men reared to think God intended them to rule the world because women didn't have the intelligence.

Chet's arrival had made her see Lantz's actions in a different light. They now seemed threatening rather than capricious, more lawless than willful. She shook her head. How could she set a self-

136

confessed gunfighter against a successful rancher and pillar of the community and have the gunfighter come out better by comparison?

Something was seriously wrong with her thinking processes. Maybe she'd been away from Richmond too long. She carried the last of the dishes from the table into the kitchen.

"You don't have to help me," Bernice said.

"I don't mind."

"You're just trying to keep from having to spend the evening sitting with Belle."

"What if I am?"

"You can do anything you want," Bernice said, setting the dishes carefully into the soapy water. They had used the best china tonight. "I just didn't want you thinking I thought you was here for my company."

"Am I that much of a snob?"

"You're better about helping than Belle ever was, and I like having company. But you didn't come for that. You came because that man is in your craw."

"Lantz isn't in my craw. If he weren't threatening the ranch, I wouldn't even think of him again." The look Bernice gave her said she'd picked the wrong answer. "Tom, either. He's a nice man, but I'd never marry him."

"I don't mean Lantz or poor Tom," Bernice said, rinsing a dish and setting it on the counter to drip dry. "I mean that man upstairs"—she nodded her head toward the ceiling—"that gunfighter fella."

"Chet Attmore is not in my craw," Melody declared, incensed. "He's—"

"He's an invitation to trouble," Bernice said, putting another dish on the counter. "I'd hate to think of the number of poor women who've taken him up on it."

Melody had never thought of Chet seducing a string of women. The picture was not a welcome one. Yet she couldn't banish it. She could easily understand how it could happen. She'd been drawn in by his looks, was certain even now that he was a wonderful human being. The fact that he was a gunfighter seemed to make no impression on her. Why should other women be any different?

"I admit he's very handsome," Melody said, "and I feel guilty over his being shot because he was riding one of our horses. But that's all. Once he's recovered, he'll ride out and I'll never think of him again."

"And I'm a bonny Irish lass with freckles and flaming red hair," Bernice said, shaking her black-as-ink braids. "You've got him in your craw, and you can't get him out."

"He's not the problem I'm worried about," Melody said, refusing to let Bernice shake her story. "It's Lantz and the ranch. Belle says I'm a fool not to marry him. She says I'd have a rich husband who'd give me anything I wanted, and she and the boys would be secure on the ranch." She picked up a cloth and began to dry the dishes.

"It sounds like a good argument to me," Bernice said as she put another load of dishes into the water. "Is this man upstairs making you reconsider?"

"It's Lantz himself," Melody said, looking Bernice square in the eye. "If he's willing to bully me to get me to marry him, who's to say he won't try to bully me into doing what he wants after we're married."

"I imagine he'll bully people the rest of his life," Bernice said as she turned back to the dishes in the wash pot. "He's that kind of man."

"Belle says it won't matter, that as long as I don't bother him about his business he won't bother me about mine."

"She's probably right."

"Have you ever been in love?" Melody asked after they'd worked in silence for several minutes.

Bernice's hands stilled. "Why do you want to know?"

"My aunt's husband was killed in the war, but she had the most wonderful memories of him. Sometimes in the evening we'd sit by the fire and she'd talk about him by the hour. Not sad or crying. They were good memories. They made her feel happy. Don't you think that would be something worth waiting for?"

"It doesn't matter what I think."

"Tell me anyway."

"Some people don't rate love as high as your aunt. They like being comfortable, safe, staying with people and things they know and understand."

"Like Belle wanting me to marry Lantz."

"Could be."

"You think I ought to marry him?"

"Do you want to?"

"No."

"Then why are you considering it?"

"Because of Belle and the boys."

"Then you have to decide what's the most important to you. Once you do, you'll know what to do."

"You're not going to give me any advice, are you?"

"It's not my life." She dried her hands and started putting the dishes in the cupboard.

"When I get old, I want memories like Aunt Emmaline had. I think I could bear anything if I had that."

"Then you'd better look for some man who can give 'em to you."

Their gazes locked for a moment.

"But you've got to remember one thing," Bernice said before she resumed putting the dishes away.

"What's that?"

"A man who can inspire that kind of memories is not ordinary. He won't follow ordinary rules. He'll make his own way. It's up to others to follow if they dare. If you begin by laying down what you will and you won't, what he can and he can't, you'll never find him."

Chapter Nine

Lantz couldn't have come at a worse time. She'd known the moment she entered her bedroom that Chet was packing to leave. She'd choked back panic and forced herself to speak calmly. And persuasively, she hoped. She was sure she'd been on the verge of succeeding. She had seen the change in his eyes and his expression. His features relaxed. He might have smiled if Belle hadn't entered with her announcement.

Now he was looking stony, as if he wanted to go back to his packing.

"Tell him to go away," Melody said.

"You can't tell a man like Lantz Royal to come back some other time," Belle said, obviously dismayed that Melody would make such a suggestion.

"I didn't say anything about coming back," Melody said. "Tell him I'm busy, or sick. Tell him anything."

"I will not," Belle said, shocked. "He came to see you, and you've got to go down and speak to him."

"All right. Tell him I'll be down in a minute."

"Now. You can't leave him waiting."

"I haven't finished talking to Chet."

"I'm sure he'll excuse you," Belle said, getting behind Melody and pushing her toward the door.

"I won't be long," Melody said to Chet. "Why don't you saddle the horses? I'll be out as soon as I change my clothes."

Belle stopped, looked from one to the other. "What are you talking about? What do you mean, you won't be long?"

"Chet and I are going riding. He needs to start building up his strength. While he's doing that, he's going to teach me how to run a ranch."

"You don't need to know how to run a ranch," Belle said quite emphatically. "If you did, Lantz could tell you anything you needed to know."

"Promise me you won't sneak off without me," Melody said, ignoring Belle. She was afraid Chet would pack up and leave before she could finish with Lantz.

"This doesn't seem like a good time for a ride," Chet said. "Suppose I—"

"It's very ungentlemanly to back out of a promise," Melody said. "I insist upon holding you to your promise."

"For goodness sake, Melody. If the man wants to bow out, let him."

"I'm not leaving this room until you promise," Melody said.

"Melody!" Belle said, beginning to sound desperate.

"Not a foot."

"For goodness sakes, don't be so stubborn," Belle said to Chet. "Promise her."

"Okay," Chet said. Melody would have sworn the light of amusement danced momentarily in his eyes. "I'll have the horses saddled and ready in an hour."

"I won't need half that long." She started toward the door but turned back when Belle didn't follow her.

"I thought I'd stay here," Belle said. "I've hardly had a chance to talk to Chet."

Melody took a firm grip on her stepmother's hand. "I'll see Lantz to please you, but I won't see him alone."

"But he came to see you."

"A well-bred, unmarried Virginia lady would never entertain an unmarried gentleman alone."

Melody didn't give a fig about propriety, but she had no intention of leaving Belle alone with Chet. Since his presence would displease Lantz, Melody had no idea what Belle might say to Chet to get him to leave, but she wasn't willing to take a chance.

"All right," Belle said when Melody would not let go of her hand. "I don't see why you're acting so formal all of a sudden," she complained as they headed down the stairs. "You never minded seeing Lantz before."

"He has to consult my guardian if he's going to ask for my hand in marriage," Melody said. "You're my guardian."

Belle continued down the stairs but turned to glance at Melody. It was clear that the notion of acting as Melody's guardian had never entered her mind.

"But you never listen to anything I say."

"You never know when I might start."

Belle clearly didn't put much hope in the possibility. "Well, I wish you'd listen to Lantz," she said. "You won't find a better husband."

Belle spoke so loudly that Melody was sure she meant Lantz to hear. When they entered the parlor to find him standing and a smile on his face, she was certain of it.

"If you'd listen to your stepmother, you'd make me the happiest man in Texas," he said.

Melody decided that his smile, as well as his feeling for her, was genuine. She might doubt he had the slightest idea what real love was, but his feelings for her were honest. It was just as obvious that he thought his courtship had proceeded along acceptable lines. If he had to rough up a few innocent cowhands here and there, so what.

After a lot of thought, Melody had finally gotten things clear in her mind. Now it was time to get them clear in Lantz's as well. Keeping a firm grip on Belle's hand, she led her across the room. They sat down on the sofa. That didn't leave any room for Lantz to sit next to her.

"Belle tells me you wanted to talk to me," Melody said to Lantz. "I hope it won't take too long. I'm going for a ride."

"Melody! That's rude," Belle protested.

"I'm sorry, but I made the engagement before Lantz arrived."

"You could cancel it."

"That would be ruder still."

"Maybe what I have to say will cause you to

change your mind," Lantz said. He was trying to be gallant and failing miserably.

"Tell her," Belle prompted. From her evident excitement and broad smile, a stranger would have supposed Belle to be the one about to receive an offer of marriage.

"I want you to marry me," Lantz said, coming straight to the point. "You know you can't get along without me."

If that was his idea of a romantic proposal, she could only assume he had carved his first wife out of a fence post.

"You haven't said anything about your regard for me," Melody said.

"Of course he loves you," Belle said, her smile still in place, her eyes anxious. "Tell her you love her, Lantz."

"I already told her when I asked the first time," he said. "I haven't changed the way I feel since then."

"So you love me and want to marry me?" Melody asked.

"Yes."

"You want to make me the happiest woman on earth by giving me anything my heart desires."

Belle squeezed her hand and sent her an imploring look.

"Now hold on there a minute. I'm willing to give you just about any horse you want. A buggy, too, if you treat me right, but I don't hold with dishing up fancy presents just so a woman can dress up and show off. I could buy a couple of prize bulls for what a ring is going to cost me."

Clearly Lantz had never even heard of the game of love, much less bothered to read the rules.

"You haven't bought the ring yet?"

Belle wrung her hand painfully this time.

"Haven't had time to get to town. I'm in the middle of roundup. We started over this way, so I could come over without losing too much time."

If she wanted to find love, she was looking in the wrong place entirely.

"You've relieved my mind," Melody said. "I'd hate to cause you to have to return it."

"Melody!" The shriek came from Belle. Lantz merely looked as if he didn't understand her.

"I appreciate your offer," Melody said, "but I can't accept it."

"Why not?"

"I don't love you."

"But I love you."

"No, you don't, Lantz. You want me. I don't know why, but you have no earthly idea what love is."

"I'm offering you my name and my house. What more can you want?"

"Your heart."

"You already got that."

"Is that why you tried to scare me into marrying you?"

"Hell, you don't know your head from your tail out here. I was just trying to hurry you a little. I don't like wasting time."

"So to keep from wasting more time, you told my stepmother that if I didn't marry you, you'd take the ranch from her and leave her and my brothers penniless."

"I mean to have this ranch," Lantz thundered. "No reason I can't have you along with it."

"I'm not a horse, or a bull, or a building, Lantz. I don't come with the ranch. Neither do I want to spend all your money on clothes and showing off.

You don't love me. I'm just something you saw and wanted. When you were told you couldn't have me, you tried to force me to accept you anyway. I would never marry a man who thought like that."

"Are you turning me down?"

"She's just saying she wants to be courted," Belle said, desperately attempting to keep Melody from saying what she obviously meant to say.

Melody looked at Lantz rather than her stepmother. "I'm saying I don't love you. I'm aware of the great compliment you've paid me in asking me to be your wife, but I can't accept now or in the future. I beg you will not ask me again."

"Don't say that!" Belle wailed. "You might change your mind."

"You're telling me you won't have me?" Lantz demanded.

"Yes," Melody said.

"And that's your final word?"

"No!" Belle practically shrieked.

"I'm sorry, but it is," Melody said. "We have nothing in common. We'd make each other miserable."

"No woman has the power to make me miserable."

Melody could have wanted no clearer proof that Lantz did not and never would love her. Her last shred of doubt vanished.

Lantz stalked across the room, then turned back when he reached the archway into the hall. "I hope you're not planning on marrying my boy. Because if you are—"

"I've already told you I wouldn't marry Blade."

"So neither one of us is good enough for your Virginia blue blood, it that it?"

"I don't have any blue blood, and I'd marry a cowhand if we loved each other."

"Then you're a fool!" Lantz thundered. "You think I've been bothering your cowhands before. You wait until you see what happens now." He turned and stalked out.

Belle let out an anguished wail. "What have you done to us, you foolish girl?"

For a moment Melody doubted the wisdom of what she'd done. She didn't have anything in the world outside this ranch, and she'd just thrown it away, for Belle and the boys as well. Maybe she ought to go after Lantz, try to reason with him, maybe even . . .

No, she couldn't marry him, no matter how desperate her situation. He might not be doing anything illegal, but he had a mean soul. He had no feelings, and he didn't understand people who did. If he couldn't get what he wanted on his own terms, he would take it.

"I can't marry him," Melody told her stepmother. "He wants to own me."

"All men want to own their wives. It's how their minds work."

"Was my father like that?"

"Of course. He was just more civilized about it. Why do you think he built this huge house, filled it with expensive furnishings, bought me all these beautiful clothes, and hired Bernice to cook?"

"Because he loved you."

"Maybe he did," Belle said, softened for a moment, "but he did it to show everybody what a success he was. The boys and I were part of it. So was keeping you with your fancy aunt in Richmond."

Melody opened her mouth to dispute Belle's

last statement, then closed it again. She'd often felt the weight of her father's absence. He'd visited her only once after moving to Texas. Even after he remarried, he had insisted she remain in Richmond. She'd told herself he wanted her to stay where she had friends, but she'd often feared he didn't want to be saddled with the worry of a daughter.

"My aunt wasn't fancy," Melody said. "She lost everything in the War. For a long time she depended on the money my father sent for her support."

"I'm not talking about your aunt," Belle said impatiently. "I'm talking about your father. And the rest of the men in this world. They think of everything around them as possessions. They can't help themselves."

"Did you love my father?"

"I doubt you and I have the same meaning for love," Belle said, "not if it leads you to throw away an offer that would have made you rich and will now make you a pauper."

"Love has nothing to do with money."

"Everything has to do with money," Belle declared, "or the lack of it."

"I can't believe that. I could be just as happy as the wife of a cowboy if I loved him and he loved me."

"What's a cowboy got to offer you? Not a house, not money to buy clothes and food, not a steady job."

"How can you think of all those things first? Don't you think of the man, what he stands for, his integrity, what you feel for him?"

"A woman who thinks like that will end up

poor. And if you're thinking of that cowboy upstairs, you'll end up a widow."

Melody felt herself flush.

"I thought so," Belle said. "A man that good-looking makes a woman feel things about herself she's never felt before. Dangerous things that make her start wanting and imagining things that can never be."

Melody jumped up, walked a few steps, and turned to face her stepmother. "Why not? Why must a woman be owned and admired but never listened to?"

"Do you think that man up there is going to listen to you any more than Lantz would?" Belle delivered herself of a mirthless laugh. "He's twenty-nine, restless, and penniless. He's also a hardened gunfighter."

"He said he's giving it up."

"Men like him can't give it up. It's in the blood. They can't settle down or stay with one woman. He'll make you feel like the center of the universe, then disappear just as quickly as he appeared."

"If he loved me, he'd take me with him."

"Don't they teach you girls anything in Richmond? *Take me with him* doesn't mean going home to Papa's plantation. It means being dragged across miles of dry, Indian-infested plains, staying in cheap hotels when you're fortunate, sleeping under the stars when you're not, eating what you can find. It means never having a home of your own or a decent future for your children."

"I didn't say I was in love with Chet or that I would think of marrying him if I were."

"Maybe not, but you're letting dreams of what you think you could find with him cause you to give up what you know you could have with Lantz."

"I want my husband to love me, not feel pride of ownership. I want to feel valued, admired. I want memories I can enjoy when I'm too old to do anything but remember."

"So you're going to throw yourself at that man and hope he'll have you."

"I haven't said a word about throwing myself at anyone, especially Chet Attmore. He'll be leaving in a few days. I'll probably never see him again."

"But you won't forget him?"

"No, I don't imagine I will."

"Fine. Remember him. Dream about him, but don't let him ruin your life. Or mine and the boys'."

Melody had stopped pacing the room and was staring out the window at nothing in particular, but she turned back to Belle.

"Blame Lantz for that, not me."

"But all you have to do is—"

"Sacrifice myself so you can have a ranch? If Lantz is willing to take this place in defiance of common decency and the law, he'll take it whether I marry him or not. No matter what I do, you and the boys will lose it."

It gave Melody no pleasure to see that her stepmother's troubled expression indicated that she realized the truth of what Melody said.

"At least he wouldn't leave us to starve."

"You won't starve," Melody said. "I won't allow it."

"What do you propose to do?"

"First, I'm going to get Chet to teach me everything he can about running a ranch."

"And after that?"

"I'm going to get him to tell me how to save the ranch from Lantz."

"Your father chose well," Chet said to Melody. "This canyon is a perfect place to winter your herd. It offers plenty of food and water and protection from the worst of the winter storms."

They had been riding for over an hour. Chet felt a little weak from spending two days in bed, but it felt good to be in the saddle. In a day or two he'd feel like his old self.

"Are you saying we've got the best ranch in the area?" Melody asked.

"Probably."

"Is it valuable enough to make Lantz determined to take it?"

"Sometimes people don't care what something costs. They just have to have it."

"Like Lantz saying he doesn't want all the land in the world, just the land that joins his."

"Something like that."

"Do you think he means to take it?"

"Don't you?"

"Maybe. I understand what you say about Texas being different, but I find it hard to believe people can just walk in and take what they want."

"It won't always be that way."

"That doesn't help me or my brothers."

"Turn everything over to Tom. Let him hire a gunfighter."

"Can't I win any other way?"

"As I see it, this is going to come down to who has the most men and guns and who's willing to use them first."

"That sounds like the War all over again."

"There's always at least one person willing to

take advantage of any weakness. Right and the law mean nothing to people like that."

"Is that the kind of men you worked for?"

He should have known it would get around to his past sooner or later. It was almost as though she thought if she asked him enough times, he would finally admit that he hadn't really been a gunfighter after all.

"I worked for people I thought were in the right. Sometimes it was a tight call, but I think I made the right choices."

"Would you work for me?"

Her request surprised him so much that he jerked his mount to a stop. The horse demonstrated his objection to such rough treatment by trying to buck him off.

"You said I had to hire a gunfighter," she said. "Tom says the same thing."

"What made you change your mind?"

"I don't like having my ranch taken away from me. And I trust you not to go around shooting people for the fun of it."

He wouldn't bother to explain that no gunfighter went around shooting people *for the fun of it*. That was a good way to die. Neither did he try to explain that if Melody hired him as a gunfighter, she'd never be able to see him any other way. That touched on areas he didn't want to have to explain to himself.

"I told you I've given up hiring my gun."

"Why?"

"If you live by the gun, you die by the gun. I decided I'd rather go on living."

"What are you going to do?"

"Find some corner of the world where there

153

aren't many people, buy myself a piece of land, and raise a few cows."

"Your wife might not like living so far from other people."

"A man like me doesn't get married."

"Why not?"

Did she always have to know everything? Couldn't she just accept some things at face value? "Because there's always some young fool trying to build a reputation. And the best way is to kill someone with an even bigger reputation. I don't want to leave a widow or fatherless children. I know what that's like. You just leave all the guns and the fighting to Tom. Now we'd better be getting back before Belle sends out a search party."

He needed to put some space between them. She'd asked him to stay. True, she wanted his gun, but she'd said she trusted him. That might not sound like much to other people, but it worked powerfully on him. She'd been thinking about marrying Lantz Royal, but she'd turned him down and was planning to fight him. Chet couldn't help believing he was somehow responsible for that change.

She was attracted to him. He'd been pursued by women often enough to be able to gauge the extent of their interest in him. Until this morning he'd thought her interest was mainly curiosity about a stranger, especially one as exotic as a gunfighter. Now he realized that serious interest wasn't just on his side. Something had happened to make her see him as a man, or at least look past the gunfighter label. She liked what she saw. That was dangerous because he already liked all he saw of her.

If he took the job she offered, in her eyes he'd be a gunfighter for the rest of his life. Besides, if he stayed, he might come up against Luke. He could never do that, not for anyone.

"Why not go home to your family?" Melody asked as they cantered back toward the ranch house.

"I don't want to bring trouble to them. They were too good to me to be served such a back-handed trick."

"They might not feel that way. I know I wouldn't if you were my family—my son or my . . . husband."

"You'd let me come back knowing what might happen?"

"Of course. I wouldn't like it, but I couldn't do anything else if I loved you."

"That's not very sensible."

"Belle says refusing Lantz wasn't very sensible, either. But I want to love the man I marry, and I want him to love me. If I did, I would never turn my back on him, no matter what trouble he got into."

Chet urged his horse along faster. He had to get back to the ranch before he started believing her. He'd faced temptation before, but until now he hadn't had so much difficulty resisting it. The longer he stayed, the more excuses he found to stay.

He forced himself to talk about the ranch, mentioning everything he thought could be of interest. He doubted she'd remember half of it, but it kept his mind off what she'd said about not turning her back on the man she loved no matter what he'd done. They arrived to find the ranch silent, the corral empty. Neill came racing out of the house as they rode up.

"Blade Royal drove off the horses," he shouted as he pounded across the yard toward them. "Tom and the men have gone to have a shoot-out. And Sydney's mad as fire they wouldn't let him go."

Chapter Ten

Chet didn't feel comfortable in the silent house. Despite Melody's saying he wasn't responsible for their troubles, he couldn't get rid of the feeling that she thought he ought to do something. Since he didn't know where Tom had gone, what he planned to do, or anything about the situation, he was at a loss to know what he could do. Even if he knew where they were, he couldn't just ride up and take over. The men wouldn't accept him. Even if they did, it would humiliate Tom. Chet wouldn't do that.

Yet as long as the men were gone, the fear of what might be happening remained uppermost in everyone's mind. Sydney stayed outside, watching for their return, hoping to find an excuse to join them, despite his mother's orders to Tom not to leave even one saddle horse in the corral. Neill ran between Sydney and the house, reporting every irrational threat the boy uttered. Melody ignored them. Belle grew more agitated by the minute.

"Blade didn't run off the horses," she kept saying. "Lantz would never let him do such a thing. It was horse thieves. They'll kill everybody."

"I doubt Tom will let that happen," Melody said.

"You should have gone after them," Belle said to Chet. "You're a gunman. You'd know what to do."

"He's been shot twice because of us," Melody said. "I don't think it's fair to ask him to risk another injury, especially since he's not recovered from the last one."

A series of gunshots caused Belle to start violently. "Why must Sydney practice his target shooting now? He knows how badly it upsets my nerves."

"He's practicing because he's angry," Melody said. "He's doing it near the house because he *knows* it will upset you. You were the one who stopped him from riding with Tom. He won't forgive you."

"I couldn't let him go. He's just a boy. And he's your brother. You ought to be as concerned as I am."

"I am," Melody assured her stepmother. "I was just explaining what he's doing and why."

Another burst of gunfire shattered the quiet.

Belle put her hands over her ears. "I can't stand it. I'll go crazy if he doesn't stop."

"I'll talk to him," Chet said, getting to his feet.

"He doesn't like you," Belle reminded him.

"I can still talk to him."

"Thank you," Melody said. "He'll probably listen to you before he listens to one of us."

"I'm not so sure." Chet doubted he could do anything more than try to take Sydney's mind off his perceived slight. Though that was a thankless task, it was better than staying inside and having to endure Belle's accusing glare.

"What are you going to do?" Neill shot out of the kitchen as Chet walked past. "You riding after them? You didn't bring your guns. Where are your guns?"

"I'm not going after anybody," Chet said. "That's Tom's job."

"But he can't shoot like you. He couldn't hit a peach can if I tossed it up a hundred times."

"It's still his job. I'm looking for Sydney. Do you know where he is?"

"Over behind the bunkhouse. He's real mad. He told me to get lost or he'd put a bullet through my hat. I'm not wearing a hat. Do you think he'll shoot me anyway?"

"I don't think so, but you can tag along with me just in case." More shots sounded from behind the bunkhouse. "Does he practice often?"

"Lots, but Melody won't let him shoot near the house. That makes Sydney mad, and he hollers at her. She doesn't back down. Tom says Melody never backs down about anything. Mama says she ought to. Mama says no man's going to marry a woman who argues with every word that comes out of his mouth."

Chet could just imagine some of the arguments that had taken place since Melody's arrival. He smiled to himself. She and Isabelle were a lot alike. Isabelle adored Jake, but she didn't hesitate to let him know when she disagreed with him. Chet was certain Melody would do the same.

159

He rounded the corner of the bunkhouse in time to see Sydney taking aim at a target he'd nailed to a corral post. He drew too quickly, fired before his gun was level, and jerked the trigger. He missed the target all three times. Tim Speers and Toby had come out to watch. Their snickers made Sydney's mood blacker.

"You need to work on making your draw smoother, one single motion," Chet said. "And you should squeeze the trigger gently. It won't matter how smoothly you draw if you jerk the trigger. It'll throw your aim off."

"I know all that," Sydney growled. "I hit everything when I'm not angry."

"You can't afford to let anger ruin your aim," Chet said. "You can be sure the other man won't."

Sydney didn't look thankful for the advice.

"You ought to move farther away from the house," Chet said.

Sydney looked belligerent. "I don't have to do what you say. Anyway, there's nobody here. No horses either. I can't hit anything."

"Your mother's worried about Tom and the men," Chet said. "These gunshots are upsetting her."

"She ought to have let me go with Tom," Sydney shot back. "Then I wouldn't be bothering her."

"She's worried about you. She doesn't want you to get hurt."

"Mama says the rustlers would shoot Sydney first because he's an owner," Neill said.

"I'm not afraid of rustlers or Blade Royal," Sydney growled at his younger brother. "I can shoot better than any of them."

Chet guessed Sydney must have some skill, but

Thrill to the most sensual, adventure-filled Historical Romances on the market today...

FROM 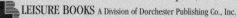 LEISURE BOOKS

As a home subscriber to the Leisure Historical Romance Book Club, you'll enjoy the best in today's BRAND-NEW Historical Romance fiction. For over twenty-five years, Leisure Books has brought you the award-winning, high-quality authors you know and love to read. Each Leisure Historical Romance will sweep you away to a world of high adventure...and intimate romance. Discover for yourself all the passion and excitement millions of readers thrill to each and every month.

SAVE AT LEAST *$5.00* EACH TIME YOU BUY!

Each month, the Leisure Historical Romance Book Club brings you four brand-new titles from Leisure Books, America's foremost publisher of Historical Romances. EACH PACKAGE WILL SAVE YOU AT LEAST $5.00 FROM THE BOOKSTORE PRICE! And you'll never miss a new title with our convenient home delivery service.

Here's how we do it. Each package will carry a 10-DAY EXAMINATION privilege. At the end of that time, if you decide to keep your books, simply pay the low invoice price of $16.96 ($17.75 US in Canada), no shipping or handling charges added*. HOME DELIVERY IS ALWAYS FREE*. With today's top Historical Romance novels selling for $5.99 and higher, our price SAVES YOU AT LEAST $5.00 with each shipment.

AND YOUR FIRST FOUR-BOOK SHIPMENT IS TOTALLY FREE!*

IT'S A BARGAIN YOU CAN'T BEAT! A Super $21.96 Value!

LEISURE BOOKS A Division of Dorchester Publishing Co., Inc.

the pristine target didn't support hi

"Maybe you can," Chet said, "bu
more experience, and that's extrem
to a gunfighter."

"I don't intend to be a gunfighter,'
the contempt in his voice indicat
thought of anyone who was. "I jus
better than anybody else."

"If you're that good," Chet said, "y
become a gunfighter just to stay aliv

Sydney didn't appear to have con
aspect of the problem. Chet suspect
nearly so enamored of guns as every
He was teetering on the edge of b
adult, eager to be thought a man bu
how to do it. He couldn't be expecte
Belle and Melody. No boy his age w
told what to do by his mother an
hadn't found a man he could respect.
he'd continue to imitate men like Bla

Chet knew he couldn't do much, b
try.

"Is that why you're quitting?" Syd

"It's reason enough," Chet replied

"What if you're better than everyb

"Sooner or later somebody will
they'll shoot you in the back like th
ther. Much better to stick with bein

"But I've got to defend my ra
know I'm good, they'll stay away."

"Some will, others won't. It's the
care that you got to worry abou
even though they know one of you

"I gotta be good," Sydney insi
putting more bullets in his gu
Tom."

"Y
few
Sy
wha
was

"I
So
was
app

"I
said

L
cou
dea
Nel
wel
reso
to
driv
refu
mer
dea
vest

"T
"A co
be o

"W
"It
those
shoo
brand
while
us if

"W
"Bla
He di

Leigh Greenwood

ou put that up for today, and I'll give you a
ointers tomorrow."

ney looked undecided. Chet wasn't sure
he would have done, but their discussion
orgotten when Speers shouted.

Tom and the fellas! I can see them."

could Chet. He could also see that someone
eing carried across a saddle. Several others
red to be nursing wounds.

n tell your sister somebody's hurt," Chet
o Neill. "I'll see if I can help."

g before the men reached the corral, Chet
tell that the man across the saddle was
He could also tell that the man was Tom
d. That angered Chet. It puzzled him as
He couldn't see any reason why Lantz would
t to killing to get the ranch. It was too easy
n off horses, rustle cows, foul water holes,
off cowhands, even pressure merchants into
ing to sell the ranch supplies. He had the
to do it, and no one could stop him. But a
would mean the sheriff and an official in-
ation.

m's dead," Curly Green said unnecessarily.
uple of the boys are shot up a bit, but they'll
ay."

hat happened?" Chet asked.

was an ambush," Curly said. "They took
horses just so we'd follow and they could
us to pieces. They had them back in a
h canyon. Tom made the rest of us wait
he went in first. They'd have gotten most of
we'd gone in together like we wanted."

o was it?"

de Royal," Curly said. "No mistake about it.
n't even try to hide."

"Cut him loose," Chet said. "We'll lay him out in the shed, then take care of the others. Just make sure you don't let the women see him."

They were too late. Melody came hurrying from the house, Belle right behind her. Neill danced around both of them like a frisky puppy. Melody blanched when she saw Tom's body, but she didn't lose her composure.

"What happened?"

"They ambushed Tom."

"Are you sure he's—"

"Yes."

Belle reached them, took one look at Tom, and started to wail. "Lantz said something terrible would happen if you refused him," she told Melody.

"I can't believe Lantz would do this," Melody said.

"It was Blade that done it," Curly told her. "I saw him."

The men had begun to dismount. Some helped the two wounded men to the bunkhouse. The others stood around, waiting, anger and dejection apparent in their faces.

"But why?" Melody asked.

"He told you he'd ruin us if you didn't marry him," Belle cried, near hysterics. "He's keeping his promise."

"See if you can get her inside," Chet said to Melody.

"I need to see to the men."

"They'll all be a lot better if they don't have to listen to her."

Bernice had come outside. She helped Melody lead Belle back to the house. Melody returned by the time Chet had gotten Tom's body into the shed.

"Is there anything I can do?"

"You can help me bandage their wounds. I can do it, but they'll like it a lot better if somebody pretty does it."

"You sound like every other man I know, thinking women are just for being pretty and bandaging up the wounded."

"Every man appreciates a woman's attention, no matter what she looks like. It puts him on his mettle, and things don't hurt so bad. But that isn't all. These men got hurt working for you. You're going to need their loyalty if you want to keep this place. They'll give it a lot more readily if you're not too proud to get your hands dirty."

"I'm not like that."

"I didn't think you were. I was just explaining why you should help."

They went into the bunk house, and she poured hot water into a basin. Chet started ripping a sheet into bandage strips.

"You're going to have to take off that shirt so I can clean the wound," she said to Peak Larson. "I'll send for the doctor to get the bullet out."

"No need, ma'am. It's nothing but a flesh wound. Milt don't have no bullet in him neither."

"We still have to make certain it doesn't get infected."

Chet was proud of the way Melody handled the men. She didn't have as much experience as he did with wounds. She kept up a steady flow of talk while he did most of the work.

"Is it too tight?" she asked Milt.

"It's fine," he said. "I'll be back in the saddle by tomorrow."

"Absolutely not. You're to stay here until you're completely well."

"Begging your pardon, ma'am, but I don't see how Peak and me can do that. With four of us down, them Royals could run off nearbout every cow on the place."

"Toby and me can ride," Speers said. "We only stayed because Tom wouldn't let us go." He looked over at the bunk that would be vacant tonight. "Now I wish I'd gone anyway."

"What's done can't be changed," Melody said. "You're going to have to help take care of Milt and Peak. What is it?" Melody asked when he kept staring at her.

"We gotta get the horses back," he said.

"I'll send some of the boys tomorrow."

"You can't wait that long. Somebody's got to go now."

"Whom do you suggest I send?"

"It's not a question of who to send, ma'am. It's a question of who's going to lead them."

"What do you mean?"

"We're all just cowhands. We're no good with guns, and we'd be no good at giving orders. You gotta get somebody to take Tom's place."

"Anybody here want to be foreman?" she asked.

Uneasy silence.

"How about him?" Speers said, indicating Chet. "Tom said he used to be foreman for his pa. Everybody knows he can shoot the eyes out of a snake. We don't know much about him, but we'd be willing to work for him until we found a reason not to."

Chet had seen this coming from the moment he realized Tom was dead. Now everyone turned to him. Some looked expectant, others hesitant or questioning. Melody looked hopeful.

"Would you?" she asked.

He didn't answer.

"I'll pay you a full month's salary even if you don't work that long."

"You can't make him the foreman."

They had forgotten Sydney.

"I know more about this ranch than he does," Sydney said. "And I know where Blade has taken the horses."

"You're too young," Melody said.

"I'm the man of the family," Sydney said, standing as tall as his five feet, ten inches would allow. He turned to the cowhands. "I want all of you who are able to mount up. We're going after Blade Royal, and we'll get him this time. He won't be expecting a second attack."

Chet could hear the uncertainty in his voice, see it in his eyes. This was a big gamble for him, a chance to show he was a man. Success meant everything to him.

The men looked at each other, then turned their gazes away.

"Saddle up," Sydney ordered. "We don't have time to waste."

Still nobody moved.

"You can go, too, Speers," Sydney said. "You look like you're healed up."

"I'm not riding with any boy." Speers looked around at the others. "None of us are."

Sydney turned white. "You letting Speers speak for you?" he asked the men.

He got several grunts in the affirmative.

"Sydney, you know you can't run this place," Melody began. "We ought to—"

"I'm going after Blade," he shouted. "Any man who doesn't ride with me can collect his stuff and get out. You're fired," he shouted at Speers. Nobody moved. "You're all fired!"

"Don't be ridiculous, Sydney. You can't fire everybody. Be sensible. Help me talk Chet into taking over until we can find someone else."

"I won't let you hire him," Sydney shouted. "I hate him. He's as bad as you are, always telling me what to do, treating me like I'm a kid. I don't want him here. I wish Blade had killed him instead of Tom!"

Chet had the feeling it was all Sydney could do to hold back tears of anger and frustration.

"Sydney Ranson Jordan, that's a horrible thing to say. Apologize this instant."

"No! And if you ask Mama to give him Tom's job, I'll hate you, too."

"Now you are acting like a little boy," Melody said.

"I'm not a little boy," he said, stamping his foot in rage. "I'm a man. I'll show you!" he yelled as he ran out of the bunkhouse.

Melody turned to Chet, a look of entreaty in her eyes. "Won't you please help?"

Chet was tempted. He could tell from the look in Melody's eyes that she meant it. She wanted him to stay. And for more than just getting the horses back.

She wanted *him*.

It was the sign he'd been hoping for, the excuse he'd been waiting for to believe there was a possibility she might care for him, that he hadn't lost the chance for normal happiness. The words of acceptance trembled on his lips.

Then he remembered her look when Belle

asked him to go after the rustlers. Horror. Disgust. Fear. She had turned to him because she didn't know what else to do. But her feelings hadn't changed. Once the horses were back, once she'd gotten over Tom's death, the horror and disgust would return.

He couldn't bear that. As much as it hurt to say no, it would hurt even more to see the look of entreaty turn to revulsion. He'd always considered himself a strong man, but he wasn't strong enough to stand that.

"Sorry, but I can't do it."

"Why?"

"I told you I've given up using my gun."

"You weren't slow to pull it on Lantz that first day you got here," Speers reminded him.

"Habit is a hard thing to forget."

"Why can't you forget it for a few more days?"

"I made a promise to myself. If I make an exception every time somebody wants a little help, I'll never escape. It took me a long time to reach this decision. I can't go back on it now."

"I don't see what is so terrible about rounding up a few horses," Speers said, unwilling to give up. "We'll go after Blade if you don't want to do that."

"Don't keep after him," Melody said. "It was unfair of me to ask, especially since he's not well yet."

"I'd think that would be reason enough for him to want to go after Blade," Speers muttered.

"It would be if he were a gunfighter," Melody said, "but he's quit. We ought to support his decision."

Chet didn't know why each word out of her

mouth seemed to condemn him more thoroughly than the last.

"Whoever you hire," Chet said, "he ought to be willing to work with Sydney. Doing his share of the work around here will give him something to think about besides guns."

"Well, it sure can't be you," Speers said angrily. "He hates your guts."

"Another reason why I shouldn't take the job. I'll leave you boys and Miss Jordan to talk about what you're going to do next. This seems like a good time for me to start packing."

She didn't say anything, but her look begged him not to go. Yet he knew there was no point in his hanging around. If he left now, he could still make it to town before nightfall. But even as he started to turn toward the door, Neill came crashing through it.

"Sydney's gone to find Blade Royal," he shouted breathlessly. "He took his guns, too." He turned to Chet. "He said he wasn't afraid of Blade even if you were. He said you'd have to treat him different now."

"Blade'll kill him," Speers said. "He's twice as fast as Sydney will ever be."

Melody turned to Chet.

He didn't wait for her to ask the question. "I'll go after him," he said.

"I'll go with you," Speers offered.

"No," Chet replied. "I have to do this alone." He headed for the house at a run. He had to get his guns.

Chet felt guilty that during the long ride to the canyon he hadn't given much thought to Melody's brother. Instead he'd thought a lot about his own.

169

In all the years Chet had followed Luke around, they'd never found themselves on opposing sides of an argument. He couldn't even consider facing Luke over a gun. But with Sydney's life at stake, he might not have any choice. He would have to do anything he could to protect the boy, regardless of who might get in the way.

He didn't know how he could face Melody if he failed to bring Sydney back alive. Just the thought of what she'd do if he returned with the boy's body slung across a horse was enough to make him want to shoot Blade Royal on sight.

He'd given up everything he loved to follow Luke, to protect him. How could he ever fire on him? He couldn't. He'd never be able to live with himself afterwards.

But what if . . .

Luke wasn't a killer. He wouldn't be involved with Blade. Chet *had* to believe that if he was to go on loving his brother.

He heard a shot before he reached the mouth of the canyon where the men had told him he could find Blade. A single shot. Nothing followed. His mouth felt dry; his nerves tight. It took only one bullet to kill a man.

Or a boy.

He tried not to visualize what might be happening, what might already have happened. It would get him too worked up. He had to remain calm. He didn't expect to like what he found, but getting angry could get him killed. That wouldn't help Sydney or Melody.

When Chet rounded a grove of trees to see Sydney on the ground and Blade on his feet with a gun in his hand, he knew it was really bad. They were on a sandy clearing next to a shallow, sluggish stream that flowed through the side canyon. A couple of dozen horses were visible farther up the canyon. Beyond that, huge boulders and scrub growth choked the canyon up to the towering walls. Blade was turned away from Chet. Billy Mason and four other men stood a little back, as though distancing themselves from what Blade was doing. They looked uneasily from one to another. Given a chance, Chet figured they might try to convince Blade to go home and forget all about Sydney.

"Why don't you get up, boy?" Blade said. His tone was biting, scornful. "You won't kill me lying on the ground."

Chet breathed a sigh of relief. Sydney wasn't dead, but Blade obviously intended to kill him. It wouldn't look too good if he killed a young boy, not even in a fair fight. But nobody would blame him if the boy drew on him again, especially when the boy was down and Blade had reason to think the fight was over.

"I've been hearing how good you are," Blade said, still taunting Sydney. "You're going to have to get up if you want to prove it."

Sydney tried to move, to lift himself up so he could get to his gun, but he couldn't quite make it. His strength gave out, and he fell back.

"You gotta try harder, boy," Blade taunted. "Your gun's still in your holster. You didn't even get it out before I shot you. But I'm willing to believe you're better than that. Maybe I just caught you off guard."

Nothing in Chet's experience told him how to go about rescuing Sydney. He obviously couldn't ride in, guns blazing. He'd be shot down in an instant. He couldn't depend upon Blade to keep talking long enough for him to attack from hiding. He decided he could gamble on the other men's hesitation. The question was, what would Blade do when he saw Chet?

He would shoot or he wouldn't. Chet wouldn't know which until he walked into the clearing. Could Chet outdraw Blade? He didn't know that, either. He thought of Melody. She wouldn't understand why he hesitated. Wasn't this what gunfighters did all the time?

Chet hoped Blade wasn't serious about killing Sydney and was only acting like this to scare the boy. But Chet had to be prepared for the worst. Nerves taut and ready, he dismounted and walked quickly toward Sydney. Blade was too absorbed to notice his arrival. As Chet had hoped, his men looked undecided about what to do. Chet hoped they would stay that way.

"You damned cheating bastard," Sydney managed to say despite the pain. "You drew before I got out of the saddle."

Blade pointed his gun at Sydney, waving it like a stick. "Nobody calls me a cheat," he shouted. "I'll kill the first man who tries."

"Looks like you already tried and failed," Chet said. "I suggest you put your gun away and go home before you do some real damage."

Blade didn't take his eyes off Sydney. "Somebody shoot that man!" he shouted over his shoulder, just as if Chet was a mad dog to be gotten rid of.

Chet turned toward Billy, hand poised to draw, but nobody moved.

Chet decided Blade was dangerously unbalanced. If he and Sydney were to get out of here alive, he had to think of some way to throw him off stride, some way to keep him from shooting them in cold blood. The only way that occurred to him was to attack his inflated opinion of himself.

"Why ask somebody else?" Chet said. "Are you afraid to do your own work?"

Chet reached Sydney's side and knelt down next to the boy.

"What are you doing here?" Blade demanded. Chet looked up. Blade was staring at him with the look of a crazy man. This was no act. He was serious.

"I came to take him home."

"Get out of the way," Blade shouted.

"I came to kill that bastard," Sydney said from between teeth clenched in pain. "I'm not leaving until I do."

Chet spoke softly. "That's just what he's hoping you'll do. It'll give him an excuse to kill you."

"Get away from him," Blade shouted again.

"Do you always pick on boys?" Chet asked.

"I'm not afraid of you," Blade bellowed. "Now back away. I'm not finished with him yet."

"Yes, you are," Chet said as he got to his feet. "I'm taking him home. He needs a doctor."

"Leave him where he is," Blade yelled, waving his gun at Chet.

Chet stood and squared up to Blade. "You going to shoot me down where I stand? I don't know just how much your men will lie for you, but an out-and-out murder will be hard to hide."

"You're wearing a gun."

"Mine's in its holster. Yours is already drawn. That would be cheating."

"Dammit!" Blade swore. "Nobody calls me a cheater."

Chet turned his back and started toward Sydney's horse.

"Don't turn your back on me!" Blade screamed.

"Are you going to shoot me in the back if I don't turn around?" Chet reached Sydney's horse and turned him. "Then you'd be a coward as well as a cheater," he said to Blade.

Blade jammed his gun into its holster. "There. You're facing me, and my gun's in my holster. Draw."

The temptation to draw was nearly overwhelming. With his temper riding him, it was almost impossible to withstand, but Chet knew he must. He might beat Blade. But the moment he went for his gun, the other men would open fire. They'd probably kill Sydney as well. There had been too many deaths already.

"I'm not going to draw on you," Chet said, though he nearly choked on the words. "I may yet get a chance to even the score between us, but right now it's more important that I get this boy to a doctor."

"I remember who you are," Blade suddenly declared. "You're that man—" He stopped, suddenly aware of what he was about to say.

"Why don't you finish your sentence?" Chet said.

Blade didn't speak. That pushed Chet's temper over the edge. "Then I'll finish it for you," he said. "I'm the man you shot from behind."

"Liar!" Blade shouted, furious.

"And Bill Mason was with you," Chet said.

"Are you calling me a liar, too?" Billy bellowed.

Chet couldn't stop now. The lid was off his temper. He leaned forward on his toes, tense, ready, anxious. "You're already a thief. Why not a liar?

Of course, if you admit Blade shot me after I'd turned and started down the trail, that the two of you left me there to die twelve miles from the nearest ranch, then you'd only be a thief."

Everything happened in a matter of seconds, but Chet was ready. Blade and Billy went for their guns at the same time, but only two shots reverberated between the canyon walls. Chet remained standing, a gun in each hand. Billy was down, shot in the thigh. Blade dropped his gun and grabbed hold of his arm.

"God almighty!" one of the men gasped, astounded. "You got them both. Who the hell are you?"

"A cowboy who doesn't like to see grown men go around shooting boys and terrorizing women. Get him home and keep him there."

Blade was swearing and shouting threats at Chet, but two men hurried to get him up on his horse while two others helped Billy.

Chet remained watching, both guns drawn, until Blade's men had left the clearing. Once he was certain no one intended to sneak back and take a shot at him from ambush, he turned back to Sydney. The boy didn't say anything as Chet helped him up on his horse and led him out of the clearing. When they reached Chet's mount, Chet swung up into his saddle.

"You got them both," Sydney said.

"I didn't have much choice. They both drew on me."

"But they started first."

"I was lucky."

"No, you weren't. I saw what you did to the peach can, and I saw what you did today."

"Don't put too much importance in it. It's going to cause a lot of trouble."

"But you beat him."

"He'll come after me. That's why I wanted to hang up my guns."

"What made you put them on to come after me?"

"Gunfighters have honor, too."

"I didn't mean it like that."

"We have rules. One of them says men don't pick fights with boys. Another says you never fire on a man when he's down."

"He would have killed me. He's faster than I am, but he would have kept egging me on until I tried to draw again. Then he would have killed me."

"Yes."

They rode for a bit in silence.

"Did Blade really shoot you from behind?"

"Yes."

"Why didn't you kill him?"

Chet didn't know why he should be upset at the question. He'd heard it often enough. Everybody thought gunfighters were bloodthirsty and cruel.

"I never killed anybody I didn't have to."

More silence.

"Blade's father's going to send his men after you. He won't rest until you're dead."

"I've managed to keep from being killed by more dangerous men than Lantz Royal. You let me worry about him. You'd better start worrying about what you're going to say to your mother. After this, you're going to have a hard time convincing her to let you ride with me."

Despite the pain, Sydney twisted in the saddle until he could see Chet. For the first time he looked like what he was, a fourteen-year-old boy in over his head and searching desperately for a way out. "You're staying?"

"I started something back there. I'll stay until it's finished."

Chapter Eleven

"I could have taken him," Blade said for the dozenth time. "I wasn't concentrating."

All the way back from the canyon Luke had listened to Blade say what he could have done, should have done, would have done if things had been different. He'd listened without saying a word. And he didn't intend to say one. Yet.

Lantz had sent him looking when Blade didn't come back when he was expected. It shouldn't have taken more than a couple of hours to run off the Spring Water horses. Blade had been gone all day. Luke arrived at almost the same time as Chet but from a different direction. He'd had his rifle aimed at Blade's heart the whole time.

"I didn't intend to kill that kid," Blade said angrily to Luke. "If I had, he'd have been dead before you arrived."

Luke had disliked Blade from the start. He was

178

a spoiled braggart. His father should have sent him to some fancy school back East. He'd have learned some manners, made friends with young men who could have had a moderating effect on his self-absorption. He might even have married a young woman who would have preferred her husband to think like a wealthy rancher rather than a temperamental gunslick.

Luke hadn't bothered to answer Blade because he had more important things on his mind. He'd been startled when he saw Chet and realized he had come for Melody Jordan's brother. He'd expected Chet would be gone from the ranch by now. Why hadn't he left? And what was he doing sticking out his neck for the son of strangers? Was it his way of thanking them for taking care of him, or was it something much more serious? Luke hadn't thought too much about it when Melody came looking for Chet. He'd been too worried about his brother, too grateful someone would take care of him, too determined to catch up with Blade to wonder why Melody would come looking for a stranger and offer to care for him in her home. Maybe he should have.

Luke knew Chet was dead set against marriage. He believed there was bad blood in the family; he'd said he wouldn't ask any woman he loved to marry a gunfighter. Luke knew this because Chet had spent years trying to get Luke to give up the trade, find some nice young girl, settle down, and raise a bunch of kids.

Chet never seemed to understand that what went for him went for Luke in spades. Chet had always been careful about the jobs he took. Luke hadn't. If he had, he wouldn't have signed on with Lantz Royal. Neither would he be worried about being ordered to kill his own brother.

"You wait until Pa hears about this," Blade said. "He'll have you and the whole crew hunting that man's scalp. He'll be dead before morning."

"You'd better hope nobody shoots him in the back," Luke said. "If they do, the sheriff will come after you."

Blade whipped around, directing a malevolent glare at Luke.

"It's going to be all over the county before nightfall," Luke said. "Everybody's going to know that Blade Royal was afraid to face that man."

"He was lying!" Blade shouted. "I never had to shoot anybody from behind. Billy can tell you—" He stopped, apparently remembering that he'd already admitted what he'd done to Luke. "It'll be my word against his," Blade said. "Nobody will believe him."

Luke didn't say anything. They'd reached the ranch house. Lantz had seen his son ride up holding his arm, blood visible on his hand. He came roaring out of the house like a bull after a wolf.

"What happened?" he demanded. He didn't spare more than a fleeting glance for Billy Mason.

"Your son ran into a little trouble," Luke said when nobody answered.

"What kind of trouble?"

"Somebody faster than he was."

"Was it rustlers? By God, I'll hire more gunfighters. I'll hire a hundred if I have to."

"It wasn't rustlers," Luke said, "and he wasn't on his own land. You ordered him to run off the Spring Water riding stock." Together Luke and Lantz got Blade out of the saddle and up the steps. The other men had taken advantage of the chance to disappear by taking the horses back to the corral.

"Then who was it? Is there some gang operating in the area?"

"Let's get Blade inside," Luke said. "He's got to be feeling pretty bad. I'll tell you all about it while we clean him up."

"I want to know now," Lantz said as he helped his son into the house and over to the large sofa that was the centerpiece of the enormous living room. "Do you know who it was?"

"Yes."

"How many of them were there?"

"One."

Lantz stopped long enough to yell for the cook to bring hot water, bandages, and plenty of whiskey. "I don't believe it. One man couldn't take both Blade and Billy."

"I saw it. So did the rest of the boys. They'll tell you the same thing."

The cook hurried in. He must have seen them ride up because he'd already laid out bandages. Blade reached for the whiskey bottle and took a big swallow.

"Go easy on that, boy," Lantz said. "I want to know what happened."

"Let your hired killer tell you," Blade said, his expression surly as he took a second swallow.

Lantz looked from his son to Luke and back again. "What's going on here?"

"Blade tried to kill Bob Jordan's older boy. A man from the Spring Water stopped him."

"I wasn't going to kill him," Blade said. "I was just trying to teach him a lesson."

"The boy was down on the ground with your bullet in him when I rode up," Luke said. "You were taunting him, trying to force him to draw. Are you telling me you wouldn't have shot him if he had drawn?"

Blade took refuge in another swallow of whiskey.

"Blade wouldn't do that," Lantz said. "That boy's only fourteen."

"I'm telling you what I saw," Luke said.

"And Billy?"

"The man called them both liars. Blade and Billy drew at the same time. The other guy drew faster."

"I don't believe it. Nobody can beat Blade."

"I can."

"But you're a gunfighter."

"Maybe this man is, too."

"Who is he?"

"I don't know." It was a lie, but the truth could get both Chet and him killed.

"Where is he?"

"I imagine he's at the Jordan ranch. He took the boy home."

"See to him," Lantz ordered the cook. "Come with me. I'll get the boys. We'll go after him right now."

"There's a little bit more you ought to hear."

"Later."

"Now."

Lantz stopped and turned, an ugly look on his face. "You ordering me?"

"Let's say I'm offering some advice you'd be wise to take."

Lantz turned back to his son. "What the hell is this all about?"

But Blade was sinking into an alcohol- and

pain-induced oblivion. He didn't even look at his father.

"Okay, spill it fast. I'm worried about Melody. No telling what a man like that would do."

"You'd better start worrying about things closer to home."

Lantz didn't like that. "What do you mean? And you'd better tell me everything this time."

"A few days ago, Blade and Billy met a man riding across your range. He was riding a Jordan horse, so they stopped him. He said his horse was worn out, that he'd borrowed one at the Jordan ranch. Blade let him start down the trail, then shot him from behind."

"You're lying," Lantz said. He started to swing at Luke. He stopped when he saw the gun in Luke's hand. "Nobody works for me who's ever pulled a gun on me."

"I don't like fighting," Luke said. "This saves a lot of trouble."

"You called my son a back-shooter."

"I found that man," Luke said. "Shortly afterward Melody Jordan drove up. The horse had returned home and she'd come to see what happened. When I found him, Blade admitted doing it."

Lantz frowned. "Why would Blade shoot him if he was just riding through?"

"For fun, the same way he was taunting that Jordan boy."

"What was that kid doing out there?"

"Trying to get the man who'd killed Tom Neland."

Lantz looked really startled now. "The hell you say! Who killed Neland?"

"Blade."

"I don't believe you."

"Wasn't he supposed to when he ran off the Jordan horses?"

"Hell, no. I just wanted to put some more pressure on Melody. Tom Neland is a good man."

"*Was* a good man. Blade set up an ambush and killed him. If Tom hadn't gone in ahead by himself, a lot of others would have been killed."

"I don't believe you."

"Ask the boys."

"I will."

Lantz stormed out of the room. Luke looked over at Blade. "How bad is it?" he asked the cook. Blade was snoring.

"It went through his shoulder. That guy came close to killing him."

"That man can put a hole in a nickel. If he'd wanted to kill Blade, he'd be dead."

The cook regarded Luke suspiciously. "You said you didn't know him."

"I've heard about him. He's deadly."

"Does the boss know he's that good?"

"He soon will."

"I'm not going to be here when he finds out," the cook said. He looked back at Blade. "He's a bad one. It would have broken his mother's heart to see what he's become."

"Maybe he'd have been different if she had lived."

The man shook his head. "She never had any say. It was always Mr. Royal." The cook gathered his bandages and picked up the basin of water. "Always wanted him to be tough, just like him. They say people get what they ask for." He shook his head again and left the room.

Luke rolled a cigarette and smoked it. He was

rubbing out the stub in the fireplace when Lantz came back into the house.

"I never meant for Blade to kill anybody," he said, "but that's not going to stop me from going after that man. I've told the boys to saddle up. I want you with me."

"Maybe you'd better think about a few things first."

"That man shot my son. I'm going after him."

"Are you prepared for a bloody fight? He saved the Jordan boy's life. I doubt they'll be willing to hand him over to you."

"Belle Jordan wouldn't—" He stopped.

"You're getting ready to kill a man just because he wouldn't let Blade kill Sydney in cold blood. After he'd already killed Tom Neland. Don't you think Belle and her crew might want to get even? And what about this man? He's obviously a gunfighter. Have you considered that he might be working for the Spring Water?"

"She wouldn't."

"Why not?"

"She's a woman."

Luke didn't bother to tell Lantz that in his experience, women were a lot more vengeful than men. "Then consider this. Blade shot this man from behind. He stole the Jordans' horses, set up an ambush, killed Tom Neland, and nearly killed the Jordan boy. You can't deny it. There are too many witnesses. If Belle or that man manage to get him into a court of law, he'll hang. People don't take back-shooting kindly. They're even less happy about killing boys. And Neland's killing was the same as murder."

"None of the boys will testify against him. Nobody would believe a stranger."

"Don't be too sure, especially since he risked his life to go after that boy. Then there's Melody Jordan."

"She's only a woman."

"I told her what that man told me when I found him. I'd almost certainly be called to testify."

"But you work for me."

"You hired my gun. Nothing more."

"Then you kill him. You don't have to do it at the ranch. Wait until he leaves if you want, but kill him."

"There are two reasons why I shouldn't do that. First, Blade has tried to kill this man twice. If he's killed, everybody's going to know either you or Blade is responsible. You'd be arrested."

"The sheriff wouldn't dare."

"If the Jordan ladies demanded it, he wouldn't have any choice."

"What's your other reason?"

"I'm a hired gun, not an assassin."

"I don't see the difference."

"There isn't much of one, but it exists. If I were you, I'd worry about that man coming after Blade. If he is a gunfighter, I imagine he'll be anxious to get even. I would."

Royal looked furious enough to ignore all danger. A groan from Blade made him more angry still. Luke had to think of some way to stop him before he lost all sense of caution.

"Look, you want Melody and that ranch. You can get what you want by starving them out. If they call in the law, I'm leaving. I can keep that man off your back if you control Blade. If he does anything else, he's crow bait."

"They'd never find a jury that'd convict Blade. This town owes everything to me," Lantz said.

"Have you forgotten that you protected Billy after he raped that girl? Folks in town hate you for that. Some of them are still convinced Blade was the other man, even though the girl couldn't identify him. I'm sure they'd like a second chance to get Blade."

Luke rolled another cigarette to give Lantz time to think. The man didn't have any sympathy for Blade's victims or care that the boy had developed evil habits. He was caught between anger that anyone would shoot his son and fear that Blade's actions might hurt him.

Luke meant to play on that fear. He didn't want to be ordered to go after Chet. He also needed to be free to do the job he'd been hired to do, find the rustlers. So far they'd proved remarkably elusive. They always seemed to know where everybody was. Clearly, they had an informant on the inside. Luke never found any trails that weren't cold. He didn't understand it, and he didn't like it. He charged a huge fee. He could do that because of his past success. He didn't want a failure to change that.

Then there was Chet. Luke had never been called upon to go up against his brother. He certainly wasn't going to do it over a spoiled, evil-minded brat like Blade Royal. But there was another reason Luke couldn't do it. If he hadn't become a gunfighter, Chet would still be where he belonged, working for Jake, living with a family he'd come to love. But he had given it up to follow Luke, to protect him.

Luke had to keep Lantz from giving him a direct order. Backing down from any confrontation, no matter what the reason, would ruin his reputation and make it difficult for him to earn the kind of living he'd become used to. But he didn't have to face that possibility just yet, not as long as he could convince Lantz that his son was in danger.

"Wake up!"

Luke looked up to see Lantz shaking Blade hard.

"What?" Blade asked, his words slurred, his eyes only half open.

"Luke says that guy who shot you is a gun-fighter. You stay in the house, you hear? Luke's going to stay with you. You're not to be out of his sight."

Blade fought to sit up, but his shoulder wouldn't support him. "I'm not hiding from any damned gunfighter. And I'm sure as hell not letting Luke babysit me."

"You're staying here until I can figure out what to do about that gunfighter," Lantz said. "I'm not losing my only kin to some filthy gunman."

Luke felt something inside him tighten. He didn't understand why Royal thought he was so much better just because it wasn't his hand that held the gun. He listened absently while Lantz and Blade argued with each other at the top of their lungs. Blade's foolish threats about what he would do when he got up were doing more to convince Lantz he was in danger than anything Luke had said.

"You're staying here, and that's final," Lantz said. "If that man can shoot both you and Billy, he can kill you if he catches you alone."

Blade cursed. Luke wasn't much happier. He didn't like Blade, and loathed being around him. He needed freedom to find out who was behind the rustling. Most of all, he had to find a way to meet Chet and convince him to leave the area.

The whole place was in ferment by the time Chet and Sydney returned to the ranch. Neill, waiting down the trail despite his mother's orders, had seen them coming and rushed back to tell everyone. By the time Chet helped Sydney off his horse, Melody and Bernice had organized the household to receive him. Melody had also sent one of the men for the doctor. Belle was the greatest surprise. After taking one look at the blood on her son and letting out a piercing scream, she pulled herself together and started issuing orders everyone ignored. But she didn't leave his side, nor did she lose control of her emotions again.

"There's a lot of blood," Chet told Belle as he helped Sydney into the house, "but he's not seriously hurt."

"I'll get some of the men to carry you upstairs," Melody said to Sydney.

"I can walk," Sydney said, embarrassed and angered at all the fuss. "I'm not going to die."

"Who did this to you?" Belle asked.

"Blade," Sydney said. "He wanted to humiliate me before he killed me."

Belle lost some color, but she retained her composure.

"I don't understand. Why would he do such a thing?"

"For the same reason he killed Tom," Chet said. "He likes killing."

They had managed to reach the top of the stairs. Sydney looked close to the end of his endurance. "Want me to carry you?" Chet asked softly.

"You're wounded yourself," Sydney replied. "I'll make it."

Chet had to give the boy credit. He had bottom. Now if he could just learn that guns weren't the answer to everything, he might make a good cattleman someday. All he really needed was someone to take him in hand, someone who wasn't his mother or his sister. Some man he could respect, try to emulate. Melody's husband. Chet refused to let his thoughts wander in that direction.

Once he had settled Sydney in the bed, he moved back to give Belle and Bernice room to work.

"Did Blade really mean to kill him?" Melody asked.

Chet drew her out into the hall.

"Don't leave," Belle called to him. "I want to know everything that happened out there."

Chet kept moving until he and Melody reached Bob Jordan's office. He motioned her inside and closed the door behind her.

"Why all the secrecy?"

"I don't want to upset Belle."

"She's already upset. So am I. What could have possessed Blade to shoot Sydney? He's just a boy."

"According to Sydney, Blade was waiting for him. He challenged him the moment he arrived, then drew on him before he was ready."

"I can't believe Blade would do anything so cowardly."

"I should have told you before. It was Blade who shot me. From behind."

Melody looked as if she could hardly believe what he'd told her. "But why?"

"He likes bullying people. I don't think he sees it as wrong, just getting what he wants."

"What does he want?"

"To be the big man around here, to have everybody fear him. I don't like Lantz, but he does have some scruples. Blade doesn't. He had Sydney down on the ground. Any other man would have left things at that, even offered to take care of him. Blade was taunting him, trying to get him to draw again."

"That's practically the same as murder."

"I have a feeling Blade can't help it. I don't think he's right in his head."

"I've got to tell Lantz. He's got to do something."

"Do you think he's going to believe anything like this about his son?"

"But if his men back up what we say—"

"They won't. Lantz is paying their wages, not you. Besides, they might be afraid of what Blade will do to them."

"Then I'll call the sheriff."

"Do, but don't be surprised if nothing happens. You weren't a witness."

"You were."

"I'm a stranger. Nobody's going to believe me if Royal's hands swear otherwise. They won't believe Sydney, either. He's a boy who got in over his head. They'll figure he's just trying to get back."

Melody looked at him in disbelief. "People out here can't be so callous. I sent for the sheriff as well as the doctor. We'll see what he has to say."

* * *

She found Chet sitting under a tree behind a corral an hour later.

"The doctor said Sydney will be just fine. We're to keep him in bed for a couple of days. He just has to take it easy after that."

That was what Chet had expected to hear, but he knew that was not what Melody had come to tell him. She looked furious. She stood there as agitated as a pot at a full boil.

"That sheriff said exactly what you said he would," she finally conceded. "He's not going to do a thing about Blade." She started to pace, the turbulence of her emotions underscored by the vigorous sway and swishing sound of her skirt. "He said it would be Blade's word against Sydney's. I asked him how he explained the gunshot wound. He said Lantz had already told him Sydney was looking for trouble. He said Blade had fired in self-defense and that he had five men who would swear to it."

"So what did you do?" Chet asked.

"I told him he was a coward and a sycophant, a disgrace to Texas, the South, and every man who'd ever had the courage to fight for his convictions. I also told him—"

Chet smiled. "Did he stay around to hear the rest of it?"

"No. The spineless worm said he had to talk to Belle about her lost horses. Horses! He was more concerned about four-legged animals then about my brother."

"Horses are very important in Texas."

"I should hope brothers are as well."

Chet thought of Luke working for Lantz Royal and his mood sobered. "Yes. Family is important to us, too."

"What are we going to do? We can't let Blade get away with this. Who knows what he'll do next?"

"I guess you're going to have to hire the gunfighters like Tom wanted."

"That'll be the same as a declaration of war."

"Lantz wants what you have, and he means to take it with guns if necessary. You have to defend it with any means at your command. I think that's the usual definition of war."

"I can't do that. It's barbaric."

"Then hire someone to do it for you."

"I mean I can't do it at all. Can't you understand that?"

"No." He'd been brought up fighting for what he wanted. Being a gunfighter was a choice. Defending your property wasn't. "If you don't fight, people will strip you bare and despise you for letting them do it."

"How can you live like that?"

"I don't have another choice."

"Well, I do. We're supposed to help our neighbors, not pick their bones."

"You can't condemn everybody because of Lantz's greediness."

"Yes, I can. It's people with attitudes like yours and the sheriff's who allow him to get away with it. This would never happen in Richmond."

"Things are different in cities, even in Texas."

"I'll have to take your word for it," Melody said. "I don't intend to stay long enough to find out. I'm going home."

"What about your share of the ranch?"

"I don't care about it anymore. I can support myself. And if I can't, I know at least one man who won't try to force me to the altar by stealing my horses or shooting my brother. How can you stand to live here?"

"It's my home."

"It'll never be mine. It's barbaric."

"There's barbarism everywhere, Melody, whether it's some banker stealing gold from poor suckers who risked their lives to grub it out of the ground, politicians stealing Indian lands and starving them on reservations, or robber barons raping the country. The only difference is that out here we're more honest about our stealing."

"Honesty among thieves. Don't you think that's a contradiction of terms?"

"Maybe, but it's true."

"Well, I can't accept it. The minute I know Sydney's all right, I'm leaving this place."

Chet watched as she turned on her heel and headed back toward the house, still talking to herself, arms flailing about as she made point after point no one else could hear. He'd grown up in Texas and expected to die in Texas. But he could see how it must be a terrible shock to someone reared in the softer traditions of a place like Richmond. Men in Virginia believed in protecting their women from the unpleasant aspects of life. Texas women had to shoulder their share of the troubles. Isabelle had managed to make the transition, but she'd been orphaned herself, then dumped into the Texas wilderness with eight homeless boys on her hands. She'd had to change, or none of them would have survived. Melody didn't have to change. She could go back to Virginia.

Chet found himself wanting to defend Texas, wanting to convince her to stay, but he kept his mouth shut. It wouldn't have been good for her.

It certainly wouldn't have been good for him. Yet, he couldn't imagine never seeing Melody again. Despite the odds, he felt she belonged in his life. She belonged *here*. Forever.

"You can't leave," Belle exclaimed.

"I can't stand it here any longer," Melody said. "They've stolen our cows, scattered our horses, and shot Tom and Sydney. They'll probably decide to come after us next. They could kill us in our beds."

"They're not Indians."

"I could understand it better if they were."

"What will the boys and I do if you leave?"

"I'll give you my part of the ranch. I'll sign any papers you want. I don't want anything here."

"That's not what I'm talking about. What's going to happen to us if we lose the ranch?"

"You grew up here. You understand the rules. You figure out how to stop Lantz. I can't, and I don't want to try anymore."

"But Melody, you can't—"

"Don't you dare say I have to marry Lantz Royal to save you. I won't be blackmailed into marrying that man, or any man out here," she declared. "They're all savages."

"I won't ask you to marry Lantz," Belle said. "I couldn't, not after what he let his son do to Sydney."

"Then why don't you want me to go back to Virginia?"

"Because you've got to convince Chet to become our foreman."

"You can do that."

"No, I can't."

"Why?"

"He won't take the job for me. He won't take it at all if you don't stay."

"Why?"

"Because he's in love with you. He has been almost from the moment he saw you."

Chapter Twelve

Melody didn't know what to say, what to think, what to do. It had never occurred to her that Chet might be in love with her. Actually, the idea scared her. Being connected to him, even in this tenuous way, seemed to draw her closer to aspects of life that she didn't understand and wanted to keep at a distance.

Yet she had to admit that the very things about him she deplored had been responsible for saving her brother's life. She didn't need Bernice to tell her Sydney was alive only because a faster gun had stopped Blade. She might not like gunfighters, she might deplore the necessity for them, but she had to be honest enough to admit she was thankful Chet was such a good one.

Deny it as strenuously as she wanted, she had to admit she was excited by the thought that he was in love with her. She'd been attracted to him from the first. The possibility that he might be in love with her raised the stakes. Did she actually like him, or was a stronger word closer to her true feelings? She'd better find out before she asked him to stay. If he did love her, asking him to stay might make him think she was offering more than a job as foreman.

Suddenly a fairly simple decision had become complicated. She couldn't say or do anything without wondering what else it might mean. She wasn't good with sticky situations, nor was she very diplomatic. But she had to be, and she didn't have much time to figure out how to do it. She had sent Neill to find Chet. She could see him walking up to the house right now.

On impulse she left the parlor and crossed the hall into her father's study. She decided to sit behind her father's desk. She hoped it would give her some sense of strength. She felt sorely in need of it.

What would she do if he refused to take Tom's job? He'd already said he didn't want anything to do with a gunfight. He'd twice refused to work for her. What made her think he was going to change his mind this time? Because he was in love with her? It would be unfair to use that. Worse, it would be dishonest. However, the temptation was great. She was desperate. People she loved were in real danger.

But if Chet loved her, she couldn't take advantage of him and still look him in the eye. That would be worse than his being a gunfighter. And if she felt more for him than liking, she wouldn't be able to look herself in the mirror. She had to find a way to convince him to be their foreman without leading him on.

She didn't know how to do that, but she couldn't throw up her hands and quit now. He had to take the job, at least until she and Belle had time to look for someone else. Despite her objections to guns and her dislike of gunfighters on principle, she didn't trust any to know better when to use a gun than Chet. Sydney had told her that Chet hadn't killed Blade even though he'd had plenty of reason and opportunity. If she'd ever had any doubt that guns were only as good or bad as the men who used them, she doubted no longer.

Chet had already proved he was willing to risk his life for Sydney. She felt certain he would do the same for anyone else on the ranch. Loyalty, integrity, and courage couldn't be bought. Either a man had them or he didn't. She would never have believed she'd find them in a gunfighter.

But from the first, she'd known Chet wasn't an ordinary man.

Her thoughts broke off when he entered the room. She was struck by the power of his looks. Maybe Belle's words had heightened her perception, but she didn't know why she hadn't realized before that he was the most handsome man she'd ever seen. Even being so blond didn't detract from his appeal. His height and obvious physical power didn't overwhelm her, but he seemed to fill the room with his presence, to gather all the energy to himself.

"You wanted to see me?" he asked.

Melody looked down at her hands and tried to organize her scattered thoughts. "Yes. Please sit down."

Chet cast her a questioning glance before taking a ladder-back chair, turning it around, and straddling it. The pose made him look on edge, poised for escape rather than relaxed and receptive.

He didn't look like a man in love, at least not like any man of her experience. Lantz had been clumsy and overbearing, but he'd tried to be near her, to capture and hold her attention. The young men in Richmond were more ardent. None had thrown themselves at her feet, but they tended to hang around making a nuisance of themselves. One had even recited poetry.

Chet simply sat there, waiting for her to speak, his expression neutral, his attitude relaxed. Belle had to be wrong. This couldn't be the way a man acted when he was in love, not even a Texas gunfighter.

"I want to thank you for going after Sydney," she began.

"You don't have to."

"Belle would thank you as well, but she won't leave Sydney's side until she's convinced he's no longer in danger."

"In that case, he's more likely to be in danger from loss of temper than from that bullet wound."

Melody smiled. "Probably, but it's impossible to convince Belle to stay away."

A silence fell between them. Once more she found herself studying his face, searching for some sign of what he might feel for her. Nothing. Belle had to be wrong.

She felt a sense of relief, but a sense of loss as well. There was something about this man that made her want to be near him. She'd liked many men before, even fancied herself in love, but she'd never felt the need of their physical presence, at least not in the same way. Her previous experi-

ences with lovelorn young men had always involved impassioned declarations, the offering of
small gifts. It wasn't at all like that with Chet. Just
knowing he was there was enough. She had felt
much the same way when he'd been upstairs, his
head wrapped in bandages, too weak to sit up.

That was nonsensical. Women didn't admire
men when they were on their backs in a sick bed.
She decided it had to be the disorientation of being in Texas, of not understanding how the men
thought or how she was supposed to react.

"Did you want anything else?" Chet asked.

"Yes." His gaze hardened. There was nothing
she could point to, but she could feel it just as
clearly as though his eyes had changed from sky
blue to deep azure. "You know what it is, don't
you?"

"You don't have to ask. I'll stay."

The sense of relief was tremendous. She hadn't
realized how tense she had become, how much
she feared he might refuse. But a sense of guilt
followed quickly. He was doing something he
didn't want to do, going against what he thought
was best for him, risking his life for people he'd
never heard of until a few days ago. What could
she give him in exchange? Money didn't seem
enough.

"I don't know how much money you usually get
paid, but—"

"I'm not doing this for money. I've put all of you
in danger."

"Don't be absurd. We put you in danger."

"Blade's not seriously wounded, but his father
is going to want me dead. He may want to take it
out on your family as well."

Melody realized she'd been completely selfish.

So had Belle. It had never once occurred to her family that helping them would put Chet in serious danger.

"Then you can't stay," she said. "Take any horse you want. I'll have Bernice pack some food for you. You can be twenty miles from here by nightfall."

He directed such an unnerving look at her that she began to squirm in her chair.

"Do you need money? I'll give you as much as I can."

"You think I would leave?"

What else could she think? It was the only sensible thing to do. "You just said Lantz was going to try to kill you."

"That doesn't mean I'll turn tail and run."

"But Tom said he had hired a gunfighter. You can't just wait for him to come after you."

Chet stood and pushed the chair away from him. "I don't intend to. The men can't do their work without horses. I'm going after them. Several of the boys are waiting for me now."

Surprise held Melody silent for only a moment. "You mean you had decided to stay even before I asked you?"

"You'd already asked me twice. I figured the invitation was still open."

The hint of a smile was back in his eyes. He'd let her sit there squirming, ready to abase herself, beg . . .

"You mean you let me sit here worrying about what I'd do if you refused?"

"I would have told you earlier, but I didn't want to take you away from Sydney."

Melody's sense of outrage continued to grow.

"You didn't think any such thing! You wanted to see me grovel."

"No, but if you were going to, I wouldn't mind watching."

He was laughing at her now. Those incredibly blue eyes were practically dancing. "Why, you—" She couldn't think of a polite word that would do justice to her feelings. "I've a good mind to—"

"Careful. You don't want to make me so angry I'll quit. Then you'll have to get down on your knees and really beg to get me to come back."

"I wouldn't get on my knees to you if—" She stopped abruptly. He was teasing her. What did he mean by having a sense of humor when she was near desperation? She took refuge in rigid formality. "My stepmother and I are deeply appreciative of what you've done for us, Mr. Attmore. We realize money can't compensate you for the dangers you've been exposed to, but you'll have our eternal gratitude."

"I liked you better when you were thinking profane thoughts and being frustrated because you were too ladylike to utter any of them."

He was still laughing at her. "A gentleman would never say anything so ungallant."

The sparkle disappeared from his eyes.

"I'm not a gentleman. I'm a gunfighter, remember? We can do anything we like."

She hadn't meant to hurt his feelings. "Despite your dependence on guns, I suspect you're as much a gentleman as any man I've ever known."

"Don't stretch your definitions too wide," he said with a wintry smile. "You'll find yourself having to be civil to all kinds of undesirable characters."

The door closed behind Chet, leaving Melody

feeling vaguely dissatisfied. She had the feeling nothing had gone right, but she couldn't put her finger on the trouble. He'd agreed to stay. He hadn't asked for more money than they could pay. He'd gone right to work with no fuss or fanfare. He'd been polite and cooperative. He'd practically apologized for getting them into trouble with Lantz. Things couldn't have gone better if she'd been able to choose the words he spoke, yet the feeling of disquiet wouldn't go away.

She felt he'd come out of this sounding noble, her looking as though she thought only of herself. He'd also put more distance between them. She'd lost her control; he'd kept his. He'd laughed at her, and that made her angry.

It was probably vanity. She liked feeling Chet was in love with her. It gave her a wonderful sense of power. It also allowed her to admit she liked him far more than she had suspected.

That was okay as long as she could believe he loved her. She was still in control. But he had out-guessed her, which left her feeling at a disadvantage again. Maybe he didn't love her, but she couldn't take back her admission to herself. She liked him a great deal and not just because he was handsome and had a great body and the most kissable lips she'd ever seen.

Melody was shocked at herself. She couldn't ever remember having a thought like that. Ladies didn't in Richmond. At least not grown-up, mature ladies, not after they turned sixteen and stopped being silly girls. But his lips *were* kissable, and it was pointless to deny that she had thought about kissing them. And that was something else. Decent women didn't kiss men.

But Chet Attmore had confused her thinking,

first by being so handsome she couldn't help being attracted to him. Next by being so nice it would be impossible not to like him. And finally by stepping in to help when she was so obviously out of her depth. And all he asked of her was that she not condemn him because he had been a gunfighter.

Little did he know that if she wasn't very careful, she would find herself in love with him.

Chet had guessed the horses would still be in the canyon, and that proved to be the case. He figured Blade hadn't taken the horses so much to steal them as to draw the Spring Water hands into his ambush. Chet directed the men to take the horses back to the ranch, but he decided to ride farther up the canyon. He kept Speers with him.

"What are you looking for?" the young man asked.

"I'm not sure," Chet replied, "but there's a lot I don't understand about this situation. Lantz Royal wants this ranch because he's greedy. I guess he wants to marry Melody for pretty much the same reason."

"That, or to keep his son from marrying her."

Chet nodded thoughtfully. "What exactly happened between her and Blade?"

They had entered a long, deep canyon that ran along the north boundary of the Spring Water Ranch. Down its center flowed a stream of cold, sweet water that never dried up even in the hottest and driest summers. A ribbon of trees provided abundant shade in summer and protection from fierce winds in the winter.

"It was quite a story at one time. Blade took one look at Melody and was lost. He made a right fool of himself over her. But Miss Jordan turned him down. Things might have died out in a natural way if Lantz Royal hadn't decided he wanted to marry her. Ordered his son to forget about her, said he should start thinking about her as his mother, not his wife."

"What did Blade do?"

"I heard him and his pa had a terrible fight, though I don't know how that could be. Lantz stands a foot taller and must weigh twice as much. He could have tossed the boy through a window without even trying."

Chet pulled his horse to a halt. He leaned out of the saddle to study some tracks in the sandy bottom of the canyon. Cows had made those tracks, not horses, and a lot of them seemed to be going in the same direction.

"Was Blade angry at Melody for turning him down?"

"I don't know, but that kind of man never likes not getting what he wants. He's the kind to do something about it."

Chet had reached the same conclusion himself, but trying to kill off most of the Spring Water cowhands seemed a little extreme, even for someone as unbalanced as Blade Royal.

"What about this rustling?" Chet asked.

"That's got me puzzled," Speers said.

"When did it start?"

"About a year ago. At first we thought it was Lantz trying to force Mr. Jordan to sell out to him, but they've been hitting Lantz worse then they hit us."

"Have other ranchers lost cows?"

"Yes, but not as many as us and Royal."

"Is that why Lantz hired a gunfighter?"

"Yes, but he doesn't seem to be making any progress. Those rustlers seem to know more about what we're doing than we do. We're never anywhere near where they strike. And they've been getting the cows out of the area without anybody seeing them."

"This might be part of the reason," Chet said, pointing to the tracks. "Nobody would see them in this canyon. Since the canyon walls are a natural fence, I imagine Tom didn't have you patrol it on a regular basis."

"We never came in here until roundup," Speers confirmed.

It was just as Chet had guessed. He, too, might have thought Lantz was doing the rustling if he hadn't gone to the expense of hiring Luke to put a stop to it. No, Lantz wanted the canyon because it was a dependable source of water, grass, and shelter. But who was doing the rustling, and where were they taking the cattle?

"Where does this canyon go?" Chet asked Speers.

"I don't know. It's more than a hundred miles long. It goes through three counties."

"Where does the water come from?"

"Lots of springs. The biggest I know of is on Spring Water land. That's what gives the place its name."

"So this canyon would give rustlers a protected route for at least a hundred miles."

"But it wouldn't be any good if they couldn't get out," Speers said. "These walls are over five hundred feet high."

But someone was taking cattle up the canyon. That meant there *had* to be a way to get them out again. All he had to do now was find it. If his guess was right, the way out was in the part of the canyon owned by the Spring Water Ranch. The rustlers had gone out of their way to shoot at several Spring Water cowhands but not wound them seriously. This didn't make sense unless they were just trying to scare them away. He would bet that the only way out of the canyon for its whole length was right here. The rustlers could hold the cattle farther up the canyon until they had enough for a drive; then they would take them out the escape route. With the Spring Water hands afraid to come near the place, they'd have plenty of grass and water and nobody to bother them.

"Ever see anything that looked like a way out?" Chet asked.

"Nothing but rock slides."

"Let's have a look anyway."

They rode for miles. It was a beautiful canyon, wild and majestic. Water had cut through the soft rock over millions of years, revealing colors and shades from cream to orange to slate grey. Long shadows filled the corners, cool breezes its depths. Smaller canyons branched off on both sides. Cactus grew in abundance. Chet also found thick tangles of shrubs and vines, a ribbon of trees, and enough grass to support thousands of cattle. But on every side the canyon walls rose steep and unbroken for five hundred feet. A man couldn't have scaled them without ropes.

"I'm going on," Chet said to Speers when they'd ridden about twenty miles, "but I want you to go back. Tell Melody I'll be back tomorrow. Don't tell her what I'm doing. Just say I'm checking on the cattle while I'm here."

"I could stay with you."

"If one of us doesn't go back, she'll send out a search party."

Chet hadn't planned to stay out overnight, but he always carried enough food and water for at least three days. That precaution had saved his life more than once.

"Keep a sharp lookout," Speers warned. "Those guys aren't going to take kindly to anybody following their trail."

No more than Chet took kindly to being shot at. Or a lot of other things that had been happening recently. Even though he couldn't explain why, he had a feeling the rustling was at the bottom of it.

Chet took his time choosing a campsite. He took even more time fixing his supper. There wasn't much he could do on the trail, but Isabelle had gotten him used to good food. He didn't get it very often anymore, but he did his best. He'd finished eating and was enjoying his coffee when he heard the sound of a walking horse in the distance.

He listened intently. The horse was walking slowly but steadily. He was probably heading toward the light from Chet's campfire. The easy pace could be taken as a reassuring sign, but Chet knew the rider could have dismounted, sent his horse on ahead, and be coming in from another direction. No one had reason to be in this part of the canyon except Spring Water riders or the rustlers, and the Spring Water hands were supposed to be back at the ranch.

Chet moved quietly into the shadows. A welcoming whinny from his horse didn't upset him. The rider already knew he was there. As his eyes gradually got used to the twilight, he made out the dark shape of a horse and rider coming down the trail. While they were still a hundred feet away, Chet realized there was something familiar about the shape of the rider. Fifty yards away, Chet's muscles relaxed. He holstered his gun, walked back to the campfire, and poured another cup of coffee.

The rider halted in the shadows, just out of the range of light.

"Light and sit a spell," Chet said.

The man dismounted and stepped forward into the light.

"Howdy, Luke," Chet said. "I was wondering when we'd run into each other."

Chapter Thirteen

Luke accepted the cup of coffee from his brother, then settled himself on a low shelf of rock. He took a swallow. "You always did make lousy coffee."

"Some things never change."

Luke took another swallow. "I thought you'd be halfway to New Mexico by now."

Chet searched his brother's face, but flickering shadows cast by the firelight obscured his expression. "I'd planned to."

"What's keeping you?"

"Your boss and his son. I can't leave those two women with no one to protect them. I'm ramroding their outfit until they can find someone else."

"It's not your problem."

"That's not the way I see it."

He could see enough of Luke's expression to

know he didn't like what he heard. But Chet hadn't expected he would.

"You know Royal is after your head."

"Blade, too, I imagine."

"He won't be allowed to leave the house until he's fully recovered. I was able to convince Lantz you might be out to kill him."

Chet tensed and directed a hard stare at his brother. He'd never distrusted Luke, but their interests had never come into conflict before. "Now why would I do something like that?"

"He figured you must be a gunfighter. You couldn't have beaten Blade and Billy if you weren't. Everybody knows gunfighters don't like people trying to kill them."

Luke might as well have put a price on Chet's head. "So now Lantz sends his men out to find me."

"So Lantz locks his son up in the house where he can't pull another fool stunt like setting up an ambush for Tom Neland and then nearly killing that kid."

Chet had hoped Luke would look out for him, but he wasn't sure what kind of game Luke was playing. He seemed to be straddling the fence, but Chet knew Luke never took any side but his own.

"Has Lantz sent you to kill me?"

"Would I be here if he had?"

"Yes. You'd tell me first so I'd have a fair chance."

Luke looked directly at his brother, his face devoid of any trace of emotion. "Do you think I would?"

The whole time they were being thrown out of one foster home after another, and later when Jake and Isabelle adopted them, Chet had been certain he and Luke would always stand together. But Luke had changed since they'd left the ranch. They both had.

But each was all the other had. That was important to Chet. In his gut he felt it was important to Luke, too.

"No," Chet said. He was relieved to see Luke relax, even allow a hint of a smile to curve his lips. "But it's got to put you in a very awkward position. Does Royal know we're brothers?"

"No. Do the Jordans know about me?"

"No, but that'll change if anybody sees us together."

"I've thought of that," Luke said. "I managed to convince Lantz I needed to stay around the house to protect Blade from you."

"What are you doing out here?"

"I can't be around that boy all the time, or I'd shoot him myself. I'm doing what Lantz hired me to do in the first place, trying to find the rustlers. What are you doing?"

"The same thing. I'm certain they're using this canyon as a holding area until they collect enough for a drive. I'm also sure there's a way out, one that's on Spring Water land."

"That's pretty much what I suspected, but I don't see how they manage to escape detection unless there's somebody on the inside feeding them information."

"Have you ever considered that somebody on the inside might be running it?"

"Why?"

"What about a foreman looking to build a ranch of his own?"

"But these two ranches have been the hardest hit. Everybody knows Tom Neland was as honest as a preacher, and the LR don't have a foreman. Who else could it be?"

"I don't know. It just feels like somebody on the inside. How else could they always know where everybody was going to be?"

"That would mean people at both ranches. Do you have any idea who on your crew could be feeding them information?"

"No. Do you on yours?"

"Any one of that group that hangs around Blade."

"Can you get rid of them?"

"No, but they won't do anything without Blade."

"He's dangerous. I think he's crazy in the head."

"Could be."

Luke got up to pour himself more coffee.

"You going back tonight?" Chet asked.

"Yeah. I can only leave when Lantz is there."

"Why don't you quit?" Chet shouldn't have asked that, but he couldn't stop himself. He hated to think of his brother working for a man like Lantz Royal.

"Why don't you leave?" Luke asked.

"I will as soon as they find another foreman."

"I'll leave as soon as I find the rustlers."

They were silent again. When they were boys, they sometimes used to lie awake all night talking about nothing at all. Now they couldn't manage a twenty-minute conversation even though what they said could affect the lives of dozens of people.

"You know you ought to give this up," Chet said. "Sooner or later some crazy fool like Blade is going to shoot you in the back."

"I thought you had given it up."

"I had until Blade shot me."

"Where you going when this is over?"

"Someplace around the Four Corners. Maybe Arizona. I hear there's some nice country in the Tonto Basin or north of the Mogollon Rim."

"Looking for a place as far away from other people as possible?"

"I'm tired of this life, Luke. I want to go someplace where I can't be found."

"Then go to New Orleans or San Francisco. Nobody'll ever find you there."

"I'd be miserable in a city. I'm a cowboy. I want a ranch."

"Then go home. Jake would be happy to have you, and Isabelle would fall on your neck."

"Will you come with me?"

"No. I don't fit there."

"You're too good to be mixing with the likes of Lantz and his son."

"I don't mix. I do my job and move on."

"What'll you have when you stop moving on?"

"Who says I'm going to stop?"

"Everybody stops someday, one way or another."

"You let me worry about myself."

Chet didn't know why he had started this discussion. They had the same one every time they met, and it always ended with them angry at each other. He had no business trying to run Luke's life. He hadn't done very well with his own. Only he couldn't bear to think of Luke dead.

"It's too late to go back," Chet said. "One day somebody would show up looking for me, and Jake or one of the boys would try to stop them. I get nightmares thinking about what might happen."

"Change your name. Jake would love to fill that valley with Maxwells. Since Isabelle can't give him any sons now, somebody's got to do it for him."

Chet resolutely put out of his mind the picture of the secluded valley he'd left, the miles of rich grass and running streams, the snug homes where the people he'd learned to love gathered to share their lives. Some stayed, some drifted away, and some came back. There was plenty of room for Chet. If only he hadn't made it impossible for himself to go back.

"Leave, Luke," Chet said. "We're bound to come up against each other if we keep working for opposite sides."

"We've managed to avoid it so far."

"But we've never been on a collision course before."

"I can't leave until I've completed the job I signed on to do."

Chet sighed. He hadn't expected anything else. He would have felt the same way. "Then let's find the rustlers before Lantz sends you after me."

Melody tried to get more comfortable, but her body was stiff, and she was tired of mending. Her neck ached from bending over her work so long. And from tension. She had been upset ever since Speers had told her Chet was staying in the canyon. By the time she'd badgered him into telling her what they'd found, what Chet suspected, and what he intended to do, she was worried. She'd only wanted him to find the horses, not go after a bunch of murdering rustlers.

She'd forced herself to read until after 1:00 A.M. to keep her mind from torturing her with horrible scenarios, all of which ended in Chet's brutal and gruesome death. The same worries kept her tossing in her bed the rest of the night. She only managed to set aside her fears when she remembered that Chet had been lying in this very same bed, his limbs resting in the very places her limbs rested now, only days before. But that set up a chain of thought that agitated her nearly as much. Never, in her entire life, had she imagined herself sharing a bed with a man. Now she couldn't get that thought out of her mind. Having seen Chet naked from the waist up made the imagining all that much easier. She could easily imagine the excitement of running her hands over his smooth chest, his firm waist, his powerful shoulders. She could just as easily imagine being held in his arms. It was frightening. It was exhilarating. It was impossible to ignore.

Then there were the kisses. Melody had only been kissed twice, neither an earth-shattering experience, but she had an excellent imagination. She could also remember the experiences of her more impressionable friends. At the time she hadn't believed much of what they said, but putting Chet in the role of lover made it all quite credible. Melody was embarrassed even to think that word, yet it wouldn't go away. How could any woman think of that man without thinking of him as a lover?

"Are you angry with me?"

"What?" Belle must have been speaking to her, but she hadn't heard a word.

"You've been ignoring me all day," Belle said moodily, looking up from her own needlework.

"Sorry. I'm worried about Chet," Melody said. "He's been gone all day. I thought he would have been back by now. I'm afraid something has happened to him."

"I'm sure he's quite safe. Sydney says he's incredibly fast with a gun. He says no one could beat him."

"Sydney ought to be very thankful that's true."

"He is. He's been quite altered by the whole experience."

"I haven't seen much sign of it." But then, Melody hadn't seen much of her brother. Belle had taken possession of the sickroom like a general of a captured enemy position. She didn't even allow Bernice inside for more than a few minutes at a time.

"It's the kind of thing he wouldn't tell a sister, but would never keep from his mother."

Melody didn't want to disparage her brother unfairly, but she couldn't see him confiding in Belle.

"What did he say?" she asked, wondering if Chet would return before dark.

"He said he knows Blade is faster than he is. He also said Blade was going to kill him even though he was down on the ground. He said Blade had his gun drawn, but Chet walked straight up to him anyway. He said Chet wasn't scared. He didn't even look at Blade. He went straight over to Sydney to see how badly he'd been hurt."

Melody already felt guilty enough that she and her family had put Chet in such danger. Learning of his bravery only made her feel worse. "I hope Sydney appreciates the risk Chet took."

"He's more impressed that Chet could outdraw Blade and the other man at the same time. He's described the entire fight at least a half-dozen times, but he talks as much about Chet's courage

as he does about his guns. He said Chet doesn't
believe in using guns to settle every argument, but
if you're going to stand up for law and order,
you'd better be as good with the criminal's weapons as the criminal is himself."

"I'm not sure I like that philosophy," Melody
said, "but it's an improvement."

The sound of horses approaching brought her
to her feet instantly and sent her running to the
window. "It's Lantz Royal!" She was surprised he
had the nerve to show up. If he'd been meaning
to apologize for what Blade did, he should have
come yesterday. If he was coming for any other
reason, he could have saved himself the effort.
She wanted nothing more to do with him. Belle
looked unhappy at having to face the father of the
man who'd almost killed her son. Melody came
to a quick decision.

"You stay here," she told Belle. "If I meet him
outside, you won't have to see him."

Melody was glad to see Belle looked relieved. It
was time her stepmother stopped being blinded
by Lantz Royal's wealth and power and saw him
for the brutal bully he was.

Melody was slightly surprised to see that Lantz
looked just as handsome and virile as ever. She
didn't know what she had expected, but she'd
imagined that somehow the evil he represented
would have become visible. He didn't appear to
be the least bit embarrassed or upset by what
had happened. His smile and swaggering self-
confidence were unchanged.

"Afternoon," he said without dismounting.
"You're looking mighty fine, as usual."

His compliments didn't interest her nearly as
much as the man accompanying him. He watched

Leigh Greenwood

her from under a hat pulled so low, it obscured all of his face except his mouth and chin. For a moment she thought he looked familiar.

"You haven't introduced your friend," Melody said, trying to keep her voice as cold and formal as possible.

"This is Luke," Lantz said. "We came over to see how your brother is doing."

Melody didn't really hear the last of Lantz's sentence. Luke! This was the gunfighter Lantz had hired to find the rustlers. But what was he doing here unless he was looking for Chet? It seemed everything Chet did for them put him in greater danger.

"I'm afraid I can't ask you to get down and come in," Melody said, gathering her wits. "Belle doesn't want to see you. She hasn't forgiven you for Blade's shooting Sydney."

"He didn't mean it," Lantz said. "It was just some of the tomfoolery boys get up to from time to time."

"He was trying to kill Sydney, Lantz. You can't put any other interpretation on it."

"You don't understand boys out here," Lantz replied. "They're nothing like the dandies you're used to in Richmond."

"In that case, I prefer dandies to *boys out here*. Is that how you behave, Luke?"

He didn't get a chance to answer. "He's a gunfighter," Lantz told her. "He'd be dead by now if he didn't have more guts than your dandies."

"Is that true, Luke?" She was determined to give him a chance to answer for himself. She'd already misjudged one gunfighter. Even though she couldn't think well of a man who would work for Lantz, she didn't want to make that mistake again.

"Of course it is," Lantz said, answering for him again. "Now, I have to see your stepmother." He started to get down out of the saddle, but just then Chet rounded the corner of the house.

If Melody had had any doubts about her feelings for Chet, she had them no longer. Relief so great it robbed her of her strength flooded her body; happiness so overwhelming it practically lifted her off the ground wrapped itself around her. Chet was back. He was safe. It was all she could do not to fling herself at him. She wished fervently that a hole would open up and swallow Lantz and his awful gunfighter. Their presence could never have been more unwanted than it was now. She looked into Chet's eyes, eager for an answer to the questions she'd asked herself ever since Belle had put the idea into her head.

Did he love her?

She saw warmth, a softening in his gaze, and her heart soared. He must love her to have risked so much. He must.

A tremendous swell of feeling for Chet swept through her. More than liking, more than fondness. It was so great, it left her speechless. She loved him. That had to be it. Nothing else could make her feel like this.

It seemed incredible that such a thing could be true, incredible that she should discover it at such a moment. It was even more incredible that she must act as though nothing had changed when everything had.

"What the hell are you doing here?" Lantz demanded. "If you had any sense, you'd be halfway to Mexico by now." It was obvious from Lantz's expression that he hated Chet.

"I don't see that's any of your business," Melody said.

"It damned well is when you're harboring a killer."

Melody's emotions, too near the surface, too much in turmoil, couldn't be contained. It passed all comprehension that Lantz couldn't see anything wrong in what his son had done, yet he considered Chet's defense of himself a criminal act. "If anybody should be called a killer, it's Blade," she said. "Have you already forgotten he murdered Tom Neland?"

"And your gunfighter shot my boy and Billy Mason."

"Even a gunfighter is allowed to defend himself when he's drawn on by two men," Chet said. "You've imposed on Miss Jordan's patience long enough. Say what you have to say and leave."

Lantz flinched. Melody realized he'd started to draw his gun, then remembered what had happened that first day.

"Melody may be foolish enough to let you stay here until you're well, but you've no say about the ranch," Lantz said.

"The Jordans made me foreman yesterday. I'm responsible for the ranch and the safety of everyone on it. As far as I'm concerned, you're a nuisance we could do without. But if they want to keep seeing you, I'll make no objection. Your son, on the other hand, is a lawless murderer. If he sets foot on this place, I'll have him arrested. If he harms so much as one hair on the head of anybody here, I'll kill him."

Melody felt something inside her go cold. She

wanted to get rid of Lantz, but Chet shouldn't have thrown down the gauntlet in such a forthright manner. It would only make Lantz more determined to kill him.

How, in the midst of all this anger and violence, could her love survive?

"How is Sydney?" Chet asked, turning to her. "Can I see him?"

Melody had begun to turn her head to answer Chet when she saw Lantz go for his gun. Before the cry of alarm could leave her throat, Chet had dropped to a crouch, his drawn gun pointed at Lantz. In that same moment Melody saw Luke's hand lash out and strike Lantz's arm at the wrist, causing him to drop his gun.

Fury and disgust filled Melody.

"Lantz Royal, how dare you draw on a man when he isn't looking!"

"Why did you stop me, you fool?" Lantz shouted at his gunfighter. "I could have killed the bastard."

"Too many witnesses," the man muttered in a harsh whisper. He pointed to the porch. Belle and Bernice had come outside.

"That was the act of a coward," Melody said. "Leave and don't come back. You can have nothing to say to us."

"You can be sure I'll be back," Lantz shouted at her, "to throw you out of this house when I take over. And you," he shouted even louder as he turned to Chet, "you're as good as dead!"

"Next time you start to draw a gun on me, I won't hold my fire," Chet said.

"Next time you'll be dead."

"Maybe I'll come looking for you first," Chet said. "That would be easier than waiting."

It was obvious Lantz hadn't considered that. He looked shocked.

"Let's go," Luke growled. He turned his horse and dug his heels into the animal's sides. His line-back dun sprang forward.

"I'm going to kill you!" Lantz shouted at Chet as he turned to follow.

Melody stood riveted to the spot as she watched the two men ride away. Lantz had sworn he'd kill Chet. It didn't make any difference to him that his own son had started the trouble or that Blade had actually tried to kill Chet and Sydney. It didn't make any difference to him what other people might think, what the law might say. He had decided Chet ought to die, and he had the money to hire more gunfighters if Luke couldn't do it.

It was beyond her comprehension, but she did understand one thing. Chet had to leave. She could never forgive herself if anything happened to him because of her.

"You must go," Melody said to Chet. "I'm grateful for what you've done, but I don't want to be responsible for you being hurt again."

"I agree with her," Belle said. She stood at the porch rail, her eyes following Lantz as he rode into the distance. "I never thought Lantz Royal could be so cruel."

"What are you going to do about Lantz's threat to take your ranch?" Chet asked.

"Let him have it," Melody said. "It's not worth dying for. Belle and the boys can go back to Virginia with me. We can sell the stock. That will give us enough money to get started."

"So you're quitting," Chet said.

Melody felt as though she'd been slapped. How could he call her a quitter when all she wanted to

do was keep him and her family safe? "Do you
think a few cows are worth getting killed for?"

"I don't care what you do with this ranch once
you're sure of its ownership. You can give it back
to the Indians for all I care, but you can't let a
petty tyrant like Lantz take it away."

"It's my ranch. I can do what I want with it."

"Fine. Sell out, run away with your tail between
your legs, but I'm staying. I'm going to teach
Lantz Royal there's at least one more man in this
world he can't bully. It's a shame the daughter of
the first man lacks her father's courage."

"I don't lack courage," Melody said, her cheeks
hot with anger. "I'm just not a fool."

Chet's expression turned scornful. "If you were
a man, you'd stay."

That hurt incredibly. All her life she'd wondered if her father would have taken her to Texas
with him if she had been a boy. Emotion, raw and
volatile, spilled over and she lost her temper. She
walked up to Chet and slapped him as hard as she
could. "Don't you ever say that again," she said,
her chest heaving from the force of her anger.

His gaze didn't falter. "I call it as I see it. And
from what I can see, you've been running ever
since you got here."

Her palm stung from the first blow, but she
itched to ball up her fist and punch him. She regretted she hadn't given him a horse the minute
he asked and let him ride out of there several days
ago. "Why do you say that?" she asked.

"You were itching to sell your part of the ranch
so you could get back to your safe and cozy Richmond. Then you were considering marrying
Lantz even though you didn't love him. You kept

tying Tom Neland's hands so he couldn't defend you or your ranch properly."

"Are you saying I'm responsible for Tom's death?" That would be too much. She'd tie him to a horse and run him all the way to Santa Fe.

"Tom made his own decisions. I'm saying you've been running from Texas ever since you got here. You don't like us, and you don't like the way we do things. It's time to find out what you're made of. Either you're soft and scared, or you've got the courage your father had when he came here by himself and carved this ranch out of land he took and held against men determined to take it from him. I say you should go back to Richmond and let your brothers fight for the ranch. Sydney's still got a few things to learn, but he's got guts."

"His *guts* nearly got him killed."

"But he didn't die."

"Because you saved him."

"That's how we do it out here. We help each other."

"Like I helped you when you were shot?"

"I had hope for you then."

"Why should you care whether I'm a man or a woman? I mean nothing to you."

Melody's surprise at her own words was mirrored in Chet's expression. She hadn't meant it the way it sounded. Yet the moment the words were out of her mouth, she knew that was exactly what she wanted to know. She was in love with this man who'd insulted her and dared to call her a coward. She wanted to know he'd done it because he cared.

But just as quickly as she recognized and accepted the change in her feelings, she realized

Chet wasn't ready to accept the truth. Even if he were, he would never consider confessing it in front of Belle and Bernice. It was unfair to ask that of him now, but she meant to do it later. If she was about to do something stupid, she wanted to know he was equally ready to be insane.

"I don't like to see anybody cheated out of what belongs to them," Chet said, "especially not women."

"How very gallant of you. How many people do you propose to kill to keep this terrible event from coming to pass?"

"None."

"How will you do that? You were the one who just accused me of tying Tom's hands because I wouldn't let him hire a gunfighter."

"You've been sitting around, waiting for Lantz to strike. I propose to carry the battle to him."

"What will that prove?"

"That he can be in just as much danger as you."

"But he's got twice as many men as we do," Belle said.

"He doesn't have to know we're acting alone."

"What do you propose to do?"

"Attack him as soon as I can get it set up." Chet turned to Melody. "Are you willing to stay here that long?"

Melody realized that question asked a great deal more than whether she was willing to stay until the confrontation was over. It asked if she understood what Chet was talking about. Quite suddenly—surprisingly—she found she did. She understood how he felt, how her father would have felt, how *she* would have felt if anyone had asked the same question about Virginia. She didn't want to fight. She wanted to live peacefully with her neighbors and let the law settle all disputes. But Lantz was threatening to take away a ranch that belonged to her, and she wouldn't let him do it. She *couldn't*. She didn't like violence, but she would do what she must. And she wouldn't apologize or feel guilty for it ever again.

She looked him straight in the eye. "I'll do more than that. I'm going to be riding alongside you."

Chapter Fourteen

At first Chet hadn't believed Melody meant it when she said she would ride with him. He had argued with her, then stated flatly that he wouldn't allow her to go with him. He'd even ordered the men to refuse to saddle her horse. But he was discovering that even though Melody Jordan had grown up in Richmond and preferred the softer life of that old Southern city, she was quite capable of being as stubborn as any Texan.

"This is my ranch, and the safety of the men who work for me is my responsibility," she said when Belle added her entreaties to Chet's threats.

"That's absurd," Belle had said. "No one expects women to act like men, not even in Texas."

"No self-respecting man would allow it," Chet added.

"You forget I own this place," Melody said. "I can fire you and lead the men myself."

Which was proof of his folly in telling her his plans before everything was over and done with. But then, he'd never met a woman who insisted upon knowing every move he planned to make. Nor had he met one willing to put on pants and learn to ride astride. That had probably shocked him the most.

"It's indecent," Belle had protested. "It would ruin your reputation if anybody found out."

"Isn't that the whole point of mounting a raid at night?" she'd asked, turning to Chet. "That no one will see us?"

"It's to give us the advantage of surprise, not to disguise females parading around in men's clothing."

"I don't see why it shouldn't do both."

"Because you'll be in the way. You won't know what to do."

"You can teach me."

"We've got only two days."

"I thought you Texans could do anything."

He couldn't take credit for her learning to ride astride so quickly. His concentration was practically nonexistent. By the time he'd satisfied himself that Melody was capable of riding in the raid, he was almost too weak to go himself. The fact that he'd spent each night tossing in his sleep hadn't helped. He'd moved into the bunkhouse with the other men, but he'd become so sensitive to Melody that he felt her presence before he actually saw her.

He'd told himself he was a fool to stay, that honor didn't require him to hang around when there was danger from two sides. But honor did require that he not abandon two helpless women and two vulnerable boys to the greed of Lantz Royal or the madness of his son. Since Chet didn't really want to leave, it wasn't difficult to decide to be honorable.

Besides, if he was going to die anyway, this was as good a time and place as any.

"If Lantz is rounding up a herd, why aren't we?" Melody asked.

Five of them were on their way to the part of Lantz Royal's range where he was holding a herd of about five hundred steers.

"You would have been if you hadn't had all this trouble with rustlers on top of Tom getting killed."

"Shouldn't we start?"

"I will as soon as we settle with Lantz."

Chet had taken care to see everyone rode dark horses and wore dark clothing. Fortunately, heavy clouds obscured the moon. He couldn't have wanted a more perfect night for the raid. Now if he could just carry it off and get Melody back to the ranch safely . . . He swore to himself that he wouldn't let her set one foot off the place ever again.

"Now remember, we're supposed to be rustlers," Chet reminded the men when they were within sight of the herd. "We can't afford for anybody to be caught and identified."

"But I thought you wanted Lantz to know he was vulnerable," Melody said.

"I do, but I don't want him to know who did this just yet. He's got enough cowhands to burn us out any time he chooses. The longer he stays confused, the better chance we'll have to do more damage." He gathered them close. "Remember, we want to drive the herd right through the middle of their camp to cause the maximum amount of damage and to delay their pursuit as long as possible. After that, we scatter the herd as far as we can. He'll set his men to rounding them up as soon as they recapture their horses. Stay low in the saddle so they won't get a good shot at you."

He could barely see the herd in the distance. Their dark shapes blended well with the ground. He didn't know how many men were on guard duty. That was the first thing to be determined, and it was his job.

"Wait until I give the signal," he said. "Anybody being seen before then will ruin the whole thing. Do you men know where you're supposed to be?"

They nodded.

"Okay. I'll need about half an hour. Watch for my signal. You'll have exactly one minute after that. Understand?"

They nodded again.

"Okay. Move out." Melody already knew she was to stay with him. It had been the only condition under which he would allow her to ride with them. He waited while the men disappeared, walking their horses slowly to keep from making too much noise. "Follow me," he said to Melody. "No matter what happens, don't speak above a whisper."

They were to take up position on the far side of the herd—after he'd checked out the crew to make sure they were asleep, after he'd disabled any night riders.

Never before had Chet felt so nervous at a time like this, but then he'd never done anything like this with a woman at his side. He'd also never felt such an urge to repeat his cautions, to warn her of the additional dangers that occurred to him with each passing minute. Only resolute exercise of willpower kept him quiet.

It didn't take them long to determine that Lantz had posted only one guard. That surprised Chet, considering the rustling in the area. Maybe Lantz figured no one would attempt a raid with so many of his crew present.

"Wait here while I loose the horses," Chet whispered to Melody. "If anything happens before I get back, head straight for the ranch." He didn't like leaving her for even a moment, but he didn't have a choice.

He was in luck. He found the camp quiet and asleep. The fire had burned down to coals, but it gave off enough light for him to make out a dozen or so men scattered about sleeping in their bedrolls. The horses were some distance away, held by a rope corral. Chet untied the ropes. They would scatter the moment the stampede started. It would take Lantz's crew hours to find them. Chet hurried back to where he'd left Melody.

"I feel useless," she whispered when he returned.

He refrained from saying that if she'd really wanted to be useful, she'd have stayed at the ranch. "Stay close when we approach the night rider," he said. "And remember, don't turn in the saddle no matter what you do. You don't have a man's profile."

She'd pinned her hair up under a hat, but even a coat couldn't entirely hide the outline of her breasts. Chet had already given that part of her anatomy more thought than was comfortable. If he didn't concentrate, he could make a mistake that would ruin the whole operation. He forced himself to look straight ahead.

233

"We can't come at him from under cover," he told Melody. "He's got to see us coming, or he'll know there's something wrong."

"Are you sure he can't see our faces?"

"I can't even see your face under that hat. Just keep your horse at a steady walk. Let me do all the talking until we come alongside. Then you've got to distract him long enough for me to get close enough to knock him out without giving him a chance to raise the alarm."

"I know what to do. You've told me a hundred times."

He knew that. He just wished he felt as confident as she did that they could pull it off.

The rider saw them coming and gave a friendly wave. Chet waved back.

"I don't like this," Melody whispered. "He's an innocent bystander."

"If he had any idea what we're about to do, he'd shoot us out of the saddle right now," Chet whispered back. "Think of that, and maybe you won't feel so sorry for him."

Chet knew the critical moment would come when the man realized he didn't recognize Chet. He was banking on Lantz's crew being so big that the cowhands didn't always know each other.

"What are you doing out of your bedrolls?" the man asked when they were still twenty yards apart.

"Lantz decided you needed help," Chet said. He hoped he'd made his voice gravelly enough to make it hard to recognize. "He's worried about those rustlers."

"But I heard him say they wouldn't attack during roundup."

"I guess he decided not to take a chance. He sent us to help out."

"It's not time for the shift change yet."

The man was getting suspicious. He kept looking from Chet to Melody and back again.

"We were awake, so we decided to come on."

"Who are you?" the man demanded. "I don't recognize you."

"Bob," Chet said, going for the most common name he could think of.

The cowhand drew his gun. "We don't have nobody named Bob. The last time we did, he was a short, fat fella. Who the hell are you?"

Chet cursed under his breath. There was no way he could get to the man before he could raise the alarm. He didn't look like one to hesitate.

What happened next was totally unexpected. Melody pulled off her hat, shook out her hair, and spoke in a sultry voice Chet had never heard her use before.

"We're lost," she said. "We only pretended to be part of your crew so you wouldn't shoot us."

The cowhand gaped at Melody, his wits apparently unable to cope with seeing a beautiful woman in a man's clothing out on the range in the middle of the night. The gun hung useless in his hand. It was a simple matter for Chet to ride in close and bring his gun butt down on the man's head right behind his ear.

"Hold his horse while I tie him up and gag him with his bandana," Chet said.

Once he was certain the man was in no position to raise an alarm, Chet led the man's horse to a protected pocket among some rocks, where he would be out of danger during the stampede.

"What did you mean by taking off your hat?" Chet demanded.

"He had a gun in his hand," Melody said as she worked to hide her hair under her hat once more. "It was obvious you couldn't get close enough to knock him out."

"But he's going to remember you when he wakes up."

"Nobody will believe he saw a woman," she said. Her hair was hidden again and she faced him defiantly. "They'll think he's been drinking. Let's get on with it."

Chet wasn't sure he knew the woman he'd turned loose by telling Melody Jordan she ought to have been a man. She obviously had a second side to her personality, one that could rise to any challenge. The question was, would she go back to her old self when the crisis was over? He wasn't sure how he felt about that. There was something to be said for both Melody Jordans.

They quickly moved in close to the herd. "Be careful," Chet said. "Sometimes a herd will panic at a sudden light." The steers hardly noticed when he struck a match. Only a few turned their heads when he ignited a small stick he'd earlier dipped in pitch.

"Do you think they'll be able to see that?" Melody asked. "It looks awfully small."

"It's the only light out here. They'll see it." He moved it slowly back and forth three times then extinguished it. "Get ready," he said to Melody as he tossed the stick away. "As soon as I fire the shots, ride toward the cows making as much noise as you can."

The minute seemed to drag by. Chet had

mounted at least a dozen nighttime attacks before, but this one had given him the most worry. He was certain that stemmed from Melody's having come along.

"This is it," Chet warned Melody. "Let's go!"

Chet fired several shots into the air and let out an Indian yell guaranteed to raise the hair on the back of any man's neck. Immediately, on either side of him, shots and shouts reverberated though the night.

In an instant, the herd was on its feet, running.

For one moment Chet experienced the exhilaration of being on a horse, galloping through the night, the woman he loved at his side.

Hell and damnation! What a time to discover he was in love! The shock was so great he nearly lost his grip. He swayed in the saddle.

"Are you all right?" Melody called.

"Fine," he lied. "Watch out for debris when we go through the camp. Can you jump?"

He was startled to hear her laugh. It seemed unreal. No delicately nurtured Southern lady laughed as she rode a horse at a breakneck pace through the night. Certainly not a woman who had probably never even been out at night except in a carriage.

"What a time to ask that question."

"Can you?" he called back, irritated at his own lack of forethought.

"Yes! Virginians may be old-fashioned by your standards, but we take pride in our ability to ride a horse over anything in our path."

Proof of her statement followed quickly. They rode through a camp reduced to shambles by more than two thousand pounding hooves. The only thing not ground to bits was the overturned chuck wagon. Melody's horse jumped a battered cook pot. They were in and out of the camp in seconds. Melody's losing her hat was the only thing that went wrong. Since Lantz and his crew were on foot and unable to follow, Chet figured it didn't matter.

He was wrong. Lantz Royal appeared out of the night like an evil apparition.

"It's Lantz!" Chet shouted at Melody. How the hell had he caught a horse? Chet grabbed Melody's reins. "Come on! Let's get out of here."

"It's too late," Melody shouted back. "Leave me. I can handle Lantz."

"Don't be a fool. How will you explain helping to stampede his herd?"

"I'll tell him you're rustlers and you kidnapped me. Now leave. That's what a rustler would do."

"I can't leave."

"You've got to. If you stay, there'll be a gunfight. One of you will be killed. I don't want that. Besides, he'll think I'm trying to steal his herd. He might even think I'm one of the rustlers. That would be worse still. Go!" she hissed. "Leave Lantz to me."

When he looked undecided, she jerked her reins out of his hand and veered sharply away from him. "Help!" she screamed and waved frantically at Lantz. Almost immediately Chet felt a bullet whistle past his head. Trusting that Melody hadn't overestimated her powers of persuasion, he dropped low in the saddle and rode beyond the range of Lantz's gun.

He rode hard. He meant to scatter the cattle so widely that it would take Lantz's crew a week to collect them again. Yet he couldn't stop worrying about Melody. He didn't share Melody's certainty that Lantz wouldn't harm her, no matter what he thought she had done.

Abruptly he pulled his horse up and turned around. He couldn't leave her. He'd let her play out this hand as she wanted, but he'd be watching in case things didn't go as she hoped.

Melody was certain she'd never been so tired in her life, not even after a day of working in her aunt's fields. Her plan had worked exactly as she'd hoped. Lantz never questioned why she would be out by herself at night looking for signs of the rustlers. In his mind, being raised outside of Texas was excuse enough for doing any number of stupid things. Throwing herself upon his protection as though he were a gallant knight riding to her rescue had made him forget he was furious at her. He was once more the all-powerful male, she the helpless female. Though it galled her pride, she played her role to the hilt.

The only scary time came when they found the cowhand Chet had tied up. She told them she'd only helped the rustlers because they'd threatened to shoot her. The other cowhands accepted that as a perfectly reasonable explanation. The fellow with the sore head seemed inclined to question her until Lantz told him to shut up.

Lantz was escorting her home. Finally. She'd spent most of the night listening to him rant and rave about rustlers and that Luke was never around when he was wanted. "You've got to promise you won't go riding out alone again," Lantz said.

"I promise," Melody replied. "I just hope Belle hasn't been up all night worrying."

After Lantz's hands had captured some of the

horses, he had sent the crew after the herd and he took Melody back to his ranch. She had wanted to go straight home, but Lantz had been certain she needed to rest before she'd have the strength to ride in a buckboard back to the Spring Water.

She hadn't enjoyed seeing Blade again. He had been just as angry and sarcastic as she expected. He seemed to have gotten it into his head that she had changed her mind and now wanted to marry his father. A declaration that she wouldn't marry Lantz if he were the last man on earth wouldn't suit her plans right then. It wasn't easy, but she kept quiet. Blade's barbs continually pricked her conscience and her pride until she climbed into the buckboard to return to the Spring Water.

"You ought to get you a proper foreman," Lantz was saying. "You don't want a gunfighter. Anyway, I'm going to kill him, so you'll have to get somebody else. I'll send one of my men over until I can find somebody for you."

Melody decided not to reply. It would do no good to remind Lantz that Blade had started all the trouble.

She would have asked Chet to leave—at least to hide for a few weeks—if she thought he'd pay any attention to her. But he wouldn't. Now she didn't want him to go, at least not until she could find out if he loved her. She didn't know what she'd do if he didn't. She didn't know what she'd do if he did. The whole concept of marrying a gunfighter was entirely beyond her comprehension. But that was part of the problem. No matter what Chet said or did, she couldn't think of him as a gunfighter. He'd not only risked his life for them, he was staying around, risking it longer, just to make sure they were safe. And he hadn't killed anybody. Wasn't that what gunfighters did? They worked for money, didn't care who was shot as long as they got paid, and left the minute their job was done, regardless of what happened to anybody else.

"I'm surprised you didn't faint when they caught you," Lantz said.

"They didn't want to hurt me," she told him. "They just wanted to use me in case you caught them."

"The rotten cowards. I can't believe anybody from Texas would do anything so terrible."

"They probably came from New Mexico or Arizona."

Lantz missed the sarcasm. She decided she'd better watch her tongue before she ruined a successful ploy.

"Will your men have much trouble finding your cows?" she asked.

"It will depend on how many those sneaking bastards ran off. I knew I should have brought Luke with me. Blade is strong enough to take care of himself now."

She had heard more than enough of Blade's anger at having Luke act as his bodyguard. Blade, too, was determined to kill Chet at the first opportunity. It seemed as though all she'd been able to do was make half the men in Concho County determined to kill the man she loved.

"They won't steal another cow from me, by God," Lantz swore. "As soon as I drop you off at the Spring Water, I'm going to get all the ranchers together. We're going to outfit a posse and keep them on the trail until they find those bastards and hang every one of them."

241

Melody felt cold dread in the pit of her stomach. She doubted Lantz or the other ranchers would distinguish between scattering a herd and rustling them, not when the man doing the scattering had already been marked for death.

She was relieved to be nearing the ranch. But this could be the most dangerous moment yet. Who would be there? What would they say when they saw Lantz bringing her home?

The worst possible person to deal with the situation was the first out of the house. Belle came fluttering down the steps acting as though she hadn't a brain in her head, babbling incoherently, and throwing herself on Melody as if she'd been brought back from the dead.

"Chet told me everything," she whispered in a startled Melody's ears. "Just agree with everything I say."

Next Belle released Melody and flung herself at Lantz.

"You're an angel of mercy, our good shepherd, our knight in shining armor," Belle trilled. "Thank God you found her." She put her arms round Lantz's waist and hugged him until his eyes threatened to pop out of his head. "We thought she was dead. I had the boys up all night, but we couldn't find a trace of her. Even Chet had begun to fear we'd never see her alive again."

By this time Bernice and Neill had come out of the house to add their bit to the scene. Even Sydney came to the door.

"Run saddle a horse and go after Chet," Belle said to Neill. "Tell him to bring the men in. Lantz has found Melody, and she's perfectly safe." She and Bernice both began to flutter around Melody, effectively separating her from Lantz, moving her quickly toward the ranch house.

"You must have been horrified."

"Terrified."

"I'm sure I would have fainted dead away."

"Did one of those murderers dare to lay a hand on you?"

"Lantz, you must go straight to the sheriff and tell him to organize a posse and go after those murderers at once. No telling who they might decide to kidnap next." Belle shuddered eloquently. "No woman can feel safe in her bed until they're behind bars."

"They'll be hanged," Lantz said, "every man jack of them. I'll see to it myself."

He started to tell them exactly what he meant to do, but again Bernice and Belle started talking at the same time. Neill and Sydney disappeared.

"She must go straight to bed," Bernice said.

"And be given nothing but thin soup until she regains her strength."

"Poor child must be running on nothing but nerves."

"I don't mean to sound ungrateful," Belle told Lantz, "but you'll have to go away immediately. I must put my stepdaughter to bed at once."

"I'll come by tomorrow to see how she's doing," Lantz said.

"Certainly, but you must not expect to see Melody," Belle said. "She's suffered a terrible shock. I doubt she'll feel strong enough to see anyone for at least a week."

Melody didn't dare turn around to see Lantz's expression—she was afraid the smile on her face would give her away—but she was certain he looked shocked and incredulous. So was she. She couldn't believe the silly, helpless Belle she'd known for the last six months could have created such a masterful charade. It was far better than anything she could have done. Melody managed to maintain her pose until she was inside the house. Then she started to giggle. It was the release of tension as much as anything else.

"How did you know what to do?" she demanded as soon as she'd recovered her power to speak.

"Chet told us what happened," Belle said. She sank down on the sofa and started fanning herself. "I think I'm going to faint."

"Don't you dare," Melody said, sitting up straight. "After the way you've behaved since Sydney was shot, I'll never believe you're a fainting, silly female again."

"Is that what you thought me?" Belle said, seeming only mildly interested.

"You know it was. Now where is Chet, and how did he know what was going on?"

"I'm here," he said, stepping into the parlor from the dining room. "I knew because I followed you."

Melody sat up with the abruptness of a released spring. Here was the man she loved. Despite facing certain death if he were caught, he'd followed her to make sure she came to no harm. But she should have expected that. He'd been risking his life for her and her family ever since he arrived.

She'd always thought he looked incredibly handsome. Now he looked tired, dusty, worried, and more handsome than ever. She struggled to make her breathing relaxed and even. There was no hope of calming her racing heart.

"You didn't need to do that," she said. "I was perfectly safe."

"Of course he should have done it," Belle said, getting to her feet. "He couldn't leave you to the good graces of that man." She shuddered again eloquently. "And to think I once wanted you to marry him. I have to check on Sydney. He shouldn't have been out of bed. He'll be wanting his dinner, I'm sure. Still nothing but soup for him, Bernice."

Bernice left the room. Belle paused in the doorway. "You're not to do this again. I don't think my heart can stand it."

Melody wasn't sure she was ready to be alone with Chet. She wanted some time to calm the tumult of her emotions, to sort them out, to decide whether she was hopelessly in love or had simply misjudged her feelings in the midst of a crisis. But one look eliminated that question. She had fallen deeply and irrevocably in love with a gunfighter, and she wouldn't care if he came wrapped in gun belts, as long as he loved her back.

She suddenly felt awkward. There was so much she wanted to say, so much she wanted to know, yet she felt she couldn't say any of it, ask any of the dozens of questions buzzing about in her mind. How did she ask a man she'd caused to be shot, practically turned into a hunted animal, if he loved her? He ought to want to get as far away from her as possible.

"I agree with Belle," Chet said, a faint smile on his face. "You aren't to do this again. I know my heart can't stand it."

Melody tried to pull herself together. He couldn't have meant those words the way they sounded—at least, not the way she wanted them to sound. She had to stop reading things into what he said.

"You didn't have to follow me," she said. "I was perfectly safe." Her voice didn't sound like itself. It seemed unusually loud. "But I'm glad you did. I was petrified somebody might say the wrong thing when Lantz brought me to the house." Suddenly remembering the danger, she turned to Chet. "You've got to be careful. He's determined to put together a posse with orders not to stop until they find and hang the rustlers."

"I'm not in any danger. He'll find all his cows as long as he keeps looking."

She couldn't understand why he never seemed upset by anything. Lantz wanted him dead and was going to put a posse on his trail, Chet had spent the better part of the night and half the day hiding in rocks, and he seemed almost cheerful. Didn't the man have any fear, or had he been living with fear so long he didn't feel it anymore?

"You really shouldn't stay here. We can get along without you." It was a feeble protest, entirely lacking in conviction. It sounded more like a plea for him to stay.

"We've already been over that. Now I'm going out. Don't bother to ask. You're not going if I have to tie you to your bed."

Melody felt she ought to protest being ordered about in such a peremptory fashion, but the truth was she didn't want to go. "What are you going to do?"

"Just burn a few haystacks at Lantz's ranch."

"He'll be ready to kill."

"Maybe, but he'll realize he's not immune to attack."

"I don't want you putting yourself in danger

again." That sounded dangerously like a declaration of something, but she didn't care.

"Now is the best time. Lantz has every man he can spare looking for his cows. I doubt there'll be anyone on the place."

"Blade will be there."

"I'll stay away from the house."

"Are you sure you have to do this?"

"We can either let Lantz bully and browbeat you until you and Belle give up, or we can convince him you're here to stay."

She sighed. He had her blocked in again. She couldn't back down without looking like a weak woman, and she did want to humble Lantz. She just didn't want to endanger Chet doing it. "Okay, but you've got to promise me you'll be very careful."

"Why?"

The question seemed completely unnecessary. Anyone would have said the same thing. But she realized almost immediately that he was asking her something very important. The hinted smile was gone.

That excited her. It scared her at the same time. This business of caring deeply about a man wasn't as easy as it seemed. Endless ramifications sprang up to demand their share of her attention. In desperation, she shoved them all aside. He'd asked a simple question, and he deserved an answer. Everything else could wait.

"Because I like you," she managed to say. This time her voice sounded fuzzy and weak. "I've so much reason to be grateful to you that it would be—"

"I don't give a damn if you're grateful or not,"

Chet barked, his voice so sharp that she jumped. "Do you like me, or is it my guns?"

"I hate your guns," she snapped, not sounding the least bit faint now. "I can't imagine why I should like a gunfighter as much as I like you, but I can't help myself. It has nothing to do with drawing fast or chasing cows about in the middle of the night or burning haystacks or—"

He'd crossed the room in a few swift strides. Before she could ask what he meant to do, he'd swept her into his arms and was kissing her so fiercely, she wondered if she'd survive. His arms wrapped around her, gripping her in an unbreakable embrace. Only she didn't want to break it. After the initial shock, she felt wonderful, exhilarated. She knew the answer to her question.

Then, just as suddenly, he released her and stepped back. She couldn't understand why he looked like a man suffering torment. It had been torment to her not to know what he felt, to fear he might despise her as much as she'd led him to believe she despised him. But now that she knew, now that she could let hope grow unhindered, she felt wonderful.

"I shouldn't have done that," he said, his voice rough with emotion. "I promise I won't do it again."

Then, before she could tell him she wanted him to do it many times more, he was gone.

She stood there, stunned and bemused, confused and delighted, weak and suddenly bursting with energy. It was an odd feeling, being in love. She hadn't known what it would feel like, but she'd never expected this. It was really quite ordinary in one sense, totally insane in another. The contrast left her feeling as though she didn't know her head from her feet. It might be a good thing if she figured that out.

Then she would turn her thoughts to Chet. It was obvious he didn't think being in love was a good thing. From the look on his face, he seemed to equate it with tooth extraction. She had to convince him that it was indeed a state much to be desired. Then she had to figure out what she was going to do about her future.

She saw storm clouds in virtually every direction.

Chapter Fifteen

Luke watched with disgust as Blade proceeded to get really drunk. The boy wasn't a happy drunk. He turned morose and bitter, talked almost without stopping. He seemed to hate just about everybody and everything, including his father and Melody Jordan. Luke was treated to a detailed account of how Blade had fallen in love with Melody the first time he saw her and how his father had elbowed him aside to pursue her himself. He was told that her refusal to marry Lantz had revived Blade's respect for her, as well as his hopes, only to have them dashed to the ground again when she threw herself at Lantz after he rescued her from the kidnappers.

"You want to know what else I think?" Blade demanded in a slurred voice.

Luke didn't.

"I think she arranged the whole thing," Blade

continued, even though he got no encouragement. "There aren't any kidnappers around here. Nobody to kidnap. I bet she changed her mind about marrying Pa. She knew he was mad as fire, so she arranged the kidnapping and stampede so she could get in his good graces again. Worked, too, dammit!" Blade took another swallow from the whiskey bottle. "And you can bet that business of staying in bed for a week is a sham, too. She's as strong as a horse. She just wants to work on his sympathy."

"You can't blame her," Luke said. "If your pa's going to take her ranch, she probably figures he owes her something."

Blade snorted. "She's just trying to get him wound around her finger good and tight so he'll do anything she wants."

Luke was irritated enough to enjoy seeing someone—anyone—manipulate Lantz.

Blade banged the whiskey bottle down on the table so hard, Luke was surprised it didn't break.

"Pa's a fool for a pretty woman," Blade said. "Hell, Belle could probably have got him to marry her if Melody hadn't showed up so fast."

Luke was so tired of hearing about the Royal men and their love affairs that he was about ready to quit. This wasn't the job he'd been hired to do. He'd wanted Lantz to keep Blade at home where he could be controlled, but Luke wasn't willing to spend all his time babysitting. When Luke had wanted to go with the posse, Lantz had said he was to stay with Blade. Lantz had considered himself invulnerable until the rustlers scattered his herd. Their kidnapping Melody had rattled him good. He had started to worry they might attempt to do the same thing to Blade. Lantz didn't even want Blade to go outside for exercise.

"You think that was rustlers went after Pa's herd?" Blade asked.

Luke nearly returned a curt, uninterested reply, but he stopped himself. He'd detected a subtle change in Blade's manner. There seemed to be some bewilderment in his attitude, as though the presence of rustlers surprised him. Maybe surprise wasn't the right word—more like confusion—and it was causing Blade to think. Luke didn't understand what there was to think about.

"Everybody knows there's rustling going on," Luke answered. "That's why your father hired me."

"I know, but—"

Blade left that sentence unfinished as he took another swallow of whiskey. He sank deep into thought again. It was clear something was bothering him, and Luke had the feeling it wasn't Melody's supposed plan to get herself back in Lantz's good graces.

"It *was* a trick." Blade said that almost defiantly, as though he was trying to convince himself.

Quite suddenly Luke was certain that Blade knew something about the rustlers. He wondered if Blade could be the insider who kept the rustlers informed. But that didn't make sense. Blade wouldn't help people steal from his own father. That would take money out of his own pocket. Besides, stampeding the herd, even if Lantz's men recaptured every animal, would cost Lantz thousands of dollars in lost weight. Still, Blade knew something. Luke took a sip from his own whiskey and settled back to wait. Blade would soon be drunk enough to tell anything he knew.

Luke got up to stretch his legs. He knew how to play the waiting game—his job required it—but he occasionally got impatient. He walked over to the window and looked out. Clouds obscured the moon for the third night in a row. He expected rain soon. All the buildings were quiet and dark. Lantz had every available hand out rounding up the scattered herd. That left no explanation as to why Luke saw a pinpoint of light on the far side of one of the buildings. Nor did it explain why the light moved and then disappeared. One of the hands must have come back. But they never used lanterns. There was always enough light to see once your eyes adjusted to the dark.

Luke's hand instinctively reached for the gun at his side. He turned, walked quickly to the gun rack, and took down a rifle. He checked it to make certain it was loaded.

Blade peered at Luke. "What are you doing?"

"Someone's outside."

Blade snorted. "Pa's got nearly thirty hands on the place. Someone's always outside."

"I saw a light."

"It's darker than the bowels of hell out tonight," Blade said.

"Has it occurred to you that those rustlers may have run off the cows to get the hands away from the house?"

"What for?"

"Your pa's convinced Melody's foreman is out to kill you. If she arranged the stampede to get back into his good graces, couldn't he also be using it to draw the men away from the house so he'd have a better chance to kill you?"

"Is that how you get work?" Blade demanded

scornfully. "Scaring old men with sons to protect?"

"How do you explain that fire?"

The disdainful look wiped from his face, Blade lurched to his feet and staggered across the room. He propped himself up against the window frame and peered into the night.

"I don't see any fire," he said.

"They're two of them now," Luke said. "Look over there, beyond the small corral."

Two small pinpoints of flickering light grew in size.

"It's the haystacks," Blade said, puzzled.

"It's not the haystacks I'm worried about," Luke said. "It's the barn."

Small tongues of flame could be seen lapping at the edges of the roof. Luke backed away from the window so he'd be out of the line of any potential gunfire. "Get down."

"Get down, hell!" Blade said. "I'm going to see if I can put it out."

Luke jerked Blade off balance and into a chair. "You're not going anywhere."

"Are you too good to put out a fire, or do you charge more for manual labor? That's our hay, our barn. What'll we do this winter without them?"

"Let the cows fend for themselves. You and I are staying right here."

The scornful look was back. "You're a coward," Blade said. "You're afraid someone might shoot at you if you go outside." Blade lurched to his feet. "I'm not frightened by any cowardly barn-burner. I'll put enough lead in him to sink him all the way to hell."

Luke pushed Blade back into the chair. "You

evil glance at Chet. "I thought of you
."
nswering glance conveyed no emotion
I go after your son, I'll do it in public
an get the credit. The added reputation
I can charge bigger fees."
was grateful Chet hadn't pointed out
en held a grudge against Blade for set-
e ambush.
Blade doing?" Melody hoped he was
;, but the less she heard about Lantz
n, the happier she would be.
ctor says he'll be strong enough to be
out in a few days. I don't think I'll be
:p him inside after that. I've given Luke
t to let Blade go one step out of the
hout him being right there with him."
ling of uneasiness that seemed to be
ll the time, the certainty something ter-
l so easily happen, grew stronger. Mel-
like to have to think about Luke. She
n Lantz meant to send the gunfighter
as soon as he felt Blade was safe. Lantz
nd of man who would never rest until
back every slight. That was one more
ody found hard to accept about the
ple seemed to live too much by the Old
:—when they bothered to remember
it all.
you for coming by," she said to Lantz.
ou'll excuse me, Chet and I have to be
le says I'm to be back before it gets too

ouldn't be up at all," Lantz said. "You
be getting over that awful experience."
iot riding far. I needed something to do

aren't going anywhere. What reason could anybody have for setting a fire unless they're trying
to get at you?"

"You're making this up, trying to hide your
cowardice."

"If you go out there, anybody could shoot you
from ambush, and you'd never even know they
were there. If I go outside, they can rush this
place and fill you full of enough lead to sink you
a lot deeper than hell. That stampede may not
have been a setup, but I'm sure this is. And killing
you is what they're hoping to do."

As if to underscore Luke's statement, two bullets shattered the glass in one of the windows.
Luke shoved Blade to the floor, put out both the
lanterns in the room, and took a position next to
the window. Several shots followed, but they
were all fired through the same window, probably
to keep Luke and Blade pinned down. Mean-
while, the fires gained a strong hold on the haystacks and the barn. Unless the rain came quickly,
it would be a total loss.

"Why should anyone want to kill me?" Blade
asked.

Luke heard honest wonder in his voice. The boy
really didn't understand. "You killed Belle Jordan's foreman and tried to kill her son. That
seems like more than enough reason to me."

The rain started, but too late to save the barn.

"Would you want to kill me?" Blade asked.

"If you'd shot me, you'd have been dead within
an hour."

Blade looked hard at Luke. Something he saw
in his gaze seemed to give him the understanding
he'd lacked until now. Luke doubted it would
change anything, but at least Blade knew the

stakes were a lot higher than he'd thought. He was no longer a kid. He was playing a man's game. If caught, he would receive a man's penalty.

This was the second time Lantz had come by to see Melody in three days. She couldn't avoid seeing him because she and Chet were about to go riding. Lantz caught them at the corral. Mercifully, he was too occupied with the attacks on his herd and his ranch to press her to reconsider her refusal to marry him. He even talked to Chet without threatening to kill him.

"The posse didn't find a damned thing but the charred remains of a campfire," Lantz complained to Melody, "the one your foreman said he made a few days ago. They disappeared into thin air, like they always do."

"Chet thinks the gang must be made up of cowhands working at the various ranches," Melody said. "He says that would account for them disappearing so easily and for always knowing where everybody's going to be and what they're doing."

Lantz cast Chet an angry look. "Your foreman may be a fast draw, but he's a fool. Our own men couldn't be stealing from us without us knowing. Besides, where are they taking the cattle? They must have stolen two hundred head by now."

"They're holding them up the canyon," Chet said. "I found the place. It's got plenty of water and grass. Nobody goes up that far except at roundup time. The walls are so steep, they're like a natural fortress."

"How are they getting out?"

"I found a narrow game trail," Chet said. "It

would be slow work, but a [ ] could move a lot of cows in [ ] the canyon, they've got the [ ] of Texas to hide in. I imagine [ ] some rancher who rebrands [ ] them in with his herd."

"That's crazy," Lantz said [ ] down that canyon just afte[ ] here. There's no way out."

Melody worried that Chet [ ] Lantz's rude dismissal of h[ ] seem the least upset.

"It's in a side canyon," Che[ ] find it unless you were looki[ ] been worked on, but I'm jus[ ] from the beginning. It's m[ ] that trail that gave the rustle[ ] place. That's another reaso[ ] own cowhands. They're th[ ] ride in and out of that car[ ] suspicion."

"It's time you hired you[ ] Lantz said to Melody, "and [ ] to his murdering ways. If [ ] whole county will soon [ ] throats."

"Did the fire do much da[ ] to get Lantz's mind off the[ ]

"I lost a good barn and [ ] place."

"Do you know who did [ ]

"No."

"Or why?"

"Luke thinks they start[ ] out of the house so they [ ]

besides think about what happened to me. I can sympathize with Blade being shut up in the house."

"Why don't you get one of the regulars to ride with you? I don't trust a fella who'd shoot an innocent young man."

Melody knew it was useless to try to make Lantz see anything he didn't want to see. "Chet is my foreman, and I trust him to take good care of me."

"He didn't take good care of you when you were kidnapped."

"That was my fault."

"You wouldn't have been kidnapped if you were my wife."

"Maybe not, but I could have been burned to death in my bed if whoever burned your barn had decided to set fire to the house instead."

"That won't ever happen again," Lantz said, embarrassed and angry at having been proved vulnerable. He had enjoyed feeling so powerful that no one dared touch him. "I'm keeping men at the house all the time."

"That seems like a wise precaution. Now I must go." She turned her horse. She thought for a moment that Lantz would ride along anyway, but he left them to go on alone.

"I don't know how you put up with his insults without losing your temper," Melody said to Chet almost as soon as Lantz was out of earshot.

"If I shot it out with every man who thought he was better than I am, I'd have been dead or hanged years ago. Men like Lantz always hire somebody else to do their killing for them. All the advantages accrue to them while the onus of being a gunfighter stays with the men they hire."

"Is that why he thinks Blade is entirely blameless in all of this?"

"It's part of it."

Melody sighed. "I'll never understand Texans."

"That has nothing to do with Texas," Chet said. "Powerful men all over the world use armies to do the same thing. They kill millions, declare it to be for the good of their country, and people believe them."

Melody wasn't prepared to discuss history or philosophy with Chet. Besides, he seemed to know a lot more about the world than she did. It occurred to her to wonder how a gunfighter would have become so well educated. She immediately felt guilty for a thought that came dangerously close to putting her in the same category as Lantz.

She was far more concerned with the fact that she and Chet were alone for the first time since the night they'd scattered Lantz's herd. Lying in her bed alone in her room for three days had given Melody plenty of time to become thoroughly acquainted with the radical changes that had occurred in her feelings. She didn't understand why she felt as she did, nor did she know how to justify some of her feelings. They just were, and that was the best she could do in the way of explaining them to herself. The real question, however, wasn't how she felt but what she was going to do about it.

And what Chet would do.

He hadn't acted surprised or pleased when she asked him to ride out with her. He seemed his usual easygoing self, and that was driving Melody crazy. After the way he'd kissed her, how could he possibly act as if nothing had happened? She'd spent hours thinking about it, remembering how it felt, wondering what he'd been thinking, torturing herself with the fear that his silence meant it hadn't been of any real importance to him. She knew men didn't feel the same way about kisses as women did. Any woman who scattered her kisses as thoughtlessly as most men did would soon be named a wanton.

Nor did men seem to consider marriage an integral part of any relationship between a man and a woman. As far as she could tell, many of them considered it an unfortunate necessity. Children, which practically every woman dreamed of having, were even further down on the list. In fact, as far as she was able to tell, men put marriage into that category of things a man did after he'd spent as many years as possible enjoying himself and was too old to do much of anything else.

In contrast, women were expected to marry in their teens, before they'd lost the bloom of youth and were considered too old and too independent to be of interest. These differences annoyed Melody. She found them frightening because she didn't understand them. She couldn't predict how Chet would feel about any of this, but she had to know. It was definitely not proper behavior for a gently bred Southern woman, but if she had to, she'd ask him.

Just thinking about it made her feel warm.

They had been riding for some time. Chet had kept up a steady flow of conversation about grazing, water, cows, roundups, market prices, cowhands, equipment, budgets, supplies—all the things Melody had been so anxious for Tom to teach her, none of which now interested her half

261

as much as knowing what Chet meant when he kissed her. Stealing numerous glances at his profile offered no hint as to what he was thinking now.

"Can we find some place to rest?" Melody asked. "I'm not used to this much riding."

She'd learned one thing about this endless plain they called Central Texas. It wasn't flat. There were hundreds of places where people or cows could hide, and that didn't count the canyon. Chet chose a place where a bend in the creek that flowed out of the canyon was shaded by a grove of cottonwoods. Melody was relieved to slide out of the saddle. She was riding sidesaddle again, but she was out of practice.

"I didn't mean to wear you out," Chet said. "Maybe you shouldn't have come."

At last he showed a little emotion. "I'm all right. I probably need a rest from all the information you've given me as much as from being on horseback."

"Sorry. I didn't mean to bore you."

Didn't this man understand anything about women? How could he be so handsome, look at a woman as if he could eat her up, and understand so little of what she was feeling? She would never have come out here if she hadn't wanted to be with him. There was nothing he couldn't tell her later, or tell the new foreman when they found one. She could have stayed in her bed. She could have gone on talking to Lantz. She could have said she needed to help Belle. She could have said any one of a dozen things, but she'd come riding with him. Alone. Surely he must know that meant something. Surely women in Texas couldn't be that different from their sisters in other parts of the country. Chet was brighter than a lot of the men she knew. What made him so slow to figure out how she felt?

Maybe nice women avoided gunfighters. She would have avoided him if he hadn't practically been forced on her and then proved himself to be nothing like what she'd expected. Maybe rejection was what he expected, what he'd always received. Looking at Chet, she found that hard to believe, but she knew practically nothing about his past. He never talked about himself.

"I just need time to digest all that information," she explained. "I helped my aunt with her farm, but farming in Virginia is nothing like this. It's like having to unlearn everything I know."

"That's why you need a good foreman."

"We've been over that. I don't mean to be this ignorant ever again."

"There'll be no point in worrying about it if you go back to Virginia."

"I'm not going."

She paused. He said nothing, but she could see the reaction in his eyes. It was slight, an infinitesimal change in the iris, a slight increase of tension at the edges of his eyes. She was gradually learning to read the expressions behind his casual acceptance of nearly everything life handed him.

"Aren't you going to ask why I changed my mind?"

"It's none of my business. I doubt—"

"Of course it's your business," she snapped, unable to contain herself any longer. "You kissed me, remember, or have you forgotten?"

"I'll never forget that."

"Neither will I. That's why I changed my mind." There! That was just about as blatant as she

263

could make it without spelling it out. He couldn't doubt what she was trying to tell him now.

"You shouldn't put so much value on one kiss," he said.

She could see the strain it took for him to speak normally. It sounded almost as if each word were prepared separately so their collective meaning wouldn't overwhelm him.

She wasn't going to let him slide over it that easily. "Why did you kiss me?"

"You're a beautiful woman."

"I'm not beautiful. Only passably pretty. Do you kiss every passably pretty woman you see? And bear in mind that includes nearly half of the female population of Texas."

She got a real smile out of him. "If I did that, I'd have been shot by at least a quarter of the men in Texas."

"Okay, why me and not Belle?"

"She's older. She's newly widowed. She's—"

"That's nonsense. She's twice as pretty as I am. Furthermore, everybody knows it's safer to chase widows than single women. Come on, the truth." She moved closer to him, put her hand on his arm, looked up into his eyes.

She was so close, their bodies practically touched and their breaths intermingled—but Chet was a tough nut to crack. She could almost see him turn to stone before her eyes. His arm was hard, unmovable. All warmth seemed to have drained from his body. It was as though he'd abandoned his body and retreated to a tiny place of final defense buried deep inside him. He was determined to stay out of reach, to deny that their kiss had meant anything to him.

She'd come too far—accepted too much, experienced too much, changed too much—to give up now. It had nothing to do with the desperateness of her position. She'd have done the same thing if the ranch had been secure and she'd had ten suitors in Richmond clamoring for her hand. She moved her hand from his arm to his chest. The irises of his eyes contracted so that the white seemed to dominate, but he remained steadfastly immobile.

"It's very pleasing to a woman to know a man wants to kiss her, especially if he likes it well enough to do it more than once." With her right hand she played with a button on his shirt—twisted it between her fingers, drew circles around it—while with her left hand she gripped his forearm and held him close. "But it would be very injurious to her self-esteem to know the experience was so unpleasant he didn't want to repeat it. You don't dislike me that much, do you?"

"I don't dislike you at all. Nor do I want to injure you."

He sounded as if the words had been unwillingly squeezed out between the granite boulders of his self-control, but Melody thought he was weakening. His irises seemed to grow smaller still, as though they, too, were retreating. She splayed her right hand flat against his chest and moved her left up his arm. He flinched visibly.

"You're doing both by ignoring me so completely," she said, her voice as close to soft and sultry as she knew how to make it. "Didn't anybody ever tell you it's impolite to treat a woman with such indifference?"

"It would be more impolite to make her think I felt something for her I didn't."

Melody winced. She guessed she'd gotten her

answer after all. But she had to admit it was a cruel shock to discover that Chet felt nothing for her.

But it was much worse than that. She loved this man, and he didn't love her. She was doomed to live with a broken heart for the rest of her life.

Melody released Chet and moved back. "I wouldn't want you to do anything like that, either. I dislike it when women attempt to entice men into saying what they don't mean."

She turned away when she felt tears start to swim in her eyes. She didn't want him to think she was so unprincipled as to resort to such an overused ploy to get what she wanted. Neither did she want him to think she was a weak, whimpering female.

"It was good of you to take the time to explain things to me," she said, fighting hard against tears that now seemed determined to come despite her most valiant efforts. She moved farther away from Chet, toward the creek. She hoped the soft gurgling sound as it flowed over the rocks and gravel in the stream bed would cover any catch in her voice. She wanted to throw herself in, let the cold water shock her back to normal. But the water would hardly come up to her ankles. "You can go back to your work now. I don't think I want to see anything else today."

She hoped he would go quickly. She didn't think she could hold on much longer.

"I'll take you back."

"I can find my way. Besides, I'm not ready to leave yet. I want to stay here a little while."

"I'll wait."

"Don't!" The word exploded from her, sounding

more like a desperate plea than the indifferent reply she'd intended.

"Are you all right?" he asked. He'd come closer. "Are you overtired?"

The concern in his voice destroyed the last of her control. A sob escaped her. In an instant he'd taken her by the shoulders and turned her to face him. She looked down, avoiding his gaze.

"You're crying."

"No, I'm not."

He put his hand under her chin and forced her head up. She kept her eyes closed. She refused to look at him.

"What's wrong?"

"Nothing."

"You're lying."

"No, I'm just trying to get used to what a stupid man you are." She opened her eyes to see a confused look on his face. "Surely even a Texas gunfighter knows it's embarrassing for a woman to throw herself at a man and be flatly rejected."

"I didn't reject you."

She angrily wiped a tear from her eyes. "Is this more of your *we do it different in Texas* philosophy?" The tears had begun to roll in earnest now, and there was nothing she could do to stop them. She dabbed angrily at her eyes. "That would qualify as a brush-off in any language. I don't want you to think I make a practice of throwing myself at men," she added, finally beginning to get her tears under control. "I didn't even want to like you. But despite your being a gunfighter, I found I liked you very much. You're kind and thoughtful and think nothing of taking appalling risks for perfect strangers. Not to mention being attractive in a way that had me thinking thoughts that embarrassed me even in my dreams. Then when you kissed me—well, I thought you might like me at least a little. But if you don't—"

Without warning, Chet grabbed her, wrapped her in his arms, and was kissing her so powerfully that it took her breath away. She started crying all over again. But that didn't stop her from throwing her arms around his neck and clinging to him with all her strength. She was certain it couldn't be very satisfactory kissing her just now. Her cheeks were wet with tears, she couldn't stop crying no matter how hard she tried, and she wasn't nearly as tall as he was. But he didn't seem to care. He just lifted her off her feet and kept on kissing her.

"I shouldn't be doing this," he said finally.

"Don't ever stop," she pleaded.

"But I'm making you cry."

"Can't you tell tears of happiness when you see them?"

Whether he could or couldn't, he kept a satisfactorily tight hold on her. "I didn't want to let myself love you," he said.

Her heart soared. He loved her. He had tried not to, but he couldn't help himself. Oh, the sound of that was music to her ears, balm to her tortured soul.

"You shouldn't love me," he said. "I'm not worthy of it."

She laid her head on his chest. "Don't say such things. Besides, I can't help loving you any more than you can help loving me."

Her words seemed to shock him. He grabbed her by the shoulders and held her away from him. "Don't say you love me ever again," he said, his expression painfully intense. "Not *ever*."

"Why?" she asked, confused. It was almost as though he didn't want to be loved, was afraid of it.

"Because I'm not the kind of man a woman like you should have anything to do with."

"I'm sorry for what I said. I was ignorant. I didn't understand—"

"I'm not talking about that."

"Then what are you talking about? You're a wonderful man. Any woman would be fortunate to love a man like you."

"No decent woman should love me. Don't you remember how Lantz treated me, like I was dirt under his feet?"

"Lantz is a horrible person. I'd never—"

"It's not just Lantz. It's everybody. I'm good enough to do their dirty work, but as soon as my job is done, they want me out of their town. Most of them won't even admit they ever knew me."

"I don't care about people like that."

"You will when nobody will give me a respectable job, when decent people don't want to be seen with you."

"I'm sure you're taking a much too severe view of things."

"It's more of my *we don't do things that way in Texas.* People like me will soon be a thing of the past. We've tamed this country so that proper, upstanding citizens can live in it. Now they want us to go away and leave it to them."

"Chet—"

"Gunfighters don't retire and grow old. They're killed by somebody hunting a reputation. You'd end up a widow with kids to raise on your own."

"Good gracious, Chet, I haven't even thought

that far. I couldn't, not when I didn't know whether you loved me."

"I've loved you almost from the moment I saw you, but I wouldn't let myself admit it. I tried to leave, but I never could."

"I know. I'm almost thankful Blade shot you. If he hadn't, I'd never have seen you again."

"That would have been better for you. It's time you hired a new foreman. I want you to talk to Belle about it as soon as you get back."

Melody decided they'd talked too much. She put her arms around Chet and held him tightly. After a moment's hesitation, he put his arms around her.

"Just hold me," she said. "Don't think about the future. Don't think about anybody else. Just us. Just now."

She didn't want to push him to make any promises. He'd made up his mind gunfighters shouldn't marry, even if they wanted to give up being a gunfighter. He couldn't stop himself loving her—he'd admitted he'd tried—but if she pushed him too hard, he might disappear.

For right now, knowing he loved her was enough. Being in love wasn't at all the way she'd expected it would be. She'd thought it would just happen and everything would work out. Now she saw it would take some thought, effort, and time to make her dreams come true. She needed time to convince Chet he was wrong. Failing that, she needed to convince him he was so desperately in love, he couldn't turn his back on her no matter what the difficulties. They could leave Texas, go anywhere he felt gunfighters wouldn't follow him.

She didn't care. She'd never expected to be given a chance for a love like this.

Now that she had it, she didn't mean to give it up.

Chapter Sixteen

Melody told Chet she hadn't said a word about their conversation down by the creek, but everyone seemed to know their relationship had changed. Since he'd given up pretending he didn't love her, they could hold hands when no one was looking. Even share a kiss when they were alone. He felt guilty about offering so little to the woman he loved—he felt even more guilty about offering anything at all when they both knew it would come to nothing in the end—but Melody seemed content.

Belle and Bernice weren't so obliging. They never let an opportunity pass to say something about how wonderful it was to be married, how well matched they thought Melody and Chet were, how fortunate a woman would be to have him as a husband, how glad they were Melody had chosen him over Lantz. Chet knew what they

272

were doing, but he couldn't stop them. One solution would have been to stay in the bunkhouse, but he couldn't stay away from Melody. Because of that weakness, he had to endure their innuendo, subtle hints, and blatant suggestions.

"I think Melody has adjusted very quickly now that Chet's here to explain things to her," Belle was saying to Bernice.

"I always thought she'd adapt to Texas ways," Bernice said. "She's too independent for a place like Virginia. Nobody but a Texas boy is strong enough to take her in hand."

"Who says I want to be taken in hand?" Melody asked. "Suppose I want a man I can manage, who'll do anything I want just to please me?"

"Then you'd better start looking in another direction," Bernice said. "I don't see any man at this table likely to be taken in by your wiles."

"What's wiles?" Neill asked.

"It's what women do when they want to catch a man," Sydney explained. "Are you wanting to catch a man, Melody?"

"Maybe she's already caught one," Belle said.

"I don't like Lantz," Sydney said. "I hate Blade."

"I don't like them either," Melody said.

"Then who are you giving your wiles to?" Neill asked. "Can I have one?"

Chet grinned. "You'll find yourself tangled in some pretty girl's wiles soon enough," he said. "And you won't find them easy to escape."

"Are you tangled up in Melody's wiles?" Neill asked. "Do you want to escape?"

"Of course he doesn't," Belle said. "Wouldn't you like for Chet to stay here?"

"Sure."

"*Are* you going to stay?" Sydney asked.

"You'd better ask Melody," his mother said as she winked at Bernice.

"I don't understand," Neill said. "If Melody has you all tangled up in her wiles, why can't I see them?"

Everyone laughed.

"Wiles are invisible," his mother said.

"I don't want nothing I can't see," Neill said, losing interest.

"You will one of these days," Melody said. "Most of the best things in life can't be seen."

"Like what?" Sydney asked.

"Like love, honor, kindness—"

"Oh, you mean that mushy girl stuff," Sydney said, obviously not impressed. He turned to Chet. "Would you stay because of that girl stuff?"

Chet didn't know how to answer that he'd give anything he owned to be able to stay for that very reason, but that he couldn't because of the things about him Sydney most admired.

"We should be talking about hiring a new foreman," Chet said, determined to change the subject.

"Aren't you going to be our foreman?" Neill asked.

"Just until your mother and Melody find someone else."

"And me," Sydney added.

"You, too," Melody agreed.

"I thought Mama said you were going to stay," Neill persisted.

"I only stopped to borrow a horse. Mine's all rested up now."

"Don't you want to find the rustlers?" Sydney asked.

"I want to stop them taking Spring Water

cows," Chet said, "but I don't need to be the one to find them."

"But Lantz's gunfighter might get all the credit."

"Good." Chet wondered what they'd think if they knew Lantz's gunfighter was his brother. He wondered if Melody would be so accepting then. It was one thing to fall in love with an ex-gunfighter. It was quite another when that ex-gunfighter had a brother with Luke's reputation.

"I bet you're faster."

"Maybe. Once I stop wearing a gun, I'll lose my edge. Soon lots of people will be faster than I am."

"I wouldn't quit," Neill said. "I'd wear my gun forever."

"You can't stay fast forever," Chet said. "Age slows you down."

"But you're not old," Neill said.

"No, but one day you get tired of hunting other men, or worrying about the man hired to hunt you, or trying to figure out how to keep from killing the young fool getting drunk at the corner saloon so he can work up the courage to test his speed against yours. You get tired of seeing men die at your hand."

"Even when they're bad men?" Neill asked.

"Even then."

"But the rustlers are taking our cows," Sydney said. "They deserve to die."

"Nobody deserves to die," Melody said.

Chet listened to Melody and Sydney argue the rules of how civilized men ought to behave. Neither of them realized that some people would never follow the rules.

"I think you ought to give some thought to the kind of man you want for your foreman," Chet said the moment he could get a word in. "It's fine to let Lantz round up some candidates, but you ought to know what you're looking for before you interview anybody."

"I wouldn't trust anybody Lantz picked out," Melody said.

"You may not approve of his character," Chet said, "but he knows the cattle business."

"I don't like the idea of having to choose from just whoever turns up," Belle said.

"You can't wait much longer," Chet said. "Whoever you hire will need time to get to know the men, become familiar with the range, before he starts roundup."

"Why can't you stay longer? That would give us a chance to look around, not take the first man offered."

"I have to be going."

"Where are you going that you have to get there in such a hurry?"

"To the Arizona Territory." Or maybe New Mexico. Possibly Colorado or Nevada. Somewhere so far from civilization, he could forget a brown-haired girl from Virginia. Somewhere so far away, he wouldn't be tempted to come back, tempted to challenge Fate. "I need to be there before the first snows start in the mountains."

It didn't matter when the snows started. He had to leave before he drove himself crazy. It was impossible to see Melody every day, be close enough to touch her, kiss her, and not hope that he could somehow figure out a way to stay. He'd spent many fruitless hours going over every minute of his life, trying to think of some way to escape the curse of his past, but nothing changed.

He couldn't condemn the woman he loved to living so far from civilization that mere survival was a daily struggle, or living in a town spurned by respectable people, living with the certain knowledge that one day someone would make her a widow. It would be extremely painful to leave, but it would be easier to accept that he couldn't have her if he didn't have to see her every day. It would hurt, but he would gradually get used to the pain. Staying here was torture.

He studied Melody's expression. She didn't seem bothered by the notion that he would be leaving so soon. If she loved him as much as she said, she ought to at least look upset. Instead she looked quite serene, sharing ideas with Belle about their foreman and patiently explaining to Sydney why gunfighting ability wasn't the first item on her list of qualifications.

If he loved her as much as he thought, he ought to be glad she was taking his departure so well. She'd known from the first that he'd leave. He'd never tried to hide it. He should be glad she was able to enjoy what time they had together without being hysterical now. It was by far the most intelligent attitude.

But knowing that didn't lighten his disappointment. He guessed he wasn't as sophisticated as he thought. Every moment he spent with her, being treated as part of the family, made it harder for him to accept having to leave. He'd even considered defying common sense and staying, but only a moment's thought told him that was impossible. Lantz Royal hated him. Any day now he might order Luke to come after him. Chet knew he would leave rather than face his brother.

If he had half the courage, honor, and just plain guts he thought he had, he would have gone before now.

Leigh Greenwood

"I think we ought to go into town the end of this week," Chet announced. Putting this off was just going to make it harder for all of them.

"So soon?" Belle asked. It seemed she hadn't actually thought he meant to leave.

"We don't need to go if you don't want to," Sydney said. "If Chet has to go, I can take over until you hire somebody."

"I agree it's time you started to learn the job," Melody said, "but I think you need someone with more experience to teach you."

Chet was pleased to see that none of the women rushed to tell Sydney he was a child.

"Chet can teach me," Sydney said. "I'd rather him than somebody I don't know."

"Learning how to run this ranch will take several years," Chet said. "You've got to see the whole cycle several times before you can really understand. It's not the normal things that cause trouble. It's the things that have never happened before."

"It won't take me that long."

"Maybe not, but it's best to be sure," Chet said. "This ranch is your family's inheritance. A lot of people would suffer if you made mistakes."

For once Sydney seemed to be considering advice. Chet began to have hopes the boy might make a good cattleman someday. A few years away at school would be beneficial. The cattle business was changing along with the rest of Texas.

Chet used to dream of going to college. Isabelle had convinced him that a man with an education was in a position to do a lot better than a plain cowboy. He'd lain awake nights talking to Luke about it. But that was all behind him now. College

278

was for boys like Sydney, boys who still had a future.

Having made the decision to go to town in two days, they began to discuss how they were going to get there, where they were going to stay, what clothes they should take, and how long they were going to stay. Sydney was disgusted to discover it would take a whole day to make the journey in a buckboard.

"I'll ride ahead," he said.

"I don't think that would be a good idea," Chet said.

"Why?"

"If a man allows his women to travel unaccompanied in a country where rustlers are active, every man in town will assume he's a coward or a fool."

Sydney bristled immediately. "Nobody'd better call me a coward. I'll shoot 'em."

"You can't shoot everybody. Besides, you'd end up in jail, and that wouldn't help anybody."

"We'll need you to drive," Melody said. "You know your mother and I can't drive that distance."

"I can drive you," Neill offered.

"No, you can't," Sydney scoffed. "You'd get lost."

"No, I wouldn't. I'd follow Chet."

"The horses would probably run away with you. I'll drive," Sydney insisted over Neill's protest that he wasn't such a fool as to lose control of a buggy horse. "But I'll tie my horse behind."

That little problem settled, Chet excused himself from the table. "I've got a lot to do before we leave."

Melody followed him to the door. "Do you

really think we have to hire a foreman just now?"

He knew she wasn't asking about the foreman. "Yes. It's time."

"You're sure?"

He nodded. He didn't trust his voice not to betray him.

"You will stay at the hotel with us?"

"If you want."

"You're still our foreman, and it's your job to protect us. Though I doubt anybody would accuse you of being a coward if you abandoned us after we've caused you so much trouble."

He wished she'd stop saying that. It made him uncomfortable. He hadn't done anything any other man wouldn't have done.

"Do you still love me?" she asked.

"Always." He held out his hands.

She put hers in his and he pulled her to him. He put his arms around her, and she looked up into his eyes. Even in the shadows of the front hall, her eyes glowed large and bright. There was something a little sad and bittersweet about her smile. Yet it felt reassuring as well, almost as if she'd reached a decision that saddened her but with which she was well content.

"You won't leave us to meet these men alone, will you?"

"No."

"Neither Belle nor I know anything about judging male character. Lantz is a prime example." She paused only a moment. "I misjudged you as well."

He kissed her so she wouldn't make any more confessions. Odd that her thinking well of him should make him feel so guilty.

"You do that very well," she said when their lips

parted. "Is that something Texas men practice from an early age?"

"We prefer to skip kissing hands and go straight to the interesting parts. It leads to a whole different appreciation of kissing."

"I see. And do Texas girls agree?"

"It was Texas girls that gave us the idea."

"Smart girls. Since Virginia is so far behind, how about giving me private instruction so I can catch up?"

It sounded like a good idea; it would have been, if Neill hadn't invaded the hall at that moment.

"You've gotta come," he said to Melody. "Mama and Sydney are fighting again. Mama says if he doesn't show some respect, she's not going to let him go to town with us."

Chet released Melody's hands and stepped back.

"I'll be right there," Melody said, but Neill didn't move. "I've got to go," she said to Chet.

He nodded and watched as she turned to Neill. He knew it wasn't the case, but it felt as if she was turning away from him. It made him feel rejected. Telling himself otherwise didn't help. Neither did knowing he was the one doing the rejecting.

She turned back, giving him a last look and a smile before she disappeared. He turned and hurried out into the night. Only outside of the house, away from her presence, could he regain any certainty of how things must be.

The silence of the night eased his troubled spirit, drained him of emotion, and cloaked him in anonymity. He felt freed of the curse his father had laid on him, a curse he'd taken up of his own free will. Only in the dark could he cease to be Chet Attmore, gunfighter.

But he couldn't live in the dark. He needed light. And light would destroy him.

"Do you intend to keep playing peacemaker between Sydney and his mama?" Bernice asked Melody. They sat in the kitchen, enjoying a late-night cup of coffee after the others had gone to bed.

"Are you asking for the job?"

Bernice laughed. "Not on your life. I've had to do it often enough, though it was your father kept him in line when he was alive."

"It was my father's death that caused all the trouble. Belle wants to protect Sydney too much, and he wants to grow up too fast. Neither one can see they're both doing it out of love."

"Boys his age never understand anything about love. They only care for excitement. A man has to get a few years on him before he can see romance in anything except being bigger, faster, or stronger than some other man. Take your fella. He's—"

"He's not my fella," Melody protested. "Oh, I'm certain he loves me, but he won't let himself belong to anyone. I'm not sure how much he understands about the power of love. Very little, if I'm any judge. He seems to think just about everything else is more important."

"Men are often like that. Your father was. I don't think he ever appreciated Belle or really understood her. He kept her acting like an empty-headed doll because he thought women were weak, foolish creatures who needed a big man to protect them. Of course, cooks are entirely different. We're supposed to perform miracles without the slightest effort."

Melody laughed. "Sounds like Lantz Royal."

"They were alike in some ways, but your pa never let his success go to his head."

"Chet wishes he weren't a success. He thinks having been a gunfighter disqualifies him from having a family like everybody else."

"Well, as much as his handsome self makes me feel weak in the knees at times, he's not far wrong. I don't know another man in his line of work I'd want sleeping in my bed."

"But you do trust Chet?" Melody asked.

"Certainly. I don't know that I would have at first, but he's not like the others. He's hurting inside. Most likely he's been hurting for years, but he hasn't let it make him hard. I saw how he reacted to something Lantz said about gunfighters not being decent like everybody else."

Melody gave a sharp, scornful laugh. "As if Lantz Royal is even close to being decent."

"That's how people feel."

"It's not fair," Melody protested.

"Texas isn't about being fair. It's still too raw. It's about power."

"Chet keeps telling me that, but I don't understand. Why should it be so different here?"

"Because the only men who could survive here were the ones strong enough and mean enough to take and hold what they wanted. This'll be settled country when your brothers take over. People will own their land so others can't just push them off it."

"Chet said we ought to buy all our land."

"He seems to know a great deal about ranching."

"He grew up on a ranch in the Hill Country. He also talks about the people who adopted him as if he'd give anything to be back there."

"He was headed in the opposite direction when he showed up here."

"He's afraid his past will bring trouble on them. He loves them too much to do that."

"It seems that man loves everybody but himself."

"He's even tried to teach me how to handle Sydney." Melody laughed again, ruefully this time. "I'm trying to get him to whisper sweet nothings in my ear, and he's busy giving advice."

"Maybe he's not as romantic as you think."

"It's not that. He's trying to teach me as much as he can before he leaves."

"I was afraid of that. He doesn't look like a man who's happy in love."

"Is it that obvious?"

"Honey, men aren't subtle. Besides, he's the stubborn kind. Once he makes up his mind, you won't change it."

"What am I going to do? I love him desperately."

"There's not much you can do with a man like him except wait."

Melody didn't want to hear that. She feared that if she waited too long, he would disappear and she'd be left with nothing but a memory. She refused to be eighteen years old and know that the only part of her life she truly wished to remember was behind her.

Chet Attmore belonged to her. He had from the moment he admitted he loved her. He didn't have the right to ruin the rest of her life out of some misplaced sense of honor. Okay, maybe he was right to worry about his past, but he didn't have

the right to protect her from herself. If she wanted
to ride a wild horse without a saddle, that was her
business. If she wanted to marry a gunfighter,
that was her business, too. It was his job to sit
still long enough for her to do it.

Chet was of two minds about entering the
little town of Timberville. The trees that had given
the town its name had been cut down to build
the town, a small collection of streets and buildings set on the tableland above a creek. The
denuded flood plain created by the creek that
flowed out of the canyon on the Spring Water had
been turned into corrals and grazing for local
livestock.

The only town of measurable size for more than
a hundred miles east and several hundred in any
other direction, Timberville had ambitions to be
the business center of several counties. But it
looked more like a leggy teenager without enough
clothes to cover its frame.

Chet never entered a town without the uneasy
feeling that somewhere—in one of the saloons or
one of the small, run-down houses that always
rimmed a town like this—a man waited, looking
for a chance to make a reputation, get revenge,
fulfill a contract. A man who might not feel con-
strained to make it a fair fight.

Neill and Sydney rode in the front seat of the
buckboard, Sydney holding the reins. Melody and
Belle sat in the back, their faces covered with veils
to protect them from the dust. Chet rode ahead.
The boys' horses were tied to the back of the
wagon. Neill had insisted that he have a horse if
Sydney had one. They entered along a street
bounded with houses on each side. It was din-

nertime, and no one was about except some cow-hands likely having a last night in town before heading out to roundup.

"I'd forgotten what a small town this was," Melody said. "I guess I still think all cities must be the size of Richmond."

Timberville wasn't. Its buildings weren't of brick or stone. Nor were its streets paved with cobblestones. Dust covered everything, and the only means of transportation had left ample evidence of its presence. With few exceptions, the buildings were single story with false fronts. The most significant exception was the hotel, built to house the tide of visitors that never grew beyond a trickle. It catered mostly to cattle buyers and ranchers who occasionally brought their families to town. Because it was getting close to roundup time, the hotel was nearly empty. The Jordan family could have as many rooms as they wanted.

"I think four rooms are enough," Belle said, despite Sydney's argument that he was too big to share a room with an eleven-year-old brother.

"I don't mind sharing a room with you," Melody offered.

"No," Belle said. "It would have been expected if I were your mother, but I'm not. You should have your own room."

"I can share with Chet," Sydney said.

"I don't want Neill by himself," Belle said.

Once it was clear that he was only sharing a room because Neill was too young to stay in one alone, Sydney agreed to room with his brother. After he'd asked for and been given his own key, he even seemed satisfied with the arrangement.

"I get to choose my bed," he called and ran up the stairs followed by a protesting Neill.

Melody looked amused, Belle distressed. "Maybe I should have left them at home."

"This place has survived cowhands and a good deal worse," said the desk clerk. "They won't hurt anything."

"Please give Mr. Attmore the room on the other side of the boys," Belle said to the clerk. "I don't want to saddle you with them," Belle said, turning back to Chet, "but they listen to you more than to me. It seems unfair to—"

"Chet Attmore!"

Several thoughts exploded in Chet's mind at once, but instinct took over. He had his gun halfway out of its holster when he turned to see Dan Walters coming down the stairs, a smile on his face, his hand outstretched. Chet relaxed, relieved to see a friend, embarrassed at his reaction. He glanced at Melody, hoping she hadn't seen. Her pallor told him she had and was horrified.

He opened his mouth to explain, then closed it again. The explanation was obvious, and nothing he might say could change that or its consequences. He was a gunfighter. He might want to change, but he could never wipe out his past, or the instincts that enabled him to survive in a business where one small mistake, one brief hesitation, could mean death.

"Dan Walters," Chet said, advancing to meet the man who was clearly glad to see him. "What are you doing here? I never expected to see you so far from Nueces River country."

"I sold up now I don't have you to keep the rustlers off my back," Dan said. "I'm looking for a place to buy, but they tell me this country is closed."

"If you knew anything about Lantz Royal, you'd understand," Chet said. "He owns most of the country and has his eye on the rest."

"You seem to be doing all right," Dan said. "Is this your family?"

Chet felt the bitter gall of a man who has no family and wants one more than just about anything else.

"This is the Jordan family. They own the Spring Water Ranch. I'm acting as their foreman until they can hire someone. Belle, I'd like to introduce you to Dan Walters. I did some work for him a few years back."

"He means he kept me from being killed by a pack of the most vicious rustlers you'll ever see," Dan said. "Thanks to Chet, we hanged the lot of them."

Despite that somewhat chilling introduction, Belle willingly shook hands with Dan. Chet thought she looked quite taken with him. But that wasn't such a surprise. Dan was on the wrong side of forty, but he was still a big, handsome man.

"I'm pleased to meet you, Mr. Walters. Allow me to introduce my stepdaughter, Melody."

Melody and Dan shook hands. She smiled in greeting, but Chet could tell she didn't feel the least bit like smiling. This further revelation of Chet's past had shocked her.

"The two boys who nearly knocked you down are my sons," Belle said.

"Fine boys. I'm sure their father is mighty proud. I'd like to meet him. Maybe he can point me to some land your Mr. Royal doesn't own."

"My husband is dead," Belle said.

Chet got the feeling his friend actually perked up at that bit of news. Dan's wife had died years ago. Apparently he hadn't remarried. Just as apparently, he found the widow Jordan very much to his liking.

"Are you and your family staying in town long?" he asked.

"We're here to find a new foreman. Since you're a friend of Chet's, maybe you can convince him to stay on. We'd much rather have him than anyone else."

"I tried to get him to be my foreman," Dan said. "He turned me down flat."

"Such a stubborn young man," Belle said.

"What do you mean talking like that? You can't possibly be more than five minutes older than Chet. You look beautiful enough to be five years younger."

"Goodness," Belle said, fanning herself. "You sure you don't come from Richmond? You sound exactly like some of the men Melody's been telling me about."

Chet had never seen Belle flustered. Silly and nearly hysterical, yes. But she wasn't either now. She was truly flustered. It wasn't much of a leap to imagine her and Dan together. They'd probably be very good for each other. Belle would love to be spoiled and pampered. And Dan would love doing it.

"My mother came from Virginia," Dan said. "A little town you probably never heard of called Williamsburg."

"That accounts for it then."

"What?"

"Your gallant manners. Chet's gallant, too, but

he insists upon doing everything without a fuss. Your gallantry is rather showy." Belle blushed. "I like that."

"Then you'll have to let me invite you to dinner. All of your family," Dan added. "We Virginians really shine at table, don't we, Miss Melody?"

"We certainly do, Mr. Walters." Melody had recovered some of her self-control. She smiled. "But I have a feeling you'd shine anywhere."

"Why, thank you," Dan said, practically bowing over her hand.

Chet had never seen Dan around women. He'd been hired to rescue a rancher about to be destroyed by rustlers. Theirs had been a grim struggle. Chet had left as soon as the rustlers had been caught. Witnessing this side of his friend amused him.

"What do you say to this evening?" Dan asked. "You've had a long journey, you're tired, and you still have to unpack. You won't have the energy to cope with ordering dinner. I'll arrange everything. All you have to do is eat."

Belle turned to Melody, who nodded her agreement. "Thank you very much, Mr. Walters. We'll be delighted to accept your hospitality. What do you say to seven-thirty?"

"Seems perfect. Now is there anything I can do? Can I help take up your luggage?"

"Thank you, but—"

"Why didn't you tell me you were coming to town?" a voice boomed from the doorway. "Tell me which room you're in, and my boys will take your luggage up." Lantz sailed up to Melody and took her resisting hand. "Are you sure you should be up so soon? I don't want you to over-do."

"Who the hell is that loudmouth?" Dan muttered under his breath to Chet.

"You're about to meet the man who closed Concho County," Chet replied.

Chapter Seventeen

Lantz Royal was just about the last person in the world Melody wanted to see. She'd never been greatly pleased with him, not even in the beginning when she actually considered the possibility of marrying him. But it wasn't until she had become accustomed to Chet's quietly efficient, self-effacing nature that she realized Lantz was so loud and overbearing. Even the good-natured swagger of Dan Walters seemed subdued in comparison.

"Good evening, Lantz," she said. "We just got here. We haven't had time to go to our rooms."

"If you had let me know you were coming, I'd have taken care of everything."

"Thank you, but Chet can handle anything that's too difficult for Belle or me."

"Or Sydney," Chet prompted.

Melody didn't know whether Chet had intended

to irritate Lantz by comparing him to a boy, but he succeeded.

"I'd be more than happy to be of service," Dan said, directing his remark more to Belle than Melody.

"Who are you?" Lantz demanded.

"This is Dan Walters," Melody said.

"What are you doing here?" Lantz asked.

"I thought I might buy a ranch in this area," he said, giving Belle a wink. "Now I'm sure of it."

"There's nothing for sale. You may as well leave now."

"You never know until you ask," Dan said, his good humor seeming to increase the more Lantz's irritation showed.

"I tell you there's nothing," Lantz said. "Get on your horse and git."

"I couldn't do that," Dan said. "I just invited the ladies to dinner."

His mood seemed as pleasant as ever, but Melody thought she could detect a hardening of his attitude toward Lantz. Chet appeared to be completely unmoved, but Melody had learned to watch his eyes and mouth closely. His lips had become hard, his eyes more narrow. That was about all the signs he would give of his anger before it burst out into the open.

"You can't have dinner with him," Lantz said, turning to Melody. "You don't even know him."

"He's a friend of Chet's," Melody said.

"That's all the more reason to steer clear of him. He's probably a killer, too."

"I think it's an excellent recommendation," Melody said. "I don't know what would have happened to us these last days without Chet. I can't speak too highly of his character. I would be willing to trust my safety to anyone he called a friend."

"You wouldn't need him or his friends to protect you if you'd married me," Lantz said.

Melody decided there wasn't even a trace of the disappointed lover in Lantz. He was merely angry that she could prefer anyone else to him. "If you hadn't been so heavy-handed, I might have." Melody wasn't sure it was wise to make that confession, but she couldn't resist letting Lantz know he'd been his own worst enemy. "But I would never marry you now. After the way you've mistreated my cowhands, I tremble to think what you'd do to me if I made you angry."

"You said your men would take the ladies' luggage up to their rooms?" Chet said. "I don't see them."

"I'll do it," Dan offered.

"The hell you will!" Lantz shouted. "I said my men would do it, and they will, by God."

"Then please find them," Melody said. "I'm sure Belle is exhausted. I know I am."

Lantz looked reluctant to leave, but he had no choice. Melody accepted the keys from a clerk who, agog with curiosity, had listened to every word of their exchange. She handed one to Belle. "Let's go before Lantz gets back. I'm too tired to deal with him."

"No lady should have to put up with such a display of bad manners," Dan said. "Just say the word, and Chet and I will get rid of him for you."

"If you really want to do us a service, you'll disappear as well. Just seeing Chet makes Lantz irrational."

"What have you been up to?" Dan asked, his glance shifting between Chet and Melody.

"It's more what Chet has kept Lantz from doing. You two can go to a saloon and catch up on old times. Belle and I are going to our rooms."

"Don't forget, dinner at seven-thirty," Dan called after Belle.

She turned and gave him a warm smile. "I won't forget."

"Belle Jordan," Melody said with mock severity the moment they turned the corner on the stairs, "I do believe you were flirting with that man."

"Do you mind?" Belle said, looking a little conscience-stricken. "Your father has been dead for nearly a year, and I have hardly spoken to a man since then. I don't count Lantz."

"I don't mind at all," Melody assured her. "I think he's charming."

"I do like men who say pretty things."

"Then you must have had a dry run of it with my father."

"Admittedly, he wasn't very good with compliments, but he was so good in so many other ways. He's very much like that young man of yours."

"He's not my young man, but I'd give anything if he were."

"He won't pay you compliments or bring you small gifts."

"I wouldn't want them," Melody said. "Just seeing him across the table, being able to reach out and touch his hand, to hear his soft breathing while he's asleep would be more than enough."

"Do you think you'll ever have that?"

"I don't know, but I mean to give it everything I've got. He's too big a prize for anything less."

Melody couldn't believe Lantz would return so quickly with two foreman candidates for them to interview. She and Belle had barely managed to unpack their clothes before they were called back downstairs. Lantz expected his recommendation would be enough to secure the job for either candidate. Belle had shocked him when she insisted on inviting Dan Walters to be present.

"He built up his own ranch in a part of Texas infested with bandits and rustlers," she explained to Lantz. "I'm depending upon him to think of all the things that would never occur to me."

Melody had angered him even more when she insisted that Chet be present. "He knows the men and the ranch," she said. "It only makes sense to ask for his opinion."

The participant all of them had overlooked was Sydney. "You keep telling me I've got to think of something besides guns all the time, so let me start learning how to run the ranch. If I'm going to do that, we've got to pick out somebody I can work with."

"The boy's right," Chet said, forestalling Lantz's explosive disagreement. "Jake made me his foreman when I was pretty much Sydney's age."

"And look how you turned out," Lantz snapped.

"That was my decision," Chet replied. "But while I was foreman, only one bunch of rustlers got out of our valley with any Broken Circle cows. I brought them and the cows back inside a week."

"If you have someone for us to see, bring him in," Melody said, furious at Lantz for attacking Chet.

"I've got two men," Lantz said to Melody. "They're both perfect for the job. All you have to do is tell me which one you like best."

Melody disliked Lantz's first choice on sight. The man did look the part—big, strong, and self-assured. Trouble came from an unexpected direction. Excited over being included with the adults, Sydney wanted to be the first to ask questions. It became apparent almost at once that the man didn't have any patience with Sydney or his questions. His answers were short and unhelpful, his attitude brusque.

"Have you been a foreman before?" Chet asked. Melody thought he entered the discussion to prevent an unwise outburst from Sydney.

"On two places," the man replied, giving the names of the ranches and their owners.

"Have you ever worked for an owner of Sydney's age?" Chet asked.

"I don't work for boys," the man said. "I'll be the one making the decisions."

"That's understood, but the boy has to learn. He'll soon be giving the orders."

"I don't take orders from boys who still answer to their mothers."

The man didn't appear to realize he'd cooked his goose. He'd not only made Sydney furious, he'd insulted Belle as well.

"I think that's all we need to ask you," Melody said, refusing to waste any more time on this man. "We'll now talk to your second candidate, Lantz."

Both Lantz and the man seemed surprised at the shortness of the interview. Neither seemed to realize that as far as Melody, Belle, and Sydney were concerned, the ability to work with cows was rather far down on their list. They certainly didn't want a foreman as stubborn and willful as the ornery beasts themselves.

"I'm Orian Meeks," the second man said as he introduced himself to Melody and Belle and shook hands with the men. "Mr. Royal tells me you're in the market for someone to manage your place for you."

"Yes, we are," Belle said. "My husband passed away, and our foreman is no longer able to continue in his position."

"I'm mighty sorry to hear that, ma'am. Are these handsome-looking young people your children? You don't look old enough to be their mama."

Melody guessed she could forgive the man some flattery—after all, he was trying to get a job—but she would have preferred a man less glib of tongue.

Belle seemed quite taken with the man, and he was soon able to smooth Sydney's hackles. Melody decided she was just prejudiced against anyone who wanted to take Chet's place. She determined to be as objective as possible, but sitting next to Chet made that virtually impossible. There was no way she could look at this man, or any other, and not compare him to Chet. She had to admit Chet was just as stubborn and determined to do things his own way as the first man. But Chet didn't ignore others or make them feel they were in his way. He'd even let her ride with him—once—and never afterward reminded her that even though she'd gotten herself out of trouble, her presence had nearly turned a carefully planned scheme into a disaster. He had been Sydney's severest critic from the first, but he'd also supported the boy's right to start being treated like a man. And he'd been kind to Belle even when she'd been acting her silliest.

Where else could you find a man who could do all that and still be the best foreman in Texas?

Melody realized that she hadn't been paying attention when she felt Chet start to tense. She looked at him, but his attention was on Mr. Meeks. Sydney was asking his questions. Meeks was answering them, but Melody gradually detected an undercurrent of mockery.

"I'd like to ask a few questions, if I may," Dan Walters said. Belle assured him he could ask anything he wanted. Meeks's attitude changed immediately. Melody thought she might have misinterpreted him, until Belle asked a question. True, it wasn't the most intelligent question Belle could have asked—Belle had to be forgiven for being more interested in the house than the cows—but the mockery was back at once. Clearly this man didn't have any respect for women or boys, a recipe for disaster if he were to take over the job at Spring Water.

That impression was intensified when it came Melody's turn to ask questions.

"We've had some trouble with rustlers," she said. "Our old foreman insisted upon arming the cowhands, but I'm against the use of guns. How would you handle the situation?"

His smile grated on her nerves. "All gentlewomen are afraid of firearms," he said. "I'd be surprised if it were otherwise. It's best to leave that sort of thing to the menfolk. We're not so high-strung, our sensibilities so refined."

"It has nothing to do with sensibilities or being high-strung," Melody snapped. "It has to do with principle."

"You're perfectly right," Mr. Meeks assured her. "I admire a woman who has principles and holds to them, but some things that need to be done are beyond a gentlewoman. Some things are beyond decent men, too. That's why we have a need for men like your foreman here. Mr. Royal explained why you don't want to keep him around any longer than you have to. Very wise, I might add."

"Mr. Royal knows nothing of the matter," Melody snapped, turning her angry glare on Lantz. "I have perfect confidence in my foreman. I've done everything in my power to convince him to stay on."

While Lantz just looked angry, Meeks tripped over his tongue to try to retrieve his words. Melody wouldn't have let him set foot on the ranch under any circumstances. She stood. "Come on, Belle. I'm afraid neither of these men is acceptable."

"What's wrong with them?" Lantz demanded. "They're the best around."

"They're too much like you," Melody told him, "stubborn, pig-headed, and contemptuous of women. Furthermore, I refuse to hire anyone who won't take the time to work with Sydney now, and Neill when he gets older. The Spring Water is their inheritance. They need to know how to take care of it themselves."

"I'll be close by," Lantz said. "After we're married—"

Melody's tiny scream of frustration stopped Lantz in mid-sentence.

"I've told you over and over, I'm not going to marry you," she said. "We appreciate your help, but you have nothing to do with what goes on at the Spring Water."

"I'll have that ranch," Lantz roared. "If you don't—"

"Do you want your herd scattered again?" Chet asked in his same quiet, unhurried voice. "Or would you rather we burned down your ranch house next time?"

Lantz gaped at him as if he were crazy.

"Didn't you ever wonder why none of your cows were missing?" Chet asked.

"My men went after them right away."

"Not for hours. And you left your ranch vulnerable. Anybody could have ridden up and set your haystack and barn afire."

"I'll have you killed for this," Lantz blazed, charging from his seat.

Dan Walters blocked his path.

"You won't do anything to anybody," Chet said. "Your reign of terror is over. The Spring Water is going to get itself a foreman who can stand up to you as well as to those rustlers. If you get up to your old tricks, I'll come back. Don't look at Melody. She won't know I'm here. Nobody will see me, but you'll see my work. When I'm done, you'll be lucky to be able to hang on to your ranch."

"You're working with the rustlers," Lantz accused him.

"If I had been, you'd be picked clean by now."

Melody was growing uneasy with the increasingly heated argument. She didn't want Chet to make Lantz so mad he'd send his gunfighter after him. "Thank you, Mr. Meeks," she said, "but I don't think you're what we're looking for."

Meeks left the room quickly, his chagrin plain to see. Lantz stayed long enough to utter a few more threats—Melody had heard them all by now—before making his usual noisy exit.

"That was very interesting," Dan said to Chet. "Would someone like to bring me up to date on what's been going on around here?"

"Chet can do that," Belle said. "Since our business is over, Melody and I are going shopping."

"I'm not going shopping," Sydney stated.

"You're staying with us," Chet said. "You've got to tell Dan what's been happening. You know far more about it than I do."

If Melody hadn't already been certain Chet was the kindest, sweetest man in the world, Sydney's proud smile would have convinced her. Lantz would never understand. She wouldn't have herself a few weeks ago. She could only marvel that two such contradictory natures could exist side by side in the same man. She didn't know how she could live without one. She didn't know how she could live *with* the other. But she intended to do her best to make sure she had the chance to figure it out.

Melody settled back while the waiter poured a fresh cup of coffee. Dan Walters was a delightful host. And once they'd gotten rid of Lantz, everyone was able to enjoy themselves. Even Neill and Sydney. They thoroughly enjoyed Dan's telling of the hunt for the rustlers. Though he made it sound like fun, Melody was certain it had been a very dangerous time for him and Chet. She didn't like Dan making it sound like such a grand adventure. Sydney had begun to show signs of maturity. She didn't want him to start regressing.

"Did you hang them all?" Neill asked.

"Yes. They had killed a lot of people both here and in Mexico."

"Are there any more bandits?"

"Too many," Dan said. "That's why I decided to sell up. I want to be a rancher, not a gunman."

"That's what Chet says," Sydney said. "He says it's not fun after a while."

"It's never fun," Chet said. "But after a while it gets to be hard to forget their faces."

"How about you?" Sydney asked Dan. "Do you still see their faces?"

"Yes," he admitted. "I guess that's one of the reasons I sold up. If I'd stayed, there'd have been more. Now, let's talk about what we're going to do for the rest of the evening."

"I'm going to look around," Sydney announced.

"Me, too," Neill echoed.

"Neill, you know you can't go off by yourself," Belle said.

"He can go with Sydney," Chet said. "Breaking in green boys is one of the things you have to learn to be a rancher," Chet said before Sydney could protest.

"I'm no green boy," Neill said.

"No, but you could pretend, just so Sydney would have somebody to practice on."

The two boys eyed each other uncertainly.

"I don't mind taking him along if he'll do what I say," Sydney said. "What's a green boy like?" he asked Chet.

"He's never been in town before. You have to show him around, tell him what to look out for. Think you can act like a green boy?" Chet asked Neill.

"Sure. I can be like Melody when she first got here. She didn't know nothing."

"I still don't know much," Melody said, smiling, "but I'm learning."

"Thank Mr. Walters for his hospitality and you can go," Belle said.

The boys mumbled their thanks and quickly disappeared.

"I'm nervous about them," Belle said. "They've

303

never been turned loose in town before."

"I know how to fix that," Dan said. "We can take a walk and keep an eye on them at the same time."

"I wouldn't want to impose on you," Belle said.

"When did enjoying the company of a lovely lady get to be an imposition?"

"Why can't you say things like that?" Melody asked Chet.

"Because I'm not a hopeless flirt. Watch out for him, Belle. He never stops talking. Women have been known to lock themselves in their rooms after only a few hours in his company."

"At least I don't bore them with long silences." Dan stood. "Come on, Belle, before I have to take him down a notch. If he doesn't say anything after the first fifteen minutes, you're welcome to catch up with us," Dan said to Melody.

"If he doesn't talk more than that, I'll go to bed."

But after Belle and Dan had gone, Melody was the one who fell silent. There was so much she wanted to say, but they'd gone over all of it before. She didn't know how to begin again without replowing old ground.

"You like Dan, don't you?" she finally said.

"Yes."

"Was his the kind of job you took?"

"When I could."

"And when you couldn't?"

"I took the jobs being offered."

"Are the other men you worked for your friends?"

"No."

"Why not?"

"Men hire me to do jobs they don't want to do themselves, or can't do. When it's over, they don't want to be reminded of that. Dan worked along-side me from the beginning."

Melody stood up. "Let's go for a walk."

"There're not many places to go."

"There's the creek. I've always been fond of moonlight on water."

Once her eyes adjusted to the darkness, Melody could see Dan and Belle strolling along the board-walk. A little way ahead she made out Sydney and Neill peeping into a saloon. She was relieved when Sydney pulled his little brother away from the window and they moved on to the next build-ing.

There were very few people out tonight, none of them women. No one seemed to be in a hurry. No one seemed to be with anyone else. They looked in windows, turned into doorways, and walked along, solitary figures all seeming to nei-ther have nor want any association with their fel-low man. Melody didn't understand it. With so few people living here, she would have thought they'd want to be friends with as many as possi-ble.

The main street of Timberville ended on the bluff overlooking the creek below. The creek ap-peared as a tiny ribbon of silver below.

"Are you sure you want to walk that far?" Chet asked.

"Yes," Melody said, anxious to have Chet all to herself.

It took all of Melody's attention to make it down the rocky path from the bluff. When they reached the bottom, they headed for the only tree left. Ap-parently others had enjoyed doing the same thing. The ground around the tree and the rocks bordering the stream had been pounded smooth.

The sounds from Timberville didn't reach down to the creek bottom.

"Aunt Emmaline's farm was on the James River," Melody said. "Sometimes we used to go down to the river at night. It was peaceful, a lot like this."

"We shouldn't be down here," Chet said. "We shouldn't be anywhere alone together."

"Why?"

"Because I'm leaving in a few days. There's no point in hoping for things that can never be."

"Why, Chet? Dan Walters likes you. Other people might like you, too."

"Dan's different. He never thought of me as a gunfighter. I was just a man willing to help him out. He paid me, but he treated me like an equal from the first. The rest are like Lantz."

"We can avoid people like him."

"You can't avoid the whole world."

"I'm not interested in the whole world. Just you."

"We can't ignore the world. I know a gunfighter who thought he could, but he was wrong."

"What happened?"

"He decided to quit. He got married and bought himself a nice little farm. He stopped wearing his gun because he thought going unarmed would protect him. A young hothead anxious to make a reputation came looking for him."

Melody didn't want to hear this story, but she knew it was useless to try to stop Chet now.

"When the man wouldn't strap on a gun, the hothead starting shooting at him, hitting him in the arm, then the leg, hoping to force him to pick up his gun. He wouldn't, and in a fit of temper, the hothead killed him. Do you know what the worst part was?"

"Don't tell me his wife had children had to watch?"

"No, she was spared that. The worst part was that the townspeople stood by and didn't do a thing. It was a clear case of murder, but they didn't interfere because he was a gunfighter. They didn't want his kind in their town."

Melody had seen Chet angry, but never as angry as he was now. "You knew that man, didn't you?"

"He sided me in a fight when I first started. I owe my life to him."

Melody was sorry for that man and his family, but she couldn't let that stop her from fighting for her chance to marry Chet. "I'm sorry for what happened to your friend, Chet, but that doesn't mean it has to happen to us."

"It does. People are the same all over."

"Not always."

"Let's not waste time talking about it, or arguing over what can't be changed."

Chet's obstinate refusal to listen to any opinion but his own infuriated Melody. Her first impulse was to argue even more vehemently. Her second impulse was to climb right back up the slope and leave him to contemplate the creek by himself. She yielded to the third, and leaned against him and let him put his arm around her. She wasn't through yet. She wasn't the daughter of a Civil War officer and Texas rancher for nothing.

She'd gotten her share of the spit and fire that enabled her father to stand up to Lantz Royal. She intended to marry Chet Attmore despite his certainty that decent people would shun her and a gunman would someday kill him right before her eyes. She didn't know how to prove to him she loved him so much she would take any risk, bear any hardship. He could have killed a thousand men and it wouldn't make any difference.

Well, yes, it would have made her very unhappy, but it wouldn't have stopped her from loving Chet. Nothing could ever do that.

"Tell me about yourself," she said. "Do you realize, I don't know anything about you—your parents, brothers and sisters, anything."

She felt him stiffen, but that didn't surprise her. She figured there was a reason he'd never spoken about his life.

"There's nothing much to tell."

"Then tell me what there is."

He started to pull away, but she held on to the arm that encircled her waist. "Don't say anything if it's going to make you pull away."

"There's nothing about me that's good."

She sat up and turned to face him, all the while being careful not to move his arm. "Everything I know about you is good. Why do you think I fell in love with you?"

"Why did you?"

"Because I couldn't help myself." She stroked his arm. "Outside of being ridiculously tall, absurdly strong, and sinfully good-looking—and believe me, a woman doesn't really need more than that!—you're the kindest, sweetest man I've ever met. There's nothing you can't do, and so far, nothing you *won't* do for me and my family. The real question is, why did you fell in love with me?"

She wasn't sure she wanted to know the answer to that question, but she'd been wondering for a long time.

"I fell in love with you the first moment I saw you."

"You must have seen many women far prettier than I could ever hope to be. And richer. And more anxious to please you. If you'd treated me the way I treated you, I'd have slapped your face, turned around, and ridden away."

"I tried to, but Blade shot me and you fetched me back."

That didn't amuse her, but she tried not to show it. "Now tell me about your past. I'm agog with curiosity. It is riddled with scandal, isn't it?"

His smile at her attempt at humor was brief. "Nothing so respectable. My father was a gunfighter, and my mother ran off. After my father was shot in the back, my brother and I were shifted from one home or orphanage to another. We probably would have been dead by now if Jake and Isabelle hadn't adopted us. The dumbest thing I ever did was leave their ranch. I spent the best seven years of my life there and was too stupid to realize it."

"Is your brother still there?"

"He left before me."

"Why did you leave?"

"I used to think it was because guns and fighting were in my blood. Now I know I followed my brother to make sure nothing happened to him. But either way, I can't marry you."

Melody felt warmth spread through her. He did want to marry her. He'd been so busy trying to convince her they couldn't have any future together, he'd never actually said what kind of future he was talking about. As much as she loved him, she couldn't have lived with him except as his wife. She might demand that men treat her like a human being with a brain capable of rational thought, but she was too conventional for any other kind of arrangement.

She settled against him, holding him a little tighter. She really felt quite sorry for him. She didn't see why a man should be punished all his life for one mistake, even in Texas. She had every intention of seeing that it didn't happen to Chet. "Tell me about Jake and Isabelle," she said. "They must be very nice people."

She laughed at his stories about Will and Drew, felt sorry for Hawk and Zeke, was glad to know Buck had finally found the family he'd been looking for. The only thing that really surprised her was Chet's desire to go to college. She supposed it was another example of her biased Easterner's view of Texans. But the one thing that struck her most forcefully, that came through in virtually everything he said, was his love for Jake and Isabelle. He called it respect and admiration. She decided anything that warm and vibrant had to be love.

It was love that kept him from going back, just as it kept him from marrying her. Melody decided men weren't as logical as they pretended. If he'd been a woman, he'd have married whom he wanted, gone where he wanted, and damned the consequences.

No, she was wrong there. She'd seen too many women do just the opposite, but she didn't intend to be one of them.

"I think you ought to go home and take me with you," she said when he fell quiet. "Don't tell me why you can't. I already know. But be warned—I haven't given up. Now, before you start to argue with me and ruin a perfectly good mood, kiss me.

I know it's horrible of me to ask such a thing, but I feel desperate and that has made me brazen."

Apparently Chet didn't mind brazen females. His kisses managed to make her forget, if only for a short while, that he was being amazingly obstinate. Honor was a good thing—she thought every man ought to have a healthy dose of it—but not when it kept her from marrying the only man she could ever love.

He liked to tease her by kissing parts of her body no proper Virginian would have touched with his lips until after he was married. No man had ever kissed her neck. She wouldn't have thought of letting him. No man she knew would have dared to push her dress down so he could kiss her shoulder. Chet didn't ask. He just did it. It had shocked her at first. Now she looked forward to it. There was something about it that was much more exciting and far more intimate than kissing the inside of her arm. She'd stopped the only man who attempted to do that. But she wouldn't—couldn't—stop Chet from doing anything he wanted. She always ended up wanting more.

She tilted her head to one side, allowing him to reach even more of her neck and shoulder. She wasn't sure exactly how he was kissing her—it seemed to involve his teeth and tongue and tiny puffs of warm air against her moistened skin as much as his lips—but she did know it stirred feelings inside her from some long slumber. She'd always enjoyed the company of men before, had even considered herself practically engaged once. But none of those feelings bore any resemblance to what she felt for Chet. With all other men, she'd kept her distance, preserved social decorum.

She couldn't imagine Chet shining in any social gathering, but that was fine with her. She didn't want to keep him at a distance, and decorum never entered her mind. She wanted him close to her, touching her, holding her. She didn't want anybody else around to draw his attention from her.

He was nibbling at her ear, sending shafts of aching weakness through her body. She slumped against him, unable to summon the energy to sit erect. Leaning against Chet was like leaning against stone covered with soft leather to make it warm and touchable. He had broad shoulders and strong arms, but she never realized his true strength and size until he held her in his arms. She liked being in his arms. She could imagine staying there for years to come. She felt safe from Lantz's predatory interest in her and her ranch.

She was safe from Chet, too, but she didn't want to be.

She wanted to feel that he was pursuing her, driving her to the edge, forcing her to give him everything she held most precious. Knowing he had enough self-control for both of them did little to heighten her romantic sense of danger.

But he didn't seem quite as much in control tonight. He had only progressed as far as tracing the outline of her ear with his tongue, but his breathing had become uncharacteristically rapid. He held her against him more tightly than ever before. His grip on her arms was almost painful.

She pulled back to look at him and immediately wished she hadn't. He wore the look of a tortured soul, a man suffering mortal agony. She didn't know if she should speak, but she couldn't help it. "What's wrong?"

He buried his face in her hair. "Nothing."

He held her so tightly, she could hardly breathe. "That's not true. Tell me."

"I was thinking this may be the last time I can hold you like this."

"Chet, I've told you—"

He quickly released her and put his fingers to her lips. "Don't," he said. "I can bear knowing I'll never see you again. What I can't bear is being promised hope when I know there isn't any."

A whole armada of arguments jostled for supremacy in her mind. She would not allow him to be defeated by fears she was certain were more in his mind than in reality. She wouldn't give him up, not for anything, but she wasn't about to waste this evening with fruitless arguments. "Then hold me," she said. "If this is going to be our last evening alone together, I want it to be one to remember."

Chapter Eighteen

His kiss was fierce and brutal, full of the anger and need that were in him. Her lips felt bruised, as if they were encircled by bands of steel. He probably didn't realize he was close to hurting her. She wouldn't tell him. It would only make him feel worse. Besides, his barely controlled attack was having a disconcerting effect on her. She felt like attacking him back. She'd never thought herself capable of feeling such wanton passion.

What was worse, she wanted to *be* such a woman.

The struggle with herself was brief, the battle a rout. Melody abandoned herself to Chet and anything he wanted to do with her.

His kisses had a desperate quality about them. They came in rapid succession, short and fierce rather than long and lingering, as though he was trying to get in enough to last a lifetime. When their seated position didn't allow him to hold her as close as he wanted, he pulled her to her feet and pressed her hard against his body. The desire that had been buried deep within her, waiting for the perfect moment to emerge, suddenly came to life.

She wanted him. It was incredible to her she should feel such an urge, should know it so certainly. Nothing in her experience with men had prepared her for this invasion of every part of her body and soul by a hunger so powerful, so pervasive, there was no possibility of denying it. There was no doubt. She wanted him—mind, body, and soul.

It occurred to her briefly to wonder why she'd never felt any part of these feelings for another man. Just as quickly she knew the answer. There was no man for her who could even begin to compare to Chet. There never would be another.

"We've got to stop," Chet said.

Mercifully he paid no heed to his own words. Melody didn't think she could have let him go. He was as necessary to her as the air she breathed. He didn't seem to know it, but she was part of him. They belonged together. If he'd had any doubt, the feeling that had exploded between them now should have convinced him.

Melody became aware of the tingling in her breasts at almost the same moment she realized that Chet's body had reacted powerfully to their closeness. The combination of the two heated her whole body. The heat of Chet's desire seemed to burn through her skin and into her own body. Her breasts grew increasingly sensitive until even the slightest movement sent delicious pleasure arcing through her. Pressing herself ever harder against his chest only served to intensify the feeling. It grew within her, filled her, growing hotter, stronger, more forceful until she felt as though she would be swept away by it.

Without warning, Chet tore her from his arms and pushed her away from him. "It's time to go back." He barely got the words out. He was breathing as though he'd been running for an hour.

"I don't want to go. I want you to hold me again." She reached out to him, but he stepped back.

"I don't want to go, either. I want to spend the rest of the night here with you."

"Why can't we—"

"Because I can't control myself much longer. Five more minutes of holding you, kissing you, wanting you, and I'll tear the clothes from your body and take you right here."

As incredible as it seemed, that matched very closely the thoughts in her own mind.

"I would never forgive myself if I did anything to dishonor you."

Melody began to think she'd much overrated honor.

Chet took her hand and began pulling her up the path to the town.

"Chet, please stop."

"No."

"Can't we talk about this?"

"We've talked too much already. We both know it has to end, so there's no use torturing ourselves, making ourselves miserable."

"I'm not miserable. I'm not—"

He stopped and turned so abruptly that she ran into him. "I am. I'm so miserable I can't stand it.

Thinking about what I'd like to do with you but can't is torture. A man can only stand so much. I've reached my limit. I'm just about to bust."

He started up the trail once more. Her protests did nothing to slow him down. She practically had to run to keep up. It seemed ironic—in the moments when she had time to think, in between dodging rocks and trying to keep from losing her balance—that after turning down several offers, she shouldn't be able to marry the man she loved. The man who loved her. Everything was mixed up.

She reached the top of the bluff out of breath. They must have been gone longer than she'd thought. Light filtered through the windows of several buildings. She heard faint sounds of music and occasionally a raised voice, but she didn't see anyone on the boardwalks. Chet pulled himself together enough to walk by her side, giving the appearance of calm, but she could sense the tempest that boiled inside him. He stopped just inside the hotel door.

"Aren't you coming in?" Melody asked.

"Later. I'm going for a walk first."

"Chet, I—"

"We've said all there is to say. Why can't you leave it at that?"

"Because I love you and don't mean to lose you because of some silly prejudice."

"It's not silly. I told you about—"

"I'm willing to take a chance."

"You don't know what you're talking about. I do, and I can't let you."

"I'm old enough to make my own decisions."

"You're not too old to regret them."

"I could never regret marrying you."

"You'd regret that until your dying day." He turned to leave.

"Where are you going?"

"I don't know."

"Be careful. Lantz could have sent that killer of his after you already."

"I'm not afraid of Lantz or his killer. I'm more afraid of you. Go to bed. Maybe some sleep will restore your common sense."

"My common sense is just fine, thank you."

But she was talking to empty space. He had gone. She started to run after him, then changed her mind. He didn't believe she loved him so deeply that she would never regret anything so much as not being with him. She had to find a way to convince him, and she had to do it quickly.

Chet sat alone at the table, an untouched drink before him. He'd walked until he was tired of looking at the same streets, sidestepping the same broken boards, hearing the same voices coming through the same open doorways. He'd found a nearly empty saloon, dropped down in a dark corner, and ordered a bottle of whiskey he didn't want. It wouldn't fix what was wrong with him, and he'd feel even worse when he sobered up. Besides, he didn't trust Lantz not to do something stupid like kidnap Melody and try to force her to marry him. He was the kind of man who would believe she'd be perfectly happy once the deed was done.

She should have gone back to Richmond and married one of her gallant cavaliers. No, she should never have come to Texas. Most important of all, she should never have fallen in love with him.

"You want me to show you how to open that bottle?"

Chet looked up to see a woman who was probably about Melody's age standing in front of his table, hand on her hip and a forced smile on her lips. She was probably tired, counting the minutes until the saloon closed and she could crawl into bed.

Chet returned a weak smile. "I remember how. I just can't decide whether it's worth the trouble."

"That bad?"

Chet had no intention of telling her about Melody, but he didn't want to force her to go away. She looked worn out. "Would you like a drink?"

"I can't drink unless the customer does."

"Bring another glass."

She must have been afraid he'd take back his invitation. She was back in seconds. He poured two drinks. He put his glass to his lips but didn't drink as he watched her take a gulp from hers.

She leaned back and sighed in relief. "Thanks. My name's Cornelia, but everybody calls me Corrie. Ain't been a man in tonight who didn't want more than company and conversation."

"I don't really want either."

She eyed him suspiciously. "You ain't going to try to talk me into going back to your room with you?"

"No."

She relaxed and took a second swallow from her drink. "You're not drinking," she said. "I'll have to leave if you don't."

Chet poured his whiskey into her glass. "There. I'm way ahead of you."

"Thanks, mister. I hope you come in here again."

"I'm leaving in a couple of days."

"Why?"

"Time to move on."

"Woman troubles," she announced. "I could tell it the minute you walked in the door."

Chet spun his glass on the table. "You see a lot of that?"

"Naw. The decent cowhands go up to the Golden Nugget. The Royal outfit hangs out at the Spinning Wheel. The townsfolk prefer the Open Door. I get mostly men down on their luck or men too mean and rotten to have anything but bad luck."

"Then go work at one of the other places."

"My luck has been about like yours. Nobody wants me."

Corrie wasn't pretty, but she was friendly.

"Ever tried waiting tables?"

"You try getting a job like that when you look like I do."

"They might give you a try if you'd ask."

"You seen those two rich women that was shopping up and down the street this morning?"

"Yes."

"You think they'd want the likes of me waiting on them?"

"I'm sure they would be pleased to have you."

"No wonder your girl threw you over. You don't have a real good grip on reality, do you?"

Sometimes he wondered if he could possibly be wrong about reality. Melody's family had accepted him. Maybe others would as well. No, Melody had rejected him at first. She'd only changed her mind after he rescued Sydney. He couldn't expect to perform dramatic rescues for everyone. There would always be rich men like Lantz who ran the towns, who decided who would be accepted and who would be kept outside the bounds of decent society. For himself he didn't care, but he wouldn't let that happen to Melody.

"Let's just say I overlooked a few very important things until it was too late."

"Didn't we both." Corrie took another swallow. "Mine was a fella who made promises I shoulda known he wouldn't keep. But a girl's gullible the first time, ain't she? After that she learns to stick to the rules."

Maybe that was why Melody thought they could make it work. She was gullible the first time.

"You're not drinking, and the boss is starting to give me the eye."

Chet filled both their glasses. When the proprietor turned away, he poured his on the floor.

"You don't even want to drink?" Corrie shook her head, looked over her shoulder, and poured hers out as well. "I don't really like it," she confessed. "But it makes the customers happy when I drink with them." She gave Chet a searching look. "I don't think I ever saw anyone who's got it as bad as you."

"It's my first time, and I was even more gullible than you were."

"But you're old," Corrie exclaimed. She lowered her voice. "I mean you're old for it to be the first time."

Chet was not amused to have Corrie think being twenty-nine meant he practically had one leg in the grave. "I guess I'd better toddle off to bed before I keel over."

"Now I've made you mad. I'm sorry. I just

thought you'd have had your first love when you was fifteen or sixteen."

He might have if his parents hadn't disappeared. Instead he was helping Jake drive herds to New Mexico and fighting Comancheros along the way.

"It's worse when you wait so long," she said.

"Well, at least my first one is behind me. It won't be so bad next time."

Corrie reached out and put her hand over his. "I've seen your kind before," she said. "There won't be no next time for you."

He'd already reached that conclusion, but having her put it into words didn't make it any easier. He pushed his chair away from the table and stood. "I've got to go. Thanks for the company."

"You talk to that girl again. You tell her I said a man like you don't come along all that often. She'd better make mighty certain she's got something better before she throws you back."

On impulse Chet bent over and kissed the top of Corrie's head. "Next time some guy starts badmouthing you, you tell him I said they don't come any nicer. I bet you can cook, too."

Corrie smiled. "You're sweet. You ought not to be wearing that gun. Somebody's liable to take you for a gunfighter."

Chet felt the warmth drain from his body. Even in a saloon, his gun condemned him.

Melody was so nervous, she couldn't stop shaking. She'd never done anything so outrageous in her life. She'd hidden in Chet's room to wait for him. She only hoped she had the courage not to run away before he returned.

It had seemed so easy when she'd first thought of it. Just slip into his room and wait. Surely he would understand that she loved him so much, nothing else mattered. But after waiting for what seemed like hours, she wasn't so certain. What if he didn't come back? What if he was with someone else? What if he got angry when he found her? What if he was drunk?

None of these things had occurred to her as she stood in her own room, undressing, furiously trying to think of some way to keep him from leaving. Now any of those things seemed more likely than that he would be pleased to see her.

She had no idea how long she'd waited. Sitting in a corner, straining for the sound of footsteps, wondering if the next would be his—almost fearful it would be—caused her to lose all sense of time. She wouldn't have been surprised to see the first rays of sunrise any minute.

She realized she had no idea what his footstep sounded like. Several times she had been jerked awake from her semi-trance only to have the footsteps stop short of the door or continue past. She had begun to catalog the difference between the sound of boots, shoes, and spurs, and the softer sound of women's shoes.

When he did arrive, she barely heard any sound at all before the door opened.

Framed in the doorway, the light from behind transforming him into a featureless black shadow, he looked huge and forbidding. For a moment Melody was certain she'd made a monstrous mistake, that she ought to hide until he turned his back and she could escape.

Then he lit the lamp, and it was too late.

He didn't see her right away. He just stood by

the lamp, apparently deep in thought. He wasn't drunk. His step was too steady, his footfall too light. After a moment he sighed deeply and turned around.

She expected a shocked reaction, some kind of stunned response. Even an outburst. She got none of that. She thought he would speak first—shout at her, at least ask what she was doing in his room—but he didn't utter a sound. She wondered if he would throw her out, if he wanted her to leave, if he wanted to throw her on the bed and force himself on her right there.

"I had to come," she said when the silence finally became too frightening. "I couldn't leave things like that."

Still he didn't speak. She felt frightened, desperate to know what was going on in his mind. Did he despise her for being so brazen?

"Aren't you going to say anything?" she asked. Despite the warmth of the night, she felt chilled. What if she had ruined her chances forever?

She pulled her arms in against her body, felt the goose bumps on her skin. She knew coming in here dressed only in a nightgown was a tremendous gamble. But she hadn't been able to think of anything else that would show Chet how much she loved him.

She couldn't back down now. She had nothing to lose by going forward. She covered the distance between them, put her arms around Chet, and held him tightly. She might as well have put her arms around a statue. He felt so stiff, his body so rigid, that she was certain he'd break before he would bend. He was fighting her, fighting his desire to give in. His arms, clamped to his sides, quivered from the tension building inside him.

This was the final battle. She had to win now, or she would lose forever.

She released him, took his face in her hands, and forced him to look at her.

"Look at me," she pleaded. "I love you. I know you don't believe that, but I do."

Much to her surprise, that broke him. He put his hands over hers. "I know you do. I never doubted that."

"Then why are you sending me away?"

"I'm not sending you away. I'm leaving."

"It's the same."

"No, it's not."

"It feels like it. I'm not going to go back to my room. I'm staying right here until that feeling goes away."

He leaned his forehead down until it touched her own. "Do you know what you're saying?"

"Yes." Her voice was barely a whisper.

"You know I can't resist you any longer, don't you?"

"I don't want you to resist me. I want—"

He put his fingers over her lips. "I know what you want. I've wanted the same thing ever since I met you."

Then he kissed her. But it wasn't the hungry, hard kiss of a man released from doubt. It was the lingering, savoring kiss of a man who intended to treasure each moment because it might be his last. Melody had every intention of changing that. Before the night was over, she meant to convince Chet Attmore that she was the one part of his life he couldn't do without.

Now that she knew he wasn't going to humiliate her by forcing her to leave his room, her body began to feel quite warm. She was in Chet's arms, he was kissing her, and he meant to keep her with him. That was all she needed to know at the moment. She still had a chance.

He was kissing her shoulders again. He had pushed her gown down her arms and was giving loving attention to her exposed skin. She surrendered to the sensation that made her bones feel as if they were melting. It was a wonderful feeling. It made her feel almost liquified, like rich, dark chocolate as the hard bars melt over heat. She felt like that. The heat came from inside her as well as from Chet. She felt warmed by it, suffused with it, overcome by it.

The feelings in her breasts, however, were quite different. As her body rubbed ever so gently against Chet's chest, her nipples grew increasingly sensitive, increasingly firm. And the more firm they grew, the more sensitive they became.

Between the two sensations, she was becoming quite distracted. Then Chet's hand closed over her left breast and all other feelings went into eclipse. The sensations were new and unexpectedly powerful. She flinched. Chet froze.

"Did I hurt you?"

"No," she hastened to assure him. To prove it, she leaned forward until her body touched his. "I don't want you to stop."

When he still hesitated, she reached up and kissed him. At the same time she struggled to undo some of the buttons on his shirt. She wanted to touch him as he had been touching her. The feel of her hand on his bare skin seemed to release Chet from further doubt. His kisses turned hard and hungry. He cupped both her breasts in his hands.

Melody gasped from the shock of his hands

against her soft, overheated skin. She tried to undo more shirt buttons, but she found it difficult to concentrate on anything beyond her body, nearly impossible to summon the energy to do more than remain on her feet. Chet was kissing her deeply, teasing her nipples with his fingertips, rubbing his leg against her inner thigh. She felt as if she were under multiple assaults, her defenses in retreat. Just about the time she felt certain her legs would give way under her, Chet picked her up and carried her to the bed.

The full reality of what was about to happen struck her with stunning force. Up until now all her thoughts had centered on doing anything in her power to make certain Chet believed she loved him passionately, would endure anything for him, to keep him by her side. While her goal remained unchanged, she recognized more fully the cost to herself. She was about to offer Chet something she could give only once. If he rejected her, she might be a marked woman for the rest of her life.

She realized that wouldn't matter. If Chet rejected her, she wouldn't care what anyone else thought of her.

Chet hesitated, looking down at her as though he could see her thoughts. To reassure him, she smiled and urged him down next to her. She put her arms around him and pulled him close. This was where she wanted him for the rest of her life. She didn't know how she could ever have had a moment's doubt.

"Take off your shirt," she said. "I want to feel your bare skin against me."

He took off his shirt, removed his boots and socks, then lay down next to her and cradled her in his arms. Instinctively Melody's hands came up against his chest. It seemed an almost unbelievable experience that she should be lying next to a man naked from the waist up, letting her hand play over the soft skin of his chest. Touching him was equally strange. He was so soft and warm, yet so hard and unyielding at the same time. He made her feel small and vulnerable, and she wasn't sure she liked that.

Then he kissed her breast through the fabric of her nightgown, and she lost all interest in theories of equality. The soft moan that escaped from her did nothing to discourage him. In seconds he had opened her gown and exposed her bare flesh to his hungry mouth. The feeling of his tongue on her nipple was far more intense than she had anticipated. Her swift intake of breath was noisy and involuntary; her muscles bunched and lifted her body off the bed. Her fingers clenched, digging into the hair on his chest. She felt him tense, but his mouth never left her breast.

When his hand moved to cover her other breast, she thought she might faint under the dual assault. Her body had never been subjected to such a barrage of sensations. Nothing had ever affected her so deeply. She felt as though each part of her body was sensually fused to the core of herself.

Even the feeling that had begun to grow in her belly seemed to have its origin in what Chet was doing to her breasts. It was a feeling unlike anything else that was happening to her. It seemed to spiral slowly outward, gradually growing warmer and bigger and more intense. As it gradually drew each part of her body into its grasp, Melody experienced a shift in the sensations ex-

ploding throughout her body. She became aware
of a feeling of moist heat that centered in her
loins. Simultaneously she became aware of a
vague need somewhere deep inside her. Ill de-
fined at first, it began to grow stronger and more
insistent. When Chet moved his hand down her
side, across her hip, and over to the inside of her
thigh, the need abruptly came into focus.

Only Chet had the power to reach that need.
Only he could satisfy it.

When his hand moved between her legs and entered her, her whole universe shifted. Before she
had a chance to accustom herself to his invasion,
he touched a spot that sent shivers racing through
her entire body.

"Oh!" The sound was involuntary, its escape
unintentional.

"Did I hurt you?" Chet asked.

"No," she managed to say, wondering if he
would touch her in that place again.

He found the magical spot and began to rub it
gently. Melody could hardly breathe. Her muscles
tensed, arching her body. They relaxed just as
quickly. She felt waves of sensation, pulsing,
throbbing, increasing in strength and intensity
until she heard herself calling Chet's name.

He swallowed her cries in a kiss, but that didn't
affect the incredible magic of what he was doing
to her body. Melody twisted and turned, pushing
against him with all her strength until she
thought she would scream from the sweet agony
of it. Just as she was certain she could stand no
more, the dam broke and moist heat seemed to
flow from her like flood waters from a broken
dam.

Before the waves had time to recede, Chet

moved above her. She felt him enter her, stretch her wide.

"This may hurt a little at first," he said, "but I promise it will last only a second."

Before she could recover herself enough to ask what he meant, she felt a sharp pain as he plunged deep inside her. The receding waves helped mask the pain, but Melody was startled by its sharpness.

"It won't hurt anymore," Chet said as he began to move inside her.

At first the sensations were entirely different. The knowledge that she was joined with Chet, that their bodies had become one, seemed miraculous. It represented everything she wanted. He must understand that they belonged to each other from this moment on, that they could never be parted. She wanted to speak, to tell him how she felt, to hear him say he felt the same way.

But hardly had these thoughts entered her mind before they were driven out by a rebirth of the sensations that had driven her wild just moments before. She clutched Chet's shoulders, but he didn't seem to notice. He appeared to be gripped by a sweet agony fully as intense as her own. Melody didn't know if she could go through this a second time so soon after the first.

Chet gradually increased his rhythm, relentlessly driving her forward until there was no possibility of retreat. Melody forgot she wanted to tell Chet anything. She forgot he probably wouldn't have heard her. She thought only of the sensations that held her in their grip, teasing and torturing her until she reached the brink.

Then, as before, she felt all restraint vanish as the liquid heat flowed from her in wave after wave. She was only vaguely aware that Chet was experiencing sensations fully as strong as those gripping her.

Finally, when the waves had receded, she relaxed into the mattress, her body totally exhausted, her breath coming more easily. Chet lay next to her. She reached over and caressed his cheek. She smiled. He was hers now just as surely as she was his. They could never be apart again.

Not ever.

Chapter Nineteen

"He's a gunfighter!" Lantz shouted at Melody. "You can't seriously consider marrying him."

"I love him," she replied, "and he loves me. There's nothing I want more than to be his wife."

"Can't you talk some sense into her, Belle? She's your daughter."

Lantz had forced his way into Belle's room as she and Melody were enjoying their coffee and talking over what to do with this last day in town. He'd found another man for them to interview for the foreman's job. He'd also come to renew his quest for Melody's hand. Melody hadn't wanted to say anything until she talked to Chet, but Lantz wouldn't take her refusal seriously. He seemed determined to go on believing she would marry him if he kept asking. Desperation had caused her to tell him about Chet. Now she wondered if she'd made a mistake. Lantz was furious. Belle looked more upset than surprised.

"She's not my daughter, Lantz. Even if she were, she's a grown woman, capable of making her own decisions."

"Not if wanting to marry that man is an example."

"Chet gave up gunfighting," Melody said. "He only put his guns on again to rescue Sydney."

"I suppose he wasn't wearing them when he stampeded my cattle and burned my barn." Lantz remembered his personal grievances. "It won't matter if you do marry him. You'll be a widow soon."

"How? Will you shoot him from behind the way Blade did?"

For a moment Melody wondered if Lantz might not be angry enough to hit her.

"He's twice as fast as you," she said. "We all saw that the first day you tried to draw on him."

"I'll have Luke do it. He's the fastest man in Texas."

Cold fear gripped Melody. "That would be murder. They'd hang both of you."

"No, they won't. Luke will find some way to make it look like a fair fight."

"How?"

"I don't know. He's a gunfighter. That's what he's paid to do."

It made her angry that Lantz could talk about killing Chet as though he was no more than an unwanted dog. That he could actually think of killing anyone without even the slightest qualm of conscience frightened her. Chet must be good to have been so successful, but not even Dan Walters claimed he was the best in Texas.

"You lay one hand on Chet, Lantz Royal, and so help me, I'll go to your house and shoot you in your own living room."

Melody was nearly as startled by her words as Lantz and Belle.

"Don't be silly," Lantz said. "Women can't shoot. You probably don't even know how to handle a gun."

"I know enough to shoot you," Melody replied. "And I will if you set that killer on Chet. Now leave. I don't want to have to look at you any longer."

Lantz sputtered, protested, even issued some threats of his own, but he soon left, promising she would be his wife yet. The minute he left, Melody jumped to her feet.

"I've got to talk to Chet."

"Are you really going to marry him?" Belle asked.

Melody stopped in her tracks. She couldn't tell Belle about last night. Her stepmother wouldn't understand.

"I intend to do everything in my power to become his wife."

"But Lantz is right, dear. He is a gunfighter."

"Was. He wants to find some place where people have never heard of him and start his own ranch. I intend to go with him."

"It won't be a thing like Richmond."

"I have no doubt I will be quite uncomfortable," Melody said, "but I love him. I couldn't think of living without him."

"If that's the case, I don't see the need for him

to go anywhere. He can stay right here and run the ranch for us."

"Are you sure?"

"Of course. It would be the perfect solution. Besides, Sydney likes him."

"I'll ask him, but he's determined that sooner or later somebody is going to come looking for him, even shoot him in the back."

"Are you prepared to become a widow?"

Coming from Belle, the question was a shock. She was certain Belle hadn't meant to hurt her, but she had. "Lantz won't send this Luke person after him. He was just angry."

"If not him, somebody else."

"What can I do?" Melody asked. "I love him. I can't live without him."

"I don't know," Belle said. "I really don't know."

Melody remembered Lantz's threat. "I've got to tell Chet what Lantz said."

"You'd better wait until you get dressed," Belle said, smiling. "It'd be a terrible shock to the poor man to open his door and find you standing there in your robe."

Melody was more certain than ever that Belle would never understand about last night.

"Just a minute," Chet called out when Melody knocked on his door.

Melody decided that after last night there was nothing she or Chet had to hide from each other, so she opened the door and stepped inside without waiting. She saw Lantz's gunfighter climbing in through the window. She pointed at Luke and started to scream. Chet clamped his hand over her mouth, dragged her out of the doorway, and kicked the door closed.

"Don't make a sound," Chet said. "I don't want anybody to know he's here."

Luke had climbed back in through the window, but he just stood there. He was wearing a gun, but he was staring at Melody, not Chet.

"That's Lantz's gunfighter," Melody said when she managed to free her mouth. "Lantz said he was going to kill you. He said he'd arrange it so it looked like a fair fight."

"He's also my brother," Chet said.

Chet might as well have hit Melody with his fist. The shock was so great, she was certain her legs would go out from under her.

"Your brother! But he was sent to kill you."

"Lantz asked me to kill him several days ago," Luke said. "I refused."

"How? Won't you be marked a coward for failing to perform the job you were hired to do?"

"I was hired to find the rustlers," Luke said.

"Then what are you doing here?"

Melody couldn't get it out of her head that Luke was a killer. Did it make any difference to a man like that whether he killed a perfect stranger or somebody he knew?

"Luke wouldn't shoot me."

"What?" Melody's guilt over her thoughts caused her to flush.

"You're wondering if Luke might not shoot me even though I am his brother."

She tried to deny it, but her tongue wouldn't move.

"It's a fair question. Everybody knows killers have no conscience. We couldn't have. How else could we do what we do?"

"I wasn't thinking that," Melody protested.

"Yes, you were. I saw it in your face."

She wasn't, not about Chet. Never about him. She could tell right then that any progress she'd made last night had just been wiped out. The worst part of it was that she'd done it to herself.

"It's not that," she said, desperately trying to think of a way out, panicked that she'd said something unforgivable, and Chet would never speak to her again. "Lantz was just in our room. He got mad when I told him I wouldn't marry him because I loved you. He said he was going to have Luke kill you. When I saw Luke climbing in the window, I thought—"

"He was climbing out," Chet said.

"What's he doing here?" Melody asked again. Then she remembered where she'd seen Luke before. He'd been the man who found Chet after Blade shot him. "Why didn't you tell me you were his brother then?" she asked Luke.

"When was that?"

"After Blade shot him?"

"I didn't know what he was doing there, who you were, anything about the situation. I thought it best not to mention it."

"And now?"

"I came to tell him I know who's behind the rustling."

"Who?" Melody asked.

"Blade."

"I don't believe it," Melody said. "Why would he rustle his own father's cows?"

"Because he's mad at his father. He blames him for stealing you away from him."

Melody didn't know what to say. She'd never been close to falling in love with Blade. She'd almost forgotten he'd ever wanted to marry her.

"That's why he's been stealing your cows as

well," Luke told Melody. "He thinks you threw him over for his father because of his money."

"But I'm not going to marry Lantz."

"That's not the impression you gave when you were at the ranch after Chet stampeded Lantz's herd."

Melody remembered that Blade had been particularly nasty that night.

"I was just trying to keep Lantz from guessing I'd had anything to do with the raid on his herd."

"Blade couldn't be expected to know that. I had something else to tell you," Luke said, turning to his brother. "Blade has sworn to kill you."

"I'm not worried about him," Chet said.

"You'd better be." Luke said. "He doesn't mean to meet you in a fair fight."

"How do you know?" Melody asked.

"It's been my job to see he didn't leave the house until he was well again," Luke said. "I've had plenty of time to hear nearly every thought that has passed through his head."

"But they'll hang him."

"He thinks his father can get him out of anything," Luke said. "Don't underestimate him. I think he's crazy."

"What are you going to do?" Melody asked Chet.

"Nothing. You're going to hire a new foreman. I'll leave. If I'm not here, it won't matter what Blade wants to do."

Something about the way he said that scared Melody all the way down to her toes. "But I don't want you to leave. Belle and I have decided we want you to be our foreman. You can—"

"No."

"Chet, you can't . . . I thought . . ."

"I'd better be going," Luke said. "I don't want Lantz to know where I've been."

Melody didn't have any attention to give Luke as he climbed out the window. She had to make Chet understand that his becoming the Spring Water foreman was best for both of them.

"I don't understand why you won't take the job," Melody said. "We've got to have some place to live after we get married. It will be a little crowded at—"

"We're not going to get married," Chet said.

There was no doubt in her mind that he meant what he said. He had looked straight at her. His gaze didn't waver. "I thought . . . after last night . . ."

"I thought so, too," Chet said. "For a few hours I thought it could work, that we could make it work. It wouldn't be easy, but I told myself if we loved each other enough . . ."

"What?"

"Nothing. It doesn't matter anymore."

"Why? What happened? Don't you love me anymore?"

"I love you as much as ever."

"Then why?"

"Do you remember what you were thinking a few minutes ago?"

Cold, deep and numbing, filled her inside. "I wasn't thinking it about you," she said, desperate to make him believe her. "I don't know your brother. Lantz had just said he was going to have him kill you."

"But you saw him as a killer."

"But—" She didn't have to finish that sentence. Chet already knew what she'd been about to say.

"But he is a killer. Isn't that what you were go-

339

ing to say? It's what anybody would say about Luke. It's what they'll say about me. It's what you'll think one day."

"No, Chet, I'll never think that about you."

"You won't be able to help yourself, because that's what I was. A man can't outrun his past. He can't deny what he was. Neither can his wife."

"I could," Melody pleaded. "I could!"

"You'd be lying to yourself, and I'd see it in your eyes. I couldn't stand that. I would leave before I let that happen." He turned to pick up his saddlebags. She grabbed him by the arm.

"Chet, please listen to me!"

"Go back to Richmond, Melody. Marry one of those nice men who's never lifted a gun except to hunt rabbits. You and your children will never have anything to reproach him with."

She pulled at his arm as hard as she could, but she might have saved her strength for all the good it did her. "Chet, for God's sake, listen to me! I'm not the same person who came out here from Richmond. I don't judge people the same way. I won't—"

He grabbed her and kissed her, fiercely and hard. For a moment euphoria flooded her. He'd changed his mind. He would stay. But when he put her away from him, she knew she'd lost.

"Good-bye, Melody."

"Where are you going? You've got to tell me where you're going!"

"I don't know, but it doesn't really matter."

Then he was gone. The door closed behind him, and she was alone.

The bed—its neatly made appearance giving no indication of the passionate embraces that had been exchanged on it just a few hours earlier—

seemed to mock her. She'd risked everything for the man she loved, then lost him because she fell prey to the same blind prejudice she thought she'd shed. She hadn't meant it, not even the thoughts Chet had suspected. She was just so afraid for him that she didn't trust anyone, especially not someone who was a killer. Didn't he understand that?

Of course he did. He'd understood it long before she did. He'd known she felt that way even when she didn't. That was why he'd gone. He couldn't endure knowing his wife thought him a killer.

And, God help her, she still did.

Returning to the ranch didn't bring Melody any relief from the terrible feeling that her life was over. She hadn't managed to solve any of her problems, either. They didn't have a foreman, the rustlers hadn't been caught, and Lantz still meant to take her ranch. They hadn't had to hire Lantz's third candidate because Dan Walters had offered to handle the job until they could find someone. That pleased Belle, but it hadn't made Sydney very happy. Even Neill seemed to feel Chet's absence.

"I'm going for a ride," Sydney announced as soon as the buggy came to a halt.

"Me, too," Neill announced.

Melody was surprised when Sydney didn't raise any objections. She was even more surprised when Belle didn't either. Apparently Belle thought Dan's presence insured that everything would be all right. Melody liked Dan a lot, but nothing felt right without Chet.

"Just don't go too far," Belle said. "This will be

our first dinner back at home. I'm sure Bernice has planned something special."

Melody knew the boys didn't care what Bernice had planned for dinner as long as it was plentiful. From the besotted look on Belle's face, she doubted her stepmother did, either.

That made Melody miss Chet all the more.

He'd disappeared without a trace. She'd even tracked down Luke to see if he knew. He answered every question she asked, but he couldn't tell her where Chet had gone.

Or he wouldn't.

She managed to pull herself together sufficiently to introduce Dan to the crew. She was pleased to see they responded well to him. She wasn't pleased to learn the rustlers had run off another batch of steers the night before.

"They didn't get so many this time," Speers said. "It was almost like they did it for spite. They took calves and yearlings, which ain't going to be worth much of nothing to them. They could have got fat steers if they'd taken a little more time."

Melody thought of Luke's saying Blade was behind the rustling. As difficult as she found that to believe, it made sense with the kind of rustling that was going on. She hadn't told Belle, but she'd have to tell Dan. If he was going to be responsible for their herd, he had to know what he was up against.

Melody found it most difficult to face Bernice. She'd never been able to hide anything from this kindly woman.

"He's gone, and he's not coming back," she told Bernice when she asked about Chet. "And it's all my fault."

Bernice made her sit down at the table. She

poured them each a cup of coffee. Then she sat next to Melody and took her hand.

"Maybe you made a mistake, but it's his fault, too."

"How?"

"A good man ought to be smart enough to see past some foolish things said in haste."

"He can. I just couldn't see past his gun. I acted just like everybody else. You should have seen his eyes. I saw something in them die, and I couldn't do anything about it."

"Did he say where he was going?"

Melody felt a momentary impulse to smile, but it was too weak to reach her facial muscles. "I've already thought of following him, but I don't know where he went."

"Do you think he'll come back?"

The question was spoken softly, almost fearfully.

"No. I confirmed what he feared. If I just hadn't been so afraid that man had been sent to kill him . . ."

"What man?"

"Luke, Lantz's gunfighter. They're brothers. Chet and Luke are brothers."

"What were you doing meeting him?"

"He'd come to tell Chet that Blade meant to kill him. He also said Blade was behind the rustling."

"Blade! Why, for heaven's sake?"

"Because he was mad at me for not marrying him and at his father for taking me away. Chet and Luke think Blade's crazy."

"He's not crazy," Bernice said with an inelegant snort. "He's just had everything he's ever wanted handed to him. Now suddenly he can't have something he wants and he's throwing a temper tantrum. He's nothing but a big baby."

"A dangerous big baby."

"Well, if Chet's gone, he won't be a danger to him anymore. But what about you? You depending on that man Belle brought home to watch out for you?"

"He's agreed to look after things until we can find a foreman."

Bernice looked skeptical. "I supposed he'll be all right if he can take his eyes off Belle long enough to know whether he's herding cows or antelope."

Melody did smile. "It's been that way from the moment they set eyes on each other. I think it's sweet."

"We'll see. Now you get yourself upstairs and lie down. You look worn out."

But Melody wasn't tired, and lying down wouldn't fix anything that was wrong with her. Only being in Chet's arms, knowing he would never leave her again, would fix what ailed her. She pulled a chair over to the window so she could look out over the wide plain between the house and the canyon.

She had to figure out where Chet had gone. The moment she had set foot on the ranch, she'd known she couldn't stay here without him. She didn't want to return to Richmond. Somehow, without her knowing, that old life had passed beyond her forever. She would stay in Texas, but she couldn't stay here without Chet.

She had to talk to Dan, find out everything he knew about Chet. If she had to, she'd talk to Luke again. She'd do anything she had to do, but she had to figure out where he had gone. When she did, she would go after him.

"I don't understand where they could have gone," Belle said for the dozenth time. "They're never late for dinner. Sydney acts like he's starved if Bernice is five minutes late getting it on the table."

"They probably just rode too far," Dan said. "They've been in town for nearly a week. Boys like to stretch their legs."

"Sydney, maybe, but not Neill," Melody said. "He's perfectly happy to stay close to the house. He only went today because he's trying to be grown-up like his brother."

"I'll look for them," Dan said. "You go ahead and eat. Let them go to bed hungry. They won't be late again."

"You can't go," Melody said. "You don't know the ranch. You'll probably get lost in the dark."

"I've found my way across half of Texas in the dark," Dan said. "I won't get lost in this little piece of it."

Belle obviously worried about Dan, too, but she also worried about her boys. The boys won out. "Take Toby with you," she said. "He's been here the longest. He knows the boys the best."

But not even Toby could find any trace of them. They seemed to have disappeared.

"I don't like to quit," Dan said after he'd allowed Belle a few moments to get over the worst of her shock, "but we can't do much now. Toby told me about this canyon you've got, but it's pitch black at the bottom. They could be almost anywhere in there, and we wouldn't be able to see them. I've told all the men to be ready to make a thorough search beginning at dawn."

"You didn't find any trace of them at all?" Melody asked. "Not even their horses?"

"No. If this were back home, I'd have said they'd gone visiting at a neighboring ranch and stayed too late to come home. But Speers tells me the closest ranch belongs to Lantz Royal and the boys would never go there."

"They don't like Lantz or his son," Melody explained.

She didn't know what gave her the idea, but suddenly she was certain Blade was responsible for the boys' disappearance. Maybe it was the way he'd taken the cows, as if he was mad at her rather than wanting stock to sell. Wouldn't it be even better revenge if he did something to her brothers?

She knew what she had to do. "I'm going to see Lantz," she announced.

"What has Lantz got to do with the boys being late to dinner?" Belle asked.

"If Blade is doing the rustling because he's mad at me, wouldn't it make sense that he might do something to the boys for the same reason?"

"What do you think he's done?" Belle said, looking deathly white.

"I don't know. If he's at home, he probably had nothing to do with it. I've got to find out."

"I'll go with you," Dan volunteered.

"I'd prefer for you to stay here with Belle. Besides, you've already been out for hours. I'll get one of the men to ride with me."

Belle put up a brief argument, but it was clear she needed someone to support her spirits through the long hours of the night. Melody was certain she wouldn't sleep. If Blade was responsible for her brothers disappearance, it would be her fault. She didn't know how much more blame she could take right now.

The ride to Lantz's ranch was long and lonely. Speers rode with her. Since she drove the buggy while Speers rode horseback, it was impossible to talk. She had far too much time to think about all the things that had happened during the last weeks, the misconceptions, the things she'd done wrong, the chances she'd missed. It was a relief to reach Lantz's ranch.

He wasn't happy at being awakened in the middle of the night.

"What in the hell did Belle mean, letting you out in the middle of the night?" he demanded. "If you get kidnapped again, you might not get away so easy."

"The boys are missing," Melody said, deciding this was not the time to explain about the kidnapping. "Nobody can sleep until we find them."

"Well, they're not here."

"Where's Blade?"

"In bed where he's supposed to be."

"Are you sure? Did you see him yourself?"

"No. Why?"

"Chet believes Blade is responsible for the rustling, that he's stealing from us because he's mad at me for turning him down."

"That's a damned lie!" Lantz bellowed. "The damned rustlers steal from me, too."

"Chet believes Blade steals from you because he's mad at you for taking me away from him."

"I'll kill him for spreading tales like that about Blade. He got over you long ago. Besides, stealing from me is the same as stealing from himself."

"Chet says he might not see it that way if he is mad enough."

"I warned you about that man," Lantz said. "I know you women can't help making fools of yourselves over a handsome cowboy—it seems like Belle is set on being just as blind as you—but they're nothing but saddle bums. Yours has already left you. I don't suppose the one Belle's latched on to will stay much longer."

Melody already knew Lantz's opinion of Chet and Dan, and she wasn't interested in hearing it again. "I want to know where Blade is. If you won't tell me, I'll look for him myself."

Lantz seemed to forget his irritation at Chet and Dan in the face of Melody's suspicions about Blade. "Why are you so all-fired anxious to know where Blade is right now?" he thundered.

"Because I think he has something to do with the boys' disappearance."

"You're a fool," Lantz said. "It's a good thing we didn't get married."

Melody could hardly believe she'd actually considered marrying this man. She must have been a complete idiot when she arrived from Virginia. "I don't care what you think of me, Lantz. I want to know if Blade is here. If you won't tell me, I'll get the sheriff out here."

"You starting blabbing your foolish accusations about town and I'll—"

"It might save a whole lot of talking if you went to see if your boy is in his bed," Speers said.

"Don't you start telling me what to do, you two-bit piece of cow dung!" Lantz bellowed.

Speers pulled his gun. "You want me to drop him right here, Miss Jordan?"

Melody should have been used to the appearance of a gun by now, but she wasn't. "No. I just want him to see if Blade is here."

"His papa seems reluctant. Do you think he'll stick his head out if I put a bullet through his bedroom window?"

"You'll just get us shot. I'll go look."

"You're not setting foot in my house!" Lantz bellowed. "I'll have Blade out here to tell you himself what he thinks of you and your accusations."

When Lantz didn't return right away, Melody knew her suspicions were confirmed. Blade was not in the house. "Let's go back," she said to Speers, unwilling to wait for Lantz to confirm what she already knew. "We have to keep looking for them tonight. I don't trust Blade not to do something terrible."

But all the way back to the ranch she couldn't think of anybody but Chet. If he were here, he'd find the boys. If he were here, everything would be all right.

But he wasn't, so it was up to her to find them. She had ridden over most of the ranch with Chet. She knew it far better than Dan. Besides, if she found Blade, she might have a chance of talking him into letting the boys go. If he saw a stranger, or a large group of cowhands, he might do something desperate. That thought petrified her. She would have to go alone.

Chapter Twenty

Melody could feel the air cool the minute she dropped to the canyon floor. It would be chilly until the sun came up. She shivered. She wasn't used to riding across open country in the dark. Even for a woman brought up on a farm, it was a frightening experience. She'd had to saddle her horse herself. She'd already stopped twice to tighten the cinch.

She wished she'd been able to ask someone to come with her. Sometimes she could barely see her hand in front of her face. Very little moonlight reached the bottom of the canyon. When it narrowed and the walls closed in, it grew darker still. Occasionally, overhanging tree branches turned the trail into inky blackness. If she hadn't been able to depend on her horse, she'd have lost the trail long ago.

She didn't know how she was going to find

where Blade was hiding the boys. She didn't imagine she'd be lucky enough for one of them to see her and give a shout. Blade was too smart to leave them where they could attract the attention of the first person to pass by. She hoped they were all right. Any man willing to kidnap two innocent boys because a woman didn't want to marry him was unstable.

At times Melody even wondered if Blade had the boys, if she hadn't made this up out of her feelings of guilt. She'd tried very hard to find another explanation, but she always came back to Blade.

Chet had told her there were several caves in the canyon walls. He'd also said there was a trail up the other side, but she didn't know where to find either. She'd asked Speers about them, but he said he'd never seen the caves or the trail out. Melody was certain they were there. Chet was never wrong.

A sound caused Melody to pull her horse to a stop. But after several minutes, the silence remained unbroken. Probably some small rodent looking for seeds. Maybe a coyote moving among the brush in search of its dinner. She had nothing to fear from either, but she couldn't forget there were steers and bulls in this canyon that might not like having their sleep interrupted. Chet had told her never to expect them to act like the cows on her aunt's farm. They were wild animals, used to fending for themselves against wolves and other predators. If they thought they were in danger, they'd attack.

A shiver of fear raced along her spine, but she rode on. Every time the horse's stride caused the saddle to shift under her, she wondered if she'd pulled the cinch tight enough, if she'd be dumped on the ground any minute. She didn't care to be left on foot this far from the ranch.

She thought of Belle and Bernice waking up to find she wasn't in the house. They'd be upset despite the note she'd left explaining where she'd gone and why, but she couldn't wait. She had a terrible feeling that if they waited until morning, it would be too late.

She tried not to think of the times she'd come to this canyon with Chet. She tried equally hard not to think of what things would be like if he were here now. He was gone. She'd driven him away. She had to get used to that.

Another sound broke the silence of the night. Again she was unable to see anything in the dark, but she had the uncomfortable feeling that something was following her. Chet had told her that her horse would sense danger long before she did. Its head up, its ears pricked, her mount seemed as calm as ever.

As she rode deeper into the canyon, Melody grew more and more certain she was being followed. She had no idea why or by what. She considered turning around, but it seemed best to keep going, to hope whatever was trailing her would lose interest and give up. Tom had once said he was certain there were cougars in this canyon. Speers said he was wrong, but Melody wasn't worried about its being a cat. It was making too much noise. Besides, her horse appeared interested, not frightened.

That meant it was a man. But who?

The rustlers!

She'd been so busy worrying about her brothers, she'd forgotten Chet said the rustlers used this canyon as an escape route. She was probably riding down the trail they used to take their stolen cattle out of the county. Knowing Luke and Chet thought Blade was responsible for the rustlers didn't help. While she might have some influence over Blade, she didn't expect the rustlers would care who she was, only that she was in their way, about to discover their hideout. They would be interested only in silencing her.

Melody suddenly realized she'd been very foolish to ride out alone in the middle of the night. If she'd been so certain they couldn't wait, she should have tried to convince Dan of the danger. She was certain Speers and several of the cowhands would have ridden with her despite their exhaustion.

Almost without knowing it, she urged her horse into a canter. When she could hear the horse behind her coming closer, she knew she was being followed. She urged her horse into a gallop, but it was too late. A rider swooped down out of the darkness, grabbed her reins, and pulled her mount to a halt. Melody tried to fight him off with her riding crop, but he easily jerked it out of her grasp and tossed it aside.

Her captor turned, and she found herself staring into the face of Blade Royal.

Her sense of relief was short-lived. This wasn't the young man who only a few months earlier had professed his undying love, who had begged her to marry him despite the fact he was a month younger than she. This was an angry man who looked very pleased at having frightened her quite badly. But she was determined he wouldn't know it.

"Let go of my reins, Blade."

He acted as if he hadn't heard her.

"Did you bring him?" he asked.

"Bring who?"

"Your gunfighter."

"What do you want Chet for?"

"I'm going to kill him."

"Well, you won't do it by waiting for him in this canyon. He's gone."

"Where'd he go?"

"I don't know. He wouldn't tell me."

He grabbed her by the throat. It happened so fast, she couldn't have stopped him.

"You're lying. He's here somewhere. Tell me where, or I'll choke you."

Blade placed his thumb over her windpipe and began to squeeze.

"If you choke me, I won't be able to tell you what I do know," she managed to say before the pressure cut off her voice. When she began to grow dizzy, she thought he was going to kill her anyway, but he suddenly released the pressure. She put her hand to her throat to try to rub away the pain.

"Now tell me where he is. The next time I won't stop."

"I don't know. You can kill me, but you won't learn any more than that."

"You're in love with him. He wouldn't pass up a chance of getting his hands on a ranch like the Spring Water. Did you know my father's gunfighter is his brother?"

"I found out when we were in town."

"I think they're in this together. Luke means to kill me. Chet will marry you. Then they'll have both ranches."

"Then why didn't Luke kill you when you were laid up?"

"It wasn't time yet. Chet wasn't sure of you."

Melody realized she couldn't reason with Blade. He was past that. "I don't know about any of that," she said, "but Chet is gone. We had an argument, and he left."

Blade glared at her. "I don't believe you. Why would he leave?"

"Because he didn't want a wife who thought he was a killer."

"But he is a killer."

"No. He'll use his gun if he thinks it's necessary, but he's not a killer."

"He shot me," Blade said.

Melody saw anger blaze in his eyes. She also saw something else, a kind of rage that wasn't quite sane.

"He thought you were going to hurt Sydney."

"The little fool thought he could outdraw me. Me!" he practically screamed. "I was going to make him draw on me. Then I was going to kill him."

"Where are my brothers?" she asked, suddenly fearful.

"I'm going to kill Chet, too," Blade said. "He shot me."

"Where are my brothers?" Melody repeated.

"I knew he'd come if anything happened to those boys," he said.

"Chet's gone, Blade. He won't know about anything that happens here."

"Now that I've got you, he's sure to come. Then I'll kill him."

Blade wasn't listening to her.

"I'll take you back to the camp, but I won't hide

355

you," he said. "I want him to see you."

Melody could tell Blade was pleased with himself. He thought he had everything figured out. She didn't know what he was going to do when he finally realized Chet wasn't coming. She hoped she'd figure out a way to help her brothers escape before then.

Blade jerked her reins out of her hands and forced her to follow him. They traveled recklessly fast through the dangerous trails along the canyon floor, but Blade seemed to know every twist and turn. Melody wondered how long he'd been trespassing on her father's land. She wondered if he'd been rustling before her father's death. She wondered how she and her brothers were going to get away from Blade, how they could get to safety before he discovered they were missing and followed. She wondered if anyone except Chet would think to come so deep into the canyon.

She knew the answers to all of those questions. Nobody except Chet would have any idea where they were. Nobody but Chet would believe the depth of Blade's hatred, believe the extent of his madness, understand the danger she and her brothers were in.

But Chet was miles away by now. He wouldn't know anything of their danger. He probably wouldn't come if he did.

No, he would. He'd done it before, and he'd do it again. Only he wouldn't this time because he wouldn't know.

"Where are we going?" she asked Blade. Maybe if she had some idea, she could think of something to do.

"A place where I can be certain he'll see you."

He turned abruptly and started up the wall of

the canyon. In the dark, Melody could hardly make out the trail. It seemed more like a rockslide than a trail. The horses struggled to keep their footing on the loose stones. Melody looked up. The rim was at least three hundred feet above them. This couldn't be the trail Chet said led to the upper rim.

A few minutes later Blade turned the horses to the right, and Melody found herself on a narrow ledge. She saw two men she didn't know sitting before a small fire. Looking around, she saw Neill huddled against a dark shape. Melody fell out of the saddle and raced to her brother. With a cry of recognition, Neill threw his arms out to his sister. He didn't come to her because his feet were bound. He broke into tears at once.

"He beat Sydney," he cried. "I tried to stop him, but they held me. I think he killed him."

Neill's gaze turned toward the dark shape lying on the ground. With a gasp of horror, Melody realized that it was Sydney.

"He shouldn't have tried to shoot me," Blade said. "I wouldn't have hurt him if he hadn't tried to shoot me."

Ignoring Blade, Melody rushed over to her brother. She turned him over. What she saw nearly caused her to be sick. Blood covered his face. His eyes were swollen shut. His lips were broken and bleeding. Cuts and bruises covered his skin. But he was breathing. She touched his side, and he groaned. He probably had several broken ribs. Blade had beaten his body as well. She got to her feet filled with such rage that she forgot to be afraid of Blade.

"If I were a man, I'd beat you within an inch of your life. He's a boy, Blade Royal. Are you such a coward that you take out your frustrations only on boys?" She slapped him as hard as she could. "If you ever touch him again, I'll kill you." She strode over to the fire and took the kettle of hot water off the stove. A cry from Neill caused her to turn. Blade was coming toward her, fist raised.

"Come a step closer and I'll throw this boiling water at you," she said. "You'd be blind. Your face would be so scarred, no one could stand to look at you."

They stood there, he afraid of the pot of boiling water, she afraid of what he'd do when she turned her back.

"Does your father know what you've done, Blade? Does he know you've stolen his cows, kidnapped a boy, and tried to kill him?"

Much to her relief, she had stumbled on something that had the power to frighten Blade.

"I hate him!" Blade shouted. "You were supposed to marry me, not him!"

Melody found it hard to believe he still thought he loved her. Still, maybe she could use this. She could see fear in his anger. Maybe she could use that, too.

"I'm not going to marry your father, Blade."

"He says you are."

"I've told him over and over again I'm not. He just can't believe anybody would turn him down."

"Nobody ever has. Everybody does exactly what he says."

"I won't."

"I won't either." He paused and peered at her. "You really aren't going to marry him?"

"No. Now move. I've got to take care of Sydney."

He didn't move, but he didn't stop her when she

walked around him. Sydney groaned when she started to clean his wounds. Every bruise, every cut, every contusion made her want to throw a basin of scalding water in Blade's face. He had beaten Sydney with methodical precision. Chet was right. He was sick.

"Will you marry me?" Blade asked suddenly.

"If you marry that son-of-a—"

"Quiet," she whispered to Sydney. "No matter what happens, don't say a word." More loudly she said, "I'm not going to stay in Texas, Blade. I'm going back to Virginia as soon as I can." She couldn't tell him the truth, that she wanted to marry Chet. He'd probably kill all three of them.

"Pa won't let you go."

"I don't intend to ask him."

"He'll find out. He'll stop you."

She stopped long enough to look up at him. "You can help me, Blade. You can help me get away from your father."

A smile instantly wreathed his whole face, then disappeared. "Pa told Luke not to let me out of his sight."

"You got away from him this time, didn't you? You can do it again."

"He's crazy," Sydney hissed. "If you let him—"

"I'm trying to save our lives," Melody said in a fierce whisper. "Shut up and pretend to be unconscious."

"Yeah, I can," Blade said. "Pa's real mad about Chet. He's been looking for him for days. Can't find him anywhere."

"Good. Then we can go while he's looking for Chet," she said, standing. "Let me get my horse. We can leave right now."

"No!" Blade's voice was as sharp as a whip.

"Chet shot me. I'm going to kill him. You're my bait."

He grabbed her and dragged her over to the edge of the ledge. For a moment she feared he would push her to her death.

"I'm going to tie you up right here where he can see you. Then when he comes, I'm going to kill him."

For the first time, Melody prayed Chet had forgotten her, that he would make it to Santa Fe before the first snow fell on the mountains.

Chet had no difficulty following Melody's trail with the occasional aid of a lantern. She didn't know the first thing about covering her tracks or even riding a few feet off the main trail. For once he was thankful she was such a novice.

"We didn't expect to see you again," Speers said.

"I didn't expect to be back."

He hadn't been able to stay away. He'd camped ten miles out of town that first night. That was as far as he got. Every time he got ready to saddle up, his limbs wouldn't move. He couldn't make his hands grip the saddle. His entire body rebelled. So he sat there, arguing with himself, shouting at himself like a fool. If anybody but his horse had seen him, they'd have sworn he was loco. In the end he'd given up and come back to the Spring Water. He'd promised to stop the rustling, and he always kept his promises. After that he didn't know what he was going to do, but he knew he couldn't leave Melody.

He'd found the household in an uproar over her disappearance. Dan was in the midst of organizing the crew into small groups that would begin combing the ranch at dawn. Chet had left immediately. Speers had insisted upon coming along.

"Do you know where he's got the boys?" Speers asked Chet.

"No, but it's got to be someplace close by. The most logical place is one of the caves in the canyon."

"And you think Melody went there after him?"

"Yes."

"Why would she go by herself? Why wouldn't she at least wait for us?"

"I don't know."

Chet thought it probably came down to guilt. She would feel it was her fault that Lantz and Blade's fight over her had put her family in danger. Maybe for that reason she thought she might convince Blade to listen to her when he might not listen to anyone else. Whatever she had thought, Chet wished she hadn't gone alone. Blade might not be crazy, but he was extremely dangerous.

"What does Blade want with those boys?" Speers asked.

That question had been bothering Chet ever since he'd learned of the kidnapping. He was convinced Blade was crazy, but he was just as certain he didn't do anything without a reason.

"Maybe he wanted to get back at Sydney, and Neill just happened to be in the way," Chet said.

"Or he wanted to catch Melody and he was using the boys as bait," Speers suggested.

"No. He couldn't expect Melody to come on her own. Still, he had to know somebody would come."

"Maybe he thought you'd come. You did before."

"I'd already left town."

"Did he know that?"

"I don't know."

There'd be no reason for anyone to tell Blade, no reason for anyone besides Melody and her family to know. The more he thought about it, the more Chet felt certain Speers had hit upon the real reason behind this kidnapping.

"Look," Speers said, pointing to a second set of hoofprints off the trail.

"Somebody's following her."

"Do you think it's Blade?"

Chet nodded. When the two trails joined, he was sure of it.

"He's got her, doesn't he?" Speers asked.

"Yes."

"What's he going to do with her?"

"Take her back to his camp. If I'm the one he really wants, this will insure that I show up."

"You come back because of her?"

"Yes."

"Then why did you leave in the first place?"

Now that he'd admitted he couldn't live without Melody, Chet wasn't sure himself. He guessed when you'd been telling yourself something for most of your life—something you didn't want to hear but something you were convinced you *had* to hear and believe—it was hard to think differently. He was still certain he was doing the wrong thing. He just knew he couldn't do anything else.

"I don't think Bob Jordan's death was an accident. I think the rustling and everything else is tied together. I won't know how until I talk to Blade."

"You think he killed Jordan?"

"I don't know, but I'm certain he knows what happened."

"But if he's waiting for you, he's not going to let you get close enough to talk."

"My first concern is Melody and her brothers."

"How are you going to get them away from Blade?"

"I won't have any idea until I know where he's holding them."

A short while later Chet realized he was fortunate to have followed before dawn. A dim glow against the canyon wall two hundred feet above told him where Blade had made his camp. In daylight, he wouldn't have seen the fire. Blade would have been able to shoot him out of the saddle before he got within a hundred yards of the trail.

"We can't ride up there without making enough noise to wake the dead," Speers said.

"I'm going up on foot," Chet said. "I'll find out where everybody is, then come up with a plan. Once I do, I'll give you a signal."

"What kind of signal?"

Chet gave an owl call. "Think you can recognize that?"

"Sure, as long as there ain't no real owls in this canyon."

"It should take me about an hour."

"You'd better hurry," Speers said, looking at the sky. "It'll be getting light about then. You sure you don't want me to come with you?"

"I want you to create a diversion. Make as much noise as you can. Use both the horses. Make him think there's a posse down here."

"Is he going to kill us?" Neill asked his sister. Though he was clearly exhausted, the boy hadn't been able to sleep all night.

"No," Melody said. "He's not going to hurt us."

"He hurt Sydney," Neill reminded her.

Yes, and somehow she'd make him pay for that.

"Why is he keeping us here?"

"He's mad at Chet. He wants to shoot him when he comes after us."

"But Chet has gone away."

"I told Blade that, but he doesn't believe me."

"He's going to be really mad when he finds out. Do you think he'll kill us then?"

"No." But Melody was afraid of what he might do. Blade had tied them up and dragged her and Neill over to the edge of the narrow ledge so anyone passing below could see them. His two men stayed at a small campfire at the far end of the ledge. She could see Blade's outline against the dark rock as he waited and watched for Chet.

"Is Sydney going to die?" Neill asked.

"No."

"He looks like he's dead."

"He's sleeping. Blade hurt him very badly."

"I tried to stop him, but they wouldn't let me."

That was another score she had to settle with Blade. Neill would always feel guilty about not being able to protect his brother.

"Don't think about that now. Try to get some sleep."

"Will Chet come after us?"

"He's gone, Neill. He doesn't know we've been captured. I'm sure Dan is organizing the men right now."

"He'll never find us. Chet would. He knows all about this stupid canyon."

The danger to her and her brothers was all she could think about right now. She didn't think she could handle thinking about Chet leaving her, too, without breaking down.

"Chet would kill all three of them," Neill said. "He can shoot better than anybody in the world."

It was the very ability that could save them that had driven him away, but Melody didn't have time to worry about irony. She had to think of some way to get free, to send a message, to warn—

She heard a soft sound, like a tiny stone falling from the rocky slope above. But she hadn't heard it bounce down the slope, just the soft plop as it landed next to her. Another stone landed near her. Melody didn't understand who could have dislodged it. Blade's men were sleeping; Blade was still waiting for Chet. Then, just as she was about to speak to Neill, she saw a blond head disappear behind a boulder next to the trail leading down to the canyon floor.

Chet! She stifled a gasp at the same moment she told herself not to be foolish. One of Blade's men was blond. She glanced back at the campfire. She thought she saw two men, but she couldn't be sure. Maybe one was hiding behind that rock so he'd be behind anybody who tried to rescue her. But even as she tried to convince herself she was only imagining that Chet had come back because she so desperately wanted him to, the blond head reappeared.

It *was* Chet. For a moment she thought was going to faint from joy and relief. Chet was here. She didn't know how or why, but she didn't care. Somehow he would get her out of this mess. Somehow she would convince him he could never leave her again.

He motioned her to keep quiet.

"Neill," she said softly.

"Yeah."

"Don't move. No matter what you do, don't make a sound."

"Why?"

"I said not to move," she hissed.

Neill turned back around. "What is it?" he whispered.

"Promise not to make a sound?"

"Yeah. What is it?"

"Chet is hiding in those rocks behind—I told you not to move!"

Neill had started to turn. At her sharp command, he settled back down.

"I don't know what he's going to do, but we've got to pretend to be asleep so Blade won't look this way."

Melody positioned herself so she could watch the men at the campfire. They were still sleeping. She lay still, waiting, straining her ears to hear even the slightest sound. She'd never realized so many tiny sounds filled the night. It seemed the entire canyon was alive. Yet when Chet suddenly whispered right behind her, she nearly jumped out of her skin. She hadn't heard a thing, not even the whisper of clothing against rock.

"Don't move," he said. "I'm going to untie you. You untie Neill while I work my way over to Sydney."

Chet didn't say anything while he untied the rope that bound her arms. Holding them close to her body so the movement couldn't be seen, she rubbed them vigorously to restore the circulation.

"Back up to me very slowly," she told Neill.

Chet finished untying her feet. "Don't move until I get back."

"What are you going to do?"

"Speers is down below. As soon as I give the signal, he's going to create a diversion to give us a chance to get away."

"Blade gave Sydney a savage beating. He can't run. I doubt he can even walk."

"Then I'll carry him."

"But how can you—"

"I'll figure out something. Just be ready to run the moment you hear an owl hoot."

Chapter Twenty-one

Melody didn't know where to run, how far, or anything else, but Chet would know. He had come after her, found and untied them without alerting Blade or his men. He could do anything. She still could hardly believe Chet had returned. His appearance had seemed magical. In the dark, it was almost possible to believe she *had* imagined it. But her hands were free. She hadn't imagined that.

Chet had returned for her.

She didn't know what had caused him to change his mind, but she was sure he'd come back for her. There could be no other reason. Even in the stress of the moment, it had been impossible to misinterpret the way he looked at her. No matter what she had to do, regardless of what she had to suffer, she vowed they would never be separated again.

A touch on her shoulder caused her to start violently.

"Sshhhh!" Chet said.

Melody forced herself to breathe slowly and evenly, willed her heart to cease its violent hammering in her chest.

"I wasn't able to get to Blade," Chet said. Light had begun to show in the eastern skies. It would soon be morning.

"He's watching for you."

"That's thrown a kink into my plans, but we'll have to get along as best we can."

"What are you going to do?"

"I've tangled the guards' feet. I couldn't tie up them up without waking them, but it'll take them a few minutes to work free, enough for me to get Sydney and Neill away. Here, take this."

Melody recoiled. His gun lay in his hand.

"You've got to hold off Blade while I get Sydney down the trail. I can't do both."

"I can't kill Blade."

"I don't want you to kill him. Just shoot at him. You don't have to hit him, just hold him off long enough for me to get the boys to safety. Once we've started down the trail, Speers will come up to help."

Melody stared down at the gun. She realized the choice that lay before her now was the same choice countless men and women before her had been forced to make, the same choice Chet had once made. It was a choice between death and life for herself and people she loved.

She reached out and touched the gun. It felt cold and hard, this black steel that killed with impunity, without regard for the sanctity of human life, with no thought for the pain and misery it created in innocent lives. How could she use it after speaking so passionately against guns, after heaping contempt on men who used them?

The mere thought caused her to recoil. She opened her mouth to tell Chet they would have to find some other way.

"If you don't shoot Blade, will he kill us?"

Neill's childlike voice, the meaning of his words, were like a stab to her heart. This child was helpless by himself. So was Sydney. They depended on her and Chet to protect them from the senseless threat of a madman. And Chet, the man she loved, the man who'd repeatedly risked his life for her, was asking her to protect him while he carried her brother to safety. He could have been hundreds of miles away by now, but he'd returned because he loved her.

She looked up at him. He had to know the thoughts going through her mind because they must have gone through his. He knew the price she would have to pay. He'd already paid it because he couldn't desert the brother he loved. And now, he'd taken up his gun again because he couldn't desert the woman he loved.

He did love her. She could see it shining in his eyes with the power of a thousand beacon fires. But then, she didn't need any proof. She'd seen it the numerous times he'd gone against what he wanted to do because of her.

She lowered her gaze to the gun. That horrid piece of metal had stood between them from the beginning. If she picked it up, she could erase the barrier that stood between them. Never again would a gun hang like a shadow over their lives. She would know what he felt because she had felt it herself.

She reached for the gun. This was a choice she'd never expected to have to make. It would leave a scar on her soul for the rest of her life, but it was something she could learn to live with. She couldn't live with the knowledge that she'd failed Chet and her brothers.

The gun felt awkward. She almost expected it to come to malevolent life in her hand. She was being foolish. It was a tool to be used if needed, and she needed it now. "What do I do?" she asked.

"When I give the signal, Speers is going to start a diversion. As soon as Blade goes to see what's happening, I'll pick up Sydney and take him and Neill down the trail."

"How long do I stay here?" The thought of facing Blade alone terrified her, but she refused to think of that just now.

"You've got to hold off Blade until Speers can reach us."

Melody felt as though she'd been thrust into the middle of a bad dream. She'd never been asked to "hold off" anyone. The closest she'd come to military maneuvers was deciding how to capture a particularly hateful rooster her aunt wanted to cook for Sunday dinner.

The sound of an owl hooting practically in her ear nearly startled a tiny shriek out of Melody. She looked up. Chet grinned and cupped his hands over his mouth in silent imitation of what he'd just done. She glanced over to where Blade stood, but he hadn't moved.

"That's the signal for Speers," Chet whispered.

They waited, but nothing happened. Chet gave the signal again. This time something happened. Blade looked in their direction, got to his feet, and started toward them.

"Sit up, both of you," Chet hissed to Melody and Neill. "Sit close together. I'll crouch down behind you. I don't want to shoot Blade unless I have to."

"You're too big. He'll see you."

"Talk to him. Distract him."

"Couldn't you sleep?" Melody called to Blade.

"It'll be daylight soon," Blade said. "Then Chet will come. What's wrong with your brother? He's backing up to you like he thinks I'm going to hurt him."

"He's cold."

Blade was drawing closer. Melody felt Chet pressed hard against her back. She heard the soft click of the hammer being pulled back on his gun. If she didn't do something, Blade would see that she and Neill were no longer tied up. Neill sat on his feet and she'd hidden hers with her skirt, but it wouldn't be long before he knew.

"Could you bring me a cup of coffee on your way over?" she asked. "I'm cold and thirsty."

"We don't have any more coffee. The boys will have to make some more."

He kept coming. She started feeling desperate. "Some water will be fine. Some for Neill, too."

He paused. "You thirsty, boy?"

Neill nodded.

"Speak up," Blade barked.

"Yes," Neill said, his voice shaky.

"I'll untie you, and you can get your sister a drink. I don't fetch and carry for anybody."

Melody was out of ideas. Blade approached and had started to lean toward Neill when a commotion broke out somewhere below. From the volume of noise it sounded like a dozen men and horses were at the bottom of the trail. She didn't know how Speers had managed to make such a racket, but she was grateful when Blade leapt to his feet with a curse and ran toward the far side of the ledge.

"Go!" Chet hissed as he jumped to his feet and sprinted to where Sydney lay.

On her feet before Blade had run six strides, Melody jerked Neill up and sent him racing down the trail to the valley below. Hardly had she done this when Chet reached her side carrying Sydney.

"Follow closely, but keep looking over your shoulder," he said as he hurried down the path Neill had already taken.

A bullet whizzed past. Melody turned to see Blade aiming his gun at her and shouting at his men to get on their feet. Then she realized he wasn't aiming at her. He was aiming at Chet, who hadn't reached the protection of the boulders along the trail. Blade was going to shoot him in the back. Rage swept through Melody from head to foot. All the arrogance of Blade and his father, their brutality toward anyone who stood in the way of what they wanted, their complete indifference to how they affected the lives of others—every bit of that was distilled in Blade's stance as he aimed at Chet.

Melody aimed her gun at Blade and pulled the trigger.

The shot startled Blade so much, he missed his target. Melody fired again. And again. The fourth shot grazed Blade's arm. When he dropped his gun, Melody turned and fled down the trail after Chet.

It didn't take Melody long to learn why Speers had been so slow in responding to Chet's call, or why they made it all the way down the trail without being pursued. The crew had talked Dan Walters into following Chet's trail. They'd caught up with Speers while Chet was making the final preparations for their escape. They hadn't been in their positions on the cliffs that surrounded the ledge when Chet signaled the first time. When Speers finally responded to Chet's signal, the crew swarmed over the ledge and captured Blade's men. The crew were taking them into town to the sheriff.

Unfortunately, Blade escaped.

"He's going to be fine," the doctor told Belle when he came out of Sydney's room. "He's got some broken ribs that'll give him a good deal of pain for the next several days, but he's young and healthy. They'll mend quickly."

"But his face," Belle protested.

"He'll look like he's been kicked by a mule for a while yet. I expect it'll look a lot worse before it gets better—the bruises will turn green, yellow, and black—but there's nothing wrong with him that won't heal."

"Thank you for coming, Doctor. Now if you'll excuse me, I've got to go to him."

The doctor cleared his throat noisily. "Mrs. Jordan, it might be a good idea if you let some of the men take care of him. No need wearing yourself out trying to please a restless young man."

Belle's look of incomprehension indicated that she had no idea what the doctor was talking about. "I'm his mother. No one will take care of my babies but me."

"That's the problem," the doctor said. "He's a young man. After what's happened to him, he's never going to be your baby again. If you really want him to get well as quickly as possible, I suggest you let this strapping young fella do most of the work for you." He indicated Chet. "From the way Sydney talked, he thinks the world of him. He's more likely to behave for him than for any woman."

"Nonsense. Sydney will do anything in the world for me. He—"

"He asked me to speak to you," the doctor admitted finally. "He said you'd smother him."

Melody thought Belle looked more upset than when they'd brought Sydney back, battered and bruised from Blade's fists. She felt truly sorry for her stepmother. Having her son turn into a man and hold her at arm's length must be terribly painful. It would take her a while to adjust to the new relationship. Melody put her arm around Belle's shoulder.

"All men are ungrateful for the sacrifices we make for them," she said to her stepmother. "You've told me that yourself many times."

"But I never expected it of Sydney."

"He's not a boy any longer," Chet said. "He's a man. I'm afraid he's saddled with all the faults the rest of us have."

"It's going to happen to Neill, too, isn't it?" Belle asked.

"I'm afraid so."

"Then I suppose I'd better mother him all I can before some bully beats him up and he turns into a man right before my eyes. You men are the strangest creatures. Who else would put up with such an initiation process?"

Dan stepped up beside Belle, slipped his arms around her waist, and gave her a slight squeeze. "We do manage to get a few things right."

"Looks like you're going to have to keep a close eye on your friend," Melody said to Chet.

"Better yet, I think I'll haul him off to town with me."

The look in Chet's eye turned her insides cold. With all the commotion of capturing Blade's gang and worrying about Sydney, they hadn't had time to talk about themselves. But she had taken it for granted that he had come back to stay. It was inconceivable that there could be any other reason for his return.

"Well, I have to be going," the doctor said. "Keep him in bed and make sure the bandages around his chest are tight. He won't like it, but it'll help those ribs heal quicker."

But as they gathered on the front porch to see him off, a rider came up, galloping hard from the direction of Lantz's ranch.

"It's your brother," Melody said turning to Chet. "What's he doing here?"

It didn't take long to find out.

"Lantz and his father had an argument," Luke said as soon as he dismounted. "I'd quit, so I'd already left the ranch, but one of the men came after me."

"What were they arguing about?" Melody asked.

"You," Luke said, banishing any hope Melody had that she wouldn't have been at the center of this argument.

"What happened?" Belle asked.

"Blade shot his father."

"I'd better get over there," the doctor said.

"No need," Luke said. "Lantz is dead."

They looked at each other, shock on all their faces.

"He shot his own father?" Belle exclaimed. "Why?"

"He's not right in his head," Luke said. "And now he's got a bullet in him that must be giving him excruciating pain."

Conscience stricken, Melody grabbed hold of Chet.

"Not your graze," he told her. "One of the boys got a rifle bullet into him before he disappeared into that cave," Chet said.

Melody experienced a tremendous feeling of relief. She had been prepared to shoulder the responsibility of having shot Blade, but she was thankful to be spared.

"Why did you come to tell us?" she asked. She'd noticed that Luke kept glancing at Chet. She had a terrible feeling those glances weren't accidental.

"Apparently the last thing he said was that he intended to kill Chet. I came to warn you."

Luke's face showed no expression, but he was a lot like his brother. Melody could tell there was more. "What else?" she asked.

"The sheriff has decided to get a posse together to find him. He wants us both to go with him."

"Why?" Melody was sure she knew.

"Blade was born here. He knows this country better than anybody else. The sheriff thinks we won't find him if he decides to hide."

"He wants to use Chet as bait," Melody finished for him.

"Yes," Luke said.

"I won't let him go."

"I don't see how you can expect him to do any more," Belle said, visibly as indignant as Melody felt. "He rescued Melody and the boys all by himself."

377

"I couldn't have done it without Speers and Dan and the others."

"Of course you could," Melody said. "You had everything arranged."

"Don't argue with her," Dan said. "She's going to make you a hero whether you like it or not."

"You're a hero, too," Belle said, looking up at him with adoring eyes. "Just not as big a hero as Chet."

"I have to go with the sheriff," Chet told Melody when everyone had stopped laughing. "If he's right, Blade could stay hidden for days, even weeks, if he wanted. Nobody here will be safe while he's at large. He's got reason to hate us all."

"But it's you he hates most of all," Melody said. "He won't care about anybody else."

"All the more reason to go with the sheriff. I don't believe in waiting for trouble to come to me."

Melody realized she wasn't going to change Chet's mind. The very qualities of courage and responsibility that had caused him to come to her rescue time and time again demanded that he not stop until the job was finished. If she wanted to marry him and be happy as his wife, she was going to have to understand that. Fighting him would only put a strain on their relationship. If she wanted their marriage to work, she had to understand that Chet would never back away from anything he felt to be his responsibility. That was why he'd followed Luke.

"You've got to watch out for him," she said to Luke. "He's been looking out for you for seven years."

"Melody, you can't—" Chet began.

"Chet says you're faster than he is," Melody said

to Luke. "If anything happens to him, I'll hold you responsible."

"I promise to bring him back in no worse shape than he is now."

Melody didn't know Luke, but she felt he meant what he said.

"I'll have to go to the bunkhouse for some more ammunition," Chet said. "If my babysitter can wait a few minutes, I'll be right back."

Melody reached out and gripped him by the forearm. "Chet—"

He looked down into her eyes and placed his hand over hers. "I promise I'll be careful," he said. "I've been trying to put up my guns ever since I got here. The end is in sight. I don't mean to fail now."

That wasn't what she'd wanted from him. She wanted to be held, to be kissed, to be assured that nothing would happen to him, but she should have known not to expect that in front of so many people. Chet was a very private man. Showing his love for her—or just about any other deep emotion—before such a gathering would be impossible for him.

"How long will you be gone?"

"It's impossible to tell," Chet said, "but I promise to send word to you every day."

She wasn't as stoic as he was. She couldn't just step back and let him go. She reached up, pulled him down, and kissed him hard. His hesitation was only momentary. He enfolded her in his embrace. Their kiss was short, but Melody didn't feel slighted. Even a few seconds in Chet's embrace could drain her of her strength.

Chet hurried toward the bunkhouse without a backward look.

Belle broke the awkward silence. "I'm still in shock," she said. "I always knew Blade had a temper, but to kill his father . . . well, I just can't believe it."

"Do you need anybody else to go with you?" Dan asked Luke. "I can bring several of the boys as soon as they get back from town."

"No. I'd feel better if the rest of you stayed here. Until we get some idea of where Blade is, I don't think it's a good idea for any of the family to go far from the house without somebody with them. I don't know what Blade may do next—there's no way to tell what a mind as mixed-up as his will think of—but I'm sure Melody and her family are in more danger than anybody else."

"I won't let them out of my sight," Dan said. He looked at Belle. "I've got an investment in this family. I'm going to—"

A shot shattered the morning, stopping Dan in mid-sentence. Melody, Belle, and the doctor stood riveted to the spot.

In the same instant Luke was running toward the bunkhouse with the speed of a startled antelope.

Chet told himself he had been a fool to enter the bunkhouse without even thinking Blade Royal could be hiding there. The men hadn't come back from taking his gang to the sheriff. There was nobody else at the ranch but Dan, and he was up at the house with Belle. This was the most logical place for Blade to hide.

He looked down at the front of his shirt. There was a dark stain over his left pocket. It was growing wider. He didn't know if he'd received a mortal wound, but he considered it a bad sign that he felt no pain. He'd been wounded several times. He couldn't remember a single one of them that didn't hurt like the devil.

"Everything was all right until you and your brother came," Blade screamed at him. "You ruined everything! I'm going to kill you. Then I'm going to kill him."

Chet looked up. Blade stood less than ten feet away, a gun in his hand. He didn't look like himself. He'd lost his hat, he'd smeared blood from the wound in his leg all over his clothes, and his irises were tiny spots of color on a field of white.

He looked truly insane.

Chet knew Blade would kill him if he didn't move quickly. He tried to will his legs to carry him back through the door, behind the potbellied stove, even behind the table, but he just stood there, barely able to stay on his feet. He would die, but at least Luke was safe. The shot had warned him. He had protected his brother just as he meant to do when he followed him seven years ago.

"You shot me," Blade said. "You shouldn't have done that."

Chet hated to leave Melody. He'd never expected to find a woman who'd see him for what he was and love him anyway. He'd told himself he would never have a family, that that kind of happiness would never be his. But he'd begun to hope, to imagine, to dream. It was so close. It was cruel of fate to take it away.

A shot rang out in the close confines of the bunkhouse. No, two shots. Why didn't he feel any pain? Why was he still on his feet?

Why was Blade sinking to the floor?

Chet felt arms around him. He looked up to see

Leigh Greenwood

Luke and Melody, the two faces he loved most in the world. He tried to speak. He had so much he wanted to say, but the words wouldn't come out. He felt himself being lifted and carried. Melody's face hovered close. Something wet hit his face. She wiped it away, but more drops fell.

He was dying. That had to be it. The end he had feared for so long had finally caught up with him. He didn't want to die. Everything he wanted was so close. He fought to hold on, but the image he loved so dearly faded, leaving him in blackness.

Chapter Twenty-two

Chet opened his eyes. Before him sunlight poured through a window framed by curtains of blue silk trimmed in white lace. A gilt mirror hung on the wall above a dressing table. On it rested a velvet box filled with cut glass, silver bottles, brushes, and an oil lamp with an elaborate shade. He smiled to himself. It looked like heaven compared to most of the rooms he'd occupied over the last seven years, a heaven on earth. It was Melody's bedroom.

"I'm glad to see you're back," Melody said. "I was beginning to think you'd sleep the week away."

He turned his head. She sat next to the bed on the other side. He smiled. It was good to see her face. She looked just as he remembered. He'd had a lot of dreams. He'd tell her about them someday. Right now he felt almost too tired to talk.

"How long have I been here?" he asked.

"Five days."

He must have come close to dying. He'd never been out for more than a few hours before.

"The doctor says you're very lucky to be alive. A quarter of an inch the other way, and that bullet would have killed you."

"Is that why you're crying?" His voice sounded so faint, so slow.

"I'm crying because you're alive, you idiot."

"I hoped that might be it." He felt so tired. It was hard to concentrate.

"Now you ought to go back to sleep. You still need lots of rest."

"Luke?" he managed to say before his voice failed.

"He's gone," Melody said. "I tried to get him to stay, but he wouldn't."

His lips soundlessly formed the word. *Why?*

"He killed Blade. Luke reached the bunkhouse just as he was about to shoot you a second time. He said he did it so you wouldn't have to kill anybody else, so you could be free to marry me. He said you didn't have worry that anyone would find him. He said he'd always wanted to see California."

Chet felt as if some part of himself had been torn away. He and Luke hadn't always agreed on things, but for most of their lives they'd only had each other. Now Luke was gone, and Chet knew he didn't mean to be found, not even by his own brother. Chet had wanted to be relieved of the curse of his guns, but the price had come very high.

"Blade didn't die right away," Melody said. "He talked a lot. It seems my father's death wasn't an accident. Blade had been rustling for some time. My father caught him. When he threatened to turn Blade over to the sheriff, Blade drove his horse off a cliff." She stopped a moment, looking at her hands. "That wasn't what Lantz and Blade argued about. Lantz didn't seem to care about Pa. He was just furious that Blade would steal from him. He called Blade a fool and said he was going to disown him. That's when Blade killed him."

Chet had been right, but it gave him no satisfaction. A family destroyed because of greed and stupidity. Much like his own. Chet vowed that would never happen with him and Melody. He didn't know where they could go or what he could do, but he wouldn't let it happen to him.

He closed his eyes. He had to rest. He had plans to make.

Melody was exhausted. She'd talked until she was blue in the face, but she couldn't convince Chet to remain at the Spring Water Ranch. Dan Walters had decided to buy Lantz's ranch. It was clear he had every intention of marrying Belle as soon as all the uproar over the deaths of Lantz and Blade settled. The Spring Water still needed a foreman.

"What could be more perfect than for my husband to run our ranch?" Melody asked for the hundredth time.

"Nothing," Chet replied with infuriating calm.

"Then why won't you—"

"But not me. I've already explained why it would be impossible."

Sounds of arrival outside the house distracted Chet's attention. Melody jumped up and closed the doors to her father's office. "You can stop wondering who that is," she told Chet. "You're not leaving this room until I talk some sense into your head."

"Melody, we've been over everything a dozen times."

"Two dozen," she said. "I can repeat all your arguments from memory."

"Then why can't you—"

"Because they're stupid. You're not a stupid man, so I don't want to hear any more of that. Now here's what we're going to do. First, I'm going to marry you. You can scream and yell and say anything you want, but I'm going to be your wife even if Dan and the boys have to tie you up to get you before the preacher. Be quiet," she said when he started to speak. "I've heard enough. Now you listen to me.

"I don't want to hear any more about you being a gunman and me some innocent from Virginia. I held that gun in my hand, and I fired it at Blade. If I hadn't been such a bad shot, Luke wouldn't have had to kill him. But that's not the point. I did fire that gun with the intention of killing Blade if I had to, so I know what it's like. It doesn't make you a killer. It's simply something you have to do. I didn't like it, but I'd do it again. So that makes me just like you. I'm the perfect wife for you."

The noise outside the office door was so loud, it was distracting. She pulled Chet up from the seat where he'd been sitting for the last thirty minutes and put her arms around his waist. Despite being the most stubborn man in the western world, he was quick to take the hint and put his arms around her. She was just as quick to accept the kiss he offered. After being assured that his objections were in no way the result of diminished love for her, Melody prepared to continue her arguments.

"We don't have to stay here if you don't want to. Dan can run both ranches. We can go to the far corners of Arizona or New Mexico if you want. We can go to Virginia if you like."

The doors flew open to reveal Belle standing there with a grin so big, it practically made her look idiotic. "How about a certain valley in the Hill Country?" she asked.

Melody felt Chet stiffen. She knew the only place he truly wanted to go was the valley he still considered home. She was angry at Belle for mentioning it. It could only hurt Chet.

"Would you go with him?" Belle asked her.

"You know I'd go anywhere with him, but—"

Belle looked at Chet and grinned even more broadly. "I thought he might have turned stubborn, but there's somebody here who's more than ready to twist his arm."

A woman a few years past the bloom of youth stepped through the doorway. Melody couldn't decide whether she was more surprised by the appearance of this stranger or by Chet's reaction.

"Are you going to stand there with your mouth open, or are you going to give me a hug and a kiss?" the stranger asked. She held out her arms, and Chet walked straight into them.

In one horrible flash of insight, Melody was certain Chet hadn't yet agreed to set a wedding date because he was already married to this woman. Melody felt her heart constrict into a tight knot. It was no consolation that the woman was probably older than Chet. She was still lovely, and he obviously loved her very much.

"Why didn't you come back?" the woman asked when she finally managed to break Chet's embrace. "It broke my heart when you left."

The tears streaming down her face and the look of love in her eyes left Melody in no doubt as to the truth of her words. A thousand explanations whirled about in her mind. They all ended in her being pushed aside by a woman Chet had walked out on years ago. She heard the sound of more people in the hall.

A man she'd never seen entered the room. The sight of Belle and Bernice watching from the hall, grinning like idiots, told Melody she must have misjudged the situation.

"I tried to leave her behind," the man said to Chet, "but she was saddled up and ready to go before I could get down the steps."

When Chet hugged this man as though he was his best friend in the whole world, Melody suddenly felt something wonderful had just happened.

If these people were who she thought they might be . . .

"I'm Isabelle Maxwell, Chet's mother," the woman said, introducing herself to Melody. "When Luke wrote that Chet had fallen in love but was about to make the biggest mistake of his life by leaving you, I knew I had to come."

"His mother," Melody repeated.

"Chet always wrote at Christmas, but Luke's letter was the first we'd had from him. We knew it had to be really important for him to write."

Jake Maxwell, for that was who Melody was certain the man was, pulled Chet over toward Melody and Isabelle. "Now introduce us to your young woman. I hear she's determined to marry you even if she has to tie you up. I'll be happy to lend a hand," he said to Melody. "He's got a passel of brothers who'd jump at the chance to help. Anybody stupid enough to turn his back on you deserves to be tossed over a cliff."

"Chet's not stupid," Melody said. "He's just—"

"Stubborn," Isabelle said.

Melody relaxed and smiled. "Yes. Very stubborn."

"We've come to help you out."

"As well as be present for the wedding," Isabelle said. "I couldn't miss that."

Chet had shown more genuine emotion in three minutes than he'd shown the whole time he'd been at the ranch. Melody wished she had a copy of the key Jake and Isabelle seemed to be able to turn so easily.

"Luke told us all about what's bothering Chet. It was a long letter." Jake glanced over at Chet. "It must have taken him a week to write it."

"First, you're coming home," Isabelle said. "There's no point wasting time raising foolish objections. I'm sure Melody has listened to them enough for all of us. I don't want to hear a word about bringing trouble on us. There's not a gun-slinger in Texas foolish enough to venture onto Maxwell land."

"But you can't come right away," Jake said. "We've got a little problem we want you to take care of first."

"Jake, I can't—"

"I know you're a little old, but I'm going to send you off to college for a year or two. The cattle business is changing too fast for this old cowboy to keep up. I want you to go learn all this stuff about crossbreeding and marketing and new grass and whatever else it is they're using to threaten to run me out of business. When you figure you've learned about all you can stand, you come back and fix it so we can make more money than anybody else in the state."

"Jake, I can't—"

"Be quiet and listen to your parents," Melody said. "I like what they're saying."

"What about it?" Jake asked.

"You forgot about the wedding," Isabelle said.

"I count four women in this room," Jake said. "That's more than enough to organize a wedding. Now let's get out of here and let Chet and Melody talk things over."

"He's marrying you and coming home," Isabelle said, giving Melody a kiss on the cheek. "No matter what argument he presents, just keep saying that. It may take a while, but he'll soon stop talking nonsense."

"Do you always tell him what to do?" Melody asked, still hardly able to believe the past ten minutes.

"Of course. It saves a lot of time." She winked. "Welcome to the family."

Jake stepped over and gave Melody a hug as Isabelle walked out into the hall to talk to Belle.

"We were praying he'd find somebody like you," he said. He gave Chet a punch in the shoulder. "I hope you've told him how lucky he is."

"Considering he's been shot three times since he arrived, I doubt he'd agree with you."

"That was nothing but a few little tests to make sure he was worthy of you. Someday I'll tell you what Isabelle and her gang put me through before they hoodwinked me into adopting the lot of them." He turned to Belle. "I seemed to remember a promise of something to drink."

"You're welcome to anything we have," Belle said as she drew him into the hall and closed the doors on them.

The sudden quiet was almost eerie. Melody felt stunned. Chet looked just as strongly affected. She decided not to waste the opportunity.

"I hope you listened carefully to everything your parents said. I have only one thing to add."

Chet pulled her to him. "Are you going to turn into a dictator like Isabelle?"

"Absolutely. It seems the only way to handle you."

He nuzzled her neck. "I could think of a few other ways."

Melody could tell the battle had been won. They'd offered Chet the opportunity to do exactly what he wanted to do, and he was being smart enough to accept gracefully. She had her man. Not on her ranch where she wanted him, but that was probably best. Sydney would soon be old enough to run it.

"I can think of a few ways of my own," she said. "Suppose we make a list and make our way through it item by item."

Chet kissed her and pulled her close.

"You are going to accept Jake's offer, aren't you?" she asked.

Silence.

She pulled out of his embrace. "I can't stand this any longer. You *will* accept Jake's offer. If it doesn't work out, we can try something else. But we've got to start somewhere, and that seems like a good place."

Silence.

"You do want to go back there, don't you?"

"It's the only place I've ever wanted to be."

Melody breathed a sigh of relief. "Good. Now let's talk about weddings."

"I'd rather start on that list you mentioned."

They were in the midst of a very satisfactory kiss when the office doors opened without warning.

"I've got to get the brandy." Neill stopped in his tracks when he saw Melody and Chet kissing. "You're not going to do that, too, are you?"

"Who else did you break in on?" Chet asked, smothering a smile.

"Ma and Dan and your ma and pa. They've kissed twice, and they just got here."

"We can't help it," Chet said. "I warned you about those feminine wiles."

"But you like them, don't you?"

Chet turned back to Melody. "Yes, I like them very much indeed."

Epilogue

"Are you sure you don't mind changing your name?" Melody asked Chet.

"It's a little late if I did. I've been going by Maxwell for two years now."

"But you were at Texas A & M. It didn't matter there. You're home now. It's your last chance to change your mind."

Chet hugged his wife and placed a kiss on the top of her bent head. She was sitting on a rock feeding their son. It was a picture he couldn't get enough of. Even though he'd seen it hundreds of times during the last six months, each time was like the first. He doubted he'd ever grow accustomed to it. Or that the noisy bundle of arms and legs with the wisps of white-blond hair was Jake Maxwell, II, the first of what he hoped would be many sons.

"It's not just that a new name signifies the start

of a new life. It makes me feel like I'm a real part of the family. Now stop worrying about me. Look around you. Isn't this the most beautiful place you've ever seen?"

Jake had wanted to pay for Chet's education, but between the money Chet had saved and Melody's income from the ranch, they'd been able to support themselves. They were going to stay with Jake and Isabelle until they decided where to build their house. Jake had said it was because he'd be working for all the ranches. Chet decided it was because Isabelle wanted to get her hands on the baby. Chet didn't mind staying with Jake and Isabelle. In fact, he'd like it for a while. But they were going to sell Melody's share in the Spring Water to buy land of their own. He wanted his own place, one he could feel he'd never have to leave again. One he hoped Luke would come to some day.

The valley opened out before them, the mountains rising on each side. Even after nearly ten years, he could remember every foot of it. Even the air seemed sweeter and cleaner than anywhere else.

"It's lovely," Melody said. "It's just like you said."

He couldn't expect her to love it as he did. She still remembered moonlight on the broad, placid James River, the majestic old houses and gnarled trees of Richmond. They were probably very nice, but they had none of the grandeur and rugged beauty of his valley. He was sure it wouldn't be long before she came to realize that, too.

A hair-raising whoop rent the air, and several riders came toward them at a mad gallop.

"That'll be Will and Pete," he said, nearly laughing for the happiness what welled up inside of him. "And unless I'm mistaken, that's Eden with them." He put his arm around Melody. "We're home," he said. "We're *really* home."

SONYA BIRMINGHAM

Song of the Lark

When the beautiful wisp of a mountain girl walks through his front door, Stephen Wentworth knows there is some kind of mistake. The flame-haired beauty in trousers is not the nanny he envisions for his mute son Tad. But one glance from Jubilee Jones's emerald eyes, and the widower's icy heart melts and his blood warms. Can her mountain magic soften Stephen's hardened heart, or will their love be lost in the breeze, like the song of the lark?

___4393-9 $5.50 US/$6.50 CAN

LEIGH GREENWOOD

"Leigh Greenwood is a dynamo of a storyteller!"
—Los Angeles Times

Jefferson Randolph has never forgotten all he lost in the War Between The States—or forgiven those he has fought. Long after most of his six brothers find wedded bliss, the former Rebel soldier keeps himself buried in work, only dreaming of one day marrying a true daughter of the South. Then a run-in with a Yankee schoolteacher teaches him that he has a lot to learn about passion.

Violet Goodwin is too refined and genteel for an ornery bachelor like Jeff. Yet before he knows it, his disdain for Violet is blossoming into desire. But Jeff fears that love alone isn't enough to help him put his past behind him—or to convince a proper lady that she can find happiness as the newest bride in the rowdy Randolph clan.

_3995-8 $5.99 US/$7.99 CAN